LOVE DIVIDED

Love Divided

George Sigsworth

[handwritten inscription]

Copyright © George Sigsworth 2005

First published in 2005 by
Serendipity
37/39 Victoria Road
Darlington

British Library Cataloguing-in-Publication data
A catalogue record for this book is available from the British Library
ISBN 1-84394-140-6
Printed and bound by Antony Rowe Ltd., Eastbourne

To Jenny and family

PART ONE 1929

Chapter 1

'Did yer knaw old Ferriday 'as gone bust then?' asked Ned, with his mouth full of bread and cheese. 'Ah couldn't believe it, but ah saw Percy Naylor int' Heverthorpe Arms last night and there's nowt he doesn't knaw.'

Ned, Ernie and Ted were sitting in the saddleroom having their packed dinner. Any connection the saddleroom might have had with horses, however, had now disappeared. There were no harnesses or horse brasses hanging on the whitewashed walls. Not even a horseshoe hanging over the door or above the fireplace. Just a few benches round the walls and two armchairs in front of the fire, with bulging springs and sacks stuffed with chaff where once there had been cushions. And as it was October and winter had set in out of turn ahead of autumn, there was a pile of wood in the alcove next to the fire.

What had once been the saddleroom at Manor Farm was now the farm men's mess room. Since the arrival of two new tractors, fewer horses were needed, and all their gear could be accommodated in the stable.

Ernie put down his flask and chucked another piece of wood onto what was already a strong burning fire. He swallowed what was left of a pickled onion and said, 'The way he's been going on, I aren't surprised. Ferriday spends more time int' pub than with his cows. And that lad of his is no better; allus out wi' that lass from up Carlton Hill.'

'Ah wouldn't mind a night out with her myself,' twinkled Ned, only too well aware that his courting days had been over for twenty years or more. 'She's got a pair of tits on her bigger than Daisy yonder.' Daisy was one of the house cows, which Ned milked every night and morning. Most farms in that part of Yorkshire were mainly arable, with sheep and beef cattle. Manor Farm was no exception, and the three cows were kept to provide milk, cream and butter for the Hall and Colonel Denehurst, manager of Manor Farm and agent for the estate. It was Throstle Nest, where Tom Ferriday had kept a dairy herd, which was unusual.

The estate had been in the Heverthorpe family for many generations.

1

Most of its 12,000 acres was let to tenants, including Throstle Nest, but the six hundred acre Manor Farm was kept in hand.

There was silence for a few minutes. Ned looked thoughtfully at the fire and said, 'Well, ah reckon Ferriday is only the first of many. He may have made a mess of things, but there are some good farmers struggling an' all.'

'There is that,' agreed Ted. 'They say that you can't give that light land up at Kirkley away; nobody wants to rent it, and only a bloody fool would buy it. We are lucky to be where we are.'

'Old Heverthorpe is worth a bob or two and he doesn't depend on farming for a living. It's the likes of you and me, Ned, that keeps him going, supping ale in the Heverthorpe Arms,' a reference to the fact that Lord Heverthorpe made his money mainly from a large brewing business in the West Riding.

As the men continued to talk and eat their packed meals, a young fair-haired, blue-eyed boy came in and stood just inside the door. He was Robert, Colonel Denehurst's youngest son. The men sitting with their backs to the door, were unaware of his presence; otherwise Ned would have been more careful in his recent reference to Lizzie Higgs, the well-endowed young lady from Carlton Hill Farm. Not that he needed to be unduly worried; there was not much that a young boy of ten, brought up on a farm and attending a rough village school didn't know about. Ned also knew Robert well enough to be sure that he wouldn't repeat the men's gossip to his father, who was very strict about the language they used. It was more than their jobs were worth to use four-letter words when he was around. The Colonel had once told Jim Slater, the threshing-tackle boss, whose favourite adjectives were 'f...' and 'bloody', that if he used those words at Manor Farm, he would find someone else to do the threshing, and Jim knew he meant it.

It was Ted, a thick-set middle-aged bachelor, with flecks of grey hair in his black, wiry, curls, who noticed Robert first.

'Now then, my lad, ah thowt you'd a'been in school,' he said amiably.

'Not this week, it's half term,' said Robert.

'Not another holiday?' broke in Ned, 'thou'll nivver learn nowt wi' all the time you get off.'

Having heard similar sentiments expressed by his mother all the morning, Robert decided to change the subject. Hesitating, slightly, he asked Ernie what he would be doing in the afternoon. He hesitated because he half expected one of Ernie's stock replies, "Helping Alice to do the washing," (Alice being one of the maids at Manor Farm), or "Making a wigwag for a mustard mill."

But even Ernie, not the brightest of men, must have realised by now that Robert had grown out of that sort of conversation. Ernie was busily eating an apple. He carved it into pieces with his penknife and then, still using the knife rather than his fingers, stuck each piece into his mouth. He spat a last piece of skin into the fire, and with his mouth still half full said, 'Ah thowt you would have known that. Hasn't gaffer said anything about threshing?'

'Yes, but that's not until tomorrow,' replied Robert.

'Ah but we shall be getting fettled after dinner. There's thatch to get off that stack of wheat and some corn int' granary to shift, and a lot more such jobs before we can start int' morning.'

'Are there many rats or mice in that stack?' asked Robert, looking forward to the start of threshing. It was always a bonus when threshing coincided with a school holiday and he, and some of the workers' children, could have fun killing the rats and mice as they tried to escape from the stacks.

'There'll be some right enough,' said Ned, 'but not that many. It's the first threshing day since harvest. There's always a lot more after Christmas when they've had time to breed a bit.'

By now it was one o'clock, and the rest of the farm men were arriving for work. Most of them lived just down the road in the estate cottages, and walked home for dinner. One or two, who lived a mile or so away at the other end of the village, were near enough to cycle home, at any rate for most of the year. But at hay time and harvest, they all brought a packed meal, and ate it when and where they could, sitting behind a stook, or in the shelter of one of the corn stacks in the stackyard.

During the winter months, all the men gathered together in the saddleroom, waiting to see if Bill, the foreman, had any special instructions for the afternoon's work. Just before one o'clock, he would arrive and join in the talk and banter for a few minutes before taking out his watch and saying, 'Right, let's 'ave a bit more then,' a signal for them all to move off, the horsemen round the corner to the stable, George and Albert to the pigs, and the general labourers to whatever the current job was. Bill himself had his own routine.

Robert often joined the men in the saddle house during the school holidays. He enjoyed listening to their talk, which was usually about their work, or farming in general – how the land was working, which varieties of wheat had given the best yield, or which of the tenants on the estate was finding it difficult to avoid going bankrupt. Farming in the late twenties was going through a very difficult period, and the men with their wage packets of thirty shillings a week were threatened with a cut of even that meagre amount or, worse still, the sack. But that didn't stop them from "farming" everyone's land better than the farmers themselves, and they always knew better than Colonel Denehurst, or Bill, what should or shouldn't be done.

By late afternoon, the weather had turned even colder and foggy. A swirling mist rolled over the pond and, through the gloom, a light from the stable door shone just strongly enough to reflect in the murky, still water. A moorhen called from under the trees, which overhung one corner of the pond.

Inside the stable, the horses were munching steadily on their evening feed, shuffling and stamping occasionally, but too tired to complain when their turn came, to be brushed and groomed. And there was plenty of vigorous brushing needed, as their fetlocks were covered in mud after a day of harvesting swedes. It had rained almost continually since the harvest was finished and the farm roads and yards were covered in a thick, clinging mud, which tired horses and men alike.

Robert was looking for Bill. He wasn't difficult to find; his routine varied from season to season. At this time of year, he was usually around the buildings, perhaps polishing and oiling the large engine, which drove the cornmill and barn machinery. Or maybe he was in the granary, sorting out the barley, which he was to grind the next day. But, in any case, there were two good clues to his whereabouts. Firstly, the old sheepdog, Rap, would not be far away; find Rap and you found Bill. But the infallible guide was a line of dark brown spittle, which made a track from one part of the farm to another. It was easiest to follow in the summer, when it made large, squat wet patches in the dust. It was more difficult to find in the winter mud. But, summer or winter, and whatever the job in hand, Bill chewed his baccy and left his trail to follow. Black twist was his favourite, and as a small boy, Robert, and his older sister, Mary, had been given it in the belief that it was liquorice, a delicacy which they bought at the village shop and dipped into halfpenny packets of sherbet and sucked on the way home from school. But the twist was sharp and bitter. Bill's false teeth were stained brown and later, when Mary had grown up and knew about such things, she wondered how Bill's wife, Nora, could bear to kiss him.

But on this particular October afternoon, Robert knew where Bill would be working. He made his way past the stable door, through the foldyard, on into the piggery, and finally through the barn into the stackyard. There, Bill was waiting with Ernie and Ted for the threshing machine.

In Bill's words, they were "Getting feckled to set." In other words, levelling off the area in front of the stack to be threshed, and collecting up likely pieces of timber to act as wedges under the wheels of the machine and elevator, if necessary. But Robert had a message for him.

'Jim has been delayed over at Church Farm, and they won't be here for another half hour or so,' he said, passing on the telephone message which Wendy, Colonel Denehurst's secretary had asked him to deliver.

Bill pulled out his old turnip watch from his waistcoat pocket yet again. It was a treasure from which he could never be parted, although the story told by the farm men was that one harvest, when they were carting wheat, Bill, who was the stacker, had lost his watch somewhere in the stack. The following winter, when the stack was threshed, Ted had found it under a sheaf, and it was still going. Robert never knew how much of this story was true, but none of the farm staff ever denied it. It was a miracle that Bill didn't lose it more often, or break it, when he was working. However, it was in good working order now.

'It'll be nearly midnight when they get here,' said Bill, and then, turning to the two men, 'We shan't get set 'til morning now, so you needn't wait on. Ah'll hang on and see them in. You can go and give Alan a hand with the bullocks; he's a bit behind this afternoon.'

It was almost five o'clock before there was a distant rumble, which gradually grew louder into a clanking and rattling and hissing of steam, as the engine, towing the threshing machine and elevator, turned in at the gate. A faint swaying light pierced the fog, and a dim shape of the engine appeared before the whole outfit jolted to a shuddering stop and Jim appeared, cursing the fog, and grumbling about being late.

Early the following morning, the stackyard was alive with activity. The engine lights were on and farm men, no more than black shapes in the half light, were moving around carrying storm lanterns. Belts were being tightened on the machine and wheels chocked. Bill arrived with a cartload of coal for the steam engine, and a long coil of hosepipe snaked across the stackyard under the fence and into the pond to bring a supply of water. Large sheets were being spread on the ground ready to catch the chaff and pulls (the short pieces of straw too long to be blown out with the chaff, but too short to pass over the straw walkers).

By seven o'clock, as the light gradually strengthened, storm lanterns were blown out; Bob blew a blast on the engine whistle as, with a belch of smoke, he put the drive wheel into gear. The belts flapped, the low hum of the machine increased to a loud, almost deafening, noise as the revs picked up, and the drum shuddered and rattled when Fred fed in the first sheaf of the day.

For the farm men, threshing meant long, hard, dusty days, but for Robert and the village children, it was a day of excitement and fun. During the morning, they played hide-and-seek round the stacks and farm buildings, but later in the day, when the stack being threshed got lower to the ground, the rats and mice started to jump off and run for safety. It was then that a crowd of children gathered expectantly round the stack.

'Look out, Bobbie, there's one just run under that sheaf there,' shouted a big raw-boned lad.

'All right, Des,' yelled Robert, 'you lift it up and I'll clout him.' He stood poised with his stick raised, and as Des carefully lifted the sheaf, a tiny shivering mouse squatted quivering, too frightened and confused to move. Robert hit it just once with his stick, picked it up by the tail, and added it to a pile of a dozen or so other mice. One more towards the daily tally.

'You'd better keep a watch over them, or Rap will 'ave 'em,' said a pretty dark-haired girl.

'Oh, he won't touch them, Maggie. He's had enough already. His inside must be heaving with mice,' said Robert.

'A pity we haven't seen any rats,' said Des, hitting his stick against the side of the stack to see if he could frighten anything out.

'I'm glad we haven't,' said Maggie, shuddering at the thought. 'I hate rats.'

'Well there won't be any now,' said another red-haired boy knowledgeably. 'They start jumping off when the stack is much higher than this. There's only three rows of sheaves left now.'

'Have you got many mice round your side?' asked Des.

'About as many as you, come round and count 'em.'

The two boys moved off, leaving Robert and Maggie together. They watched for a few minutes as Ted started to lift another row of sheaves onto the machine. 'Come on, Maggie. Let's go up into the granary. I've had enough of mice for one day.'

'OK. We'll run up the planks before dad takes another sack.' Of all the jobs on threshing day, the hardest was carrying corn. A sack of wheat weighed 18st. Every few minutes, throughout the day, a sack would be filled ready to be carried to the granary. To get up there, there was an elaborate arrangement of planks, one from the ground to a strategically placed rully, and another from the rully onto the top of the granary steps, a height of fourteen or fifteen feet. The only mechanical aid was a sack lift to raise the sack onto the carrier's shoulders. Then off he went, a hundred yards or more across the stackyard, up the planks and into the granary, where the grain was shot out of the sack onto a huge golden heap. It was up this arrangement of planks that Robert and Maggie, rather gingerly, made their way to the granary.

Usually it was the bigger, stronger men who carried the corn. But there were plenty of small men, who weighed a good deal less than a full sack, who could carry corn all day. One of these was Harry Jackson, Maggie's father, and waggoner at Manor Farm. He was only of average height, but broad-shouldered, tough and wiry. He had worked at Manor Farm for over twenty years. He was highly thought of by Colonel Denehurst, and a favourite of Marjorie, the Colonel's wife. He was devoted to his family, particularly Maggie, who was the eldest of three girls. As a small child, she often came to the farm with her father, and she and Robert had been childhood playmates ever since they were old enough to go to school.

It was quiet and peaceful in the granary compared with the noise and hustle near the steam engine and drum, where everybody had to shout to make themselves heard.

'I'll race you to the top of the heap,' shouted Maggie, jumping on to the heap of grain which reached to within a few feet of the great thick oak beams which held up the roof.

'Hold on a minute then. That's not fair. Let's start together.' Robert joined Maggie on the heap and, as they struggled up the side, the loose grain slipped under their feet so that for every foot gained they slithered back almost as far.

'Give me a hand, I'm sinking,' yelled Maggie. Robert reached over, took her hand and, struggling and laughing, they reached the top to slide down again, scattering grain all over the floor of the granary.

'What do you two think you're playing at? Out of the way, or you'll get this sackful over yer.'

Harry Jackson had arrived with another sackful of wheat and, leaning forward with the sack over his shoulder, he expertly guided a stream of grain, which cascaded onto the heap.

'Ah'm surprised at you, Master Robert, scattering grain about like that. Ah thowt ah'd trained yer better than that. And you, Maggie, it's tahm you were going home. Yer mother will be wondering where you are.'

Harry seemed more disappointed than angry. But he was, in any case, a patient man, and seldom raised his voice in anger. Folding the sack under his arm, he made his way back through the door and shouted, 'You'd better find a brush and get it swept up afore Bill comes.'

The two children sat down and emptied their shoes and socks before Robert went to find a brush, and Maggie, with a cheerful, 'See you tomorrow, Bobbie,' went off down the granary steps, rather than risk the planks on her own. She always found it more difficult going down than climbing up.

Chapter 2

It was a bright, mild morning for mid-October. Colonel Denehurst was riding over to Elm Farm to see the tenant, George Coleman. The Colonel was a tall, well-made man, with steel-grey hair and hard blue eyes. But, in spite of his army training and regular exercise, hunting and shooting, he was fighting a losing battle with his figure. He was too tall to be portly, but he had an obvious paunch and difficulty keeping his trousers hitched up, which was one reason why he usually wore britches and leggings. He had a reputation for being a hard man, but fair. Often he rode round the estate in the early morning before breakfast. If he found any broken-down walls or fences or gates needing repair, whoever they belonged to would be firmly told to get them put right. However poor a tenant might be, there was no excuse for carelessness or neglect, but if a tenant was in real difficulty, through no fault of his own, the Colonel would be helpful and considerate. Nevertheless, he was a formidable man who expected to have his own way, and usually got it. His daughter, Mary, was the only person who could really influence him. She was grown-up now and married to Stephen Langley, a fortunate young man who owned his own land on the edge of the estate. Ever since she had been a little girl, she had been the Colonel's favourite. Now, as an adult, if he was depressed and worried, she could comfort him; if he was angry, she could turn him to laughter, and when he was being obstinate in argument, she could sometimes make him change his mind.

But on that particular morning, as he rode to Elm Farm, the agent, in spite of his problems, was in an optimistic and cheerful mood.

At Manor Farm, the threshing had finished for the time being, and the cold, foggy, weather had departed along with Jim Slater and his threshing tackle. John Denehurst was pleased to see them go. He didn't like threshing so early in the autumn; there were more important seasonal jobs to do, but he was short of bedding straw and needed some seed wheat. He hoped that the land would soon be dry enough to drill. The day-to-day running of the farm he could safely leave to Bill. It was the depressed state of farming, and the effect it was having on the estate, which most concerned him. Several of the tenants were in serious financial trouble. He had been as tolerant as he could about unpaid rents, but there came a time when it was in the best interest of both the estate and the tenant to issue an ultimatum: Pay up or get out. As farms became vacant, it was becoming increasingly difficult to relet them. Some of the nearer land he could take back and farm it from Manor Farm. This would mean more capital for labour and machinery, but it might be preferable to an uneconomic rent. But the outlying farms, some of them five or six miles away, were a difficult problem. He hated the thought that land might just be left idle to revert to scrub and weeds, with the houses and buildings empty and left to ruin.

Colonel Denehurst's immediate concern was Throstle Nest. He wasn't particularly worried about Ferriday – he was a foolish man and a bad tenant – but a dairy-farm would be particularly difficult to let. However, he hoped George Coleman might provide the answer.

As he rode into the farmyard, he was impressed, as always, by George Coleman's high standards. There were neatly thatched rows of stacks; hedges were well looked after; there were no implements standing out getting rusty and the long, low, farmhouse looked comfortable and welcoming. It wasn't long before the Colonel and George were settled in front of the sitting-room fire with cups of tea and some of Dorothy Coleman's fruit cake – a delicacy for which she was a frequent prize winner at the local Women's Institute shows.

In true Yorkshire fashion, the discussion at first was general — the weather, of course, the result of the harvest and prospects for the autumn-sown wheat. Farmers worked their way slowly to the main business, arriving almost by accident at the reason for calling. The Colonel knew this well enough, but, after a second cup and some talk about George's new rams, he decided the time was opportune to sound out his tenant.

'Well, George,' he said at last, 'I expect you know that Tom Ferriday is bankrupt and under notice to quit Throstle Nest?'

'Ah 'ad heard,' replied George, carefully, never being a man to elaborate, and having some trouble with his aitches, which were frequently missed off where they should be and emphasised where they shouldn't.

The Colonel went straight on. 'It seems to me you would be the best man to take over; his land adjoins yours. You are doing a good job here, and with that eldest boy of yours now grown up, you need to expand.'

'But hold on a minute, sir,' said George more sharply than usual. 'Ah don't know nowt about cows.' In George's case the double negative didn't mean that he therefore did know about cows – in his mind, it emphasized the fact that he didn't. He added, 'Ah don't much like 'em. And you couldn't do nowt but milk at Throstle Nest.'

'I realise that, George. It's what I expected you to say, but think about it. John is a good worker and an ambitious lad from what I've seen of him. I know he has been engaged to George Turner's girl for – well, it must be over a year. Surely it's time they were married. And it's not a bad house at Throstle Nest.'

George stirred his tea, looking absently at the fire. It was certainly true what the Colonel had said about John. Dorothy had been nagging him for some time about finding a house for John and Joyce. But cows, how would John take to milking? And what about the rent? He wasn't finding it easy to pay his way as it was.

Colonel Denehurst watched him closely. He knew he had scored a point, and guessing George's thoughts correctly, he continued, 'No need to rush about it; talk it over with John and Dorothy.'

George was weakening, but still reluctant. 'Well, sir, that's right enough. But milking. My father always said, "Nivver be tied to a cow's tail," and ah've always told John the same. But we need to do summat for the lad. Ah'll be like t'old hen and brood on it a bit.'

'Good man. I'm sure you are doing the right thing,' said the Colonel. 'Let me know when you can. I won't rush you, but I do want to get this business settled without too much delay.'

With the departure of the threshing machine, work at Manor Farm had returned to normal. The three labourers, Ned, Ernie and Ted, were clearing up the mess left in the stackyard. There was old straw from the stack bottom to cart away, and heaps of chaff and pulls to tidy up. Any loose grain was scattered in the paddocks for the hens to pick over; the rest was carted into the foldyard.

Robert had been with them for an hour or so, looking for mice hiding under the loose straw. He and Rap had killed a few, but in a somewhat aimless and restless mood, he decided to take Rex, his father's gun dog, for a walk to see how the horsemen were progressing with the ploughing.

Robert was the Denehurst's third child. His elder brother, Robin, who was in the army, and his sister, Mary, were a good deal older. In fact, Robert's unexpected arrival ten years after Mary had been greeted by the farm men with vulgar amusement. In his early years, Robert had been a sickly, clinging child, spoiled by everybody, particularly his mother. Now he was taller than average, broad shouldered and physically strong. He spent most of his free time with the men on the estate, or around the fields and woods, shooting rabbits and pigeons. Occasionally he rode over to Holme Green to visit Mary and Stephen, but he was not keen on riding and apart from going to an occasional meet, he did not follow the hunt.

It was a lonely life for a young boy. At the village school there were no children of his class or social standing. Consequently, his only companions were the children of the estate workers, in particular Desmond Parker, the head gamekeeper's son, and Harry's daughter, Maggie, who was Desmond's cousin. This friendship had never been thought of as desirable, especially by the Colonel, but, in the early years of childhood, he and Marjorie had reluctantly accepted it. But now, as Robert grew older, the social gap was becoming more pronounced. The Colonel had wanted to send Robert to preparatory school when he was eight, but Marjorie, assisted by Mary, had persuaded him that this was too young for the boy to leave home. It was something which John Denehurst was now beginning to regret.

The horsemen were ploughing in a field on the far side of the park. It sloped gently from the boundary wall up to Beech Wood. The trees were just beginning to turn to a rich, golden, brown, in contrast to the dark brown strips of upturned earth left by the plough. Robert could easily pick out Harry's team of two grey horses, Jack and Bonny. He timed his approach along the headland to coincide with Harry's reaching the end of the furrow.

'Whoa then,' shouted Harry, before making his turn for the next furrow. The horses stopped, and Robert went up to his favourite, Bonny, to rub her nose and have a quiet word. Harry adjusted his cap, kicked a bit of soil off one of his boots and, turning to Robert, said, 'Now mi lad, 'ave yer come to give us an 'and?'

'I wish I could,' said Robert.

Harry's reply took him by surprise. 'Well, why not? Do yer think yer can manage to steer the plough? 'Osses will go on their own, they're no bother.'

For a moment, Robert was not sure whether Harry was teasing him. But there was no tell-tale twinkle in his kind grey eyes, and Harry had already shown him how to do several jobs, such as harrowing and loading corn, at harvest time.

'All right then, but you'll have to help me.'

Harry turned the plough round on the headland and ploughed a few yards of the next furrow before stopping. 'Come on and get 'od o' these handles. An' get your reins in your right hand. That's it, now off you go.'

Robert started, unsteadily at first, surprised how awkward and heavy the plough was. It seemed so easy when Harry did it. But as he felt the traces tighten and the share bite, he felt his confidence growing. The mouldboard turned the stubble over against the previous row, but every now and then the plough lurched away to his left, and he realised he was missing a strip, and not going very straight. But he was ploughing.

It was hard work, as much as he could manage to keep the plough from keeling over and his feet from stumbling in the furrow. He had no time to drive the horses.

About halfway across the field, his arms and back began to ache, and he almost lost control of the plough.

Harry, who was following up behind, shouted and stopped the horses. 'Well, that's not bad for a start. Not very straight, but ah can put that right next tahm around. If yer 'ang on a bit and get your breath back, yer can 'ave another go in a minute.'

Later the same evening, as the Danehurst family started dinner, the Colonel, in a good mood after his visit to Elm Farm, turned to Robert. 'Well, Robert, what have you been doing with yourself today?' he asked, carving the roast pork that Alice had just brought in.

Robert chose his words carefully. 'I went over to the twenty acre at Beech Wood to see the men ploughing.'

'Ah yes. How are they getting on? I told Bill I wanted that field sown with wheat as soon as it is dry enough.'

'They've nearly finished. Harry thought it should be ready to harrow down on Monday if it doesn't rain over the weekend.'

There was a pause for a moment as Marjorie helped them to vegetables and gravy. Then, as she sat down, she said tactlessly, 'Robert was telling me that Harry has been teaching him to plough.' Robert was horrified and gave his mother a telling look, knowing full well what was coming.

The Colonel turned angrily to Robert. 'How many times do I have to tell you that I don't want you working on the farm? You spend far too much time with the farm men and the village children. You'll end up being no better than they are. And you shouldn't encourage him, Marjorie,' he added, turning his anger onto his wife.

'Come on, John,' she said calmly, 'be reasonable. What do you expect the boy to do all day? Anyway, I think it is a good thing that he is learning something useful.'

'If I'm going to be a farmer when I grow up, I shall have to learn sometime,' broke in Robert, not being overawed by his father.

'What chance is there of your ever being a farmer?' said the Colonel, but in a more normal voice. 'There's no future in farming. Farming is only prosperous when there is a war and a shortage of food. Even the best farmers are struggling now, and have been ever since the last war.'

'Stephen and Mary seem to be doing well enough,' persisted Robert.

'Stephen's family have always had money behind them. His father was a good farmer, and Holme Green is one of the best farms in the area.'

Alice came in with an apple sponge, and when she had taken the empty plates, the Colonel continued. 'I've been up to see George Coleman today, trying to persuade him go take over Ferriday's place. I know Ferriday was never going to make a go of it at Throstle Nest, but he is only one of many who are going to go under.'

John Denehurst was now well into one of his favourite themes.

He was a pessimist by nature. If anyone showed any initiative and a will to succeed, it seemed almost as though it gave him pleasure to prophesy doom. His first reaction was always, 'You can't.' If asked why not, a simple, 'Because you can't,' was the reply.

Unfortunately, what he was saying, in this particular case, was only too true. Farming was in a very deep depression, and it was difficult to view the future with any optimism at all.

Marjorie, too, recognized the truth of his argument. As a farmer's daughter, she had seen her father struggle to make a reasonable living all his life. On his recent death, he had left only a few hundred pounds. There would be no money coming to Robert from her side of the family and the Colonel, although comfortably off, had not sufficient capital to start farming on his own account.

But Robert found his father's view of life difficult to understand. They lived in a beautiful Georgian house. His mother had two maids, and there was Albert, the "back door man," who looked after the Colonel's hunter and the ponies, brought in the logs and vegetables, and cleaned the Colonel's boots and leggings. Lord Heverthorpe held regular shooting parties throughout the winter, and his father went hunting every week. Life seemed very sweet.

For the moment, however, Robert was relieved that his father seemed to have forgotten his ploughing lesson with Harry. A career seemed a long way into the future. He was more concerned that Harry wouldn't be blamed for encouraging him to work on the farm.

Chapter 3

'Will your anchor hold in the storms of life;
   When the clouds unfold their wings of strife ...'
It was Sunday morning, and at No. 4 Estate Cottages, Dunmere, Harry Jackson was having his weekly bath. He paused for a moment in his hymn singing to look for the soap which was somewhere on the hearth rug. There wasn't much room for Harry in the tin bath, and not much water either. On the side where the fire was it was warm, hot enough to make the bath hot to the touch, but on the side away from the fire, there was a strong draught under the door from the kitchen. At least the hearth-rug was soft and comforting when he stepped out to dry himself.

The rug was one of Emily's pricked mats. The design was of a large setting sun behind a hill and a clump of trees. The sun had been a yellow blouse belonging to Mrs Denehurst; the trees were all that was left of an old green woollen dress, and a pair of Harry's old trousers had been used to make the hill. Most of the stone flagged floor was covered by similar rugs of various patterns and designs, and all were made from cast off clothes which had been cut into strips and "pricked" into an old corn sack. They were cheap, hard-wearing and not unattractive.

'When the strong tides lift and the cables strain,
   Will your anchor drift or firm remain'
Harry had found the soap and was in voice again. It was his favourite hymn, well-known to Jack and Bonny, who had no alternative but to listen to Harry's singing as they trudged up and down the rows of mangolds when he was scuffling, or to and from the corn field to the stackyard at harvest time.

Harry was just getting launched into the chorus:
'We have an anchor, that keeps the soul, steadfast and sure...
'Oo, ouch, that was hot.'
He was so carried away with his singing that he had not heard Emily come in with a kettle full of hot water, which she had heated on the kitchen stove, and was pouring into the bath.

'That will have to do you,' she said, squeezing out the last few drops.

'There's no more in the boiler, and it will take ages to boil up the kettle again.'

The boiler was the main source of hot water. Heated by the fire, it had to be filled by bucket from the tap outside the kitchen door, and, as Emily and the three girls had already had first use of the bath, Harry was having to top up with water from the kettle.

'Ah'm about finished anyway. Ah'd better be out of here before the girls get back from Sunday school. Pass us that towel.'

'Wait a minute, I'll get you a clean one.'

'This'll do. Ah want dinner in good time. You know ah 'have to be at Darren Beck by half past two. It will take me at least an hour – longer if Maggie is coming with me.'

'She *is* going with you,' said Emily, 'you know she would not miss a visit to Darren and a chance to see Gilbert's hens.'

Harry was a Methodist local preacher. Almost every Sunday, except when it was his turn to feed the horses, he would be "planned" to preach at some village chapel. Services were held on Sunday afternoons and evenings. Often he would be double booked, preaching at the afternoon service, and then being entertained to tea by a stalwart of the chapel before taking the evening service at six o'clock. He always walked, whatever the weather, sometimes five or six miles each way. If the weather was fine and the distance not too great, Maggie kept him company.

'Stop fussing,' said Emily, 'dinner is in the oven. We are having that pig fry Mrs Denehurst sent with Maggie yesterday. I don't know how we could manage without her kindness; she is always sending us a parcel of something.'

'They killed a pig last week,' said Harry, towelling himself in front of the fire. 'It won't be long before Henry is fat.'

Henry was the Jackson's own pig, which they kept in a small sty at the bottom of the garden. They fattened one every year, and he was always called Henry. Harry was privileged to live in one of the end cottages in a row of four. Bill lived in No. 1, at the other end. He also kept a pig, and the two families usually shared, each having a half of whichever pig was killed. This made it easier to deal with all the pork, a whole pig giving too much offal for one family to eat.

The cottages on the estate were identical. Downstairs there was a living-room at the front and a lean-to kitchen and scullery at the back. The stairs were partitioned off from the living-room, access being gained through a door, which opened directly onto the bottom step. Upstairs there were two bedrooms. In the Jackson's case, Harry and Emily had one, and the three girls shared the other. They were fortunate. Some families with more children, and of both sexes, were packed into the two rooms, like sheaves in a corn stack. There was no bathroom and the "privy" was under an apple tree at the far end of the garden, near the pigsty. But the two end cottages had much bigger gardens than the middle ones, with room for a hen run, as well as a pigsty. Without the home-produced pig meat, eggs and vegetables, plus an occasional rabbit, mealtimes would have been more frugal than they were. A farmworker's wage of less than thirty shillings a week, with a bit extra for overtime at certain times of the year, was barely a living wage in the late twenties and early thirties.

Harry finished drying himself, and put on his clean underwear, followed by his best shirt. On weekdays he wore the traditional farmworkers' blue striped flannel shirt with a stud at the collar, the sleeves being rolled up and held in place with an elastic band – probably one of Emily's garters. But on Sundays and special occasions, he put on a white shirt, with starched cuffs and collar. He also wore a tie. Bow ties were his one luxury in life, and he had an impressive selection of them, mostly bought by Emily and relatives as Christmas and birthday presents. He chose one with blue spots to match his thick serge, blue, Sunday suit, which he had worn every Sunday since Edwin Brown, the village tailor, had made it for his wedding, over twelve years ago.

But for all the special care which he gave to his "best" clothes, and in spite of Emily's meticulous starching and ironing, Harry appeared not quite pulled together and strangely ill at ease in his finery. He was more himself and appeared much more comfortable, in his patched old jacket and waistcoat, his baggy corduroys, tied at the knees with a piece of binder band, and his clumsy hobnailed boots, which were, in fact, much more comfortable than the highly polished, pointed black shoes, which completed his Sunday wear. The one and only garment, which was common to all days of the week, and all occasions, was his flat, peaked cap.

Harry Jackson preached from many different texts, but in reality he only had one sermon. Whatever text he announced, the message was the same – simple and direct. If you kept the commandments, and believed in the birth, death and resurrection of Jesus Christ, you would go to heaven. If you didn't, then you joined the devil in Hell. There were no refinements, and no compromise.

Harry had no natural gift with words, and very little learning. His reading was limited to the Bible, and he believed every word of it. But as a preacher, he did have his compensations. Being a quiet and rather shy man, it was natural for him to be brief; unlike many local preachers, who could bore everybody for half an hour, or even longer. His sermons were neither long, nor boring. And the congregation could always be sure of a good sing. The hymns he chose had rousing tunes, and usually a chorus. So long as "Will your anchor hold," was one of your favourite hymns, you would enjoy a service conducted by Harry Jackson.

The congregation at Darren Beck chapel knew what to expect. Harry preached there at least once a year, and they accepted him for what he was – a hard-working, honest, good-living man, who gave much of his limited spare time to the cause of Methodism, and the spreading of the gospel message. In his work and his way of life, he was one of them. His shortcomings were recognised, but forgiven. He was well liked, and nobody stayed away from chapel because Harry Jackson was the preacher.

As usual, Harry ended his sermon with a short prayer, and announced the last hymn, "When I survey the wondrous cross." It wasn't Easter Sunday – not for another two weeks, but it was near enough, and in any case it was a good tune. The organ, played by Gladys Cook, Gilbert Dawson's housekeeper, wheezed into life. Gilbert himself, sitting near the wall in the third pew, woke up with a start as the congregation shuffled to its feet and launched unevenly into the first verse. The singing was wholehearted if not tuneful or in time with the organ. A large, fat lady in a pew on the front row, just below the pulpit, had what Harry described as a voice like a swathe rake. Somehow she produced a remarkable volume of sound through her teeth and without ever fully opening her mouth. If ever she had opened it fully, she could have been heard as far away as Dunmere. A singer who could provide a good lead in a small congregation was a blessing. Emma Wiles achieved this effortlessly; it was just unfortunate that she was a semi-tone or so flat. The rest of the congregation did their best to drown her out, but with little effect. Her husband, who for some reason sat on his own at the back of the chapel near the door, had a strong voice. So, too, did Gilbert Dawson, and Harry himself had a good tenor voice, which he kept well tuned when he was ploughing or having his bath, but even their combined talents could not muffle the heavy, flat, monotone of Emma Wiles.

The singing ended, Harry pronounced the benediction and descended from the pulpit to join Maggie and meet his friends in the congregation. 'Pick that one up, it's number 118,' said Gilbert Dawson. It was a game he enjoyed playing with all visitors to Newlands Farm, and one he had played many times with Maggie ever since she had been a little girl and first accompanied Harry when he was preaching at Darren Beck.

Maggie bent down and carefully lifted up the hen, taking hold of a leg to see the number on its ring.

'Yes, of course, you're right. How do you do it – tell the difference between one hen and another? They all look alike to me.'

She put number 118 down and, picking up another, asked, 'What about this one then?' thinking that perhaps Gilbert had a few favourites which he could distinguish and that if she chose at random, she might catch him out.

'Seventy-two,' chuckled Gilbert, obviously enjoying himself. He had a laugh, which sounded a bit like a cockerel. In fact, thought Maggie, not for the first time, he looks a bit like a cockerel with his large beaked nose, receding forehead and sharp little eyes. Harry always said that people start to look like the animals they keep, especially middle-aged women with ugly little dogs.

'That one was easy. She has two curly feathers in her tail,' said Harry.

'They all have some distinguishing feature when you examine them closely. And when you see them as often as I do, you soon notice even very small differences,' replied Gilbert.

'It's time you three came in for tea,' called a voice from the garden. It was Gladys Cook, who was not only Gilbert's housekeeper but also his head poultry girl, although girl was no longer an apt description. Gladys was now well into her forties, only a few years younger than Gilbert. She had been with him over twenty years, and had started to work there as a young girl when she left agricultural college. Now she was in charge of the girls who worked on the farm and responsible for the running of the home.

Nobody quite knew what sort of relationship there was between Gilbert and Gladys. At one time, there had been a good deal of gossip in the neighbourhood and idle speculation about the sleeping arrangements. The common gibe about housekeepers was "Meat for work and sleep wi' maister". However, the local cleaner, who went to Newlands to do the housework, had rather spoilt the fun by announcing very firmly that the two bedrooms in use were at opposite ends of the house, and that both beds were slept in regularly. But as time passed the relationship, whatever it was, had come to be accepted.

In those early days, when Gladys had first started work at Newlands, it had been run as a mixed arable farm, with a large poultry unit. But, over the years, the poultry had become increasingly important. Some of the outlying land had been sold off, and Gilbert had introduced a pedigree flock of Rhode Island Reds. These produced hatching eggs and breeding stock for sale, and the Newlands strain was now recognised not only in Yorkshire, but all over the country.

The management of a pedigree flock meant long hours and hard work. Every hen was identified with a numbered ring on its leg and an accurate record kept of the number of eggs each hen laid. The birds were kept in separate breeding pens with twenty-five hens and two cockerels in each. The nest boxes were constructed so that when a hen started to lay, a door dropped over the entrance to the box, so that after laying she was unable to get out until someone came to release her and, at the same time, note her number. Two or three times a day visits were made to the laying boxes and the eggs recorded. It was a very labour-intensive system.

Not surprisingly, boiled eggs were always served at Sunday tea.

'I know you'll have two, Harry, but what about you, Maggie; you are growing a big girl now, can you manage two?' asked Gladys.

'No, just one please, auntie.' Although Gilbert was only Emily's cousin, the children had always called him uncle, and somehow it seemed natural to call Gladys auntie, even though she was no relation at all.

'She wants to leave room for some of that trifle,' said Gilbert jokingly.

'Ah've got my eye on that an' all,' said Harry. 'Ah like to get well stocked up before evening service. I could nivver preach on an empty belly.'

'Some would say you can't preach on a full one,' said Gilbert. 'Don't be so rude,' chipped in Gladys.

'He knows I don't mean it, don't you Harry?'

'Ah don't see how you could know anyway. Yer always asleep,' said Harry, not missing an opportunity to get his own back.

'It's the only chance I get for a bit of rest. It's been a bit hectic round here just lately. How are things on the estate, Harry?'

Harry knocked the top off his egg.

'Not very good. You would know Ferriday went bust. The Colonel is worried there will be some more yet. And ah don't see how Manor Farm can be paying its way. Everything we produce is worth less money than it was last year, and our expenses don't go down. And he hasn't laid any men off.'

'I'm surprised he hasn't mechanised more. You still only have two tractors, don't you?'

'Two too many. You can only use them when it's dry. They soon make a mess on any land that's a bit wet. Give me a pair of 'osses any day.'

Gilbert didn't pursue that reply. He knew how Harry felt about horses, and if he got launched onto that topic they could well be late for evening service. Instead he turned to Maggie.

'You're very quiet, young lady. What are you doing these days?'

'Getting into mischief,' said Harry before she could reply.

'Her and master Robert were larking about in the granary when we were threshing last week. They'll have Bill after them if they're not careful.'

Maggie blushed slightly and said, 'Rather him than Colonel

Denehurst. He really does scare me.'

'Well, I hope you are taking school seriously,' said Gladys. 'Jobs are difficult to find now. You'll need a good education if you are going to get anywhere in the future.'

Harry and Maggie were walking back to Dunmere after evening service. The valley below was shrouded in mist, thick enough to hide the lights of Kirkley, but there was no fog up on the hill road and a crescent moon floated in a clear sky.

'You are very quiet; are you getting tired? We've only about a mile to go now.'

'No, I'm fine, dad,' replied Maggie. 'It's just that I was thinking about what auntie Gladys was saying at teatime.'

'What was she saying?'

'You know, about school and work. Do you think there's any chance of my going on to secondary school when I'm old enough?'

'Ah don't rightly know,' said Harry hesitatingly. 'Ah'm not very well up in school topics. You'll have to ask your mother, she knows more about it than me.'

'Perhaps Robert might know,' said Maggie, after a pause.

'He might, but he won't be interested in a secondary school around here. He won't be needing a scholarship or anything like that. He'll be going to boarding-school soon. Come to think of it, ah'm surprised he hasn't gone already.'

'I shall miss him if he does go.'

'Well, he's grown up now. You both are. You can't expect Robert to be interested in playing with you much from now on. It was different when you were both little, but when he gets away from here, he'll be meeting friends of his own type.'

'You mean I won't be good enough any more?'

Harry paused awkwardly. 'Well, yes, ah suppose so. Ah didn't mean it quite like that. It's no reflection on yer. Yer know how I feel about yer. But, after all, he *is* the Colonel's son and ah'm just one of the farm men. Once he goes away to school ah reckon you can say goodbye ti Robert.'

Maggie didn't reply. She was hurt by what Harry had said. She found it difficult to analyse her feelings about Robert, but he had been her companion and friend ever since she could remember and she couldn't imagine life in Dunmere without him. Her commonsense told her that what her father had said was true, but her heart hoped otherwise. She felt a lump in her throat, but forced back the threatened tears. Instead of crying, she took her father's hand – it was a rough, coarse, hand, the fingers cracked by years of hard work, but it was warm and comforting to Maggie.

'Come on,' said Harry encouragingly, 'let's have a sing over the last half mile.' As they dropped down the hill into Dunmere and the mist finally blotted out the moon, it seemed natural that he should lead off with, "Lead kindly light amidst the encircling gloom." For Maggie, it had an added significance. An omen perhaps?

Chapter 4

It was dinner-time at Dunmere Council School. Robert, along with most of the village children, had been home for a hurried meal, and was back in the playground twenty minutes or so before the start of afternoon school. Children from the outlying farms, some of whom had a two- or three-mile walk over fields or rough tracks, brought a packed meal, which they had eaten even more quickly. In the boys' playground, an improvised game of football was in progress. Facilities were scarce. A pile of coats substituted for goal posts and a frayed tennis ball was being kicked around on the gravelled surface. There were two sides, of a sort, but no referee, and a distinct lack of team work. In fact, it was difficult to know who was in each team, and frequently play was held up to try and bring some sort of discipline to the game, or to retrieve the ball from the adjoining field. Only about half the boys were playing, and the remainder either stood around shouting and arguing or played in a separate part of the playground behind the toilets, generally referred to as "the bogs".

Suddenly, for no other reason than the ball happened to come in his direction, Frank, a big, rather gormless lad, wearing very short trousers and hobnailed boots, but who was not a member of either side, took a huge swipe at the ball, which he sent high over the brick wall into the girls' playground.

'You stupid twit; what did yer do that for?' shouted Albert. 'Yer know the girls won't let us 'ave it back.'

Albert Lloyd was nearly fourteen, the eldest of a family of three boys and two girls, who all attended Dunmere School. They were a rough, crude bunch. Although they quarrelled frequently amongst themselves, there was a strong family loyalty; if anyone from outside threatened one of them, the rest quickly rallied round.

Albert and his brother, Jimmy, worked on their father's small farm at weekends and during school holidays. They also helped with the livestock before and after school, often arriving late and smelling strongly of pigs. Beatrice, the eldest girl, was as rough and uncouth as the boys. She, too, worked on the farm, feeding calves and looking after the poultry.

It was Beatrice who had now taken possession of the boys' tennis ball.

'Come on our Beattie, chuck it back or I'll deal with you on the way home,' shouted Albert.

'You and who else?' taunted Beatrice, and started to get the girls organised for a game of rounders.

'It's no good bothering about them,' said Jimmy. 'Let's get that bugger, Frankie.'

'Yeah, let's debag him. Come on lads, grab him,' shouted Albert.

A group of big boys, led by Albert and Jimmy, got hold of the kicking and struggling Frank, dragged him over to the wall and pulled off his trousers.

'Come and have a look at this, girls,' yelled Jimmy, as Frank's private parts were exposed.

There was a lot of shouting and jeering from both boys and girls and in the general melee, Maggie Jackson, in a misguided effort to restore peace and harmony, threw the ball back into the boys' yard.

Beatrice was furious. 'You silly little bitch; what the hell did you want to interfere for? Come on girls, we can't be beaten by those louts over there,' she screamed.

Four or five girls then got hold of Maggie, holding her down while Beatrice triumphantly pulled off her knickers and waved them in the air.

By now there was a line of boys scrambling onto the wall at the base of which Maggie was lying with her skirt over her head and her bare, white, thighs spread-eagled on the rough ground. Before she could recover herself, Albert, who was seldom without a piece of chewing gum in his mouth, dropped a large cockle of spit right onto where her pubic hairs were beginning to show.

Robert, who had been on the fringe of all this horseplay, suddenly found himself involved. Normally the village boys were careful how they behaved towards Robert. Although he was at school with them and took part in their playground games, he was never quite one of them. He would never have been a target for debagging. Robert was not a prude, but Albert and Beattie's behaviour disgusted him, especially as it was Maggie who had been the victim of their bullying.

'You filthy swine,' he shouted at Albert, grabbing hold of his legs to pull him off the wall.

'Get your dirty paws off me,' yelled Albert, at the same time lashing out with his feet. Robert hung on and, as Albert fell down off the wall, the two boys squared up to each other.

'You think you are God Almighty just because your old man is a bloody Colonel.'

'You keep my father out of this,' snapped Robert.

23

'Keep him out? You can't keep his long nose out of anything, telling everybody what they should or shouldn't do. Anybody would think it was him, not Lord Heverthorpe, who owned the bloody estate.'

Robert was not going to stand by and hear his father insulted by Albert Lloyd, or anyone else. He aimed a blow at Albert's face, but Albert, who was older and bigger than Robert, retaliated, catching the younger boy a blow to the eye. But just when the skirmish looked like developing into a real fight, Desmond and Jimmy pulled them apart just as the bell sounded for afternoon school.

They were both hot, red-faced and short of breath, but neither of them appeared to have suffered any serious damage. If the schoolmistress, Miss Blakey, noticed anything amiss, she tactfully avoided passing any remarks. She had difficulty enough keeping order in the classroom without worrying too much about what went on outside. As it was, afternoon school passed without incident, and when it ended at half past three, Robert and Albert kept out of each other's way.

It was only when Robert and Des were walking home that Robert became aware of mistiness and watering of his left eye. Turning to Des he asked, 'Can you see anything wrong with my eye?'

'Cor, not 'alf, you're going to have a real shiner there.'

'Go on, pull the other one.'

'No, honest, it's beginning to puff up and turn black.'

'Bad?' asked Robert, feeling his eye, and, for the first time, becoming concerned.

Desmond's reply was not encouraging. 'Well not too bad yet, but it's now quite noticeable and it will probably get worse.'

'Christ, what am I going to say when I get home?' asked Robert anxiously.

'You can hardly pretend it was an accident,' said Des as the two boys walked on. 'In any case, the Colonel is sure to find out from somebody what happened. Ah reckon you'd better come clean.'

There was silence for a time as the boys walked on considering the events of the afternoon.

'Maggie wasn't hurt, was she?' asked Robert, breaking the silence.

'No, I don't think so. A bit shaken up. It can't have been very comfortable lying half naked on that rough gravel.'

'If she's scratched or bruised herself, at least it won't show,' said Robert ruefully.

Des didn't reply. He was picturing again the fleeting glimpse of bare thighs and midriff. Although he felt guilty about it, after all she was his cousin, he was rather annoyed that he was on the end of the line on the wall and hadn't a better view!

'I'm taking the short cut home,' he said as they came to a stile on the side of the road.

'Hope you don't get into too much trouble at home. See you on Monday.'

'I hope so too,' shouted Robert over his shoulder as he turned in at the white gates of Manor Farm drive.

Usually, when he came home from school, Robert went straight into the buildings or the stackyard, to see if any of the farm men were about. But, on this occasion, he was anxious not to be seen with his black eye, so he crossed over the yard, passed the stable and pond, and sneaked unobtrusively to the back door, observed only by Rex, who wagged his tail in response to Robert's whispered, 'Hi, fella.'

Once in the house, he slipped quietly passed the kitchen door and up the back stairs to his bedroom. Not exactly trusting Des's opinion, he wanted to see for himself the extent of the damage to his eye. One look in the mirror was enough. There was no way he could hide that.

He fingered the swelling gingerly. It wasn't particularly painful, and Robert concluded that it looked worse than it was. He pottered around his room for a while in a reflective mood, putting off as long as possible the inevitable confrontation with his mother and, much more daunting, his father.

Through the window he could see across the yard to the pond. As a small boy he had spent many hours there watching the horses coming out of the stable for a drink. The stable door was close to the side of the pond, and on Saturday and Sunday afternoons, the horsemen let out the horses one at a time to drink. They each had their idiosyncrasies. Bonny stamped on the water with a front foot, stirring up the mud before drinking – perhaps it tasted better that way. Jack pottered about, sniffing and taking an occasional sip, but if the weather was cold and the water uninviting, he would turn back at the stable door without drinking at all. And, for some reason known only to himself, Punch, who in any case was a rather stupid and stubborn animal, pushed his nose right into the water above his nostrils, and when he found he couldn't breathe, panicked, tossing his head and snorting as he clattered back to the stable. He had been one of the first horses to be sold when the tractor arrived.

Sometimes on Sunday afternoons, Maggie came with Harry, and Robert would sneak out to join her in a game of hide-and-seek round the stacks, or go to watch Ned milking the cows. There, in the cow shed, they would often be joined by two or three expectant farm cats, and Robert would dash over to the kitchen to borrow a saucer from Alice.

But those innocent days seemed a long time ago. On this fine, spring afternoon, only a few ducks and geese ruffled the still water on the pond, and there were fewer of them than usual, as most of the birds were now penned up for the breeding season.

Robert turned reluctantly from the window, took one final look in the dressing table mirror, and went apprehensively down stairs.

'Cor, what happened to you?' asked a startled Alice. 'Has your mother seen it?'

'Have I seen what?' asked Mrs Denehurst, as she entered the room carrying a tea tray.

'My eye, mother,' said Robert, turning to face her.

'Oh, my poor boy, what on earth have you been doing? Come to the bathroom and let me find something to bathe it with.'

Robert followed Mrs Denehurst meekly to the bathroom. 'Now tell me all about it while I bathe it with some lint,' she said gently.

Choosing his words carefully, Robert outlined the events in the school playground. It wasn't easy. He could not possibly tell his mother the full story of what had led up to the fight. He left out all reference to the debagging of Maggie and concentrated on Albert Lloyd's bad behaviour, especially his insulting remarks about the Colonel. Mrs Denehurst listened patiently and sympathetically while she bathed Robert's eye. She knew enough about the Lloyd family to accept that part of the story, but she had a feeling that she had not been told all there was to know. However, she did not press the point and, putting away the lint, said, 'There now, that should take out the worst of the swelling. Does it feel any easier?'

'Yes, thanks,' said Robert, hoping that his mother asked no more questions.

'I don't know what your father is going to say when he comes home. You know how he feels about the village children and he has told you repeatedly not to get too closely involved with their squabbles.'

'How can I help it when I'm with them all day?' said Robert plaintively.

'I know it's not your fault, darling, but you should know to keep well clear of the Lloyds. Stick to Maggie and Desmond and the estate children.' She paused for a moment, gave Robert a kiss and added, 'Now off you go. Fortunately your father will be late home from York and you won't see him until breakfast time.'

'I sent Alice to bed. There was no point in her waiting up after ten o'clock. Do you want me to get you a hot drink?' asked Marjorie.

'No thanks, darling. It's been a long day; I'll just help myself to a Scotch. Do you want anything?'

'Just a small sherry. I want to talk to you about Robert before we go to bed.'

John and Marjorie Denehurst were sitting in front of the sitting-room fire. The Colonel had caught the last train from York to Kirkley, where Albert had met him with the pony and trap. It was almost half past ten when they arrived at Manor Farm.

'Can't it wait until the morning?'

'I suppose it could, but I would sooner talk now. I shall only keep turning it over in my mind all night. Anyway, there's never time at breakfast and I want you on your own.'

John sipped his drink. 'All right, what's the problem?'

'I won't go into all the details,' said Marjorie, 'But Robert has had a fight with Albert Lloyd. You know...'

'Good God, why?' interrupted the Colonel. 'He knows only too well...'

'Don't start all that again, darling.' It was Marjorie's turn to interrupt. 'Of course he knows. Let me finish. In a way I'm rather proud of him and you will be too when you've heard the full story.'

The Colonel grunted and Marjorie took a sip of her sherry before going on to explain Albert's behaviour and Robert's reaction.

'Is his eye bad?' asked John when she had finished her story.

'No, not really. I think Desmond and some of the other boys stopped them before any serious damage was done.'

'Well, I'm glad he stood up for me. After all, young Lloyd is a good deal older, and a tough youth. But I shall have plenty to say when I see him in the morning.'

'Don't be too hard on him, John,' said Marjorie, putting a hand on his arm. 'I know I spoil him, but it is not really all his fault. I have been sitting here thinking all the evening, which is why I wanted to talk to you tonight. I blame myself. I have been selfish and short-sighted. You were quite right; I see that now. We should have sent him away to boarding-school ages ago, where he could be with boys of his own sort. There is really nobody about here he can be friendly with.'

The Colonel was silent for a moment. He sipped his Scotch, staring into the fire, and casting his mind back to the many conversations they had had since Robert was eight. He felt a bit out of touch with his young son and was only now realising that Robert must be leading a rather lonely life.

'All right, my dear,' he said eventually. 'I won't say anything much about the fight. I'm as much to blame as anybody. I've left the boy too much on his own wandering about the farm. I shouldn't have let you and Mary talk me out of sending him away. I'm too soft with that girl; always have been. We'll talk it over with the family when Mary and Stephen come over on Sunday.'

27

He stood up, walked over to Marjorie's chair, and stooped to kiss her upturned cheek.

'Thank you, darling,' she said smiling. 'I can go to bed and sleep now.'

Chapter 5

'Well, my boy, we are going to make a man out of you now,' said Colonel Denehurst at breakfast the following morning. 'Your mother has told me all about your fracas with young Lloyd. I could have a lot to say about that, but I won't. As far as I'm concerned, that particular episode is closed.' He paused for a moment to take a drink and start to butter a piece of toast. 'Perhaps I'd better rephrase that,' he added jokingly as he looked at Robert's half-closed eye. 'How is the eye this morning, still a bit sore?'

'You'd better bathe it again after breakfast, dear,' said Mrs Denehurst.

'It looks worse than it is,' said Robert, not wishing to dwell on the subject. He looked at his mother questioningly. He had dreaded breakfast with his father, and now he couldn't understand his jocular mood. It wasn't that the Colonel was a heavy-handed father or a bad-tempered man, he had sufficient authority without, but he wasn't usually in a frivolous mood at breakfast. More often than not, he had almost finished breakfast by the time Robert came down, and was in a hurry to see Bill about the day's work or ride off round the estate.

'Your father and I had a long talk last night,' said Marjorie, taking her cue. 'We decided it's time you went away to boarding-school.'

For a moment Robert was stunned. He had just taken a mouthful of bacon and egg, but that was not the reason for his being tongue-tied. As his mother frequently reminded him, his manners were not so impeccable as to prevent him from talking with his mouth full if he had something he needed to say. But for the moment he had nothing to say. He quickly tried to sort out his feelings. He had always expected to go to boarding-school some time, but it was the suddenness of the decision, which had taken him unawares. Normally important decisions in the family were discussed at length, and carefully analysed, but he realised now that the skirmish in the school playground had quickly brought things to a head, leaving "no time" for discussion. It was an outcome, which he had not anticipated, and he did not know whether he was pleased or sorry.

'When, and where, am I going?' he said at last. 'We don't know yet,' said the Colonel. 'I shall have some to enquiries to make. Probably next September. Obviously we should like you to go to Oakfield if they have a vacancy. I expect we shall be able to arrange it. As an old boy, I have a bit of influence there, and as Robin went there as well, there is a strong family tradition. However, I must go now. I want to see Bill before he goes home for breakfast. There were a few ewes likely to lamb during the night and they haven't finished preparing the lambing shed yet.' The Colonel took a last drink of tea, rose and walked towards the door. 'We will talk more about school tonight. But the sooner you can go, the better,' he called as he closed the door behind him.

'I expected father to be angry about my fight with Albert Lloyd,' said Robert to his mother as soon as they were alone together.

'That was his first reaction when I told him last night. But on reflection, it made him – it made us – both realise that it was more than time you got away from the village school. You need to meet children of your own type.'

Marjorie finished her toast and marmalade. 'Do you want to go away?' she asked.

'I don't know. I need to think about it. It has come up rather quickly and unexpectedly.'

'I realise that, darling, but we shall both have time to get used to the idea before September. Now if you don't want any more toast, I'll send Alice in to the clear the pots.'

It was a cold, but sunny, March morning. Bill, with the help of Ernie, Ned and Ted, was busy preparing the lambing quarters. Four or five bays of the wagon shed had been cleared, and hurdles were being put into place to form a series of small pens. The open ends of two bays had been closed in with a stack sheet to give additional shelter for the new arrivals. Later, the whole area would be spread with straw, and if the weather really turned cold, the hurdles would be clad with more straw. The ewe flock had been brought into the home paddocks several days ago, and every day expectant mothers would be brought into the nursery to lamb. After a few days of warmth and shelter, mothers and lambs were turned out to fend for themselves, and make room for late lambers.

'What happened to you then? It's a fair shiner you've got there!' said Ned as Robert came into the shed to assess progress. 'You should see the other fella,' said Robert quickly, hoping to forestall the next quip which he knew for certain would be coming.

'You and Des had a fight then?' queried Ted.

'A back-hander from young Maggie, more like. Trying something on were you?' said Ernie, grinning.

Robert felt his colour rising. He had been prepared for some leg-pulling and sarcastic comments when he saw the farm men, but the reference to Maggie was a bit of a shock. Had they heard the full story of the playground antics? You could never tell with Ernie, and gossip in a small village spread quickly, being amply embellished as it went. Robert sought safer ground.

'How many lambs so far?' he asked, walking over to Bill, who was expertly tying two hurdles together.

'We 'ad fahve last neet,' said Bill. 'Yer can come and give us an 'and toneet, it looks like ah'll be busy.'

He took a large penknife out of his waistcoat pocket, cut a loose end off the binder twine, and before putting it away again, he took a roll of black tobacco twist out of another pocket, cut a piece off and pushed it into his mouth with the penknife.

'Ah don't suppose ah can tempt yer wiv a bit,' he added, more as a statement than a question.

'No thanks,' said Robert.

'It'll make your hair curl,' shouted Ernie, never backward when it came to trotting out the well-worn quip.

Robert ignored that gibe. He was not in the mood to spend time idly talking to the men. He needed somewhere quiet to think, and decided to take Meg, his pony, out for a ride. Although he had been taught to ride almost as soon as he could walk, Robert was not an enthusiastic horseman. He much preferred walking round the woods and lanes with Rex and an air rifle, or, preferably, an old shotgun if he knew the Colonel was away for the day and unlikely to find out who was shooting in the woods. Consequently, Meg did not get enough exercise. For a time, she was too frisky and mettlesome for Robert to relax, but by the time they had reached the bridle-road, which skirted the south end of the park before joining the Kirkley Road, she had settled down to a quiet walking pace. It was an ideal morning for a ride. The rooks were noisily building in a group of oak trees. Along the bank, on the side of the road, cowslips and primroses were just beginning to emerge, and Robert hoped that the daffodils in Beech Wood would be in flower. They had been in bud when he and Maggie had been bird nesting up there the previous week. Soon, the swallows would arrive, skimming over the farm pond, and finding their old nesting sites under the eaves of the stable.

The bridle-path rose steeply, and when they reached the top of the ridge, Robert dismounted and left Meg to graze by the edge of the road. He sat down at the foot of an old elm and looked back towards the village and Manor Farm. He could see clearly the two tractors moving up and down the twenty acres as Alan and Tom prepared the field for a crop of turnips. Further across, and nearer to the deer park and the hall, two of the horse teams were rolling a field of winter wheat. Looking the other way, he could see Kirkley lying by the river Dun at the bottom of the dale, and over to the far side of the valley the hills rose up to the moors and the sea beyond.

For Robert, this was what life was all about. It was this beautiful, unspoilt countryside and the life on the farm which he would miss when he went to boarding-school – apart from his home and family. There would be no lambing, no sowing, no hay time. No animals; no Rex. There would be no Harry or Des or Maggie. He would miss her terribly – her gaiety, her laughter and bubbling fun. How could Ernie think of his making a pass at Maggie? Not that he knew much about these things, but, in any case, Maggie to him was just a friend. He didn't really think of her as a girl. She was, and always had been, just a part of the farm and his life on the estate.

Of course he would still see her in the holidays, but he felt it would never be quite the same again. In fact, it wasn't quite the same now. A lot seemed to have happened since he had walked up to Beech Wood with her. For some reason, which he didn't quite understand, he had not wanted to see Maggie following the incident in the playground. Perhaps once he had talked to her he would find their relationship the same as it always had been. But he had the feeling that he would not be seeing as much of her and Des during the Easter holiday as usual.

He got up from the grass under the elm. His trousers were stuck to the back of his legs – obviously the grass was still wet but he had been too preoccupied to notice until now. He walked over to Meg, took her reins, mounted and rode thoughtfully back down the hill towards Dunmere.

'Does your eye hurt? It looks nasty,' asked Maggie, as she and Robert walked home from school.

Robert was getting bored by people asking about his eye.

'It probably looks worse than it is,' he gave her his stock reply. 'What about you, did you hurt yourself on the gravel?'

'Just an odd scratch and bruise – can you see them?' Maggie asked, unconsciously lifting her skirt to look at the back of her legs.

'Nothing to worry about,' said Robert. 'She's a real cow, Beattie Lloyd. Almost as bad as Albert.'

'He's going around saying he's going to do you over well and truly. I should keep out of his way if I were you.'

'Well, he's leaving school at Easter. He was fourteen last month. I don't suppose we shall see much of him after this week.'

'Did you tell the Colonel about your fight with Albert?'

'Yes – well sort of. I couldn't really hide it or make up an excuse. I didn't go into any details. What about you? Did you say anything? After all, your cuts and bruises are not as obvious as my eye.'

'No, I didn't tell mum. There was nothing I could say; I mean, I couldn't tell her what Beattie and Albert did, so I didn't say anything.' She paused, and there was silence for a few minutes. 'Was your father angry? I'm glad I didn't have to tell him.'

'No, that's the funny thing. I thought he would be furious, but it turned out differently from what I expected. I'm going away to boarding-school in September.'

So dad was right after all, thought Maggie. Even so, the knowledge had come sooner than she had expected. It was still a shock. She paused before replying and then, to hide her concern, I asked rather casually, 'Where to?'

'I'm not sure yet, probably Oakfield – that's where Robin went. I'll still see you in the holidays though, won't I?' she asked, rather anxiously. And then, before Robert could reply, she blurted out her own news. 'I may be going to grammar school in September if I get a scholarship. Mum talked about it to Miss Blakey after chapel yesterday. She's going to find out about it, and help me to prepare for the exams next term. Des may go as well.'

'He hasn't said anything to me about it,' said Robert.

'No, well it's still a secret really.'

Robert thought about it. 'But how would you get there? It's ten miles or more.'

'I should have to cycle to Haggs Cross and get a bus from there.'

'But it's four miles at least – all right in the summer. But in winter it could be raining, or even snowing. I wouldn't want to do it.'

'You're lucky. You don't have to. Your dad can afford to send you to a posh boarding-school. But I don't want to end up as a maid, or work in a shop or something crummy. I need to get a decent education and make a career.'

'What do you want to do?'

'I don't know. It's no good building castles at this stage. I'll have a better idea when I'm older and have passed my exams.'

Robert had no doubt about Maggie's ability. She was a clever girl. But whether she had the stamina to travel every day to Beacroft and then do her homework at night, he was not so sure. He pursued his thoughts with Maggie.

'I'm sure you can pass your matric. But the travelling. You won't get home 'til after five. It will be dark in the winter.'

'I know all that, silly. Anyway it hasn't happened yet. And don't say anything to anybody in the village. Mum hasn't mentioned it to anybody yet.'

'You needn't worry about me, Maggie. We have often had secrets in the past. Anyway, I shall seldom be seeing any of the village people from now on.'

'Not even me?' asked Maggie, turning her head to look into his eyes. She wanted to test his reaction.

'You are different. I shall always want to see you.'

'Always? Always is a long time.'

'Always.'

Chapter 6

The house at Manor Farm dated back to the eighteenth century. It was a fine house, built of stone in the traditional Georgian style. It was larger and more elegant than the traditional Yorkshire farmhouse, being built originally by one of Lord Heverthorpe's ancestors as a dower house. The buildings had been added at a later period but now the farmstead and house formed a complete entity, situated on the edge of the deer park on the outskirts of Dunmere village.

At the rear, the house backed onto the buildings and pond, but the front overlooked the park with a terrace and large lawns sloping down to the river Dun, which curved round behind the walled vegetable and fruit garden to run through the centre of the village. The east was sheltered by a planting of tall elm trees, noisy with building rooks in the spring and carpeted with a mass of snowdrops and daffodils. To the west, a shrubbery dominated by old-fashioned roses backed onto the boundary wall of the park. It was a stone wall, over twelve feet high, but even that was not always stockproof. One year the snow had drifted against the wall high enough for the deer to jump over the top and escape during the night. There is nothing safe from a herd of hungry, marauding, deer, and after stripping the vegetable garden they had moved on into the turnip field before the men could round them up the following day.

But now it was a hot, rather sultry, Sunday afternoon. Mary and Stephen had driven over from Holme Green for the day, taking the opportunity of a quiet period on the farm before the start of harvest. The family were having afternoon tea on the terrace and Marjorie, pouring out a second cup for John said, 'This tea is beginning to look like brown gravy. Be a darling, Robert and ask Alice for some more hot water, would you?'

'Oh, all right,' said Robert resignedly. It was over a week since he had arrived home for the summer holidays.

He had been at boarding-school for two years now, but it still took him several days to adjust to the very different lifestyle. His mother, too, had still not become accustomed to his comings and goings, and she seemed to forget that he was now a teenager.'

'You should have let me go, mother,' said Mary when Robert had disappeared out of earshot. 'You should treat him as an adult and not send him off as if he was an errand boy.'

'He doesn't mind,' said Marjorie.

'You shouldn't exploit his good nature. Anyway, what is he going to do all the holidays? You should put him to work on the farm,' said Mary, turning to the Colonel.

Her father answered rather sharply. 'We have only just managed to wean him away from the farm men and the village; I don't want to undo the good work of the last two years.'

'Nonsense,' said Mary, as usual not overawed by her father. 'What harm can the men do? Are you frightened he might pick up a few juicy titbits, or learn some new swear words? You are always saying yourself that the men watch their language. Come on, dad, he's nearly fifteen.'

'I'm not worried about that aspect. It's just that I don't like the idea of my son and, of course, your mother's as well, not to mention you as his sister, working as a paid farm man.'

Mary stood her ground. 'It's no different from the army where you had officers and men living and fighting together.'

The Colonel sensed that if the argument went on, he might come off worst. 'I'm not going to argue with you, Mary. I'm not going to be influenced by you again; you and your mother between you persuaded me to delay sending Robert to Oakfield and we all know the results of that.'

'No real harm has been done,' said Marjorie.

'Of course it hasn't,' added Mary. 'The poor lad has to fill his days in somehow. He may as well do something useful.'

Robert returned, carrying a hot water jug. 'I thought I may as well save Alice a journey. What's that about me doing something useful?' he asked.

'About my doing something useful,' corrected Marjorie. 'Don't they teach you anything at that school?'

'I was just suggesting to dad that you should be working on the farm instead of poking around the fields and woods all day with a gun, or larking around with Maggie and Des,' said Mary.

'I don't lark about with Maggie and Des. I've hardly seen them since I went to Oakfield and they went to Kirkley,' said Robert.

'Well, I've got a suggestion to make,' said Stephen, who had been sitting quietly for some time. 'Go on then, darling, let's hear it,' said Mary.

'If John doesn't want Robert working here, he can come and help us at Holme Green. I can do with all the help I can get. We can find a bed for him, can't we Mary?' he asked, turning to his wife.

'It's a bit sudden to ask, but yes, of course we can. How about it, Robert?'

'Yes, smashing, if you really mean it, but I shall expect to be paid. No slave labour.'

Stephen was amused by his quick response.

'All right, we will see how you shape. If you get down to some hard work, I'll make it worth your while.'

'You won't mind, will you mother?' asked Robert, suddenly realising that he had no sooner arrived home before being away again.

'I shall miss you darling. It's bad enough when you are away all term, but by all means go if you want to. You can come home at the weekends and even during the week if the weather interferes and Stephen doesn't need you.'

'You have been very quiet, dad,' said Mary. 'Have you any objections?'

'No, if that's what everybody wants,' he replied, a little taken aback by the rapid turn of events.

He wasn't very enthusiastic about the idea, but he was far happier for Robert to work with Stephen than having him working at Manor Farm.

Colonel Denehurst walked round the stackyard feeling worried and depressed. Normally by the end of September the stackyard would be full of rows of pikes and stooks. Thatching would be well on the way, each pike being finished off with a cockerel on the top.

The cockerels were home-made affairs. A piece of tin was cut out to form the outline of a rooster and fastened by a swivel to a round piece of wood – often the shaft of a broken pitchfork. The shaft was then pushed firmly into the pinnacle of the pike, leaving the cockerel free to swing backwards and forwards in the wind in the way of a weathervane. There was no finer sight than a neatly thatched row of pikes proudly flying a red painted cockerel. They were a landmark for miles around Dunmere.

But the harvest this year was still not finished, and the thatching not even started. John Denehurst was not only anxious about his own harvest at Manor Farm, but even more worried about the effect a bad harvest would have on the estate. There were two or three tenants who were depending on a good harvest to stay solvent, and the Colonel knew of others who were only hanging on through the goodwill of the bank manager. There were signs of the agricultural depression all round, with stone walls falling down, broken gates and fences unrepaired, hedges left uncut, and even fields no longer cultivated and covered in charlock and thistles.

Already, the autumn nights were drawing in. The air was warm and muggy. The heavy overcast sky brooded ominously over the farmstead. Bats flitted low over the still, black, water of the pond. There was no reflection of the moon or stars; no shadows round the buildings, just a quiet eerie feeling which reminded the Colonel of the night before the battle of the Somme. He walked slowly back to the house for dinner.

'We thought we'd lost you, John. Dinner has been ready for ages,' said Marjorie. 'If you want a Scotch, you'd better make it a quick one.'

'There's nothing I need more,' said the Colonel, going over to the drinks cupboard. 'I've just been walking round the stackyard. I reckon that we have at least three days threshing less than we would have in a normal season.'

'That's just what Stephen said the other day. Although three days is more serious for him, as he doesn't have as many acres of corn as we do here,' said Robert.

'If we can avoid a storm tonight, we should finish harvest tomorrow. We shall be a man short, but if Bill gets himself properly organised, they should manage to finish that last pike.'

'Is it Jim's case at court tomorrow?' asked Marjorie.

'Yes, it is, and I'm pretty fed up about it,' said the Colonel irritably. 'It's bad enough when I have to lose a day sitting on the bench, but it's even more frustrating when you are dealing with one of your own men.'

'That means that Albert and Jimmy Lloyd will be up as well. Make sure you clobber them, won't you, dad?' Robert was keen for revenge, remembering all too well the black eye he had received from Albert in the school playground.

'They'll get what they deserve,' said the Colonel, anxious to show impartiality and justice.

Jim and the Lloyd brothers were well-known for their poaching exploits. Not for the first time they had been caught by the estate game-keepers, and the Colonel was quickly running out of patience.

'If Jim is caught again after this, I shall sack him. I can't afford to carry irresponsible young men these days. It's not as though he was a married man with a large family to feed. Every man counts in a year like this, and his absence tomorrow will upset the balance of the whole team.'

The following morning, the Colonel was in the estate office, talking over the day's work with Bill before going off to the Crown Court at Bridborough. 'Just how much wheat is there left still to bring in?' he asked, signing some letters, which Wendy had typed the previous day.

'There's about half that far twenty acre. It's a rough lot, a bit green in the bottom, but it should be safe enough to put on top of that last pike.'

'You think it will be dry enough to cart today, do you?'

'It should be, wi' a bit o' luck. We turned worst o' stooks over yesterday, to try to get arse ends of the sheaves dry. It hasn't dried much, it's too muggy and no wind, but at least it hasn't rained again, yet.'

The Colonel put down his pen and started going through his 'In' tray. 'Well, if it's anything like at all, get it stacked before it does rain again. The forecast is for thunderstorms later in the day.'

'We shall have a job ti' get it all in afore night,' said Bill pessimistically. 'It's a long way up to that twenty acre. You need five wagons to keep stack going, and don't forget we are one short with Jim being away.'

The Colonel looked up sharply. 'I'm not likely to forget about him,' he snapped. 'Make no mistake, Bill, I want that field finished today. I'm fed up with harvest this year.' He rose and moved towards the door, almost bumping into Wendy, who was coming in with some files. 'Is Albert ready with the trap?' he asked.

'Yes sir, he came a few minutes ago. He knows you were with Bill.'

'Right then, I'm off. Remember, Bill, no excuses. If that wheat isn't finished when I get back tonight, your head is on the block.' The door slammed and they heard his footsteps crunch on the gravel as he walked quickly towards the waiting gig.

'I'm glad he's away for the rest of the day. I hate it when he's in a bad mood,' said Wendy, putting her files down on the desk.

Bill was moving towards the door. 'He'll be in a worse mood when he comes back tonight. The court always has a bad effect on him. But, anyway, there's no way we can finish that field without five wagons. We shall be hanging about at the stack after every load, waiting for the next wagon to arrive, and then Ted and Ernie will be waiting for an empty wagon at their end.'

'But the Colonel must know that,' said Wendy, somewhat at a loss to know what all the fuss was about.

'Of course he does,' said Bill. 'He just feels like letting me have it sometahms, but you wait and see. Ah can be as cussed as him. Ah know how we can get finished, and it'll annoy him more than ever when he finds out.'

Normally at Manor Farm, the work was done harmoniously and efficiently. The Colonel and Bill had a mutual respect, and had developed a good working relationship. But, once in a while, usually when they were both under more pressure than usual, and tempers became frayed, there would be a real row. They were both obstinate, and liked to have their own way. In the end, of course, the Colonel had to win, but Bill was devious, as well as obstinate, and he plotted ways of getting his own back.

For instance, Bill was a skilled stacker, but he had one fault which irritated the Colonel every harvest. When building his stacks, he over-filled the middle, especially when making a pike. It was a good fault to have, because it ensured that the stack was water-tight, and there was never any waste because of seepage through the thatch. However, it meant that Bill's pikes were seldom straight. As often as not, the tops would lean slightly to one side, or the outer courses would bulge a bit, so that it was necessary to prop them with a long, stout, piece of wood. Colonel Denehurst fell out with Bill about this every year, threatening to let Harry do the stacking instead. Bill regarded this as an attempt to undermine his authority. It was customary on all farms that the foreman did the stacking, and to bring in someone else in his place would have been a serious blow to Bill's pride. It was, perhaps, foolish of Bill not to correct this fault, which he could have done easily enough, but he knew that it irritated the Colonel, and he perpetuated the fault purposely to prove his independence. He knew the Colonel well enough to know that although he would shout and rant, his bark was worse than his bite, and he would never carry out his threat.

Since his return from Holme Green, Robert had been glad to relax for a few days before going back to school. He had spent much of the time giving Meg some badly needed exercise.

He went into the stable for a halter to go and catch Meg in the horse pasture. To get to the field he took a short cut through the stackyard. Harry and Ned were unsheeting the stack, and Bill was filling up the tank on the little petrol engine, which drove the elevator. Harry's wagon was standing ready to be unloaded, having been left sheeted down since the last day of harvesting.

'Robert, here a minute, just the chap I wanted to see,' shouted Bill. Robert walked over, wondering what could have happened to make Bill call over to him so urgently. He hadn't long to wait.

'How would you like ti take Jim's wagon and horses for the day?' Bill asked, screwing the filler cap back onto the tank. 'We've got ti get that last bit of wheat in today, and we could do wi' some help.'

Robert was completely taken aback. Bill knew as well as he did about the Colonel's instructions not to work on the farm.

'I'd like to help, but I don't see how I can,' said Robert hesitatingly.

'But we're desperate. The Colonel gave me strict orders to get harvest finished today, and we can't possibly do it wi' only four wagons.' Robert thought for a few moments. Why not, he concluded. If it is as important as all that, father should be pleased rather than angry.

'Yes, I'll help,' he said. 'Are Brisk and Depper in the stable?'

'Ah expect so. Have a word wi' Harry. He'll help you to harness up. Yer can go off with Ted straight away and Harry will follow as soon as he has unloaded. The others are already there. We shall 'ave to keep moving, it could rain afore night.'

By late afternoon, the pike was past the eaves, and Bill had started to top up. Robert finished unloading his wagon just as Harry arrived with another load. Bill came down the ladder from the pike, as he did after most loads, to check round the outside course of sheaves and make sure he was keeping a regular line.

'How many more loads are there still to come, Harry?' he asked anxiously looking up at an ominous bank of heavy, black, clouds gathering over Kirkley. There was not a breath of wind, and the air was full of little black thunderbugs, which crawled everywhere, and got into the men's hair. You didn't need to be a meteorologist to know that a thunderstorm was imminent.

'Ah reckon that if Robert goes back, and I follow him, we shall about get the lot,' said Harry. 'So long as it doesn't rain first.'

By the time Robert had loaded, it was almost dark.

'Now you've cleared up this row, Harry will take the rest easily,' said Ted, moving the horses on a few yards until the wagon was opposite the next stook. He forked up the remaining sheaves, and Robert packed them in. It was a bigger load than normal, but he was confident it would carry home safely. In fact, he had barely lost a sheaf all day. Ted threw him a rope to climb down, they pulled it tight, and Robert tied it to the hook under the wagon shelving.

'Another rope on the back and she'll ride to London,' said Ted. 'Ah'll go and help Ernie to finish loading Harry. You get off home.'

Robert climbed between the horses' heads onto the wagon pole and hoisted himself up onto Depper's back. Horses always sensed when knocking off time was approaching, and they set off across the field with more urgency than usual. It was soft going after all the rain, and the wagon wheels cut shallow ruts across the stubble which, after the day's comings and goings, had the appearance of a tramway junction.

Robert turned his team onto the headland of the next field, a bare fallow already mucked out and partly ploughed ready for winter wheat. The sky over Kirkley was inky black. Suddenly there was a sheet of lightning, followed by a rumble of thunder.

'Thank goodness it was sheet and not forked lightning,' said Robert to the two horses. They responded with a twitch of the ears and plodded on, the traces tight, and the muscles rippling across their flanks. The storm grew nearer and more violent. There was a sudden flurry of large raindrops, which stopped almost as soon as they started. At the end of the fallow headland, Robert had to pass through the gate, cross a culvert over the brook, and make a sharp right-hand turn onto the lane which led down to the farmstead, still some half mile away. He negotiated the

gate, drove onto the culvert and, just as he turned the horses onto the
lane, there was a crash of thunder immediately overhead. Brisk, who
lived up to her name, and was a mettlesome horse at any time, gave a
sudden start, and lurched towards the right, pulling the front wheels of
the wagon and Depper with her. Robert pulled hard over on both horses'
bits, but he was not quick enough. The front offside wheel started to slip
down the bank of the brook, threatening to pull wagon, horses and all
with it. Robert stopped the horses. At the critical moment, when it
seemed that the load would fall into the stream, the wheel caught on an
old tree stump. The wagon stopped slipping, but was left precariously
balanced, leaning dangerously towards the beck. Fortunately the horses
stood still; even Brisk remained calm, as though she too sensed the danger. Robert carefully dismounted, his knees feeling weak and wobbly.
His hands trembled as he unhooked the traces, and quietly eased the
horses onto the lane. He reasoned that if the wagon did suddenly top-
ple over, the horses would be unable to hold it, and would be dragged
into the brook.

It was now raining hard, but the intervals between the thunder and
lightning were growing longer and the worst of the storm was over.
Robert was not sure what to do for the best. He could do nothing about
the loaded wagon. He considered taking the horses home but, realising
that the rain would have stopped Harry, if he had not already finished
loading, he decided to wait for him and the two forkers. As he was wearing only a shirt and trousers, he was now wet through. He had brought
a jacket with him, but had not had a chance of putting it on. There was
no point but he squatted behind the stone wall, to keep as rain out as
possible. The horses stood hunched with their backs towards the storm,
heads lowered and a hind hoof bent over to rest a weary leg.

As he waited in the rain, Robert pondered on his unhappy situation.
He had control of his emotions now, but he was cross with himself for
not realising the danger. Looking back, he realised that he should have
stopped and held the horses until the worst of the storm was over. Not
that he had had much warning and, in any case, the horses were used
to thunderstorms, and normally showed no fear. But he had known
about Brisk's nervous temperament and should have been prepared.

He had no illusions about the reaction of the farm men. Harry would
feel let down and be more hurt than angry. Ted and Ernie would consider it a huge joke, and he would be teased about it for months. But it
was his father's reaction that really worried him. It had, perhaps, been a
rash reaction to help out when asked by Bill, but he had agreed with the
best of motives. He had genuinely wanted to help.

'You've gotten into a bit of a pickle here,' said Harry as soon as he, and the other two, arrived.

'Were yer trying to take a short cut?' said Ernie grinning.

'You should 'ave stopped and waited until the storm had passed,' said Harry.

'I realise that now, but there seemed to be no danger at the time. It all happened so quickly,' replied Robert.

The three men gathered round the wagon for a closer inspection.

'What can we do about it? Will it have to be unloaded?' asked Robert anxiously.

Harry lifted his cap and scratched his head. A sure sign that the grey matter was working.

'It could have been worse,' he said eventually.

'If it hadn't been for that tree stump, you would have ended up int' hole,' said Ted, rather obviously.

'We 'ad better do something about it afore it gets dark,' said Harry, undoing the ropes on his own load. 'Ah reckon if we hitch Jack and Bonny to the front end corner, we can drag that wheel back up. It's not gone far.'

Ted bent down to take a closer look. 'You'll need a steady pull. If you jerk at it, you'll break t'wheel.'

Already Robert was feeling happier and relieved. His confidence returning.

The farm men were always so philosophical and practical. Whatever went wrong, they knew instinctively how to put it right.

What had seemed to him an insurmountable problem, they took in their stride. To them it was just part of the day's work.

Harry and Ted hitched Harry's team to the roped wagon. Gently, Harry took Jack and Bonny's head, one hand to each bridle. He moved them forward, slowly, until the slack of the traces was taken up. Then he paused before urging them to take the critical pull. The wagon shuddered and creaked; the horses struggled for a better grip on the slippery road, but gradually the wheel slid upwards. As it reached the top of the bank, the wagon wobbled alarmingly for a second before levelling off onto all four wheels. At one stage, it almost toppled over the other way, but Harry stopped the horses at exactly the right moment. Ted peered at the wheel.

'Ah can't see any damage. No cracks nor nowt,' he said confidently.

'Right then, get those 'osses hitched up, Robert. Let's see how she goes.' Ernie helped Robert to hitch up whilst Harry and Ted tied Harry's ropes back on and 'returned Jack and Bonny to their own wagon. Then they set off for home, the wagons following in tandem, and Ted and Ernie walking behind, carrying their forks and lunch bags. For them, the harvest was over for another year.

It was dark by the time Colonel Denehurst arrived back from the court at Bridborough. As Herbert dropped him off in the yard, he noticed that the lights were on in the stable, and he went straight in to find out how the day had gone. He found Harry brushing down the horses. His quick eye had already seen that Depper and Brisk were having their evening feed along with the other horses.

'What are Jim's horses doing in the stable, Harry? Why aren't they out in the horse pasture?'

Harry continued to brush down Jack for a moment, unsure how to respond.

'Come on, man,' said the Colonel. 'What's going on?'

Harry decided to tell all. The Colonel was sure to find out what had happened sooner or later. He tried to make Robert's accident sound as trivial as possible, and emphasised that, in spite of that and the thunderstorm, they had finished the field. Something they would never have managed without Robert's help. The Colonel listened intently, not interrupting, and Harry thought he was keeping remarkably cool.

'Where is Robert now?' he barked, when Harry had finished his story.

'He 'as gone int' house. I said ah would see to his horses.'

'And where's Bill?'

'Sheeting down in the stackyard. We shall have two wagons to unload in the morning,' replied Harry, moving round to brush Jack's other side.

'I want some words with him,' said the Colonel sharply, and turned and walked purposefully out of the door.

Bill was coming down the stack ladder to tie down the sheet when he saw a figure emerge from the barn. It was too dark to see clearly, but he knew it was the Colonel. He had been expecting him.

'And just what do you think you've been doing?' bawled the Colonel when he was still several yards away. 'I thought that at last I'd got it into even your thick skull that Robert does not work on the farm. From what Harry tells me, he could have had a serious – even fatal – accident, and then where would you have been?'

'But you ...'

'Don't interrupt,' snapped the Colonel, even though Bill was only trying to reply to his question. 'You know that when I'm away you are in charge. If anything serious had happened to Robert, or the horses, you would have been responsible. You might well have been charged with negligence.'

He paused and Bill came in quickly. 'Ah know that well enough, sir.' It wasn't often Bill gave him a "sir" but in view of the gravity of the situation, it seemed appropriate. 'Ah thowt it was the only way we could finish that field, and you'd left me very definite instructions this morning.'

'You should know by now not to take me too literally. I knew well enough you could never finish with only four wagons, but if I hadn't taken a strong line, you would have dawdled about all day and we should never finish harvest,' said Colonel Denehurst, a little less fiercely. In fact, he was relieved that harvest was over, that Robert had probably learned a salutary lesson and that Jim, too, might learn better ways following his appearance in court.

'But what would you have said if we hadn't finished?' asked Bill, still worried and alarmed by what the Colonel had said about being charged with negligence. He had never really given any thought about his own position following the accident.

'Bawled you out,' said the Colonel, suddenly laughing. The tension eased, and even Bill managed a sheepish smile.

'Master Robert did a good job today, sir, in spite of the accident.'

'I am glad he did, but it's for the last time,' and the Colonel was confident that it really would be. He looked up at the pike. 'Can you get those two loads up there; you haven't left yourself much room?'

'Ah'll pack 'em in,' said Bill, following his gaze.

'Well, watch how you do it. I don't want something looking like an abortion. One or two of those over there are on a bit of a lean. I think I might let Harry have a go next year.'

Later that evening, the Denehursts were having pre-dinner drinks. The Colonel poured Marjorie her usual sherry, and a large Scotch for himself. 'You have been going a bit hard on the Scotch recently, John,' said Marjorie, noticing the size of the Colonel's drink.'

'It's been a long, trying, day, darling, but don't worry, I'll keep control. I've seen too many chaps in the mess get hooked on the hard stuff.' He turned to Robert, who had been sitting quietly, wondering just when and in what form the storm would descend.

'Harry tells me you've also had a hard day. Would you like a drink as well? How about a sherry? It's as good as anything to start with.'

Robert had never been offered a drink before, and, for a moment, he wasn't sure if his father meant it. In the circumstances, it was the last thing he expected.

'Come on, you are nearly sixteen. You've done a man's work today. I think you've earned it, don't you, Marjorie?'

She was almost as surprised as Robert, but, after a pause, said, 'Yes, I suppose so. I didn't have a drink until I was twenty-one, but perhaps that's being old fashioned.'

Robert took the glass. 'Thanks, dad. I still feel a bit shaky after today, and I expected you to be angry with me, especially in view of the accident.'

'I was angry,' said the Colonel, 'but Bill bore the brunt of that. I'm more disappointed that you let me down after promising not to help out on the farm again. Anyway, I hope you are now sensible enough, and old enough, to discuss this whole business responsibly.'

'Oh, I am,' said Robert, much relieved. 'I realise now that I acted foolishly, but it was with the best of intentions. I've never known Bill so worried as he was this morning.'

'Well, I did lay it on the line. You've both disobeyed my orders, and your circumstances are different from his. He's a paid employee. You are not.' The Colonel paused to take a sip of his whisky. 'Now, just supposing,' he continued, choosing his words carefully, 'what sort of position would we be in if your mishap had really been serious? The horses could have been badly injured, even killed. For that matter, so could you.'

'I know that only too well. For a few minutes, I was really scared,' said Robert.

'Don't say any more about it now, darling. I shall be worried every time you go out riding, or if you help Stephen again next year,' said Marjorie.

'It was the sort of accident that could have happened to Harry, or any of the horsemen. It was the sudden clap of thunder that did it.'

'Accidents happen on farms all the time. The difference is that the farm men are covered by insurance. You're not. The men are paid to take risks. You're not. And think of Bill's position, if the accident had been fatal, he would have had to carry the can. Make sure you never put him in that position again,' said the Colonel, finishing his Scotch, and rising to pour another one.

'And another thing,' he continued. 'In the end I'm the one who carries the responsibility for the farm and the estate. I have to answer to Lord Heverthorpe. What would he say if I had to report a fatal accident to him? An accident caused by my own son, who had no business to be involved in the first place.'

Neither Robert nor Marjorie replied. There was no need to. The Colonel knew from the look on their faces that his point had gone home.

PART TWO 1933

Chapter 7

The following Saturday, Marjorie Denehurst and Alice were preparing and packing Robert's clothes for his return to school. It was a job that Marjorie hated; sewing on name tapes, mending socks and checking lists to make sure that nothing was missing. It always seemed to her that the boys lived in one another's clothes. Half the socks and the rugger shorts and vests had someone else's name on them, and the other half had no name at all. As the day went on, Marjorie became increasingly irritable, and Robert kept out of the way as much as possible. He viewed going back to school with mixed feelings. When he was at home, he missed friends of his own age and similar background, but he knew that as soon as term started, he would miss the farm and the open-air life of the countryside.

By nature, he was a quiet boy, in some ways a bit of a recluse. There was nowhere at school where he could be on his own.

After lunch, a cold meal, as Mary and Stephen were coming for dinner, he took is 2.2 rifle and went up to Beech Wood to see if there were any pigeons or rabbits about. He didn't take Rex with him as he had been out with the Colonel all the morning, and, in any case, a dog would have been a nuisance when he needed to sit quietly to wait for a flock of pigeons to settle, or a rabbit to venture into the open.

Beech Wood formed the boundary of Home Farm on the far side of the park. It was a good place for wildlife. Pheasants roosted there, being close to their feeding grounds on the barley stubble. A group of tall beeches attracted wood pigeons, and there was plenty of cover for rabbits. On the side, adjoining Manor Farm, a ditch ran between the side of the wood and a grass field. There were a lot of rabbit holes in the bank, and Robert remembered losing a ferret there the previous winter.

He soon found a good place to hide, behind some tall blackberries, where he had a clear view of the burrows, and was also within shooting distance of some trees, which looked as though they might be attractive to pigeons. There was no sign of either rabbits or pigeons, but he was quite happy to sit quietly and wait. He had been there about twenty minutes when he heard a rustle of leaves behind him, as though somebody was moving about. It was unlikely to be a poacher in the middle of the day, and the gamekeepers did not normally work on Saturday afternoons, except for shooting parties.

Turning round, Robert caught sight of a figure bending over some briars. It was a girl. She was wearing a blue and white spotted dress, and as she leaned forward to reach some blackberries, he caught a glimpse of bare legs and a mass of dark hair which was unmistakable. It was Margaret Jackson. She obviously hadn't seen him. He didn't want to call out and frighten her, so he watched and waited to see if she would turn for him to see her face.

Over the last two years, Robert had hardly seen Maggie, although he had thought about her often enough, and wondered how she was enjoying Kirkley High School. He had seen her once or twice to wave to in the village, but she never came to the farm as she had so often done when they were young children. Their relationship had never been the same after the accident in the playground during their last year at Dunmere village school. Robert had not wanted their friendship to end, but as they outgrew their childhood games, he became increasingly conscious of the social gap between them. As children, this hadn't seemed important. The farm men were accustomed to seeing them playing round the farm, but if they were seen together now, people would raise their eyebrows, and gossip round the village would be rife. Robert had no idea what Maggie thought about their relationship, but perhaps she, too, thought it prudent not to meet. But for the moment, in the shelter of Beech Wood, they were alone.

Maggie was intent on picking her fruit, and still had not seen him, although now she had turned so that he could see her clearly. She had changed. She was no longer a young schoolgirl, but more adult and sophisticated. He felt a sudden thrill through his body, something he had never experienced before. Stepping out into the glade, he called: 'Can I give you a hand? They are hardly ripe yet. You can't be finding many.'

Maggie looked up quickly. 'Oh, Bobbie, you startled me. I wondered who it was.' As she spoke, she coloured slightly. Then, recovering herself and seeing his rifle, she added, 'I hope that thing isn't loaded; I hate guns. If you're sure it's safe, you can come and help me. I haven't anything like enough for a pie.'

Robert unloaded his rifle, stood it against a tree, and went over to join her. 'I'm so pleased to see you. I go back to school on Tuesday. I haven't seen you for ages. In fact we've never had a chat together since we left Dunmere School.'

'Whose fault's that? You know where I live. You used to be keen enough to see me before you went off to that posh school. I thought, maybe, you were avoiding me these days. You once said you would always want to see me. Remember?'

'Oh, Maggie, of course I remember. It's just not so easy now. It was different when we were younger. But now I'm expected to stay away from the village. Dad doesn't even like me to work on the farm.'

'I suppose the village people are no longer good enough. Is that it?' said Maggie sharply, her blue eyes flashing.

'No, well yes, I suppose so,' said Robert rather uncomfortably. 'I don't think that, but you must understand why dad sees it that way.'

'I can see the difficulties. Our backgrounds are certainly different, but I don't see why it should stop us being friends and seeing each other occasionally.' And then, very quietly and uncertainly, almost to herself, and wondering if she should really say it, she added: 'It's not easy for me, either.'

'Why not?' said Robert rather surprised.

'Well, it's dad. You know how old-fashioned he is.'

'How does that affect it? I've always got on well with him.'

'Oh, yes. He thinks the world of you. Never stops saying how well you can do skilled work on the farm – better than some of the men. And now that you go to boarding-school, you are quite the young gentleman. Growing up to be a fine chap. He told us last night all about your mishap yesterday. Not your fault, of course. You couldn't possibly do anything wrong. But all that only makes our position worse. He doesn't think you should be involved with the likes of me either.'

By now, Maggie had worked herself up into quite an emotional state. Whatever doubts Robert may have had about her feelings before, it was now clear that she wanted their friendship to continue.

Robert stopped picking blackberries for a moment, and turned to look at her. He had never thought about it from her point of view, but now, as he considered what she had just said, he could see very clearly what Harry's attitude would be, particularly if their friendship ever developed into something more meaningful. And, suddenly, he knew that he would like it to.

He put a hand on Maggie's arm. She stopped picking, and came close to him, noticing that he had suddenly become serious and intent.

'You know, Maggie – I don't know quite how to say this,' he began awkwardly. 'You seem different, grown-up and changed from what you used to be. I feel different as well. I'm shy and nervous, in case I say the wrong thing. I...'

'Shy?' interrupted Maggie. 'Don't be silly,' she said laughing, showing her large, rather prominent teeth.

'I'm not being silly. I mean it. You *are* different, more grown-up and sophisticated, and more difficult to approach.'

Maggie stopped laughing, as she realised that Robert really did feel what he was saying. She looked up at him, tall, broad-shouldered, a thoughtful look in his eyes and furrows on his brow half hidden by his fair hair, which had flopped forward as he stooped over the briars. Robert was usually good-natured and full of fun. He never seemed worried about anything. Normally they laughed and joked together, gossiping about life in the village, and what was happening on the farm. But now, she too became serious and a little apprehensive. Perhaps she had changed; certainly something was different between them. It wasn't usual for Bobbie to be short of words, and she herself was not at all sure what to say. She wanted to encourage him but was frightened of being thought "fast" or "cheap". As she hesitated, Robert asked: 'Why are you looking at me so intently – is something wrong?'

'Oh, no,' said Maggie quickly. 'It's just that your hair is falling forward,' and she reached up to brush it out of his eyes. As she did so, she felt Robert's arm round her shoulders. For a moment she thought, and hoped, that he was going to kiss her.

But he turned suddenly aside, and said quickly, 'Come on, we'd better go. I'll walk with you as far as the stile, but I'd better leave you there, as from then on we're in sight of the road, and we'd better not be seen together,' and, picking up his rifle, he waited for Maggie to join him with her basket. They were both subdued as they picked their way quietly through the wood. It was not easy to hold a conversation when most of the time they were walking in single file to avoid low-hanging branches and bunches of nettles and briars, which grew profusely in the open glades. As children, they had romped in Beech Wood by the hour, playing hide-and-seek, or building tree-houses where they could sit quietly and watch the squirrels chasing each other up and down the beech trees. But there was no lingering now, and no frolicking or laughter. They walked apart, each thinking over their conversation at the bramble patch, childhood behind them, but not yet old enough to realise their deepening affection, and sexual desire, for each other.

Robert reached the stile first, turned and waited for Margaret to catch up with him. He watched her closely as she approached, her long, black, hair swept down to her shoulders and her large, blue, eyes, usually so bright and intelligent looking, more thoughtful than normal. He noticed, too, that she had developed quite a bosom, emphasised by her dress, which fitted tightly round her slim waist. She smiled when she saw him looking at her. She had a pretty mouth, in spite of the overfull lips and prominent teeth. Robert had a great desire to kiss her, as he had a few minutes before, at the bramble bush, but he did not have the nerve to do so.

He had, of course, kissed her before, many times, at Christmas parties in the village hall, when they played postman's knock and shy widow. But that was just innocent child's play. Now he wanted to kiss her properly. He didn't know much about it, really, but he had seen Mary kissing Stephen goodnight before they were married, and it seemed to go on forever. And his friend, Peter, who was the dormitory authority on all things pertaining to the fairer sex, said that you put your tongue into each other's mouth. Robert was not sure whether to believe this – it was difficult to know with Peter whether he was just teasing or really telling the truth, but he would have loved to experiment with Maggie, if only he had had the courage.

All this went through his mind (as it had done most of the time he had been talking to her) as she joined him at the stile.

'Am I going to see you again before you go back to school on Tuesday?' asked Maggie, adding with a slight touch of sarcasm, 'Or do I have to wait until the Christmas holiday?'

'I don't know. I want to see you again, but it's not really possible, is it? How can we meet? It's Sunday tomorrow, and you know what Sundays are like, chapel for you, church for me, and then you are back to school on Monday.'

They were both silent for a moment, and then Robert made what even he knew was an impossible suggestion. 'Why don't we try to meet after service tomorrow night?'

'Don't be funny,' said Maggie. 'I couldn't just disappear on Sunday night. There is nowhere I could possibly go on my own. Anyway, you have no idea how strict dad is about my going out.'

'Come to think of it, there's nowhere I could be going either,' said Robert ruefully. 'It was a stupid suggestion, but I really would like us to meet. Anyway, to be realistic, what about the Christmas holidays? Will you be helping, as usual, at the tenants' shoot on Boxing Day?'

'I expect so. In fact, I'll make sure I do. Mother is in charge of the helpers, so perhaps we can arrange something then.'

'It's a date. And now we must go. I promised mother I would be back to make sure everything was packed for school. You go on first, and I'll wait here until you reach the village road.'

'Bye-bye, then,' said Maggie, as they both hesitated.

'See you at Christmas,' said Robert.

She climbed, quickly, over the stile and went off down the path. When she reached the gate onto the road, she turned and waved, and Robert, feeling sad and cross with himself for not having made more of his opportunity, waved back. After waiting for a few minutes, he followed down to the road and turned for Manor Farm.

'You've been a long time picking those few,' said Emily, when Maggie arrived home with her chip basket, less than half full of blackberries. 'Anyway, there should just about be enough for a small pie.'

'They aren't quite ready yet, and they took a lot of finding,' said Maggie. She had been prepared for her mother's reaction, and had her answer ready. But she had also been considering whether to confide in her mother about the chance meeting with Robert. After all, it had been innocent enough, and she was anxious to test her mother's reaction. She finally made up her mind.

'Actually, that wasn't the only reason. I met Robert up in Beech Wood, and we got talking, and ...'

'You mean you had arranged to meet him?' interrupted Emily rather sharply.

'Oh, no, it was just accidental.' Maggie blushed, hesitated and added quickly to cover her confusion, 'he was up there on his own, shooting pigeons. He goes back to school on Tuesday.'

Emily noticed Maggie's embarrassment, but said nothing for a moment. Instinctively, she realised that something had happened. Maggie had grown up a great deal over the past few months, and Robert, too, probably, although boys were usually slower to mature than girls. She sensed something more than just a chance meeting between child-hood friends. Robert was a fine, good-looking boy; it was only natural that an impressionable, young, girl would be attracted to him.

'You've always been good friends in the past,' said Emily eventually. 'You would have plenty to talk about.'

'Oh, yes, well no, not really. It wasn't very easy. He was different somehow – more grown-up. Not as he used to be at all.' Maggie was blushing again, and finding it difficult to continue. Emily smiled, in spite of herself.

'Come on, you can tell me all about it. What did he say?'

'He wants to see me again – we both want to see each other. But, of course, we know we can't. I thought he was going to kiss me. He did-n't, but I'm sure he wanted to, but was too unsure of himself.'

'Did you want to kiss him?' asked Emily, somewhat relieved that the affair had not progressed as far as she had feared.

'Yes, of course,' said Maggie. 'There's nothing wrong with that, is there? You aren't cross? You don't mind, do you, mother?' she said anx-iously.

'No, I'm not cross at all. But I *am* a little worried. I don't want you to get hurt. Robert will meet all sorts of girls. Remember who he is and who you are.'

'I know that, and so does he. You are beginning to sound like dad, or the Colonel. You won't say anything to dad, will you? I shudder to think what the Colonel would say if he knew.'

'No, your secret is safe with me. But I'm glad you told me. Now, off you go and find out what has happened to those two girls. I sent them off to the village shop ages ago. I want a few minutes' peace to finish off the baking.'

What Emily really wanted was time to think. She was not worried that Maggie had started to think about boys; she was now nearly sixteen. But why did it have to be Robert Denehurst? But then, why not? It wasn't really surprising. Sooner him than some of the rough farm boys, such as the Lloyds. In an isolated village such as Dunmere, the choice of teenage companions was limited. Emily was an ambitious woman. She came from a better social background than Harry. Her family thought she had married below herself, and could have done better. But, in spite of that, Harry Jackson was a good husband and a kind and loving father. Emily had no regrets. However, she was not popular in the village. Workers' wives on the estate thought she was a social climber. She considered herself too good for them and had ambition above her station in life. This was unfair, and probably stemmed from jealousy. The whole Jackson family were held in high regard by the Colonel and Marjorie Denehurst, and the other estate workers did not like it.

Emily knew all this, but she was not a fool. Far from it. She was shrewd and calculating. She obviously wanted the best for her family, and worked hard to try to improve their status, but she realised that nothing could ever come of an affair between Maggie and Robert Denehurst. It could only end in tragedy. On the other hand, she thought none of the other boys in the village good enough for her daughter. No harm had been done so far, and she decided to let things take their natural course.

Chapter 8

The only farmer to have benefited from the exceptionally wet summer was George Coleman, at Throstle Nest. After much deliberation, he and his son, John, had taken up Colonel Denehurst's offer of the tenancy of the farm, following Ferriday's bankruptcy, and during the past four years, built up a herd of Ayrshire cows. The wet summer had been beneficial to his new leys. Ayrshires were not a common breed in North Yorkshire, but George had well thought out reasons for choosing them. Throstle Nest was a light, land, farm, which had been neglected and run down by Ferriday for many years. Much of the land was high and exposed, with little shelter from the prevailing east wind. Ayrshires were noted for their hardiness and thriftiness, and these characteristics had influenced George when choosing the breed. He had also planned, carefully, for the future. If the venture proved successful, he intended to establish a retail milk round in Kirkley, and Ayrshires produced good quality milk, with a higher butterfat content than either the traditional Shorthorn, or the recently introduced Friesians.

The Thursday after Robert had returned to school, George Coleman had an appointment to see Colonel Denehurst in the estate office. Like most farmers, George was happier on his own ground. Although he had a high regard for the Colonel, he was never completely at ease in his company, especially when they met in the estate office.

'Hello, Mr Coleman,' said Wendy, as he entered the outer office. 'The Colonel is expecting you. He's on the telephone at the moment, but he won't keep you long. Do you want to leave your cap?'

'Naw, ah'll take it in wi me, if yer don't mind.' George never liked parting with his belongings, particularly his cap, although what he thought would happen to it if he left it on the office coatrack Wendy couldn't imagine.

'Not a bad day for time o' year,' he said. 'Drying up nicely now.'

'Yes, it makes a change not to have to bring an umbrella to work,' said Wendy. 'I don't have very far to walk, but it rains wet in Dunmere.' Wendy lived with her mother, who kept the village post office, less than half a mile away.

'It's made t'grass grow, but it's been a rum old harvest. Ah'm pleased ah decided to go in for cows. Ah dean't 'ave all mi eggs in one basin noo,' said George, beginning to get launched on what had become his favourite topic.

The telephone extension clicked off.

'The Colonel is free now, you can go through,' said Wendy, as she opened the door to the inner office.

'Hello, George. A sharp dry morning,' said the Colonel, as he rose to shake hands with his tenant. 'See if you can find a cup of tea for us, Wendy. I'm sure George can do with one.'

George sat down on the edge of the offered chair, opposite the Colonel. In spite of the friendly welcome, he looked nervous and uncomfortable, balancing his cap on one of his knees.

The Colonel chatted with him for a few minutes about the harvest and the poor price of wheat, before asking him how the cows were milking. He was sure it was the cows that George wanted to discuss with him.

'They've been milking well, sir. Plenty of grass about and I made some good hay early on.'

Wendy came in with the tea, and he helped himself to two large spoonfuls of sugar before balancing his cup, precariously, on his free knee.

'It was about t'cows ah wanted to see yer,' George continued. 'Ah want to increase the herd, but ah've nowhere to put any more.'

'You mean you want a new cowshed?' said the Colonel, somewhat surprised, but pleased to have something positive to think about as a change from the usual gloom and despondency.

'No, ah don't want another shed. Ah want to convert that old building where ah keep my young heifers. It joins the cowshed at one end, and could easily be made into an extension which would give me room for another ten or twelve cows.'

'So what you'll need then is a building for your young stock?' suggested the Colonel, seeing where George's thoughts were leading.

'Aye, that's just it, sir. Ah reckon a covered, or even half-covered yard, so they can run out and get a bit o' sun on their backs would do the job.'

'Well, that seems a reasonable suggestion. I think we can agree to it in principle. We shall have to charge you a bit more rent, of course. Will that bother you?'

'Naw. Ah think ah can manage, so long as yer don't overdo me.'

'Right, well I don't think we can discuss this much further at present. I shall have to come to see you and we can go into details, and get some plans drawn up.'

'Thank you, sir,' said George, obviously relieved. The Colonel rose to see him to the door.

'I will be in touch, George. It's a pleasant change to have a tenant who is planning to expand.'

'I'm not very good at slow fox-trots, Maggie,' said Des, treading on her foot yet again.

'You never will be if you don't try. This floor doesn't help. Wouldn't it be nice if we could go to one of the big dances at Bridborough or some-where? This place really is a bit of a dump.'

They were at the Dunmere Cricket Club dance, which was held every October in the village hall. Hall was perhaps too grand a name for what was a wooden hut, which had been used by the army in the First World War. It was long and narrow, with a stage at one end which, when nec-essary, could be curtained off. This only occurred twice a year, at the school Christmas concert and the Women's Institute annual play.

Running parallel with the hut, and attached to it by a covered walk, was a more substantial stone building, known as the Reading Room. Its name dated back to a time when one of Lord Heverthorpe's benevolent ancestors had supplied the parishioners with second-hand books and magazines no longer wanted in his library. But nobody read there now. When not drinking in the Heverthorpe Arms, the young men of the vil-lage met there to play snooker or darts, and the old men played dominoes, or sat round the fire gossiping.

On most Friday nights during the winter, the hut was booked by one or other of the village organisations for fund-raising events, such as whist drives or dances. The football and cricket clubs, the farmers' dis-cussion groups and the WI all held annual events in the hut. Apart from the church, chapel and pub, it was the social centre of the village.

The cricket club dance was the first major event of the winter pro-gramme. It was well supported, drawing people from the surrounding rural areas as well as Dunmere itself. As it attracted both young and old, it was customary to have a mixture of dances, with a large proportion of old-time numbers in the early part of the evening, giving way to more up-to-date dances when the young men arrived after closing time at the Heverthorpe Arms.

Des and Maggie struggled along for a few more times round the floor before deciding to sit down for a while until the band played a quick-step or waltz. It was a four-piece band; Wendy played the piano, Ernie the drums, and two chaps came, from Kirkley, with saxophones. They hired themselves out, and augmented many village events all round the area.

There was a line of benches and some wooden tip-up chairs round the walls of the hut, and Des and Maggie sat down at the end farthest away from the band, as the noise near the stage would have made conversation impossible. It was not very comfortable "sitting out".

Apart from the hardness of the seats, dancing couples came dangerously close, and Maggie drew her feet back under her chair to stop them being trampled on.

'There isn't much talent here tonight,' said Des, looking round at the assortment of couples on the floor.

'There never is. We know everybody who is likely to be here. What sort of glamour were you hoping to see?'

'Nobody I suppose really; not that it matters,' said Des resignedly. He paused for a moment, and then added, 'You are here. I'm not bothered about anybody else.' Maggie didn't reply. She knew that Des had always been attracted to her even though they were related. She liked Des in a friendly, brotherly, way, but was careful not to give him any encouragement, or hurt his feelings.

They watched the couples in silence for a few minutes. 'You're very quiet tonight. I'll bet I know where your thoughts are – a good many miles from here,' said Des eventually.

'How do you mean?' said Maggie, suddenly startled by Desmond's perceptive mind reading. 'Why should my thoughts be miles away? Where had you in mind? Come on, let's be a bit more specific.'

Des turned to look at her, but she avoided his eyes, absently watching the dancing. He knew that he had guessed correctly, and they both knew who he was referring to.

'I know you're smitten. It's no use, Maggie. He'll never be interested in you.'

But Maggie was not giving way. 'Who won't?' she asked. 'Stop talking in riddles,' she added, trying to sound unconcerned and appear composed. It had never occurred to her that Des could suspect anything between her and Robert, but it was obvious that this was what he was hinting at.

Des watched her intently. He could see that she was becoming agitated, and he now knew that what he had only suspected a few minutes ago was, unfortunately, true. 'My God,' he said to himself, becoming suddenly aware of the consequences of such a relationship. He regretted now that he had started to tease Maggie, but having got so far, he thought it best to find out the whole truth. Maybe it was just wishful thinking on Maggie's part.

'So, when did you last see your friend, Robert?' he asked.

Maggie thought for a moment before answering. She decided to tell

Des everything – not that there was really very much to tell, but he might as well know. He was a good friend of them both, and could well be a helpful ally in the future.

Desmond was a little hurt and confused by Maggie's story. He had always hoped that he might win Maggie's favour one day. After all, it did happen occasionally – that cousins married. If she really had fallen for Robert, there was no hope for him. But it just didn't seem possible. He knew well enough they had always been close friends as children. They all had. But he hardly ever saw Robert now, and didn't expect to. How could Maggie possibly see any possibility of a serious relationship with a boy of Robert's social background? What would happen if his family found out? The more he thought about it, the more incredible it became. There may be a brief flirtation but it could never develop. Robert would meet a girl of his own class, and that would be it. 'And better for all concerned,' he said to himself. And then to Maggie, 'So you expect to see him at the tenant farmers' dance? And then what? How are you going to meet after that?'

'I don't know. We'll think of something.' Then she asked, 'Have you any ideas?'

'Not at the moment, but it isn't my problem, is it?'

'No, but you will help if you can, won't you, Des?' said Maggie, squeezing his arm affectionately, and looking at him beseechingly with her large blue eyes.

Enough to melt any heart, thought Des as he said, 'I don't see why I should encourage you, but I suppose I'll help, if I can. God knows why.'

'For old time's sake. Come on, it's the valeta; even you can manage that,' and she pulled him onto the dance floor. It was now after ten o'clock. The hut was hot and airless. The dusty, wooden floor sprang up and down in rhythm to the dancers' heavy feet. Traces of blue tobacco smoke swirled round the oil lamps, which hung dangerously low from the wooden rafters, swaying just above the dancers' heads. A knot of wary, young farm lads hung around outside the door, peering in occasionally, and then quickly withdrawing their heads to exchange banter with their friends standing under the porch outside. Red cigarette ends glowed in the dim light, and there were spasmodic outbreaks of bawdy, but good-humoured, laughter as the odd bottle of beer was handed out. Eventually, two or three of the more adventurous drifted in, fumbling in unfamiliar trouser pockets for the shilling entrance fee.

Maggie and Des were dancing a general excuse-me quickstep, always a favourite with the shy youngsters, who needed some sort of stimulus to encourage them onto the floor. Unfortunately, it was also a good opportunity for some of the less desirable partners to grab a girl who would otherwise refuse a conventional request. An attractive girl like Maggie was a favourite target, and she seldom managed even a single round of the floor with the same partner. It was not long before she lost her partner to Albert Lloyd, the one person in the room whom she really did want to avoid. Ever since the crude incident in the school playground four or five years ago, he had leered familiarly at her and made suggestive comments when they chanced to meet. He had smartened himself up since those days, and fancied himself when it came to finding a girl. He was wearing a heavy blue serge suit and brown suede shoes, with a flamboyant silk scarf tucked round his neck. His lank, black, hair was plastered down with greasy, sickly-smelling hair cream, but even that was not strong enough to mask the beery smell which swamped Maggie, his spotty face close to hers and tried to draw her body close to his.

''Ello mi luv,' he breathed. 'Ah've been trying to get 'old of yer all night.'

'No you haven't,' said Maggie. 'You've only just arrived from the pub and you are too drunk to dance.'

'Not with you I'm not,' he said, holding her even tighter. 'Come on, why not come outside wi me for a bit o' kiss and cuddle?'

Maggie could well have done with a breath of fresh air, but there was no way she was going outside with Albert Lloyd, or anyone else. It was a regular ploy by the lads to try and persuade a girl to go outside with them, but it seldom happened. Any girl who did so would have been thought common and fast.

'Don't be ridiculous, and don't hold me so close,' said Maggie, hoping that someone would come and excuse her, but realising that nobody would want to tangle with Albert.

'You can do the last waltz wi me then and ah'll take you home afterwards,' said Albert, winding himself up to do a last elaborate swirl as the music ended. As he did so, he lurched clumsily to one side, lost his balance and almost dragged Maggie down to the floor.

'You clumsy oaf,' said Maggie crossly. 'I'm going home with Desmond, thank you.'

'You stuck-up little bitch. Ah suppose yer think ah'm not good enough for yer, just because you won a bloody scholarship, but ah'll get yer one day and gi yer summat you can't get from yer bloody cousin,' said Albert, flushing with anger and resentment. He staggered off to join his mates, and Maggie, feeling hot and dishevelled, went to find Des to rail at him for not coming to her rescue.

Maggie linked her arm through Desmond's as they walked home along the village street.

'Are you going home across the park or round by the road?' asked Maggie.

'All the way round. The footpath is too wet when I've only got my thin shoes on. In any case, the deer are rutting now, and I don't fancy an argument with one of those stags.'

'I would be scared living where you do in the woods. All those trees. It must be very eerie.'

'You get used to it. After all, I've lived there all my life. I love it. Particularly on cold spring nights when the owls are hooting, and you can hear the vixens calling.'

'Do you want to be a gamekeeper, like Uncle Fred?'

'I don't know. Maybe. I wouldn't want to live in a town.'

'Me neither. I wonder where we shall be in, say, three years' time?' said Maggie wistfully.

'I know where we are now,' said Des, killing any romantic notions. 'Outside your garden gate. There's still a light on downstairs.'

'That'll be mum. She won't go to bed until I'm home. Dad'll be up in four hours time. Off to feed his precious horses.' They stopped and stood for a moment before parting.

'Thanks, Des. You will help Robert and me, won't you?' said Maggie, and reached up to give Des a sisterly kiss before running down the path. Des saw her go in safely and stood a moment looking up through the trees at the floating moon. Then he set off on his long, lonely walk home with a heavy heart, disturbed by the behaviour of his two friends.

Chapter 9

The tenant farmers' Boxing Day shoot traditionally ended with a dance at Manor Farm. It was very different from the dances held in the village hall, which Maggie and Desmond frequently went to, being restricted to the families of the tenant farmers on the estate and friends of Colonel and Mrs Denehurst. Normally it was an event which Robert attended only out of loyalty to his parents. But this year was different. Maggie was going to be there – not of course as a guest, but as one of the helpers serving refreshments organised by her mother.

'Come on, Bobbie you can do this with me,' said Mary.

'Where's Stephen? Why aren't you dancing with him?' replied Robert as he led his sister onto the dance floor.

'Oh, he's with dad and a farming crowd at the bar. The last I heard they were planning next week's shoot – moaning about the shortage of pheasants and grumbling about the new parson, the Rev Nigel Heyfield-Jones. Apparently he is not only a first-class shot, but he thinks that every bird which flies over is his, and then shoots it before anyone else can get his gun up.'

'He must be quick if he can shoot Stephen's bird. Sorry old girl, you know slow fox-trots are not my strong point,' said Robert, standing on Mary's foot.

'That's the first time,' said Mary encouragingly. 'You've improved a lot since last year. You must have the next dance with Celia. Have you met her yet?'

'No, who is she?' 'You know, the Rev Heyfield-Jones's daughter. She is over there, with him.'

'Not that fat wench in the glasses,' said Robert, pulling a face of disapproval. 'I saw her in church on Sunday and wondered who she was. Thank God mother didn't introduce us. What is she like? Have you met her?'

'I've met her, yes, but obviously I don't really know her. She only came home from school a few days ago – just before you. She seems a pleasant enough girl, quite bright. Not exactly an oil painting though, I agree, but there's not much choice around here, is there?'

'Well no,' said Robert hesitantly, his thoughts turning immediately to
Margaret Jackson. He wondered if he should take Mary into his confidence.
He had always been good friends with his sister in spite of the
age gap. When they were young children, she had been a "bit bossy" –
like many older sisters, but she had been really super when Robert
stayed with her and Stephen to help with the harvest. He now thought
she might prove to be a needed ally. Attractive too, with her blonde hair
and blue eyes, very like his own. But whereas Robert was tall for his age,
Mary was only average height and tended to be overweight. For the first
time Robert noticed that she had a large bosom – particularly prominent
in her low-cut evening-dress. He couldn't help looking at the two jutting
points as he glanced down to talk to her, and he felt them pushing
against him whenever they did a turn. And, not for the first time, his
thoughts wandered back to the summer holiday when he had met
Maggie blackberry picking.

'Now my lad, take your eyes off there,' said Mary laughingly. 'I didn't
know you were old enough to notice things like that!'

'You can't help noticing. I'll bet dad will have something to say to you.
Anyway, you forget, I'm sixteen now and you soon learn a few facts of
life at boarding-school – never mind Dunmere School,' he added,
remembering the antics of the crude boys like the Lloyds.

'Well you had better behave yourself with Celia,' twinkled Mary. 'She
will have had a strict upbringing – none of your crude, country ways
with her.'

'Do I really have to dance with her? I'm glad the boys from Oakfield
are not here to see me. I would never live it down.'

'Come on,' said Mary. 'She's not as bad as all that. I'll take you over
at the end of the dance. I shall have to go and see if I'm needed to help
with the hostessing during the interval, but I expect mother and Emily
Jackson will have everything organised. And no sneaking off to chat up
young Maggie Jackson; I saw you eyeing her when she was taking visitors'
coats in the hall. A pretty little thing, isn't she?'

Robert didn't reply because, unusually for him, he did not know what
to say. Did Mary really know something? Was she just teasing, or was it
a veiled warning? Maybe there was some gossip in the village. But really
nothing happened. He had only been alone with Maggie on that one
occasion last summer. Anyway, Holme Green was over four miles away.
Mary did her shopping in Kirkley; she had very little contact with the
village or the men at Manor Farm. It was fortunate that the dance ended
and Mary was not aware of his uncomfortable silence – or if she had
noticed, she was too tactful to say anything.

It was the dance before the supper break, a waltz, and Robert was doing his best to be gracious and friendly towards Celia. Close to, she had quite a pleasant face. The glasses didn't help, but her red hair (ginger would perhaps be a more accurate description) waved naturally, and when she smiled, she showed her small, neat teeth. But after Mary, who was not exactly what one might regard as slim, dancing with Celia was like pushing a sack of potatoes about. She didn't so much dance close as lean on him. Not in any sexy way, but just a heavy, unyielding, weight. And she never stopped clacking, an endless prattle about her friends at school and her pet dog who had been so pleased to see her on her return from school.

Robert found it heavy going, both physically and mentally. He was pleased that she did all the talking. At least he only needed to half listen, with his thoughts elsewhere. He was anxiously turning over in his mind his earlier conversation with Mary, but even more urgently, he was wondering how to ditch Celia at the end of the dance. He didn't want to have supper with her and 'mummy'. Somehow he had to find Maggie and arrange to meet her where they could be alone and undisturbed.

The dance at Manor Farm was held in, what was normally, the inner hall. It was a huge room with the stairs sweeping up and round to meet a balcony across one end. Members of the dance band were seated under the balcony, and at the opposite end of the room was a temporary bar. The rest of the room, being cleared of furniture, allowed sufficient space for about thirty couples to dance. Not everyone danced though. The farmers tended to bunch together near the bar and talked farming or hunting or shooting. The farmers' wives formed another group, and it was usually long after supper, when the beer began to take effect, before they managed to break up the knot round the bar and persuade their reluctant husbands to take the floor.

Supper was held in the dining-room. It took the form of a buffet, the guests helping themselves before finding somewhere to sit, or stand, only to find they needed an extra hand as they tried to balance a glass and a plate of food and still have a hand free to eat with. Emily Jackson and her helpers served tea and coffee and brought fresh supplies of food from the kitchen. Robert had decided that the best way to free himself from Celia and make contact with Maggie was to offer to make himself useful. He slipped into the kitchen, where several village women were making more sandwiches and cutting up pies and cakes.

'Anything I can do?' he asked, as he saw the friendly face of Emily Jackson.

'You shouldn't be out here,' she said. 'You should be enjoying your supper with the guests.'

'Just thought I would make sure there was no slacking,' said Robert jokingly, helping himself to a piece of pork pie.

'Well, as you are here, you can go and get another jug of milk from the dairy. And Margaret, take that little oil lamp and go with him; it will be dark down the passage,' said Emily.

There were no hanging lamps down the passage or in the dairy. It was dark and musty. There were large bowls of milk and cream on slabs that lined the whitewashed walls. Over by the separator were pats of freshly made butter and nearby a bowl of thick cream was set aside for the next day's churning. Robert found a churn half full of milk and ladled out a jugful. Maggie's lamp cast large shadows on the walls and ceiling.

'It's a bit cold and spooky in here,' whispered Maggie. 'I shouldn't like to be on my own.'

'Well, you are not on your own,' said Robert, also talking in a low voice, as though anxious not to disturb anything. I'm so glad to see you,' he continued. 'But we can't stay here. Lord and Lady Heverthorpe will be coming to the dance after supper. They always put in an appearance, and Lord Heverthorpe does the valeta with my mother. I shall not be missed for a few minutes, so meet me in the maids' sitting-room. Elsie and Betty are busy in the kitchen, so it will be empty.'

'You might have to wait for me. I shall have to help with the washing-up,' said Maggie. 'But I'll sneak off as soon as I can.'

'Right, see you soon. We had better get back to the kitchen now.'

It was half past ten. The dance was beginning to warm up. Some of the farmers had left the bar, and having taken their jackets off, had started to enjoy the dancing. Lord Heverthorpe was in earnest conversation with the Colonel, the rector was dancing with Lady Heverthorpe and Stephen was doing his duty by partnering Celia, no doubt prompted by Mary.

The position looked favourable. Robert slipped out into the back hall, hoping that the washing-up would be finished. It was warm and cosy in the maids' sitting-room. He fanned the dying fire into life, turned the table lamp down even lower and waited anxiously for Maggie. He was nervous and apprehensive. Too excited to sit down, his thoughts concentrated on Maggie and the problems of being able to see her again during the holidays.

What should he say? He had not doubted that she would agree to join him, but did she feel about him as he felt about her? And what did he feel about her? Just a strong physical attraction, or something deeper and more serious. The only hint of anything at all between them had been in Beech Wood last September, and that had been innocent enough.

Robert stood with his back to the fire, facing the door. After a few minutes, but which to Robert seemed like hours, the door clicked open, and Maggie came in looking flushed and a little guilty. Her dark hair shielded most of her face, but in the dim light he could *see* a warm look in her eyes as she came towards him. Neither of them spoke. He held out an arm, and, as he drew her close towards him she raised her face to his.

It wasn't a very successful first kiss. They were too excited and nervous, aware of their vulnerable and embarrassing position if someone came into the room unexpectedly.

'Oh, Maggie, I've wanted to do that for ages – ever since we met in Beech Wood,' said Robert huskily.

'Then why didn't you? I was sure you were going to when we parted at the stile.'

'I didn't know how you would react. Perhaps I was a coward.' And then, after a pause, Robert added, 'I was afraid of the future. I didn't want to start something we might regret.'

'But you've started it now.'

'Yes, and there's no going back now is there?'

Maggie was still in his arms, and as he bent to kiss her again, she put her arms round his neck and pushed her warm, moist lips long and hard against his, leaving Robert in no doubt about her response.

For a few moments their world stood still. They forgot about time, forgot about the dance and their surroundings and almost, but not quite, forgot their guilt and hopeless position. Although they stood holding each other so close, there was a divide between them that could never be bridged. One from a comfortable, privileged, home and one from a farmworker's family, who barely had enough to eat. They were victims in a way of life governed by tradition, which over hundreds of years the feudal system had established rules which were never broken. The landed gentry, the tenant farmers and the farm labourers lived and worked in the same countryside. The farmers' children and the workers' children sat side by side in the schoolroom and their fathers worked the land in a close-knit team. But the families never mixed socially, everyone knew their place and anybody stepping out of line was ostracised.

Robert and Maggie were still locked in their embrace when suddenly the door opened. They disentangled themselves and stood red-faced and horrified, waiting to see who was coming in. It was Mary.

'Oh, I'm sorry if I disturbed you. I was looking for Alice. You haven't seen her around, I suppose?' she asked calmly, as though seeing her younger brother kissing one of the village girls was an everyday occurrence.

'Er, no,' replied Robert.

'She hasn't been in here,' replied Maggie.

'No, obviously not,' said Mary wryly, and went out, quietly closing the door behind her.

The young lovers looked at each other but before either could speak, there was a loud knock at the door, a moment's pause, and then Mary poked her head in and said, 'By the way Maggie, they've finished in the kitchen, and your mother was getting ready to go home. I shouldn't be too long, she will be wondering where you are.'

'Oh, thanks for telling me. I'll be there in a moment,' said Maggie, pulling herself together, both physically and mentally, as well as she could. Once again the door closed and Bobbie and Maggie were left alone. They stood quietly holding hands, not in the mood to kiss again, each left with their own thoughts. The silence was broken by Maggie.

'Oh, Bobbie, what will happen now?' she whispered anxiously.

'I don't know. It's been a bit of a shock,' answered Robert. He was quite bewildered. Had Mary guessed they were in there and come in purposely? She had certainly behaved very calmly, showing no surprise or emotion of any sort. But he was fairly confident that Mary would not say anything to his parents or Emily Jackson – certainly not before she had seen Robert on his own again.

Maggie was obviously very distressed and he wanted to reassure her. He drew her to him, kissed her gently on the lips and then said, 'I don't think we need to worry at the moment. Mary is a good sort. She won't go telling tales. We must meet again as soon as we can – I don't know how, but we'll manage something. You do want us to meet again, don't you?'

'Of course, I don't want to leave you now, but we had better not wait here too long.'

'You can go back to the kitchen then. I'll wait here and then go back to the dance. I expect it will be over soon.'

'Yes, OK then.' Maggie was more composed, but there was still a worried look in her eyes. 'I must see you again and find out what action Mary takes. Goodnight, Bobbie.' She reached up, kissed him lightly on the mouth, and went very quietly out of the room.

Robert moved back to the fire. He looked in the mirror over the mantelpiece, straightened his hair and his tie, and checked that there were no traces of lipstick anywhere. There weren't. Maggie didn't wear much make-up – she didn't need to. In any case, she could not afford such luxuries. It was difficult enough finding a decent dress to wear. She and Emily made all the family clothes themselves, often by altering items passed on by Mrs Denehurst.

A deafening noise greeted Robert on his return to the dance floor. It was the Gay Gordons. All the farmers were now on the floor. Red-faced and sweating, they threw their partners around with loud shouts of laughter and ribaldry, an enthusiasm, which considering their earlier reticence, was remarkable. But this was nothing unusual; all country dances were the same, dead for the first few hours and then, when the beer and spirits began to take effect, the last hour or so was chaotic, with hunting horns being blown and a stampede not unlike the weekly cattle market at Kirkley.

Robert was in no mood to join in. Not that there was anyone to partner if he had wanted to dance. Even Celia was looking happy and vivacious as she hurtled past throwing him a wave as she disappeared into the mass of gyrating bodies. He stood quietly watching just inside the door, trying to sort out his thoughts. He felt elated, apprehensive and dejected all at the same time. He was excited by the memory of that first kiss and, although encouraged by Maggie's warm response, he was anxious about how Mary might react. He was also frustrated because her unfortunate intrusion had left them no time to arrange another meeting.

The Gay Gordons ended. After a short break, the tempo and the mood changed as the band started to play the last waltz. Robert came out of his trance and thought it would be courteous, and tactful, if he asked Celia to dance. Most of the guests were now with their regular partners and Celia was on her own. She was obviously happy to join him on the floor and moved close to him. Whether it was the low lights or the sentimental music that had affected her, he was not sure, but she seemed more attractive and easier to dance with than earlier in the evening. Even so, he could not help wishing it was Maggie who was in his arms.

'My young brother-in-law seems to be in a quiet, pensive, mood,' whispered Stephen to Mary as they passed close to the young couple. 'He was standing near the door with a glazed look in his eyes a few minutes ago and even now, dancing with Celia, he looks as though he would rather be somewhere else.'

Mary gave a wry smile and said, 'You mean with someone else. I found him in the maids' room half an hour ago necking with young Maggie Jackson.'

'You mean Harry Jackson's lass? The young devil. Mind you, I admire his choice, she's a real looker – a few more years and she will have half of Kirkley running after her. But, my God, what would John say if he knew? You are not going to tell him, are you?'

'Of course not. And I'm not going to say anything to Bobbie, not yet anyway. Let him sweat a bit.'

Stephen smiled. 'You are a hard bitch,' he said, dropping a light peck on her forehead. Then, more seriously, he added, 'You don't suppose Harry and Emily know about this do you? I could imagine Harry really would blow a fuse if he thought there was something going on between them.'

'No, I'm sure they won't. I don't think there's anything to it really. After all, they played together as children, almost like brother and sister, except for the obvious differences in background. She is an attractive girl, and there isn't much talent about here. He hardly sees anyone of his own sort during the holidays, and there's no hope of meeting girls at a boys' public school.'

It was well after midnight when the guests had gone and the Denehursts were left alone. Marjorie has sent the staff off home, leaving the rooms to be tidied up and put back to normal the following morning. Robert had hoped to catch Mary on her own before she and Stephen went home, but she had already got her coat on and was standing by the door, with John and Marjorie, as Stephen brought the car round. She offered her cheek to Bobbie for a brotherly peck as usual, saying, 'You must pop over for a day before you go back to school. You could ride over with Celia. I'll give you a ring and fix something.'

'Thank goodness that's all over for another year,' said the Colonel when they had gone.

'Don't pretend you didn't enjoy it,' replied Marjorie. 'I always feel flat when it is over. What about you Bobbie? Did you enjoy yourself? I saw you were dancing with Celia. Such a nice girl. You will have someone of your own type around now during the holidays. I'm pleased the Heyford-Joneses have moved into the rectory. A real asset to the village already.'

Chapter 10

It was a sharp, cold, morning and, in spite of the sun, the cobwebs still ribboned the hedgerows with thin trails of delicate white cotton. Robert and Celia's ponies walked at a brisk pace and their hooves, chattering on the hard road, slipped now and again on the frozen puddles. A bitter wind whipped across the fallows and stirred the slowly, melting snow that still lingered defiantly in the furrows.

Robert had spent an anxious week since the Boxing Day dance wondering if Mary would say anything to his parents about her embarrassing encounter with him and Maggie in the maids' sitting-room. It was a relief when she had telephoned to suggest that he and Celia should ride over to Holme Green for the day. He was not overjoyed at having Celia for company, but it was a small sacrifice to make for the opportunity it gave to have a quiet conversation with his sister.

'It was jolly decent of Mary to invite me along,' said Celia as she drew her pony alongside Robert's. 'After all, she hardly knows me.'

'Well you haven't had the chance to get to know any of us yet. You've only been here a couple of weeks or so.' Robert paused and then asked: 'How do you like living in Dunmere?'

Celia thought carefully about her reply. Her first impression was that it was a bit of a dump, but she was careful not to give offence. 'It's a lovely village, but where are all the young people? I haven't seen any in church, and almost all the guests at the dance were our parents' age.'

'I'm afraid that's how it is. Just the farm and estate workers' families in the village and then the surrounding farms.'

'What is Kirkley like? Is there much social life there?'

'There's social life in Dunmere, if you regard the weekly whist drive, the WI meetings, the church and chapel anniversaries and the cricket club dance as social occasions,' said Robert. And then, so as not to make life appear too mundane, he added: 'There are various organisations and clubs which hold dances and events in Kirkley or even at Bridborough. The Hunt Ball and all the snob events are held there. The problem's transport. It's eight miles to Kirkley and twenty to Bridborough, so you really need a car.'

'Your father has a car.'

'Yes, he does now. He only bought it about three months ago. I some-times wonder why. He still seems to go everywhere on his hunter.'

'I shall have to persuade daddy to buy one. We didn't really need a car in Bury St Edmunds.'

'Why did your father leave a town parish to come and live in a vil-lage like Dunmere?' asked Robert, wondering if perhaps the conversation was becoming a little too personal. He had no reason to be cool towards Celia, but he did not want to develop too close a relation-ship. He could see that they were going to be together quite a lot anyway if the friendship between their parents developed.

'Oh, he hated living in a town. He was brought up on my grandfa-ther's estate. Very similar to this. He's a countryman at heart, and loves shooting and hunting. I'm sure he'll be very happy here.'

Robert made no comment, but it made sense of the snatches of con-versation he had heard at the dance, which alluded to Nigel Heyford-Jones's skill with a shotgun.

'We seem to have talked all the time about me,' said Celia after a short silence. 'Tell me about Mary and Stephen. I need to know a bit of back-ground if I'm to make a contribution to the conversation over lunch.'

Remembering her prattle at the dance, Robert could not foresee any circumstances in which Celia would be tongue-tied, but he saw her point and told her of the tragic death of Stephen's father, and how this had precipitated his marriage to Mary when he was only in his early twen-ties, and Mary not long left college at nineteen. Robert had quickly realised that Celia was something of a snob, so he left her in no doubt that Stephen was a wealthy young man, already the owner of one of the best farms in the district.

As they left the main Kirkley road and turned towards Holme Green, they rode head on into the strong north wind. He told Celia it was the sort of wind that Bill described as lazy – too idle to go round, so it went straight through, but he didn't think she understood, or appreciated, the witticisms of the farm men. She had a lot to learn if she was going to be happy living in an isolated rural community such as Dunmere.

Holme Green was every townsperson's dream of a country house. It was long and low, whitewashed with dormer windows and a porch over the front door. Parts of it dated back to the sixteenth century, but it had been altered and enlarged several times over the years, but fortunately always in sympathy with its period. Even the pantiles, which had replaced the thatched roof, had not spoiled its character. Behind was a courtyard, surrounded by traditional buildings, now used as stables, tack room, and, more recently, a garage. The main block of farm buildings were on the other side of the lane which led down from the main road. They were typical of the area, with a stable for the farm horses, fold yards, Dutch farm and implement shed. In addition, however, there was a large, modern Danish-type piggery, which had only been built a few years ago. Mr Langley had always had a special interest in pigs and, following a visit to Denmark with a party of farmers, he came home determined to copy their ideas. Stephen was now following a similar pattern of breeding, so it was not surprising that the conversation at lunch should turn to pigs. Robert was keen to learn all he could, and the discussion between him and Stephen soon became technical, with talk of live weight gains and food conversion. Mary let it go on for a while but, conscious that Celia knew nothing at all about pigs and probably cared even less, she thought it was time to change the conversation to something more general.

'Come on, you two,' she interrupted. 'That's enough about pigs. I have to listen to farming talk all day, but I don't see why Celia should have to suffer.'

'Oh, I don't mind,' said Celia politely. 'It sounds fascinating. I always imagined pigs were dirty, smelly animals, happiest when rooting about in...' She hesitated before continuing, as though not sure what word to choose, '. . . in what I suppose you would call muck.'

'Not at all. In fact, they are the cleanest animals on the farm. I'll take you round and you can see for yourself,' said Stephen.

'A good idea,' said Mary, 'but first a cup of coffee in the sitting-room, and then we'll find some boots for Celia.'

'If the piggery is as clean as Stephen suggests, I shall be all right in my shoes,' joked Celia.

'You could have had your lunch off the floor,' said Stephen.

As soon as they were alone, Mary asked Robert how things were at home.

'Much as usual. Father worried about the farm and the estate and mother fussing about as though I was still unable to look after myself.'

'Come on, Bobbie, be fair. She's only trying to find something of interest for you. She realises you are missing your school friends. It was her idea that I should invite Celia to come with you today.'

'Exactly, that's just what I mean. It doesn't surprise me, she is always making suggestions about Celia. I'm quite happy wandering about the estate with Rex, or going out for a ride. I miss the open spaces and the countryside when I'm at school. Playing cricket or rugby is not the same.'

'Don't you miss seeing Maggie Jackson?' asked Mary rather pointedly.

Robert had expected Mary to raise the question of Maggie at some convenient moment, but that was a rather unexpected gibe. Seeing his hesitation, Mary continued with a follow-up question. 'Do you see her often?' Have you seen her since the Boxing Day party?'

'No, I haven't. I mean, how could I? I can hardly go round to Harry's cottage and ask if she is in, can I?'

'I'm glad you realise that, but don't you think you are making a fool of yourself chasing after a girl like Maggie? What do you think father or mother would say if they knew?'

'You haven't said anything to them, have you?' asked Robert anxiously.

'Of course not. We have always had our secrets, as well you know. But that does not mean I approve of what I saw in the maids' sitting-room. Have you thought what it might mean to Maggie? A girl in her position is bound to feel flattered, and perhaps think there is more to it than a quick kiss and cuddle on the side. She could end up getting hurt.'

'It's not like that,' said Robert feeling resentful. 'I care a great deal about Maggie. After all, we've known each other all our lives. We've been friends for years.'

'Of course you have. That's all the more reason for being careful. You are both still young, but old enough to realise what an affair, however innocent, could lead to.'

Obviously, Mary thought that all there was between them was a strong, physical, attraction. Robert was not sure just what his feelings towards Maggie were, but he felt they were much deeper than that. He was tempted to discuss it further with his sister but, on second thoughts, he considered it prudent to let her think that it was no more than a passing affair which they would both grow out of, so he simply said, 'I will not lead her on. The last thing I want to do is hurt her feelings.'

'Well, make sure you don't. Maggie is an attractive girl, and intelligent too. But she is ambitious. And, remember, she is her mother's daughter. Emily is thought of in the village as a social climber who tries to live above her station in life. If Maggie thought there was even a remote chance of one day becoming Mrs Denehurst, she would have the full support of her mother. So don't get carried away by Maggie's sexual charms. If she thought she could use them to her advantage, you could end up in real trouble.'

'Chance would be something. I have only kissed her a couple of times and there is no likelihood of our ever being alone together. Anyway, I shall be going back to school in two weeks' time.'

'Well, if you are as keen on Maggie as you seem to be, I dare say you'll find a way to see her again. It's probably just as well you are going back to school.'

Most of the farms on the estate carried a small herd of breeding sows or bought-in store pigs to fatten for bacon. It was a sideline that integrated well with the main arable enterprise. Some of the barley grown was of a sufficiently high quality to be sold for malting, but most of it was used for feed and it formed the basis of the pig ration. There was ample straw for bedding, and the muck produced from the pigs and cattle was essential for maintaining fertility. It would have been impossible to sustain the regular growing of cereals on the thin upland limestone land without the folding of sheep and a generous supply of farmyard manure.

But Mr Langley, and now Stephen, recognised that what was traditionally a useful, but minor, enterprise could be developed into something much more important. With relatively little capital input, other than some extra housing, pigs could be a profitable alternative to corn growing, for which there was currently a very depressed market. It was one of the main reasons for the large number of farmers going bankrupt.

Stephen explained this background to Celia as they stood leaning over a pen wall watching a sow suckle her litter. He had been surprised by the intelligent interest she had shown as they wandered through the farm buildings.

'She's remarkably patient,' said Celia, as the piglets jostled and fought over the teats. 'Do they always have as many as this?'

'Not always, no. I wish they did. We average about eight reared. We are all the time trying to improve the strain of pig by better breeding and, of course, even if a sow gives birth to ten or a dozen, as this one has, you often lose one or two. Sometimes a heavy, clumsy sow will lie on one, and there's usually a wreckling which we have to knock on the head.'

'You mean you kill it?' queried Celia, somewhat shocked.

'Yes. They never do any good. You can't be sentimental. There's no point in feeding an unthrifty pig.' They walked on down a central passage with pens on each side. In some were expectant mothers. One or two were empty, but in nearly all of them were sows and litters of various sizes, the piglets varying in age from a few days to several weeks.

'I'll take you to the Danish piggeries now,' said Stephen, and they crossed over a wide concrete road, which separated the old breeding pens from the new fattening house. This was similar in layout to the one they had just left, with pens along each side of a central feeding passage. But there was one crucial difference.

Behind each pen was a separate dunging area, to which the pigs had access through a door, leaving the main part of the pen clean and comfortable to lie in.

'Do they always go into the passage to...' Celia hesitated, 'to...?'

'To dung,' broke in Stephen, seeing her embarrassment, and coming to the rescue. 'Yes, that's why I said when we were having lunch that pigs were clean animals. Cows or bullocks would just lift their tails and let fly anywhere – sometimes in their feed trough or water tank.'

'So, when you clean out, it's only necessary to clean the passage?'

'Yes, every day we close the pen doors, shutting the pigs into their pen and then we have a straight sweep down the passage all the length of the building. We only need to freshen up the bedding straw in the pens once or twice a week. It also saves straw as well as work.'

'There's so little smell,' said Celia.

'That's because we control the ventilation. You need fresh, moving, air, but no draughts. And it must be warm. Pigs won't thrive in a cold building with stale, moist, air. But I mustn't get launched. I could talk about pigs all day, and I had strict instructions from Mary not to bore you.'

'I think it's fascinating. I'm sure that people who live in towns have no idea about life on a farm. I don't and I was brought up in Bury St Edmunds, which is only a small place compared with somewhere like Hull or Leeds.'

'Do you think you could live on a farm?'

'Oh, I'm not sure about that. I've never thought about it. I find life very different even in Dunmere. It would be a very quiet life if I wasn't busy at school most of the time. I think even Robert finds it a bit lonely, and he has lived here all his life. Do you think he is?'

'What? Lonely? Oh, I don't think so. He enjoys mooching about the farm. He's a real country boy. Last summer, he came and stayed with us and helped with the harvest. He can do almost any of the jobs on a farm as well as a skilled farm worker.'

Stephen did not want to give Celia the impression that Robert was starved of friendship. She would have been a much more suitable companion for him than Maggie Jackson, but that was for Robert to decide. Stephen could see very clearly why Maggie was a more attractive girl to a young teenage boy than Celia.

It was dark by the time Robert and Celia arrived back in Dunmere. A pale, crescent moon hung over the trees surrounding the churchyard and there were welcoming lights in the rectory windows.

'It's been a lovely day, said Celia, as they approached the gates of the rectory drive. 'Thank you for taking me. I've enjoyed every minute.'

'It was a pleasure to have you with me. It's a long ride on your own, especially in the winter,' said Robert, surprised to realise that he meant it.

Celia seemed in no hurry to go. 'Perhaps we could go for a ride together one day,' she said. 'I don't know the country roads round here very well yet. You could show me where all the bridle ways are.'

Robert realised that she had been a pleasant enough companion – much more interesting than he had thought when they first met – but he did not want her to get any ideas of their relationship being more than "good friends". However, he saw no reason for refusing her request, as he said, 'Yes, why not? One day next week. We could arrange details after matins on Sunday. I think your father and mother are invited for pre-lunch sherry, so we shall be together anyway.'

'I shall look forward to that, to both seeing you again on Sunday and then riding next week.'

They chatted for a few more minutes before parting, but the ponies were getting restless, and by the time they had fed and stabled them, it would be time for dinner.

Robert rode on through the village at a gentle, walking, pace. As they passed the farm cottages, he noticed a light on in the Jackson's window and his thoughts turned immediately to Maggie.

Why did life have to be so unfair? If only she had been the parson's daughter, life would indeed have been much simpler and very sweet.

Chapter 11

The top fields of Manor Farm, from where Robert had carted wheat on the ill-fated day of his accident with the harvest wagon, were surrounded by woodland, known as Hagg Wood. It was a remote area. At appropriate seasons of the year, the farm men went there to plough, drill and harvest. The Colonel rode up there to keep an eye on the growing crops, but for most of the time the only visitors were the gamekeepers. It was an area familiar to Desmond, who frequently accompanied his father to check his snares, or see if there were any fresh fox earths or badger setts. There was plenty of cover and its quietness and isolation made it a relatively safe place for wild animals to breed.

There was a group of tall elms in one of the woods and in their shade stood an old shepherds' hut. It was many years since it had been used for its intended purpose. At some time, it had been dragged into the wood for use as a store for the gamekeepers, but, for some time now, it had been left unused even by them. Desmond had forgotten all about the hut until the Monday after Christmas, when he had been sent, by Fred, to see if there was a dogfox lying up there following the Saturday hunt. After a long run, the hounds had lost their scent, close by the woods, and it was a likely spot for a fox to take temporary refuge.

On his visit, Desmond found no trace of a fox. There was no smell of one and his spaniel bitch, working through the undergrowth, put up nothing other than a couple of rabbits. But, as he decided to call off his search and turned for home, Desmond came across the old hut.

Solidly built of wood, with iron-spoked wheels and a corrugated iron roof, it appeared to be still sound and weatherproof. The door was padlocked, but, balancing precariously on one of the wheels, he peered in through the wire mesh, which now covered the glassless window. Inside was a wooden bench, a pile of old corn sacks, a corn bin, a couple of buckets, one without a handle, and a spade with a broken shaft. Hanging from a nail in the far corner were some ferret nets. There may have been some other neglected items tucked away in the corners, but Desmond had seen enough to start him thinking.

Ever since the cricket dance, he had pondered on the affair between

Maggie and Robert. He had wondered how he should respond to Maggie's request to help them to meet. He sometimes felt it was morally wrong to encourage them, and would try to dismiss, from his mind, any idea of assistance. But he was too fond of Maggie not to try to give her something she obviously desired, even though his commonsense told him that any serious relationship between her and Robert could only lead to tragedy. Perhaps, subconsciously, this was what he wanted. With Robert out of the way, there could just be a chance for him.

As he walked back home, he came to the conclusion that the old hut would make a safe place for Maggie and Robert to meet. It was not particularly comfortable, but they were unlikely to be seen. At any rate, given a chance, he would have been more than happy to spend a few hours there with Maggie. The only problem was the padlocked door, but he was fairly certain that he knew where to find the key.

The Denehurst family usually walked to church, the Colonel going on ahead a few minutes early. As one of the churchwardens, he liked to be there promptly to greet the rector, put up the hymns and welcome parishioners, showing them to their seats, and making sure that everybody had a hymnbook and a prayer book. As most of the congregation worshipped regularly, each week and sat in the same pew every Sunday morning, and, as the necessary books were permanently placed in the racks in front of every seat, his enthusiastic attention to their welfare was not really necessary.

At one time, when the Denehurst children were young and all living at home, they filled the family pew, which was situated at the front, close to the choir stalls and lectern. Now, however, John and Marjorie usually had the pew to themselves, except when Robert was home on holiday, or Stephen and Mary came over to spend the day at Manor Farm.

On the Sunday after Robert and Celia's visit to Holme Green, Robert walked, with his mother, to church as usual. At the entrance to the porch, Marjorie stopped to have a word with Mr and Mrs Coleman and as Robert waited on his own for her to catch up, Desmond, who was also with his parents, slipped a piece of crumpled paper into his hand and whispered, so as not to be overheard, 'I can't talk now. Read this and then eat it!'

Taken by surprise, Robert thought he must have misheard, but, when he glanced at the note, he smiled, appreciating the message and the typical Desmond humour. There was just one sentence on the paper: "Meet Maggie in the old shepherds' hut, in Hagg Wood, at half past two."

Robert quickly pushed the piece of paper into his trouser-pocket. As he followed his mother down the aisle and passed Desmond's pew, he gave him what, he thought, was a meaningful look, which he hoped would be interpreted as "Message received and understood".

As he sat waiting for the service to begin, Robert turned over and over in his mind the significance of the message. How was he going to escape from home after lunch? More importantly, how was Maggie going to escape from her home after lunch? What would happen if one of them failed to turn up? And, the most worrying question of all, why was Desmond involved in this intrigue?

As far as Robert knew, the only person who knew about his involvement with Maggie was his sister, Mary, and probably Stephen. He could not believe that Mary would not have discussed it with her husband.

Robert realised how pre-occupied he must have been when he was suddenly aware that they had reached the general confession.

'We have erred and strayed from our ways, like lost sheep – we have left, undone, those things we ought to have done and have done the things we ought not to have done. And there is no health in us ...'

The familiar words took on a new significance. He felt guilty, deceiving his family, taking advantage of Harry and Emily, for whom he had the greatest respect, and playing on the emotions of an innocent, young girl who had been his childhood friend and companion.

Why did he go on? Why start something that he might regret for the rest of his life? What was there about Maggie, which so thrilled and excited him? Was it just physical attraction or was he really falling in love? He raised his head and glanced across at Celia. At the same moment she raised hers and, briefly, their eyes met before they each turned quickly back to their prayer books. How much easier life would be if it was Celia he was arranging to meet. She was pleasant enough girl, but she had no attraction at all for Robert. For him it had to be Maggie. She had been constantly in his thoughts ever since Boxing Day and, in spite of all the doubts and difficulties, he felt a warm glow inside at the prospect of being with her. And, for the first time, they would be alone and undisturbed.

Later the same morning, the Heyford-Jones were having pre-lunch drinks at Manor Farm.

'Well, Celia, how did your visit to Holme Green go?' asked Marjorie. 'Robert tells me you spent most of the afternoon in the piggery.'

'Not quite all afternoon. I enjoyed my day very much. It's a lovely, old, house, but a bit too isolated for me.'

'You don't fancy being a farmer's wife, then?' queried John.

Celia blushed. 'It depends who the farmer is,' she said, laughing.

'There's no future in farming. I wouldn't start looking for a farmer's son if I were you.'

'Don't start on that topic again, John.' Marjorie came in quickly before he got launched. 'The plight of farming is a favourite topic of John's,' she said, turning to the rector.

'We all enjoy talking about our own occupation. Anyway, I find farming interesting. I wouldn't be much good as a parson in a country area like this if I didn't have some sympathy and understanding of their problems. I want to learn a much as I can,' said the rector.

'How about you, Robert? Are you going to be a farmer?' asked Rosemary. Robert was only half listening, his thoughts far away – in Hagg Wood to be precise. As he was slow to respond, Marjorie broke in: 'Come on, Robert, wake up. You were daydreaming all the way through the service this morning.'

'Particularly during the sermon,' said Celia, teasing her father.

'I would like to farm, more than anything else, but you don't think it's a good idea, do you dad?' said Robert, turning to the Colonel.

'The only time farming pays is when there is a war and we are short of food,' said the Colonel.

'In that case, now would be a good time to start,' said Nigel. 'I don't like the way things are going in Germany. We shall have trouble with this chap, Hitler.'

'We had a team of young Germans to play hockey at school last term,' said Robert. 'Very smart young chaps they were, too. And good players. They beat us easily. The frightening thing was that at the end of the game they lined up and gave the Nazi salute.'

'Your older boy is in the army, isn't he?' asked Rosemary.

'Robin? Yes. He's a captain in my old regiment. In India at present.'

'We haven't seen him for nearly two years,' said Marjorie.

'What about you, Robert? If you are not going to farm, how about a career in the army?' asked Rosemary.

'I'm in the OTC at school, but that is as far as it goes for me,' said Robert.

'Two army people in the family are more than enough,' said Marjorie. 'He is going to Cirencester to study estate management if he passes his exam in September. But enough about our family. What are you going to do when you leave school, Celia?'

'I'm not sure. I want to get a degree, if I can, and then probably, teach.'

'I think it's important for a girl to have a good education first, and then worry about a career. Celia has a flair for languages. I would like her to spend some time in France, but the first essential is to qualify for university. It seems that both she and Robert will have to wait to see what happens in September,' said Rosemary.

When the visitors were ready to go, and put on their hats and coats in the hall, Robert and Celia stayed behind in the drawing-room to plan their ride.

'Tuesday, or Wednesday, would be a good day for me,' said Celia. 'Daddy usually tries to have Monday off and, later in the week, mummy wants me to spend a day with her in York.'

'Let's say Tuesday, then. Morning is the best time of day. It gets dark early at this time of year. I will meet you outside the rectory at ten o'clock.'

'Come on, Celia,' called her mother. 'What are you two discussing so urgently?'

'We are just arranging to go riding together – we are not doing anything on Tuesday morning, are we?'

'No, I don't think so.'

'Don't be late back home. John is going to market on Tuesday and will want an early lunch,' said Marjorie, having overheard the conversation.

'You can stay and have lunch with us, Robert,' said Rosemary. 'It won't matter if you are late so long as I know when you are likely to be home.

Come on, Nigel, you can win the next war another day. It is today's lunch I'm worried about. I put it in the oven before church.'

Lunch at the rectory was not exactly what Robert had in mind, but he could do no other than accept graciously, and, needless to say, Marjorie was delighted.

After lunch John and Marjorie settled in front of the fire with a book. Robert, who had plenty of homework to catch up with, joined them for a time, anxiously watching the clock. It was not long before the Colonel fell asleep, and Marjorie, engrossed in her book, barely responded when Robert announced that as it had stopped raining he was going out for some fresh air.

He quickly discovered that there was certainly no lack of air as he faced a cold, blustering, wind on his way up the farm road towards Hagg Wood. He was always surprised to find how the farm road changed with the seasons. At harvest time, a layer of dust, which the horses kicked up in clouds as they plodded up and down carting home the corn, covered it. In a long, dry, spell the hedgerows became covered in a grey film. In winter, the road turned into deep ruts and potholes, often filled with water, and the horses' fetlocks became clogged with thick, clinging, mud, which they were made to wash off in the pond before going into their stalls for their evening feed.

But, as he pushed on, Robert's thoughts were not concerned with the weather, or the state of the road. He would shortly be seeing Maggie, and nothing else mattered.

Maggie did not possess a watch and was not sure what time it was when she reached Hagg Wood and found the old hut under the elms. There was no sign of Robert, so she turned her attention to the padlocked door.

For a moment she wondered if Desmond had given her the right key as she struggled to turn the stiff, rusty, lock. Eventually it yielded, and she opened the door carefully and went in, rather hesitantly, as if expecting something to jump out. Nothing did. Once inside she thought it looked rather more promising than the impression given by Desmond. She picked up the heap of sacks, shook them outside to get rid of the accumulated dust, and then spread them on the bench. As she sat and waited for Robert, all the pent-up emotions of the last few days welled up. She had been constantly worried that Mary would report the incident in the maids' sitting-room. At times she reproached herself for having acted foolishly and rashly, but at the same time, she knew that anything was worthwhile if she could continue to see Robert.

The excitement of the last few days, since Desmond had told her about the hut and now the immediate prospect of being in Robert's arms, were almost more than she could bear.

It was not long before he arrived, windswept and breathless, following his struggle against the wind. She rushed out of the hut to meet him and they held each other close before she eventually lifted her tearful face to be kissed.

'Oh, Bobbie, it's so marvellous to see you. I've had a miserable few days. Put me out of my misery and tell me what's happened. I can't bear not knowing.'

'You don't need to worry any more,' said Robert, fishing for a handkerchief to wipe her tears. 'Mary hasn't said anything to anybody.'

'Thank God. I prayed in chapel this morning,' said Maggie, laughing, in spite of her tears. 'There is nobody I can talk to. Sometimes I feel we are all alone in an alien world.'

Robert was surprised by the intensity of Maggie's feelings. He had never seen her like this before. Mary was quite right in one respect. She was very vulnerable and he must be careful not to hurt her.

'Come on, Maggie. There's no need to be upset, now that I'm here. We shall be able to see each other more often now.'

He guided her into the hut where they sat on the bench, huddled close together and holding hands. In the wood outside all was quiet except for a robin, which piped a plaintive, sad, song from the shelter of a bramble thicket under the bare, swaying, trees.

'I'm not as confident as you about our meetings in the future. I had an awful job trying to think of an excuse to leave the house. I had to tell a lie at the end and say I was going to borrow a book from Des.'

'Des seems to figure, very prominently, in your life,' said Robert, a bit resentfully. 'How is that he found this place and arranged our meeting here? I thought nobody, other than Mary, knew about us.'

'Well, I didn't tell him, not in so many words anyway. He had his suspicions and started to tease me. I had to admit it in the end.'

'Admit what?'

'That we were hoping to meet at the Boxing Day dance, and that I was... well...' Maggie hesitated, '...very fond of you, and that I thought you felt the same way about me.' She paused and turned her large, blue, eyes to look into his. 'You do, don't you?' she added, testing his reaction.

'Of course I do,' said Robert, squeezing her hand. 'I couldn't wait to see you again. It seems ages since the dance and it's only a few days. I suppose we should be grateful to Des.'

'Yes, he is very sweet, really. He said he would help us if he could. He thinks he's in love with me and will do anything I ask. I'm sure we can trust him not to tell anybody about us.'

'So, the only obstacle is to find excuses to get out of the house. It's not very easy for me, but I can see it will be even more difficult for you,' said Robert.

'I can't go on telling lies,' said Maggie. 'I hate deceiving mum and dad. It should be easier in the spring and summer when the weather is better. I can always just go out for a walk then, but would who want to go for a walk on a day like this?'

'Me,' said Robert. 'It was the only thing I could think of!'

They both laughed. The laughter eased the tension and, for the first time, they were able to relax. Slowly their worries left them and they settled into the close, happy, relationship they had enjoyed as children, except, now, they were conscious of a strong, physical, attraction and sexual desire. They had lost their innocence and now faced the responsibility of continuing their maturing relationship in an adult world.

Chapter 12

Gilbert Dawson was a shrewd businessman. He was intelligent, capable, and successful. During the difficult years of the twenties and thirties, when all farmers all around him were struggling to make a living, he had prospered. He had achieved his success by specialisation. When other farmers were spreading their risks by mixed farming, in the belief that if one enterprise did not pay its way, another one might, he had specialised even further by becoming a pedigree breeder. His strain of Rhode Island Red hens was one of the best in the country. He won major awards at national shows and egg-laying trials organised by feeding stuff manufacturers. More recently, he had taken a leading role in the National Farmers' Union and was in line for the chairmanship of the poultry committee.

He should have been a happy and contented man. To all outward appearances he was. He always seemed cheerful, enjoyed a joke, and had plenty of friends. But, underneath the facade, he was a sad and lonely man, who longed for a wife and children, but had neither. He was fortunate to the extent that Gladys had been a loyal friend and constant companion for over twenty years. That she had loved him for the whole of this time, there was no doubt, but it was a love which he was not capable of returning. He had the highest regard for her; he depended on her both in the home and on the farm; he trusted her completely, but he did not love her. It was, perhaps, because he had no wife that he was able to be so single-minded in his business affairs. The love and devotion he would normally have given to his family he had bestowed on his hens.

Gilbert had been an only child. His closest relative was his cousin, Emily Jackson. But whilst he prospered, life had not been so kind to her. At least not in a material sense. Being married to a farm wagoner and bringing up three children on a wage of less than thirty shillings a week meant a standard of living far removed from Gilbert's. But Emily had a devoted husband and three loving children, which had given her a kind of happiness, and fulfilment, that Gilbert could never hope for. Although their lives had gone in opposite directions, Gilbert had maintained a close relationship with Emily, whom he thought of more as a sister than a cousin. He called in frequently to see her and welcomed Harry to his home whenever he was preaching at Darren Beck Chapel. He also made sure that the family lived more comfortably than the average farm workers.

Every spring, he provided them with young pullets, gave them the corn to feed them and regularly took gifts of food and clothes for the children. Perhaps, even more important, Emily knew that if she was ever in need of real help, she could rely on Gilbert's support.

On Easter Sunday, as Harry was planned to preach both afternoon and evening at Darren Beck, Gilbert had arranged for the whole Jackson family to spend the day at Newlands Farm. It was a long way for Emily and the younger girls to walk, so he drove to Dunmere on Sunday morning to take them back home in time for lunch. Emily, who wanted a quiet talk with Gilbert, did not have an opportunity until they returned from afternoon service. Harry had taken the younger girls to see the hens, Maggie was helping Gladys to prepare tea, and Emily, at last, found herself alone with Gilbert.

'I have wanted to catch you on your own all day,' she said to him. 'I want to talk to you about Maggie. She will be leaving school in September.'

'I hadn't really thought about it but I suppose so,' said Gilbert. 'She seems, suddenly, to be a young woman. I don't know where the years have gone. It seems no time at all since she was a little girl.

I shall never forget the day she was being chased by one of the cockerels. He was a vicious bird and ran her all round the pen. Harry picked up a stone, threw it and knocked him on the head – a chance in a thousand!' Gilbert gave one of his cackles, not unlike the sound of a cockerel learning to crow. 'At least the experience did not have any long-term, detrimental, effect. She has always enjoyed coming here to see the hens.'

'That is the point. When she leaves school, she wants to go to agricultural college and take some sort of course in poultry husbandry,' said Emily.

'A splendid idea,' said Gilbert enthusiastically. 'Farming is in a very depressed state at present, as you well know. But, long-term, I think there will be plenty of opportunities for a girl to make a career in poultry. But does she really need a career? I should have thought an attractive girl like Maggie will be married before we know where we are.'

'There's plenty of time for that.'

'Don't be too sure. I thought there was plenty of time, and look at me. A miserable old bachelor.'

'You could have married if you had wanted to. It's easier for a man. There are not many young men here with much to offer. Maggie is ambitious; she needs to get away to meet people as well as study for a career. Harry and I don't know what courses are available or what qualifications she will need. Then, of course, it's the cost.' Emily hesitated. 'We are just hoping that she can get a scholarship. We couldn't possibly afford to pay for her.'

'Of course not. Don't worry, she's a bright girl. I'm confident she will be able to get a scholarship, or bursary, from the county council. If not, I shall pay for her myself,' said Gilbert.

Emily was taken off guard by this offer of financial help. It was the one thing which she had not intended. She was worried now that Gilbert had interpreted her request as being one of obliquely asking for money and that was the last thing she had wanted. She was too proud and independent to seek charity. On the other hand, she could see that Gilbert really meant what he had said and to refuse could be hurtful to him.

Gilbert saw her hesitation and understood her embarrassment. 'Don't be upset, Emily. I know you want to be independent. The last thing I want to do is hurt your pride.'

'And the last thing I want is come begging for money,' said Emily.

'You are not begging. I'm offering. Maggie means a great deal to me. You all do. It would give me a lot of pleasure to see Maggie go to college and do well. I shall be very hurt and disappointed if you don't accept. So think no more about it.'

'I don't know what to say,' said Emily, losing her composure. 'I'm sorry. Pass me your handkerchief. It's silly to cry, but you have no idea what this means to me,' she said between sobs.

'I think I have some idea. It has affected me, and, after all, Maggie is only my niece. You are her mother.'

'But what will Harry say? You know how obstinate and independent he is, you know what his reaction will be.'

'I know you and Harry well enough to be sure that in the end he will do whatever you want. Your happiness and the children's welfare are all he cares about.'

'Apart from his precious horses,' said Emily, trying to laugh between her sobs.

'Well, yes, we can take them for granted. But, in any case, I don't really think it will be necessary for me to help with her fees. I'm sure she will win a scholarship. Leave it to me and I'll make some enquiries. I know who to talk to.'

Emily was now back to her normal self.

'Well, I'm still not sure. You are kind and generous. I can't tell you how grateful I am. Not just for the help, but also your understanding, I won't say anything to Harry, or Maggie, about money. Let's see what sort of results she gets in the autumn.'

'One other thing, Emily. I think it would be a good idea if Maggie got some practical experience. It would help with her application for a grant, and I'm sure an agricultural college, or farm institute, would regard it as a necessary qualification for entry. She can come and work here during the summer holidays.'

'That sounds a marvellous idea,' said Emily, who was quite happy to accept that kind of offer, as she felt that Maggie would be paying her way.

'She will have to stay here, you realise. At least during the week. It means long hours with an early start and a late finish.

'I shall miss her,' said Emily, suddenly realising that Maggie had never before slept away from home or spent time away from the family. 'It will also do away with the eight-mile cycle journey. When she comes home from school now, she is almost too tired to do her homework.'

Robert and Maggie were now seeing each other at their secret rendezvous as often as possible. However, with the longer days and fine spring weather, it was easier than it had been during the Christmas holidays. They had managed to meet on Easter Saturday, but on the Sunday, as the Jackson family were spending the day at Newlands Farm, Robert had finally given in to Celia's request to take her up to Beech Wood.

Although they had been riding together on several occasions since coming home from school, Robert had managed to find excuses for not going for a walk. If he had been asked to explain the difference between taking Celia out riding and going for a walk with her, he would have found it difficult. But, illogical though it may seem, there was a difference. He regarded a walk as something more intimate. On horseback, you were physically distanced, and intimate conversation was difficult. And, in any case, Beech Wood was somewhere special. It was where he and Maggie had spent so much time together as children. An even more precious memory was the occasion they had met there blackberry picking and perhaps for the first time realised that there was more to their relationship than childhood friendship. It was, therefore, with some reluctance that he called for Celia at the rectory and they set off along the lane leading up to the woods. As the lane left the farmstead, it passed between trees and hedges, which were just coming out into pale green leaf.

In the large arable fields, rows of wheat and barley glistened after overnight rain. Robert soon found himself in the role of teacher, as Celia asked a host of questions: How do you recognise wheat from barley? Why were occasional fields bare with no crops at all growing in them?

What were wethers and gimmers?... and so on. He was surprised by her keen interest and the perception of her questions. It also flattered him a little to be thought of as an authority.

Their progress along the lane was slow. As they climbed gently up towards the higher wold, the character of the countryside changed. White, flinty, stones covered the thin soil between the rows of barley; the hedges gave way to stone walls. There was no cover for pheasants or magpies. The song of the thrush and blackbird gave way to the constant cry of gulls and, in the distance, the wild cry of the curlews. Clumps of cowslips and primroses nestled in the grassy banks.

'If we scramble up the bank, we shall probably find some violets in the shelter of the wall,' said Robert, taking Celia's hand to help her up the slope. It was an impulsive action and he suddenly realised it was the first time he had touched Celia apart from the Boxing Day dance.

She followed him willingly, but she was a bigger, heavier girl than he had realised, without any natural agility. Without warning, she stumbled, and Robert almost lost his foothold on the slippery grass as she fell against him. For a moment he held her, conscious of her body against him. She looked up, laughing. Briefly their eyes met and, taken off-guard, Robert bent and kissed her gently on the lips. Celia just let it happen. She made no response, but did not resist or pull away.

Robert felt guilty and cross with himself. As they scrambled back onto the lane, now oblivious to wild flowers, Celia asked: 'What made you do that, Robert?'

'A sudden impulse I suppose. Why? Didn't you want me to?'

'It was just a surprise, that's all.'

'Well, it's a lovely spring day and in the spring a young man's fancy ...'

'Turns to what a girl has been thinking about all winter,' broke in Celia, finishing the well-known saying for him.

'Have you...been thinking about it all winter?

'Perhaps not all the winter, but we have been out together several times – and I would have at least expected a goodnight kiss.'

They walked on in silence for a few yards, as Robert thought about his reply. The kiss had meant nothing to him but it had at least given him an opportunity to find out how Celia regarded their friendship. She did not attract him physically. In any case, he would never be unfair to Maggie. But he did not want to hurt Celia's feelings, or give her any encouragement. He was quite happy to have her companionship. There were not many young people of his own social background in the area with whom he could be friendly. Celia was in a similar situation. It was to their mutual benefit to remain friends.

'Yes, I suppose so,' said Robert eventually. 'But I didn't want to start something which we might regret later. After all, we are sure to be in each other's company a great deal. It could be embarrassing if we had an affair which didn't work out.'

'But how can we know it might not work out if we never give it a chance?' said Celia, with a strength of feeling that Robert had not expected.

'We are giving it a chance. We see each other two or three times a week, and visit with our families.'

'Yes, I know that. But it's not leading anywhere, is it?'

Robert felt that the conversation was now becoming more serious than he had intended. He was tempted to give a flippant reply such as, 'It has led us up to Beech Wood,' but that was unfair. Celia was obviously hoping for a more serious relationship than Robert was prepared to give.

'Where do you want it to lead – bed or the altar?' he asked crudely. 'We are much too young to be tied down now. In the autumn we shall both be going away to start new lives. We shall live a more social life than we do here and meet new people.'

Celia had blushed slightly at the mention of bed. 'I was not looking for either a sexual relationship or marriage,' she said. 'But a little more warmth and affection would be nice. Don't you find me attractive, or is there someone else? A girl you have met at school, perhaps. There are only the village wenches around here. Nobody of our social background.'

That both hurt and angered Robert. 'There's nothing wrong with the village girls, or boys,' he said sharply. 'They may not have much money or enjoy the privileges which we take for granted, but most of them come from honest, hard-working families. Remember, I went to school with them until I was eleven and have known them all my life. When you have lived here a few years, you will begin to recognise just what sort of people they are.'

'I'm sorry, I didn't mean to be critical,' said Celia, realising that she had unintentionally hit a sensitive spot. 'It's simply that however worthy they may be, I cannot see how either of us can have anything in common with them. As you keep reminding me, I haven't lived in Dunmere very long, but one thing is already obvious, the feudal system is as strong today as it ever was. I don't want to sound snobbish, but the different classes just do not mix socially.'

Robert smiled wryly. He did not need to be told that. He was conscious, however, of the danger of pursuing this particular theme, as he might be driven into a position where his justification of the village people might lead to Celia becoming suspicious of his motives. He did not want her to think there was another girl and certainly not one of the farm workers' children.

'We seem to be getting away from the point,' he said, steering the conversation back to themselves. 'I don't see why we can't continue as we are, good friends and no complications.'

'If that is how you want it, fair enough. At least we know where we stand,' said Celia, realising that to push Robert any further might lead to a definite end to their friendship. She was disappointed not to have had a more positive response from Robert, but as he had quite rightly said, there was plenty of time, and she could not believe there were any rivals around Dunmere.

Chapter 13

The sheep flock at Manor Farm was too small to justify a full-time shepherd. On a day-to-day basis, Bill looked after the sheeep himself, but at certain times of the year, particularly at lambing and shearing times, he called on the general labourers to help him.

The folding of sheep on a green crop, such as kale or rape, and then, later in the winter on roots, was an essential part of the crop rotation. In a normal season, the hoggs were folded on turnips from November until the end of April, or early May. Three times every day, including Saturdays and Sundays, as well as Christmas Day, the sheep had to be fed.

The turnip field was divided into strips by a wire-netting fence which was moved across the field every day to provide new feed. The turnips were pulled by hand, topped and tailed with a special turnip knife, and then fed into the turnip cutter which chopped them into small pieces. It was a simple machine consisting of a wooden frame through which passed a rotating chopper driven by a hand operated wheel. The roots were fed in with a pitchfork. The turnip slices fell out at the other end either onto the ground to form a pile, or more often, straight into a scuttle to be carried to the feeding troughs.

Work in the sheepfold was one of the least popular jobs on the farm. Bill hated it. When the roots were covered in snow, lifting them was a nasty, cold, task, being particularly hard on the hands. When the ground was frozen hard, the only way of lifting the roots was by using a pick-axe. Roots were most frequently grown on the high exposed fields, where the folding by the sheep improved the fertility of the thin, impoverished, soil. There was no shelter from the wind, and, even on a reasonable winter's day, the roots were cold and wet to handle.

It was with some relief, therefore, that on the Tuesday following Easter Monday, the hoggs were moved onto the last strip of turnips and the next morning Bill sent Harry and Ernie up to the sheep fold to collect the sheep nets, stakes, troughs and turnip cutter. Harry harnessed Bonny to one of the farm carts, and the two men set off along the road leading to Beech Wood. The turnip field was about half way along the track, and Robert and Celia had passed it on their Easter Sunday walk.

As usual, the talk was about work on the farm and life in the village, but when they reached the sheep fold, Ernie was reminded of a piece of information which he thought would interest Harry. He jumped down to open the gate and, when he got back in again, he said, 'Did yer know Maister Robert has gotten a young lady?'

'Naw, ah can't say as I did,' replied Harry. 'But it's not really surprising at his age, he'll be eighteen soon. Ah knows that 'cos he's the same age as our Margaret. Anyway, ah know thou knaws most o' what goes on in Dunmere, but how do yer knaw that?'

'Well, on Sunday, Ted an' me was up 'ere cutting turnips. Yer knaw Bill won't do t'job if 'e can 'elp it. And we saw Robert walking up Beech Wood wi' parson's daughter. Yer knaw that ginger-haired lass wi' glasses? Celia or summat like that ah think 'er name is.'

'Very suitable ah should say,' said Harry. 'From what Emily tells me, Mrs Denehurst and rector's wife are very friendly.'

'Ted reckons they've been out riding together a few times an' all. We ain't seen much of Robert about lately. 'Appen he's got summat better to do. Ah wouldn't mind an hour or two wi' a lass in Beech Wood meself.'

'Come on, Ernie, enough of that, your courting days were over a long tahm ago. Come and get this net rolled up. Bill will be up here soon wi' Rap to get hoggs shifted down 'ome. He'll be wanting to start clipping tomorrow, ready for Kirkley Market on Friday.'

'A lousy job that is an' all. Their wool looks to be all clagged up wi' soil an' muck. It's worse than dipping. Ah allus said sheep were more trouble than rest o' t'farm put together.'

Later that day, when the Jackson family were having tea, Harry introduced the news about Robert and Celia. It came as a terrible shock to Maggie. She just couldn't believe it. She and Robert had met regularly all through the holidays and every time they were together their feelings for one another had become deeper and more intense. She had trusted Robert implicitly. She could not accept that he had been unfaithful to her, stringing her along while all the time he was seeing Celia Heyford-Jones. And then a whole wave of doubts and fears welled up. Supposing it was really true? She had no reason to doubt Ernie's word. He was a known gossip, but not a liar. In any case, there was no reason for him to make up such a story.

So far, she had listened, in silence, to Harry and Emily's conversation, struggling to control her emotions.

'You've been very quiet, Maggie,' said Harry suddenly. 'You 'ave allus been close to Robert. Ah'm surprised you or Des didn't know what was going on.'

'I don't see much of Robert these days, and Des has never said anything,' said Maggie, hoping that her voice sounded normal. She also looked closely at her mother. After all, Emily knew that Maggie had seen Robert since he had been away at school, although Maggie had not talked to her about him since the blackberry picking incident. For the moment she gave no indication at all that she knew anything more than Harry.

'Well, it's only to be expected,' said Harry. 'We don't see him round the farm much these days. Not since 'e started to help out at Holme Green. He'll be going off to college, or somewhere, next ah shouldn't wonder, and we shall see even less of 'im then.'

For the moment it seemed to Maggie that the subject was closed. Somehow, she managed to sit through the rest of the meal hoping that she appeared to be her usual self.

Gradually, the hurt and anguish changed to anger. Her pride was hurt. She had arranged to meet Robert the next day. It would serve him right if she failed to turn up.

As soon as possible, Maggie disappeared upstairs and lay on her bed, sobbing. When she went back downstairs, the rest of the evening passed in an unrealistic haze. She spent a sleepless night lying awake for what seemed to be hours. Sometimes she persuaded herself that there must be some explanation, and then she would wake in a cold sweat, fearful that her affair with Robert was over before it had barely started. In the early dawn, before going down for breakfast, she had made up her mind. She would meet Robert as arranged, challenge him about Celia, and never see him again.

The morning passed slowly. Maggie thought that two o'clock would never come, but she was determined not to arrive first in Hagg Wood and was pleased to find Robert already there, waiting for her. She approached slowly, trying to appear cool and controlled, instead of rushing eagerly into his arms as she usually did. When he tried to kiss her, she turned her face away, her body rigid and unyielding.

'Come on, Maggie, what's the matter? Aren't you pleased to see me?' asked Robert, puzzled by her unusual behaviour.

Maggie already felt her resolve slipping. Just seeing Robert, and being close to him, had weakened her determination to go through with her plan. 'I'm hurt and angry. Very angry. I trusted you and now I find you are not being straight with me,' she said.

'How do you mean?' asked Robert, suddenly sensing real trouble, and becoming even more puzzled. 'What have I done wrong?'

'You know well enough. Don't try to be innocent with me. You've been seen out, riding and walking, with Celia Heyford-Jones. But what you can see in that ginger-haired cow, God only knows.'

Maggie had wound herself up into quite a state now, and Robert was surprised by the uncharacteristic venom, almost hatred, in her voice. Maggie had always been volatile and passionate, but he had never known her as petty, and spiteful, as she was now. However, he was pleased to find out the cause of Maggie's behaviour and also relieved that it was something that he felt he could put right.

His friendship with Celia was so innocent and meant so little to him, compared with his regard for Maggie, that it had never crossed his mind that Maggie would consider her to be any sort of rival.

'Thank goodness that's all that's worrying you.'

'How do you mean, all?' snapped Maggie, her eyes flashing and her temper now completely out of control. 'How would you like it if I was seeing someone else? And don't think I couldn't. Half the boys in Dunmere would be after me, given a chance.'

'Oh, Maggie. I know that, but you are all wrong about Celia. She means nothing at all to me. No more than Desmond, say, means to you. She's just a companion. Her mother and father are friendly with mine, as you must know, so, obviously I see her quite often. She's rather lonely living in Dunmere, with no friends. You can't be jealous of her.'

Maggie now began to realise she had, perhaps, acted hastily. She could see the logic in what Robert was saying, and already felt relieved and reassured to hear his explanation, but she was still hurt, and not totally convinced.

'Well, even if that's true, you should have told me,' she said, a little more calmly. 'Instead of that, it seems that everybody in Dunmere knows about it, except me.'

'You know what village gossip is. A good job really. It's a help to us. If everybody thinks I'm having an affair with Celia, they are not likely to suspect the truth. And, just imagine how terrible it would be if the gossip going around was that you and me were the ones who had been seen together. But, I'm sorry, I've behaved unthinkingly. I should have told you about Celia myself. But really, the whole thing is so innocent that it never occurred to me that you could mind. Am I forgiven?'

Maggie had calmed down now. She smiled sheepishly. On a sudden impulse she said, 'We'll start again. I'm going back down the path. Close your eyes and count to ten, then you can open them again.'

Robert did as he was told. Maggie was nowhere to be seen, but, in a few moments, she appeared from behind a clump of trees and ran towards him. 'Hello,' she said, when Robert eventually released her. 'Sorry I was late.'

It was a lovely, late, April afternoon. The early morning mist had been slow to clear, but now it was warm and sunny with only a breath of wind, which stirred the pale, emerging, leaves of the ash trees. Bees were busy amongst the May blossom and, quite close by, a cuckoo was calling excitedly. Robert and Maggie were oblivious to the beauties of nature around them as they lay, entwined, on the grass under the elm trees.

Each time they met their lovemaking became more and more passionate. Robert moved his hand from inside Maggie's blouse and slipped it under her skirt, slowly inching it along her thigh until it reached the bare flesh above the top of her stocking. It was at this point that Maggie had always stopped him, gently moving his hand away. But, on this occasion, to Robert's surprise and gratification, all she did was intensify the movement of her tongue between his lips and murmur something which, in the circumstances, was quite unintelligible.

As his fingers probed forward she widened her legs and he felt a warm, moist, patch under her blue, serge, knickers.

Robert recalled their childhood days at the village school when, in PT lessons, the girls unashamedly tucked their skirts into the tops of their knickers.

'Why do you have to wear passion-killers like these?' he said, fumbling to try to feel under the elastic.

'To stop you getting any further.'

'I could always pull them off.'

'Why don't you then,' said Maggie, teasingly.

'You wouldn't let me.'

'You wouldn't even if I did. We are both too well brought up. But, if you're a good boy, I'll give you a treat next time we meet and wear my cami-knickers.'

'What's so special about them?' asked Robert, not very well versed in the niceties of girls' underwear.

'Don't you know? They have buttons on the piece that goes between your legs. Very handy, don't you think?'

'It's a good job you haven't got them on now. The temptation might be too great. But, anyway, why this sudden change in behaviour. You've always been so prudish in the past.'

'Not prudish, just careful. I want to make love just as much as you.'

'But you have never gone as far as this before.'

'Well, I don't really know why I have now. Relief, perhaps, after all the doubts over the past two days, or just the happiness of being with you, knowing that all is the same as ever between us. It nearly wasn't, you know. When I came here today, I vowed I would never see you again.'

'Well you won't see me now for a long time – not until the summer holidays. We had better make the best of the rest of today.' And Robert held her close to him to start a new wave of heavy petting.

'Oh, Bobbie, don't get me all worked up again. I might not be able to resist next time,' said Maggie, as soon as she had a moment to speak.

As she walked home in the later afternoon sunshine, Maggie reflected on the events of the past two days. She realised now that she had perhaps over-reacted to her father's news about Celia and Robert. She should have trusted him and her own convictions. However, it had been enough of a shock to make her realise that she really was in love. She could not bear the thought of losing him. It was likely that in the autumn they would both be leaving Dunmere. Robert would meet girls of his own social background. Attractive, sophisticated girls whom his parents would approve of and whom he could bring home. How could she hope to compete? And then she remembered her recent behaviour with Robert. Why had she acted so irresponsibly? Most boys would have made the most of this opportunity. She loved and respected Robert all the more because he had not taken advantage of her. But supposing that next time they met she really did seduce him? She knew that if her father and Robert's parents found out about their affair, they would stop them from meeting. And, looking even further ahead, she realised that they would never consent to their getting married. But what if she became pregnant? An illegitimate baby would be an even bigger disgrace. They would have to get married. And then she felt guilty and ashamed even to consider such a thing. She wanted Robert, but she would win him fairly and honourably.

As she approached the village, Maggie suddenly realised how late she was returning home. She noticed that the cows were no longer grazing in the cow pasture at Manor Farm, which meant that Ernie must have already taken them in for the afternoon milking. It must be at least four o'clock. As she passed the church, she looked up anxiously at the clock. Almost four-thirty. She knew that her mother would be wondering where she was but at least her father would not be home for another hour or more.

All through the holidays, Maggie had felt guilty every time she returned home from her illicit meetings with Robert. Maggie loved her parents. They were a close, united, family and she hated deceiving them. She had not said any more to her mother about Robert since their meeting when out blackberrying. She had wanted to be absolutely sure that she loved him before upsetting her. After today, she was convinced that her future happiness was linked with him. She decided it was time to confide in her mother.

'I was getting worried about you,' said Emily when Maggie walked into the back kitchen looking rather dishevelled and windswept. 'You must have had a long walk.'

'Well, yes, I suppose so...' Maggie paused, wondering how to go on. 'Oh, mum,' she suddenly burst out, 'come and hug me for a minute. I have a lot to talk to you about – things to explain.'

Emily was wondering what there was to explain. Being late for tea could not account for Maggie's emotional state. She was obviously upset and close to tears. She put an arm round her daughter, gave her a kiss, and waited.

As her tears subsided and she became aware that her mother was sympathetic and understanding, Maggie found that talking about her problems was a great relief. She started her story right back at the beginning, the conversation with Emily following her meeting with Robert when picking blackberries, the Boxing Day dance, Mary's intervention, Desmond's involvement and finally her meeting with Robert in Hagg Wood.

'I'm so glad you've told me,' said Emily when she had finished. 'But why didn't you come to me sooner? You know that I would have understood and tried to help.' As she said these words, Emily wondered how on earth she could help. She was shattered by Maggie's news, but tried to keep calm and in control of the situation. It was not the first time her daughter had come to her with a problem, but it was certainly going to prove one of the most difficult and significant.

'I was afraid of upsetting you. After all, it may just have been a passing phase. I wanted to be sure it was serious before telling you.'

'You are sure you love him? You are still very young and innocent. You've never been out with other boys or even given them a chance.'

'What other boys? There are no other boys worth considering,' said Maggie, thinking of Albert Lloyd and his cronies. 'And remember, I've known Bobbie – Robert – all my life. This isn't a sudden impulse. It's not unnatural, or surprising, for a childhood friendship to blossom into love.'

'And do you think Robert feels the same way about you?' asked Emily, still trying to come to terms with her daughter's bombshell and not finding it easy to control her feelings. 'What about Celia Heyford-Jones? You heard what your father said yesterday.'

'Oh, don't worry about her. That's just a platonic friendship. Robert has explained everything. It's difficult for him when the families are friendly and, naturally, Robert sees Celia quite a lot. I think the two mothers are trying to do a bit of matchmaking, which, I suppose, is understandable. On the face of it they are suitably matched.'

'One other thing I must be sure about. Can you rely on Mary Langley not saying anything to Mrs Denehurst or the Colonel?'

'She has promised not to. Of course she won't know anything about recent developments. She probably regards it as just an innocent flirtation.'

'Yes, you are probably right,' said Emily. She realised that if she had been in Mary's position, she would have thought nothing more about it.

For a moment neither of them spoke. Each was busy with their own thoughts.

'You are not going to stop me from seeing him, are you?' said Maggie suddenly. 'I couldn't bear that.'

Emily had not yet had time to decide what she would do, but she had already realised that there was nothing to be gained by trying to stop them meeting. If the affair was as serious as Maggie had implied, and she had no reason to doubt it, it was unlikely that she could prevent it anyway – "love would find a way".

'I'm not sure what I shall do yet, but it would be pointless trying to stop you seeing Robert. If it was just one of the village boys there would be no problem at all. It's to be expected that a girl of your age would have several boyfriends, in your case, a whole raft of them, being the pretty girl you are – and fall in love several times. It's only because Robert is who he is. I need time to think.'

'Thank you, mum,' said Maggie, giving her mother a kiss and a quick hug. 'It's such a relief to have told you. I'm so happy.'

Emily smiled to herself. 'It's what mothers are for. If you couldn't have come and talked to me, who else is there?'

Over the next few days, Emily gave the whole matter a great deal of consideration. She thought of discussing it with Harry or with Gilbert. She even wondered if she should talk to Robert or Mary Langley or Mrs Denehurst. She knew Mrs Denehurst well and saw her regularly at the WI. In the end she decided to tell nobody. In a few days, Robert would be going back to school. Maggie would not see him again until the summer holidays. And now that Maggie had taken her into her confidence, she would be able to monitor progress. The time for important decisions was still a long way into the future.

Chapter 14

Marjorie Denehurst was expecting Mary for afternoon tea. It was one of those days, which flattered to deceive. Indoors it was warm and pleasant, but outside there was a sneaky wind and Marjorie went out to see if it was warm enough to have tea in the garden. She was soon wishing that she had stayed indoors, not because of the wind, but rather that as she walked across the lawn she became aware of the decimated appearance of her shrubs and herbaceous borders. It was a bad year for pests and diseases. Her favourite climbing rose, Dorothy Perkins, was covered in mildew. The leaves of almost every shrub were smothered in greenfly, and when she went into the vegetable garden, the cabbages and broad beans were being ravaged by caterpillars and black spot. She walked, dejectedly, along the gravel path back to the verandah and through the French doors to the sitting-room, sighing deeply as she sat down to await the arrival of her daughter.

But it was not only the state of the garden, which was causing Marjorie's unusual depression. She was becoming increasingly worried about John's state of mind. It seemed that the continuing problems of the farming industry and the deteriorating political situation in Europe were beginning to affect him. He was gloomy, increasingly irritable and, for a man who was normally level-headed and sensible, some of his recent decisions were ill-considered, if not irrational.

Marjorie was also worried about Robert. John had overruled everybody and insisted that he should make a career in estate management. This would entail a three-year course at the Royal Agricultural College, but before that, Robert was to spend a year as a pupil with a firm of estate agents in London. Marjorie knew that Robert would be miserable living and working in a city, and had suggested that he could gain the necessary experience with a country-based firm. However, the Colonel was determined that only the best was good enough and, through an old army friend, had arranged for Robert to join a leading firm in the West End.

Some time later, towards the end of tea, Marjorie suddenly turned to Mary and said, 'While we are on our own, there's something I want to ask you. It's to do with Robert. How much do you know about his friendship with Celia? Do you think it's serious?'

It was an unexpected question, and Mary wondered if Marjorie had some ulterior motive in asking it. In any case, it was something she did not have much knowledge about. She remembered Robert's first reaction on seeing Celia, and they had ridden a few times over to Holme Green, but she had never discussed it with Robert, and neither had she talked to him about Maggie Jackson.

'I don't know,' she said eventually. 'I think they are good friends. They seem to have an easy relationship but it seems rather low key.'

'But is there not more to it than that? I was talking about it to Rosemary the other day and she seemed to think that Celia was rather smitten, but that Robert doesn't feel the same way.'

So that's it, thought Mary. The two mothers have been trying to do a little matchmaking. She was not surprised, and found it rather amusing. She was not surprised either that it was Celia, rather than Robert, who was making the running.

'I should think that sums it up quite well, mother,' she said.

'But why?' asked Marjorie, 'I would have expected a young boy of eighteen to be chasing after girls, not running away from them. After all, there's not much choice around here and Celia is so – well – suitable.'

'You and Rosemary might think so, but I would have thought Robert was old enough to make up his own mind. Anyway, glamour is important to a boy of his age. Celia is a pleasant enough girl, but hardly what you would call attractive. But if you really want to know what Robert thinks about Celia, why not ask him? You are his mother.'

'Oh, I couldn't do that. He never confides in me. Since he went away to school, he seems to have drifted further and further away from me. And from John too for that matter, not that he and your father were ever very close. But you seem to be able to talk to him; can't you find out?'

'Do your dirty work for you?' said Mary laughing.

'Well, if you put it like that, yes, I suppose so. I know you think I'm interfering, but I am worried about Robert, so I would appreciate your help. You should have plenty of opportunities to talk to him during the holidays.'

'I will see what I can do. No promises though. From my experience of boys when I was that age, they seemed to keep their thoughts to themselves. Not like girls who spent hours discussing in detail their experiences with boys.'

Maggie had never written a love letter. She had seldom written a letter of any kind. As a young girl, her mother had insisted that she should write letters of thanks when she received Christmas and birthday presents, but this had not happened very often. Most of the people she knew could not afford to buy birthday presents. The few gifts she did receive were from family and friends who lived locally and they were delivered in person.

A love letter was something different. In the first place, she was eager to write it. She had given it thought for several days; ever since she had talked to her mother and Robert had returned to Oakfield. In her thoughts she had plenty to say, but now that she was sitting with pen in hand and an empty page in front of her, she did not know how to start."Dear Robert" seemed rather formal and cold."Dear Bobbie" – well now that they were grown-up she really should not continue to call him Bobbie. She must get out of the habit and, at the same time, insist that he called her "Margaret" rather than "Maggie". He always said that he liked "Margaret" as a name, but still continued with "Maggie", probably just out of habit. She tried "Dearest Robert" and then "Darling Robert". That did not come to her naturally. She knew that in the Denehurst family, and in families of similar social standing, everybody referred to everybody else as "Darling". She did not think it meant a great deal. She dearly loved the members of her own family, but her mother never called her "Darling" and not even her father.

Eventually she settled for "My Dearest". After that it was easy. She wrote just as she would have talked to him if he had been there. She told him all about her conversation with Emily, ending the last paragraph as follows: "… so, you see, it will be much easier for me to meet you now. No more lies or excuses. And you can write to me. The post doesn't arrive until dad has gone to work, and now that mum knows all about us, she will keep your letters until I come home from school. I miss you so much my dearest, and long to be in your arms. It will be another ten weeks before I see you again. Make sure that you write soon. All my love, Margaret XXX."

A week passed, and every day Margaret returned home from school in anticipation of a letter, and then, on the Saturday morning, she went to meet the postman herself. It was there. A blue envelope with unfamiliar writing, rather scrawny, really; not a firm, bold hand. Robert must have waited and timed his letter to arrive on Saturday morning when he knew she would be at home to receive it herself. She had no need to tell her mother. Emily knew by her excited look and slight embarrassment that Robert had written. She went upstairs to her bedroom to read it and treasured it in peace.

"My Dearest Margaret. From now on and for always, you will be Margaret. Not that I shall ever forget Maggie. She is too precious a memory ..." The rest of the letter was not of significance, except for the last few sentences." ... If only I dared to tell my mother and father about us, how much simpler life would be. At present I have not the courage and perhaps it would not be prudent even if I had. In the autumn, when we have left both school and Dunmere, it should be easier. I hope so, for your sake as well as mine. In the meantime, I will write to you every Saturday until the summer holidays. I love you and always will. I think I always have. I know I have not told you before, but I will the next time we meet. Until then, Yours always my Dearest, Love Robert XXX."

Robert arrived home from school on Thursday and the following day he rode over to Holme Green to discuss his holiday harvesting work with Stephen. As he rode slowly along the bridle-path leading onto the main Bridborough road, he noticed that Harry was scruffling turnips. It was a very particular job, which needed all Harry's attention, even with an experienced horse like Bonny. Such was his concentration that he did not see Robert on the bridle-path. Normally, Robert would have stopped to have a word but since his secret affair with Margaret, he felt guilty and ill at ease in Harry's company and rather avoided meeting him. On the far side of the field, Ernie, Ted and Ned were singling roots using the traditional hand hoe. This, too, was a skilled and tiring job, particularly when the weather was hot. The sun beat down mercilessly across the shoulders of the stooping workers as they carefully chopped out the unwanted seedlings to leave a nine-inch gap between the plants. They did not notice Robert either and he rode on in a pensive mood and yet instinctively noticed everything around him; the fields of winter oats almost ready for harvest; the cleared hay meadows greening over again and a heavily laid crop of wheat which was going to be very difficult to cut.

Robert had mixed feelings about leaving Oakfield. He had enjoyed his school days and knew that he would miss the companionship and feeling of camaraderie peculiar to a boys' public boarding-school. The last few days of term had been more emotional than usual because of the deteriorating political situation in Europe. Several boys in his form were intending to make a career in the army, and, if there really was a war, they all knew that they may never see each other again. However, his closest friend, Peter Buckley, was planning to join a firm of solicitors in London, which meant they could continue their friendship later in the year. Even so, Robert had no wish to spend a year in London and was worried about his own future. The bright lights were not attractive to him. He would have been much happier, and have found life more satisfying, if he could have spent the year working for Stephen.

But all these thoughts were overshadowed by his relationship with

Margaret. They had corresponded regularly throughout the summer term and had arranged to meet on Sunday afternoon. The fact that they had been able to write to one another had made life much easier from a practical point of view, but it had made Robert realise more strongly than ever than they could not continue their clandestine meetings indefinitely. One day he would have to tell his parents and face the consequences.

On his arrival at Holme Green, Robert found Mary in the garden picking green peas for dinner. 'Hello, I was expecting you ages ago,' she said. 'I think I have enough of these now. You can help me to shell them whilst I catch up on all your news. Does it feel any different to be no longer a schoolboy?'

'No, not really. I haven't felt like a schoolboy for a long time,' said Robert, giving her a brotherly peck of greeting. 'Anyway, it's good to be home. I can't wait to start work. I passed one or two crops of winter oats that are almost ready for the binder.'

'Yes, I think Stephen is planning to start harvest next week. He'll tell you about it later. We can sit under that apple tree to deal with these. It's too nice to go in.' Mary thought this was a good moment to follow up Marjorie's request to find out about Robert's friendship with Celia, so she said as casually as possible, 'I don't want to organise you, but if you want to bring Celia over for lunch one day, you are very welcome.'

'Oh, thanks,' said Robert. 'I'll bear it in mind, but I don't really expect to be seeing her often. After all, as you say, I shall be harvesting most of the time. I hope so, anyway, as I want to earn some money ready for when I go to London.'

Mary would have liked to follow up on the London theme, but she was anxious not to be drawn away from the subject of Celia. She was already beginning to realise that if she was going to find out what she wanted to know, she would have to be more direct. 'You don't sound very enthusiastic. Have you and Celia fallen out, or has it just cooled off?'

'It was never very warm. Nothing more than a platonic friendship.'

'And as opportunities for meeting girls at school are limited, life must be a bit dull,' said Mary, trying to sound as casual as possible.

Robert was not deceived. His sister was obviously fishing, and he wondered if he should give her something to catch. Perhaps this was the opportunity he had been waiting for. 'I wouldn't say that. Celia isn't the only girl around here.'

'No, but I can't think of anyone else who is – well, let us say, suitable.'

'It depends what you mean by suitable.'

Mary was now fairly certain that what she had suspected was true – that Robert was continuing to see Maggie Jackson. She decided to be bold. 'Come on, Bobbie,' she said, 'Let's stop playing games. You're still seeing Margaret Jackson, aren't you?'

'And what if I am?' said Robert defiantly.

'That's up to you. You are both old enough to know what you are doing. I'm not going to try to stop you. I know I couldn't even if I wanted to.'

'And don't you want to?' asked Robert, seeing a chink of hope.

'Look, Robert, we understand one another well enough to be frank,' said Mary. 'I have nothing against Margaret. She is an intelligent, ambitious and very attractive girl. I can understand why you are interested in her, and if you want to continue meeting her, that's up to you. How seriously involved are you?'

'Up to here,' said Robert, pointing to his chin. 'It's not just a strong physical attraction – a passing affair – we are both serious.'

This was what Margaret had feared. They were not foolish. They knew what the stakes were. The risks were too great just to be involved in a casual affair. She did not know how they were managing to meet without being seen, but overcoming all the difficulties involved could only be worthwhile if they were in love – or at least thought they were.

'Does anyone else know, apart from me?' asked Mary.

'Margaret has told her mother, and Desmond Parker knows. In fact, in the early days, he was very helpful – carrying messages – you know, suggesting ways we could meet.'

'Well, if you really intend going on, in spite of all the problems, when are you going to tell mum and dad. And, equally important, when is Margaret or Emily going to tell Harry?'

'I just don't know,' said Robert. 'Neither of us do. So far, I haven't been too worried. It has always been a bridge to cross when I come to it.'

'And now you have reached it?'

'Yes, exactly. I don't want to upset mother and dad. And Margaret is worried sick about Harry's reaction. He is devoted to her.'

'You always got on well with Harry when you were a young boy. I should have thought he would be pleased.'

'Yes, I know, but Harry is a much more complicated character than you think. He's always thought highly of me. He's taught me all I know about the practical side of farming, in spite of knowing how strongly dad was against my working on the farm. But he wouldn't expect Margaret to marry someone like me any more than dad would. However much he loves Margaret and admires me, he would think it wrong for us to be involved. He would regard it as a breach of the trust there has always been between us.'

'It would break mother's heart as well as his,' said Mary.

'Yes, I know, which is why we have to be absolutely certain before we tell them. Our separation this autumn will put us to the test, which is another good reason for not saying anything to them at this stage. What do you think?'

'You are probably right,' Mary paused. 'That's my first reaction. I really need time to think. But I'm pleased you have told me, and that you felt you could trust me. I shan't say anything – except to Stephen, of course. We tell one another everything, but you can rely on him not to mention it to anyone.'

'I'm pleased I told you, too. You've no idea what a relief it is to talk to someone about it. Margaret felt just the same when she told her mother. I feel guilty all the time and I hate being deceitful.'

Mary realised just what Robert had been going through. He was so young and vulnerable, younger in many ways than most boys of eighteen.

'I'm so sorry it has to be like this for you – for both of you. I'll help if I can. But it's up to you. Do you think it would help if I had a word with Emily? It must be very difficult for her. She sees mother regularly at WI meetings and events in the village. And, of course, mother is always sending parcels of food and clothes round. She must be very embarrassed.'

'Oh, I would be so grateful if you would,' said Robert, only too pleased to have some support.

'I don't know quite what I shall say. I don't know her all that well, but I'm sure it will help just to have an ally in the opposite camp.'

'Thanks, Mary. And, remember, this summer, if I'm suddenly missing or not around when perhaps I should be, you will know where I am.'

'I won't know where you will be, you haven't told me, but I shall know who you are with,' laughed Mary.

'I'll tell you all about our secret meeting place one day. And just one last request, try and discourage mother where Celia is concerned.'

'I'll try, but you know what she's like, and Rosemary is just as bad. I believe Celia is rather fond of you.'

'Yes, I'm afraid so, but she is in no doubt about where we stand. I've nothing but goodwill towards her. She's a nice girl, but she will never be anything more than a friend to me.'

'I have got to say this to you, Robert. I'm trying to give you moral support, and I understand your position, but that does not mean I approve. I think you are both playing with fire, and, at the moment, I can't see anything but a sad end. You know as well as I do that there are traditions and understood codes of practice in Dunmere, and one of them, perhaps the most important; you do not marry out of your class, or, if you do, you suffer the consequences.'

Sunday afternoon was a happy and important occasion for Margaret as, for the first time, she was able to meet Robert with a clear conscience. Harry had left early for a preaching engagement, the two younger girls had gone to visit their aunt, so Margaret was free to spend time choosing what to wear. She did not have a large selection of clothes, but now that she had left school and was going away to college, Emily had spent a good deal of time and more money than she could really afford in extending Margaret's wardrobe. Not many of the clothes were new. Most of them came either from Gladys, at Newlands Farm, or from Mrs Denehurst. Others had been bought cheaply at village jumble sales. But, at least, there were more of them, and a choice could be made. As she was meeting Robert, she could hardly wear something handed on by his mother, so she chose a long navy blue skirt, which had belonged to Gladys, matched with a new, white, blouse. The skirt had been shortened by Emily, but it was still longer than the dresses she normally wore, and as it was drawn in tightly round her waist, it gave her an appearance of being longer-legged and taller than her five feet six. She had also changed her hairstyle. Instead of a long mane reaching to her shoulders, she had cut it shorter and fastened it at the back of her head in a kind of pony-tail. The effect was to emphasise the clear moulding of her cheekbones, and make her widely placed eyes appear larger and a deeper blue than ever. As a final touch, she persuaded Emily to lend her a lipstick.

'You look so lovely, I'm almost scared to touch you,' said Robert as he greeted Margaret at their usual rendezvous. 'Is that kiss-proof?'

'Why not try it?' she said, revealing her large, white teeth as she smiled and enticed him with her blue eyes.

Robert took her in his arms and gave her a long, passionate kiss.

'I've been waiting twelve weeks to do that and it was worth waiting every minute,' said Robert. He looked at her for a moment and then added, 'I just do love you. I said in my letter that I would tell you when we met. I love you, and I don't care what happens so long as we can always be together.'

'I love you, my dearest. But I'm frightened. I wake up in the night scared that I shall lose you. And then I wake up thinking it is all just a dream. Twelve weeks was an awfully long time.'

'How do you mean, lose me?' asked Robert, holding her close to him. 'I've just told you I love you. I can't do more than that.'

'It's silly, I know. But in October you'll be going to London and you'll meet lots of attractive, much more sophisticated girls than me.'

'So what? They won't interest me when I know I've got you to come home to. And anyway, you'll meet lots of boys at college looking for an attractive girl.'

'Yes, but it's different for me. I'm just a humble village girl who has been fortunate to be loved by a boy from a completely different class. I couldn't better myself whoever I met. For you, it is the exact opposite. Almost anyone you meet would be considered more suitable than me.'

'I see what you mean. But you mustn't worry about any other girls. Just trust me. There is nobody else and never will be,' said Robert, and then, after some reflection, added: 'But I'm also worried about our future, only for a different reason.'

'Because of the Colonel?'

'Yes. Just your calling my father Colonel is sufficient in itself to show how difficult it is. He could be your future father-in-law.'

'It's just not possible, is it? The whole thing is ridiculous. I was frightened to death of him as a child. A big, stern man on a horse is how I thought of him. I made a point of keeping out of his way. I still do. I haven't spoken to him for ages.'

Neither of them spoke for a few moments, but it was Margaret who expressed what they were both feeling and wondering: 'When are you going to tell him about us?'

Robert paused awkwardly. 'I just don't know. I feel such a coward about it, but I don't want to lose you. I just have a feeling that the time isn't right and that I should wait until the end of the summer when we shall be going away. But it's not all gloom. I've made some progress. I decided to tell Mary.'

'When? Why haven't you told me before? What did she say?' The questions came tumbling out one after the other.

'Just a minute,' said Robert, laughing. 'Give me a chance. I only saw her on Friday. But she was marvellous. Understanding, sympathetic and helpful.'

'And approving?' asked Margaret.

'Well, no, not really. But she didn't condemn us altogether. I think she just feels sorry for us.'

'Tell me about it. I want to hear everything. I won't let you kiss me again until I've heard every word.'

It took Robert some time to tell Margaret everything, particularly as she kept on interrupting, but she was obviously pleased to know that Mary was willing to talk to her mother.

When there really was no more to be said, Robert asked: 'Can I kiss you now?'

'No. I'll kiss you. An extra big, passionate one,' she said, slipping her tongue between his open lips.

'Don't start that again. Not yet,' said Robert. 'We have to talk about the holidays. If you are working at Newlands all the week, and I'm at Holme Green, we shall have to make a different arrangement.'

'Surely it will be much easier now that Mary and Stephen know, and I shall be free once I've finished work. We can meet whenever we like.'

'Yes, but it's a question of where. The old hut here is too far away for both of us.'

'What do you suggest?'

'I'm not sure. It would be easiest if we met half way. You could cycle to Pinfold Bridge on the Bridborough Road. It will be about three miles. I can cut across through Grange Farm and over Rudland Rigg. It will be quicker for me to walk than cycle all the way round by the main road.'

'Will you be free in the evenings?' asked Margaret, suddenly realising that in harvest time the men often worked until eight o'clock or even later if they wanted to get a field finished. Quite often it was almost dark when her father arrived home.

'Not every night. It will depend on what we are doing. We shall work later when we are carrying corn than when we are cutting. We shall just have to arrange a date and hope I can keep it. If I don't turn up, it will because I am meeting Celia Heyford-Jones!'

'Don't you mention her. Not even in joking,' said Margaret. 'I was very angry and upset at the time.'

'Don't I know,' said Robert. 'You really had me worried. But it was worth it for what followed.'

Margaret blushed slightly as she remembered their lovemaking. She was a sensitive girl and had wondered since why she had so easily lost her self-control.

'Have you got your cami-knickers on under all that finery?' asked Robert teasingly.

'Never you mind. You're not going to find out. Not now anyway. As soon as we're sorted out when and where we are going to meet, I'm going home. The only thing mother said when I left home was: Don't be late for tea, and remember, it's chapel tonight.'

Chapter 15

'That's enough. If yer put any more on, it'll only drop off getting out o' this 'ole,' shouted Harry.

'You've got nowt like enough on yet,' said Ted.

'Naw,' added Ernie, grinning under his peak cap. 'Ah reckon yer worried that yer 'osses will get stuck up that slope.' He winked at Ted as he said it and threw another forkful of muck on just for devilment. They enjoyed pulling Harry's leg, particularly about his horses.

But, on this occasion, Harry did not rise to the bait. He was already on the wagon, and with a loud "Gee up" and a flick of his rein on Bonny's back, the horses lunged forward and scrambled up the rutted exit from the fold yard, their shoes slipping and scraping on the wet stones. It had always been a difficult pull out of that yard. Every autumn, at muck-leading time, the men grumbled about it, and every autumn, Bill promised they would find time to improve it before next year. But they never did. It was one of those jobs, which was put off because there was always something more urgent that needed attention.

It was a mellow, late, September morning, ideal for carting muck onto the stubbles. A thick mist hung over the farm, and small white plumes of breath rose from the horses' nostrils as they ambled steadily down the farm road to the twenty-acre wheat stubble.

"Getting the muck out" was the first job after harvest. Half of it went onto the bare fallows, which were followed by a winter wheat crop, and the rest was spread on the wheat or barley stubbles which would be ploughed and sown the following spring with mangolds or swedes.

Plugging muck was one of Robert's favourite jobs. As a young boy he had often ridden out to the field with Harry. He drove the horse on whilst Harry stood on the load and forked the muck off, spreading it evenly round the wagon. Then Robert would move the team on a few more yards. He wasn't really needed, as the horses would move themselves on at a word from Harry. When he grew older, he too had a fork, and spread one side of the wagon whilst Harry did the other and the back. It was hard but exhilarating work; more difficult than it looked. There was a certain knack in throwing and twisting the forkful of muck at the same time, and all too easy to lose one's balance, or drop the fork over the side of the wagon. But when he went to boarding-school, Robert missed the muck carting, unless it was a particularly early harvest.

Colonel Denehurst had gone out early on his morning ride round the farm. He was worried by the lateness of the season, and anxious to see when they could start drilling the winter wheat. It had been a better harvest than last year, but much later than usual.

There were fifteen acres of tick beans stooked, but not yet ready to cart. A late harvest meant that autumn drilling was delayed, and some wheat would not be drilled until the spring. Spring-grown crops at Manor Farm never yielded well. In any case, they ripened late, which meant another late season and the yearly cycle of work got later and later.

As John Denehurst rode slowly back down the bridle road which led from the Kirkley road, he barely noticed the beauty of the autumn countryside. The sun had already broken through the mist at the top of the ridge, but the farmstead and lower lying fields were still hidden from view. The oaks in Wakeman's Wood were changing to a pale yellow and the beeches stood half naked in a sea of gold and copper leaves. Pheasants were feeding on the edge of the wood and a hare loped unconcernedly across the furrows of a newly-ploughed field. Suddenly a cock pheasant rose noisily and clumsily whirred over the hedge. He startled both horse and rider. The Colonel, jolted suddenly out of his deep thoughts, instinctively checked his hunter and, at the same time, made a bold, critical, perhaps even rash decision. A decision which was going to have a disturbing influence on the lives of several families on the estate, including his own.

Friday was pay-day at Manor Farm. At the end of the day's work, the men queued at the farm office to collect their pay packets. Bill always went last, so that he could have a talk to the Colonel.

'We are getting way behind with the autumn work, Bill. We must try to catch up. I've decided to ask the men to work overtime tomorrow afternoon and Sunday.'

Bill was flabbergasted. The men often worked Saturday afternoons, but Sunday was always observed strictly as the Sabbath. Not even in harvest time were the men asked to work on Sunday. Of course animals had to be fed and the house cows milked, but only absolutely essential work was done on Sundays. There was a strict rota for the horsemen to feed and water the horses night and morning. Apart from Harry, none of the men was particularly religious. They might go to church or chapel on Christmas Day and for the harvest festival but, even so, Sunday was still precious. It was the only day they had at home with the family, or to catch up with the gardening. They all grew their own vegetables, and with such meagre pay, overtime was welcome. But not on Sundays.

Seeing that Bill was temporarily speechless, the Colonel went on, 'I know I've never suggested working on Sundays before, I don't like the idea myself, but I don't know what else to do. We shall never get the wheat drilled, or even those beans carted.'

'Well, sir,' said Bill at last, 'if it's an order, ah'll pass it on to the men in the morning, but ah don't know what they'll say. They won't like it, ah know that.'

'I can imagine their reaction, but, make no mistake, it is an order, and I don't want anybody making trouble over it. If you need any support, I shall be in the office before seven.'

Although the horsemen and Alan came early at six o'clock, the official starting time was seven. As usual, the following morning, the men gathered in the old saddleroom to wait for Bill and receive their instructions for the day's work. He arrived early, and took part in the general banter and conversation until, punctually at seven, he said, as he always did, 'Right, men, we'll have a bit more then.' And then he added his bombshell. 'But, before yer go, ah've to tell you that we shall be working this afternoon and on Sunday.'

There was silence for a moment as the order took time to sink in.

'But we never work on Sunday,' said Ted. 'You don't mean it. You are having us on,' said Ernie. 'The Colonel would never work on a Sunday,' said Harry. 'Missus wouldn't let him,' quipped Ernie. It was always a joke amongst the men that, though the Colonel might be full of talk and bluster, it was really Mrs Denehurst who influenced the home and family life.

'When yer've all finished,' interrupted Bill firmly, 'ah'm not kidding. It's an order. The Colonel is a worried man. He may well be in here in a minute, so yer had better be off and make sure yer 'ere in the morning. We shall probably be carting beans, so get yer wagons cleaned up after muck loading.'

There was a bit more grumbling and banter, but Bill thought the men had taken it rather well – better than he had feared. He realised that some of them, with large families, would be glad of the extra money. There would normally have been no more overtime until the spring.

They had all moved off, except Harry. He was looking unusually sombre. His normally warm, twinkling, blue eyes were hard and cold. There was a determined line about his mouth and jaw, which Bill had never seen before.

'Ah shan't be coming in the morning,' said Harry flatly.

'Now don't be stupid. Yer not a fool. The Colonel has given an order and that's all there is about it.'

'No it isn't. Ah've nivver worked on a Sunday and ah'm not going to start now. Apart from anything else, another day won't make a damn bit of difference.'

Bill realised that Harry must be very upset. He had never heard him swear before, not even a mild "damn".

Bill played for time. He took out a piece of black twist, cut a piece off with his knife and, before putting it into his mouth, paused long enough to say: 'Ah'm not going to argue with yer, Harry. If yer really don't intend working tomorrow, you'd better go and see the Colonel. He'll be in his office by now. Ah'll make sure somebody gets loaded up before yer so there'll be no waiting about,' and he stumped off towards the fold yard.

Harry watched Bill go, waited for a few minutes, thinking about what he might say to the Colonel, and then set off through the stable and across the yard to the office. He paused a moment before the door, adjusted his cap, knocked and went in.

Colonel Denehurst was standing at his desk, looking through the morning post, which had just arrived.

'Come in, Harry,' he said, without really looking up. 'What can I do for you?'

Harry came straight to the point, something that he seldom did. 'Ah'm not coming to work tomorrow, sir. It's not right to work on the Sabbath. Ah don't believe in it.

The Colonel looked up quickly and saw immediately the expression on Harry's face. A mixture of determination and stubborness. He sensed serious trouble.

'Come on Harry. You know how far behind we are with our work. You also know how many farmers have gone bankrupt. We are fortunate here, but we can't go on every year losing money. If it's fine tomorrow we can cart those beans. It's not asking much.'

'As far as ah'm concerned, they can rot int' field,' said Harry sharply. 'Anyway, there are enough chaps about without me. Some of 'em will be glad to 'ave a bit of extra money.'

'That's not the point. I've given an order. I expect you to obey it, like everybody else. I know nobody likes the idea of working on the Sabbath. I know you go to chapel every Sunday. I go to church. But for years you've taken your turn feeding the horses when, as a wagoner, you didn't need to.'

'Ah know that, but ah don't expect the other horsemen to do what ah'm unwilling to do. Ah stand mah corner. Yer can't leave 'osses to starve just because it's Sunday. Christ himself picked ears of corn to eat on the Sabbath, but the Lord said the seventh day should be a day of rest. And, as far as ah'm concerned, it is.'

The Colonel thought this was going too far, even for a Methodist local preacher. It was narrow-minded and unreasonable. He was not worried about being one man short for the day, but he could not have insubordination. He knew he had to make a stand, however unpleasant the consequences might be.

'Harry, we have known one another for fifteen years. I've nothing but the highest regard for you, both as a skilled, conscientious worker and as a fair, upright man, but you must understand. I've given an order. If you disobey it, for whatever reason, you know what the consequences will be. I don't want to lose one of my best men. I'm sure you do not want to lose a good job. You can't afford to. In these hard times, you would have difficulty in finding another. Think of Emily and the girls. In fact, don't say any more about it now, and when you go home at dinner-time, talk it over with Emily. But remember, I want you here tomorrow.'

Harry shifted uneasily, fiddling with his cap. After a moment's silence, he turned towards the door. As he went out, he said with one last act of defiance: 'Right, sir, but it won't make any difference.'

He closed the door with a definite "click", as though that was the end of an episode, and strode purposefully off towards the stables, no doubt to discuss his problems with Jack and Bonny.

Colonel Denehurst swore at the closed door, flung the letter down onto his desk, and went thoughtfully for his breakfast, pondering how best to confront Marjorie.

As soon as Harry walked into the cottage at dinner-time, Emily knew there was something wrong. However, she said nothing, and continued to prepare the meal. Dinner passed more quietly than usual, and as soon as it was over, the two young children went out to play, and Margaret went through into the kitchen to start the washing-up. The parents were left alone.

Harry went over to his chair, and sank slowly into it with a sigh. 'Ah'm in a mess, lass,' he said, turning to Emily, and went on to repeat the conversation he had had with Bill and the Colonel.

'So, if you don't turn up in the morning you think the Colonel will give you the sack?' said Emily, after listening quietly to his story.

'Ah'm sure he will.'

'Well I'm sure he won't. The Colonel is a fair and reasonable man. He probably admires you for sticking to your principles. I refuse to let it worry me,' and, bending over the chair, she kissed him lightly on the forehead.

'You are a great comfort, lass. Ah don't think you are right, mind, but ah'll try not to think about it.'

'Well you stay and have a rest. As soon as we've finished the washing-up, I'm going to arrange the chapel flowers for tomorrow. I'll take the girls with me so you won't be disturbed.'

As soon as he was alone, Harry went over to the sideboard where he opened a drawer and took out a cardboard box. On the lid was a picture of the wise men visiting the manger in the Bethlehem stable. It was rather like a religious Christmas card. Inside was a file of fifty or so texts from the Bible. The box had been a Christmas present from Gilbert Dawson and was one of Harry's main sources of comfort and encouragement. Whenever he felt in need of help and guidance, he drew out a card, and took it back to his chair before reading it. It said: "I go to prepare a place for you. And if I go to prepare a place for you, I will come again and receive you onto myself" – John 14.2.

That was all Harry needed. He was now convinced that the Colonel would give him his notice, and that he would be leaving Manor Farm, perhaps even leaving Dunmere. Where he would be going, or what would happen to him and his family, he had no idea. But he believed implicitly in the text, and his simple faith was strong enough to assure him that "The Lord would provide." On this occasion, both home and employment. He knew now exactly what he was going to do. He was a man of pride as well as stubbornness. He had no intention of waiting for Colonel Denehurst to give him the sack. He would take the initiative, and hand in his notice. But, first, he must see Emily, and, putting on his cap, he set off in high spirits down the village street, humming to himself as usual his favourite hymn, "Will your anchor hold in the storms of life." He stopped and smiled wryly, saying to himself, 'It looks as though mahn is shifting just a bit now, but it'll cum to rest in a quiet haven somewhere.'

Colonel Denehurst was a man of unpredictable temperament. A mood of friendly cheerfulness could suddenly change to one of glooming intro-spection. Although quick to anger, a scowl could just as quickly turn to a smile. Those close to him were accustomed to these sudden changes of mood, but recently, Marjorie had noticed that his periods of depression were lasting longer, and his moments of good humour appeared only briefly. She was not, therefore, surprised when he came into breakfast looking anxious and irritable. She knew that he was worried about the late season and its effect on Manor Farm and the tenant farmers. This was something he had learned to live with. His present expression reflected something more immediate.

'You've been longer than usual, John. Alice will have your bacon and eggs ready. No trouble, I hope?' she queried, when her husband eventually arrived.

He sighed and sat down wearily at the table. 'I'm afraid so. You had better prepare yourself for a shock. I'll tell you all about it as soon as Alice has been and gone.'

Marjorie, obviously shaken, greeted John's news with a grim expression and silence.

'But if he doesn't come to work in the morning, you won't really give him his notice, will you?' she asked eventually. 'I mean, you don't have to. He's entitled to his Christian beliefs. He's being honest and straightforward with you. He could just not have turned up, and said he was ill or something.'

'Come on, Marjorie, you know Harry better than that. He's never told a lie in his life. I admire him for that, and sticking to his principles. It just makes it all the more difficult for me. I have to take a stand. You must see that.'

'Perhaps you should think about your own principles, John. After all, when the men are working in the morning, you'll be reading the lesson in church. What are you going to say to Nigel? You can't expect the rector to condone the men working on Sunday. And what sort of example is it to the estate tenants?'

John buttered another piece of toast more vigorously than necessary. He had known the conversation with Marjorie would be difficult, but it was not going the way he had planned. He expected her to defend Harry Jackson, but not attack himself.

'You think I lost my temper and acted rashly, Marjorie. Well, I may have been annoyed, but I didn't – act rashly I mean. I didn't sack him on the spot. I told him to go home and talk to Emily about it. She is a sensible woman, and he takes notice of what she says. I've been giving it a lot of thought and I shall continue to do so. Times are changing. You accuse me of being old-fashioned and not keeping up with the modern generation. Well, I'll bet Stephen would understand. He would have done exactly the same. Well, no. On second thoughts, he wouldn't. He would have sacked him on the spot, and have never given it a second thought.'

'Well, you'll soon be able to find out. He and Mary are coming for dinner tomorrow night. Mary 'phoned when you were out. Anyway, it may not be necessary. Harry may change his mind when he has talked to Emily. It is her and the children I feel most sorry for. Where can he find another job?' And then Marjorie suddenly stopped. It was not just the job but also the house. Harry's job was tied to his cottage. No job, no home.

'John,' said Marjorie in alarm. 'You can't go through with this. What about the tied cottage? You can't turn the family out onto the street with nowhere to go.'

The Colonel saw the anguished look on her face. She was quite right, of course. He would have to give Harry his notice, but he knew that he could never throw the family out of their home.

'Don't start and worry about that, my dear,' he said more gently. 'Just one step at a time. I won't do anything in a rush. I shan't be replacing Harry. We need to cut down on labour. It's just a pity it has to be Harry. He would have been the last man to go if I hadn't been put into this position.' He paused, feeling that there was really no more to be said. The next move was with Harry.

'Pour us both another cup of tea,' he said. 'Let's talk about more cheerful things. I can't think of anything at the moment, but there must be something.'

Chapter 16

The news of Harry Jackson's departure from Manor Farm came as a shock to the whole estate. Never before had an honourable, conscientious worker such as Harry been dismissed, or put in a position where he felt obliged to hand in his notice. There was a great deal of gossip about the circumstances, which had been the cause of such a drastic decision. Most of the village people were amazed by Colonel Denehurst's unprecedented action. He had broken tradition by asking the men to work on Sunday and had disregarded a man's principles and strong Christian beliefs. The Colonel had a reputation for being a strong disciplinarian. He was not popular with everybody but he did have the respect of his men, and was regarded as being a good employer and a fair-minded man. His treatment of Harry was thought to be out of character. There were even whispers that the increasing responsibilities of running the estate were proving too much for him and were beginning to affect his judgement.

On the following Monday morning, the men at Manor Farm met, as usual, in the old saddleroom to wait for Bill and their orders for the day. It was a more subdued gathering than usual.

'Ah nivver thowt ah would see the day when Harry was sacked,' said Ernie.

''e wasn't sacked. 'e gave in his notice,' said Ted. ''e was as good as sacked. All he did was try an' save face,' said Ned, who had never got on very well with Harry, and was not particularly sorry to see him go.

'Just because he was well in wi' missus 'e thowt 'e could do as 'he liked. 'e got too big for his boots.'

'Nivver,' said Ted. ''e was best 'ossman for miles around. There was nowt he couldn't do wi' a pair of 'osses. 'e looked after 'em as if they were his own children. They understood every word 'he said to 'em. This spot will nivver be the same wi'out him.'

This was an opinion held by most of the men. They may have teased Harry about his horses, and sometimes even his religion, but they respected him, both as a worker and as a man. Their opinion of Emily Jackson, however, was more critical. She had always enjoyed a much closer relationship with Mrs Denehurst than the other men's wives, mainly through her work as secretary of the WI and her membership of the village hall committee. It was with a certain amount of gratification, therefore, that Ned said, 'Ah wonder what will 'appen about the cottage. Colonel will want another man in there. Ah reckon the whole family will 'ave to get out.'

'Naw, they won't,' said Ted, who was getting a bit sick of Ned's carping. 'Colonel would nivver put 'em out ont' street. Anyway, the way things is going on, wi' new tractors and implements, ah don't suppose he'll want another wagoner.'

'It sounds as though you were fancying Harry's job, Ned,' quipped Ernie.

'Ah nivver said owt like that,' snapped Ned, starting to get irritated.

It was just as well as at that moment Bill arrived. 'Let's have a bit more, then,' he said as usual. 'We shall be a man short now. It's back to muck-leading today. Alan will be taking Harry's 'osses for now, so we shall 'eve five wagons for most o' t'day – 'til Alan 'as to feed up tonight. You can stop plugging muck about four o'clock and give 'im an 'and, Ted.'

The men moved off and Bill, anxious to know more about the Colonel's plans for managing the work force without Harry, made his way to the farm office.

Meanwhile, at No 4 Estate Cottage, Harry was eating a leisurely breakfast. Considering he had no job, or prospect of one, and could even be without a home at any moment if the Colonel so decided, he was remarkably cheerful.

'Ah reckon ah'll get on wi' a bit o' gardening today, Emily. It should be dry enough to do a bit o' digging,' said Harry, spreading a layer of Emily's home-made marmalade on his toast.

'That will keep you busy for today, but what are you going to do tomorrow and the rest of the week?' said Emily, not relishing the prospect of having Harry hanging about the house all day.

'Ah shall busy misself wi' summat. Ah shall 'eve ti get a sermon ready for Sunday for one thing.'

'You have prepared a service most weeks and had no difficulty in finding the necessary time, even though you were at work every day.'

'Ah, but ah'm at Kirkley next week, main chapel and a big congregation. Ah want ti give 'em summat extra special. Is there another cup of tea in that pot?'

'It will need some hot water. I'll go and see if there's any left in the kettle,' said Emily, going out into the kitchen.

'And what will you be doing with yourself all day?' asked Harry, turning to talk to Margaret. 'You're out of a job as well.'

Margaret had spent most of the holidays working at Newlands Farm, but she was spending a few days at home before starting her poultry husbandry course at Askham Bryan.

'I've plenty to do, dad. I only have until Wednesday to do my packing before going away,' she said. She had also arranged to meet Robert in the afternoon, and was relieved to hear that Harry was going to be busy in the garden. Otherwise, he might have suggested accompanying her when she went out for her afternoon walk.

'It's a good job you won that scholarship. Ah can't think what you would have done if you hadn't. There aren't many jobs about here for a girl leaving school.'

'That applies to men out of work as well,' said Emily, overhearing the conversation as she returned with the teapot.

'Another cup for you as well, Margaret?' She poured out two cups.

'What are you going to do about finding some work yourself?' she said to Harry. 'We can struggle on without your wages for a few days, but we have to eat.'

'Ah wasn't planning ti do anything. There'll be a job somewhere. Yer know what that text said. Ah reckon we shall be leaving here in a week or two.'

Emily was astounded at his complacency. She was a devout Methodist too, but she had more imagination than Harry. She did not share his simple faith. It was one thing to have a Christian outlook on life, go to chapel on Sunday and say one's prayers, but Emily did not believe that the good Lord intervened directly into life in the practical way Harry did. She had not slept since Saturday, and was far more worried than she would admit, even though, unlike Harry, she knew that, if necessary, Gilbert would make sure they had enough to live on.

Margaret was enjoying her last few days prior to going to college. As Robert was also back home, they had arranged to meet at the old hut in Hagg Wood. Margaret set off soon after dinner, her thoughts concentrated on the news of her father's departure from Manor Farm. It had affected her deeply. She had nothing but happy memories of playing there as a child; going with Harry to feed the horses on Saturday and Sunday afternoons; enjoying the bustle and excitement of threshing days and, above all, the lasting friendship of Robert, which now, as she approached womanhood, had blossomed into love. The future now seemed more uncertain than ever. She found it both exciting and frightening. As she passed each familiar landmark, and reacted, almost instinctively, to the subtle colours of the early autumn countryside, she wondered if she would ever walk up to Hagg Wood again. She was worried about her forthcoming separation from Robert and apprehensive about leaving home for the first time. And yet, in spite of all her forebodings, she felt a surge of hope and optimism as she approached the edge of the wood. As soon as she was with Robert, she knew that all her worries would disappear.

Robert had arrived early in Hagg Wood. He had purposely left home sooner than necessary, as he wanted time to sort out his thoughts. Like Margaret, he had still not come to terms with the fact that Harry was no longer wagoner at Manor Farm. For the whole of Robert's childhood, Harry had been his hero and mentor. He remembered, as a small boy, being given rides on Bonny's back. How Harry had answered so patiently all his questions. And later, when he became old enough, taught him to plough, drill, load a harvest wagon, and all the other skills practised so expertly by the farm men. Throughout, Harry had been kind and considerate, good tempered and cheerful, friendly, but not familiar. In Robert's eyes, Harry was irreplaceable. Manor Farm would never be the same again.

It was a warm, mellow, afternoon, too nice to be indoors, and Robert and Margaret were lying together under the trees, discussing what was uppermost in both their minds.

'You know, dad lived for his work,' said Margaret. 'He spent hours talking about the farm. In fact, he hardly ever talked about anything else, and he was always full of admiration for your father.'

'How has he taken it?' asked Robert. 'Father thought the world of him, which is why it all seems so stupid. He must be very hurt and also worried about the future. There are no jobs around here. How will you all manage with no money coming in?'

'I don't know. Mother is worried sick. But the funny thing is that dad seems quite unconcerned. He just says: "The Lord will provide" and has no doubt at all that He will. He has no intention of even trying to find another job.'

'He'll have to one day,' said Robert. 'And then suppose he did find work away from here, what would happen to us then?'

'If we both continue to work in the holidays, as we do now, we can go on in the same way as we have been doing.'

'But you would presumably go home at the weekend, and it would be difficult during the week in winter. Where could we go when it was cold and wet?'

Margaret understood the truth of what Robert had said, and did not reply immediately. Robert continued, 'And then, in a year's time, anything might happen. I suppose I shall be going to Cirencester, and where will you be? What are you planning to do when you leave Askham Bryan?'

'I don't know. I would like to stay at Uncle Gilbert's, but I don't know if he would want me once I'm qualified and trained. I should have to look for a job somewhere. I could go anywhere, maybe miles away.'

They were both quiet for a moment as they contemplated what appeared to be a very uncertain future. Robert squeezed Margaret's hand and held her close to him. He realised she was upset and close to tears.

'Don't let's try to look too far ahead. Anything might happen in a year. Look what has happened just in the past six months,' said Robert, trying to find some words of comfort, and then added: 'There's one thing I am thankful about. It's a good job that I didn't tell my father about us. For one thing, it would have looked as if he had taken revenge and attempted to move you all away from Dunmere so that we couldn't see each other.'

'Yes, I hadn't thought of that,' said Margaret.

'And now, depending what happens in the next few weeks, it should make it easier to tell him. The fact that Harry no longer works at Manor Farm does distance the problem. I mean, I'm not planning to marry one of the farmworkers' daughters. As a family you will be independent of the estate.'

'Does that mean you are going to tell your father before you go to London?' asked Margaret.

'No. I think I should wait until we see what happens next. If you leave the village, I'll tell him when I come home for Christmas.'

As the sun sank behind the copper-tinted trees, it started to turn chilly in Hagg Wood. The sky was a clear, pale, blue, with not a cloud in sight. Soon the grass would be turning damp and the evening mist was already gathering in the hollows along the bridle-path leading down to Dunmere.

Robert stood up and offered a helping hand to pull Margaret up after him. 'It will be nearly Christmas before I see you again,' she said, smoothing down the creases at the back of her dress and then instinctively tidying her hair.

'Do you remember the Christmas of the Boxing Day dance?' asked Robert, anxious to see what Margaret's reaction would be.

'Don't remind me. I shall never forget Mary coming into the maids' sitting-room.'

'I hoped you might say, "I shall never forget the first time I kissed you,"' said Robert wistfully.

'That goes without saying,' said Margaret. 'But it took you an awful long time to get round to it. You don't kiss me like that any more. Very innocent we were then, but at least it was warm and comfortable. Wouldn't it be marvellous if we could be like any normal couple and snuggle up together on a settee in front of a warm fire instead of always having to meet in cold, uncomfortable, surroundings?'

'It would be even nicer in a warm and comfortable bed. I would love to see you in a pretty nightdress – you know, something pink and frilly, which was always riding up round your waist, and ...'

'Stop tormenting yourself,' interrupted Margaret. 'Nothing like that's going to happen until we're married, and there's not much hope of that just yet, is there?'

'No, I realise that. I was only teasing really. But I do have a serious suggestion to make. When are you leaving Askham Bryan to come home for Christmas? Do you know the date?'

'I can't remember. About the twelfth, I think. Why?'

'Well, whenever,' said Robert. 'I can leave London on the same morning and we could meet in York. I could then take you out to a restaurant for lunch – dinner, whatever you want to call it – anyway, a nice, leisurely, meal. And then we could go to the pictures before catching a train to Kirkley. We don't necessarily have to catch the train if you think there is a risk of our being seen arriving together.'

'Now that is a wonderful idea,' said Margaret excitedly. 'I've never been to a proper restaurant, and it would be lovely to see a film with you.'

'There's just one snag,' said Robert. 'We don't know where you'll be living. It depends on when, and where, your father finds a job.'

'I could always spend the night at Newlands and go on home the next day. I'm sure we can arrange something,' said Margaret eagerly.

They walked arm-in-arm in a thoughtful, but optimistic, mood to the edge of the wood, knowing they would soon have to part. What happened during the next few weeks would be critical to their plans for the future. They were events out of their control, but whatever happened, they now felt grown-up and independent, with freedom to manage their own lives. Nevertheless, it was a sad and tearful parting under the elm trees.

PART THREE 1938

Chapter 17

On his move to London, Robert lived in Bayswater with Mrs Hartley. She had known John Denehurst during his army days when he and her husband had been fellow-officers in the yeomanry. Major Hartley had been killed in the second battle of the Somme, leaving Mrs Hartley childless and a widow. The terraced, four-storeyed house, with its iron railings and steps leading to the basement, was typical of that part of London. Robert had found it to be conveniently situated for the offices of Kitchen, Kitchen and Drew, the Knightsbridge firm of estate agents with whom he was gaining practical experience before going to the Royal Agricultural College.

Rather than take a tram, he frequently walked to work across Hyde Park, particularly on fine October mornings. A pale sun shone through the mist shrouded trees; the paths were covered in fallen leaves and the grass still wet from the overnight dew. Horse riders weaved their way through the glades and along the well-worn bridle ways. He stopped for a few minutes to watch the ducks on the Serpentine – small, dull, birds compared with the Aylesbury ducks and geese on the pond at Manor Farm. He pictured the horsemen harrowing and drilling the winter wheat and wondered how they were managing without Harry. Ernie and Ted would be busy thatching the wheat pikes and Bill, no doubt, tinkering with the oil engine before starting to grind the cattle feed. He walked slowly and reluctantly on into Knightsbridge to spend another dull day sitting at his desk with little to occupy his mind.

He had been warmly welcomed by Mrs Hartley and was happy living there, but in spite of that he did not enjoy London. He hated the busy streets with the rattle of trams instead of farm wagons; the clip of high-heeled shoes on the pavement instead of the scraping of horses' shoes in the stable, and when night came, it was the hooting of car horns, not barn owls, which disturbed his sleep.

The one thing which made life tolerable was being able to renew his friendship with Peter Buckley who was now articled to a firm of solicitors in the city. Harry Jackson had been out of work for two weeks. During this time, he had made no effort to find employment and seemed quite contented to potter about the garden, go for a stroll round the village, and spend more time than usual preparing his sermon for the following Sunday. In fact, he had been able to build up quite a stock of sermons, which would keep him supplied for the next few weeks. One of the advantages of being "planned" to visit different chapels throughout the area each week was that the same sermon could be repeated at different venues. He had even begun to think about his sermon for Christmas, but this was not really necessary, as he was never planned to preach at the same chapel two successive Christmases, and, even if he had been, it was unlikely that the congregation would remember his sermon from one year to the next. In any case, the Christmas message never changed. It was always the same theme, particularly if preached by Harry Jackson.

In contrast to Harry's complacency, Emily was becoming increasingly worried. Unlike her husband, she had the family to feed and household bills to pay. She was a good manager and a thrifty housewife, but however carefully she managed her meagre budget, one day soon she would no longer be able to pay her debts. Margaret had now gone to Askham Bryan, which meant one fewer to cater for, but the two young daughters were still at home and, even though Harry was no longer doing a hard day's work, his appetite was as keen as ever.

The garden at No 4 Oak Cottages had never been in better shape. All the remains of the summer vegetables had been cleared, and Harry had started his autumn digging. The runner beans still continued to produce but the pods were becoming old and stringy. The first frost would finish them off completely and Harry decided it was time to take down his framework of bean sticks to enable him to dig and manure another patch of ground. He was not even sure if he would still be there to plant it again in the spring, but Harry was a true countryman who believed in good husbandry. It would have hurt his pride not to leave the garden in good condition for his successor. His motto was that gardeners, as well as farmers, should live as if they were going to die tomorrow, but look after the land as though they would live forever.

As he concentrated on bundling and tying together his bean sticks, he was surprised to see a visitor walking towards him down the garden path. It was George Coleman.

'Thou's getting well gardened up, Harry,' he said as he approached.

'Aye, well, ah ain't much else on just now,' said Harry, wondering what George Coleman could have come for. They knew one another well enough to have a casual word if they met, but as far as he could remember, George had never visited him at home before. For a while they talked about farming – the late harvest, the poor state of the industry –

the usual farm gossip. Eventually, Harry asked George how he was getting on with his cows.

'Well, it were that ah came ti see yer about. Ah 'ad heard yer were out of a job and ah wondered if yer might like ti come and do a bit for me.'

Harry was taken aback. For a moment he was not sure what to say. 'Yer mean milk cows? Ah nivver milked a cow in me life. Ah've allus been wi' 'osses at Home Farm an' ah've nivver worked anywhere else.'

George knew that well enough. 'No, ah don't need any help wi' milking – not now we've gotten this machine. Marvellous it is an' all. Ah want somebody to deliver round Kirkley. Did yer know ah'd gotten a retail licence?'

Harry paused for a moment, lifted his cap and scratched his head. He had heard that George was doing well and expanding his dairy but he had not known about the retailing.

'Yer mean tek on a milk round?' he asked eventually.

'Aye. You would have to collect milk churns every day, tek 'em to Kirkley and deliver milk from door ti door. Ah hope soon to get a bottling plant, but for now yer will 'ave ti ladle it out ont' doorstep.'

Harry thought for a while. 'Ah don't know,' he said. 'Course I want a job, but ah've nivver done nowt like that. What about money?'

'Oh, ah would pay yer well enough ...'

'Ah don't mean that,' interrupted Harry, a little embarrassed at being misunderstood. 'Ah mean would ah 'ave to collect money? Ah don't knaw nowt about money. Emily looks after our bit. Ah just give her mi wage packet every Friday night, except sixpence for mi collection. Ah nivver spend nowt.' Harry had forgotten for the moment that there was now no wage packet to collect.

'Aye. You would 'ave to keep a record and collect money on a Saturday morning, but we would 'elp yer wi that. John's wife is good wi figures. She looks after all t'farm books.'

The longer this conversation went on, the more perplexed Harry became. It was taking time for him to take it all in.

'Well, ah'm fair capped. Ah nivver thowt ah would end up working in a town. Not even a small spot like Kirkley,' he said.

'Did yer ever think yer might live in one?' asked George, moving on to the next consideration.

'Naw, but it's not likely ti happen, is it?' said Harry, completely unprepared for George's next proposal.

'But you won't be able ti stop 'ere. Colonel will want this cottage for another man.'

'Naw 'e won't. Not just yet anyway. 'e said ah could stop 'ere for a bit. Ah don't think 'e is going to replace me. Cutting down a bit now, things is bad.'

'Well it is up to you,' said George. 'But there's a house for yer in Kirkley. It goes wi t'job. There will be a bottling plant there eventually. Ah want somebody there ti look after it.'

A new job and a house. Light dawned. Harry suddenly remembered the text: "I go to prepare a place for you."

'Well ah nivver,' he said, still bewildered. 'Ah'll give it a go, but ah shall 'ave to talk it over wi Emily. Ah don't knaw what she'll think. Fair capped probably.'

'Ah should think so,' said George. 'It must 'ave been a worrying tahm for both o' yer.'

He was delighted that Harry had accepted. He would obviously find it a very different life from the one he had been used to. He would have a lot to learn. But George knew his man. Harry Jackson was a good worker, conscientious and well regarded. Customers would take to him and, most important of all, he was absolutely honest and reliable. No short measures, no fiddling the small change and no lying in bed when he should be up and on his rounds.

Harry, too, must have begun to realise that from now on life would be a new experience.

'Well, at least ah shall still be working wi' 'osses and a rully,' he said.

George laughed and said, 'Aye, we wouldn't part you from 'osses altogether. But think about it over the weekend. There's a lot to consider. Let me knaw on Monday morning.'

Left alone, Harry quickly bundled together the remaining bean sticks and put them in the shed at the bottom of the garden near the pigsty. Any more digging would have to wait. He went indoors to talk to Emily.

Askham Bryan was a revelation to Margaret. Life was obviously going to be very different from Dunmere, but it was even more of a change than she had expected. She was prepared to find living away from home something of a trial but even when the excitement of the first few days had passed, she was not in the least homesick. She missed home, of course, but she was too busy to think much about anything other than settling into her new surroundings and exciting lifestyle. There were lectures every morning, and either work in the laboratories or practical work on the farm during the afternoon. The evening was spent writing any notes or reading textbooks. Any spare time she had was spent with her fellow-students, gossiping in the common room or playing table tennis. Her colleagues on the poultry husbandry course were mainly girls of her own age, but from a variety of backgrounds; farmers' daughters and girls from the town who were attracted to a life in the country. All of them seemed to come from middle-class homes whose experience of life so far was completely different from her own.

There were plenty of boys around on various agricultural courses, and Margaret had a strong suspicion that it was considered more important to "catch" a wealthy farmer's son than to pass the examinations at the end of the year. This was something which she had never even thought about and she felt rather smug when she realised that most of the girls there would have given up everything to be in her place and have a boy like Robert waiting for them.

Students' letters were placed on the noticeboard. Every morning, after breakfast and before lectures, Margaret went expectantly into the common room to see if there was a letter from Robert or, perhaps, from home. Emily had promised to write every week but, so far, nothing had arrived from Dunmere. However, on the Wednesday following her first weekend in college, there were two letters, one with a London postmark and one from Dunmere. She decided to read her mother's first and keep Robert's until she had time to enjoy it at leisure. She casually opened the envelope and started to read as she climbed up the stairs to the first-floor lecture theatre. On the half landing she stopped, hardly able to believe what she was reading. After a few conventional sentences referring to health, settling in and being missed at home, Emily had gone straight to the point.

"Your father starts work next week for George Coleman, retailing milk in Kirkley, and we shall be moving to Kirkley to live there in a house which goes with the job."

Margaret read and re-read that sentence, slowly taking in its significance. Her immediate reaction was one of great relief and excitement. She was delighted that her father had found work so near to Dunmere and comforted to know that her mother's financial worries were over. However, she was less sure about their going to live in Kirkley. It would no doubt be a bigger and better house. It could hardly be otherwise. But she wondered how her parents would adjust to living in a town, even a small market town with which they were already familiar. Conscious that she was, perhaps, being selfish, she was also concerned from her own point of view. It was going to be difficult to arrange meetings with Robert when they were both at home on holiday. On the other hand, their lives were going to change so much that it probably made little difference where her parents lived. Whatever happened at the end of the year, she would almost certainly be leaving home and Robert would be in Gloucestershire.

Suddenly aware that people were rushing past her up the stairs, she realised that she must move quickly or be late for the lecture. Arriving breathless and rather flustered, she found concentrating on the subject of the various systems of poultry-keeping rather difficult.

'The free-range system is only possible on the larger, specialised, farms or on mixed farms. On a small acreage, there is a danger of over-stocking. The land would become poultry sick with a high risk of disease such as gapeworm and coccidiosis. On this system, one hundred hens per acre is a maximum for adult birds ...'

The lecturer droned on and Margaret's thoughts kept drifting back to Dunmere, to her father's new job, and, of course, to Robert. She must write and tell him. Perhaps he already knew. Maybe Mrs Denehurst had written; she was sure to know. News travelled quickly on the estate. His mother might even have telephoned. She decided she would telephone herself. She knew his address and would have no difficulty getting the telephone number. Then she was worried about the cost. Could she really afford it? Would he be in during the evening? If not, where was he? She suddenly had a completely illogical panic, imagining him out with another girl and all her fears of losing him welled up inside her.

Margaret forced her mind back to reality and the lecturer. 'The large flock has almost disappeared. It has been replaced by smaller houses holding fifty or up to a maximum of one hundred birds ...'

Margaret glanced at her neighbour industriously writing in her note-book. She had almost filled a page. She was determined to listen. Somehow she managed to concentrate to the end of the lecture, but for the remainder of the morning her mind was far away and she was left with a hazy and incomplete knowledge not only of the systems of poul-try keeping, but also the principles of breeding, which was the subject of the following lecture.

Colonel Denehurst was spending Monday morning in the farm office as he often did. It was a good opportunity to plan the week's farming operations with Bill, sort out the office work with Wendy and make sure that orders with the various farm suppliers were up to date. With the long, drawn out, harvest at last finished, he could now concentrate on the autumn sowing and buying bullocks for winter fattening. He was becoming more and more convinced that the winter fattening of cattle was a luxury he could no longer afford. Nothing gave him as much pleasure as a yard full of sleek, contented bullocks lying chewing their cud half buried in clean straw. He was sure that they made a loss, or at best broke even, but his farming rotation depended on them. They were an integral part of the farming system, as the farmyard muck they pro-duced was essential for the root crop and the bare fallows. Store cattle sales were held at all the local livestock markets during October, but the

Colonel preferred to go to York where there was usually a good selection of Irish stores. He was about to ring up the auctioneers when Wendy knocked on his door and came into the office.

'A visitor for you. Have you got a moment?'

'Yes, I suppose so. Who is it? Not one of those reps... I hope. If it is, I'm not in.'

The Colonel had his regular suppliers of feed, fertilisers and seeds, whom he had traded with for years. Nothing annoyed him more than salesmen pestering him for custom.

'No, it is only Harry Jackson,' said Wendy, who knew from past experience never to introduce a salesman into the office.

'Good God,' said the Colonel, surprised and rather taken off guard. 'What does he want? You had better show him in.'

His ex-waggoner was the last person he had expected to see. Colonel Denehurst was just getting used to the idea that Harry was no longer working at Manor Farm. The furore over his departure had now settled down, and the work on the farm seemed to be going well enough without him. He bore Harry no ill-will. In fact, in some ways he rather admired him for sticking to his principles, although he would never have admitted it openly – not even to Marjorie. He wondered what he could have come for. Not his job back surely.

'Well, Harry, how are you getting on?' he asked as the familiar, friendly face appeared in the doorway.

Harry hesitated uncomfortably just inside the door.

'Come and sit down,' said the Colonel. 'What can I do for you?'

'Well, sir, ah don't think there is owt yer can do 'cos ah don't want nowt. But ah thowt ah 'ad better come and tell yer ah shall be moving out o' t'cottage at end of t'week. Ah thowt mebbe yer would want it for somebody else.'

This was something the Colonel had not expected.

'That was very considerate of you, Harry. Especially in the circumstances. But where are you going to live? Have you got another job?'

'Aye, ah'm going to work for George Coleman.'

'Not milking cows?' interrupted the Colonel rather more sharply than he had intended. After all, in Harry's position, any sort of work was welcome.

'Naw, ah'd nivver do that,' said Harry. 'Ah'm going ti deliver milk in Kirkley an' there's a house wi' t'job.'

The Colonel knew something of George Coleman's plans to start retailing milk, but he had not realised they were so far advanced. As he thought about it, he could see the advantages both for George and Harry.

'Well, I'm delighted for you, Harry. You know I never wanted to lose you. I'm pleased both for you and Emily. It must have been a worrying time for you both. It will be a big change for you, though. How are you going to like living in a town?'

'Well enough, ah reckon. We shall be 'andy for t'chapel. Ah shall miss t'farm though, especially 'osses. But it will be an easier job than trudging up and down furrows all day or plugging muck.'

'An early start though. Earlier than coming here to feed the horses.'

'Aye, but ah don't mind that. Ah could allus get up of a morning. Best part of t'day. An' ah shall be finished by dinner-time.'

The Colonel was pleased to have had a word with Harry, but there was a danger that he was going to become engaged in a long conversation. He had a busy day ahead and there was really no more to say. He stood up.

'Well, the best of luck, Harry. No hard feelings, I hope,' he said, extending his hand.

'No sir, none. Ah think noo things 'as turned out for t'best,' said Harry, as they shook hands.

'If you want a horse and rully to help you to move, you are very welcome. Have a word with Bill, and he will fix you up.'

'Thank you, sir, but ah think George will 'elp me ti shift. We 'aven't got much stuff to 'andle.'

Harry turned and moved towards the door. 'By the way,' said the Colonel as an afterthought. 'I hear that Margaret has gone to Askham Bryan. She has done well; you must be proud of her. I don't know where the years have gone. It seems no time since she and Robert were playing round the stackyard together.'

'Aye, she's a grand lass,' said Harry, pleased that the Colonel had commented on her success. 'We don't see much of her now. She spends most of 'er 'olidays at Newlands wi' Gilbert Dawson. Keen on 'ens, she is. Allus 'as been.'

'I'm sure she will do well. Make somebody a good wife one day. Goodbye, Harry, and give my regards to Emily.'

Harry closed the door and walked slowly across the farmyard, past the pond and down the drive into the village. He was in a reflective mood. He had enjoyed his years at Manor Farm. He was going to miss his life in Dunmere, but he was reconciled to his move to Kirkley. The Lord had pointed the way and He had never let him down.

Chapter 18

Robert switched on his bedside lamp. After years of living with oil lamps and candles, it was a luxury he was only just getting used to. Even at school, there had only been the main dormitory lights, and once they had been officially switched off, anyone daring to switch them on again did so at the risk of a prefect's wrath and a sore backside. In spite of a long day out in the fresh East Anglian air, he could not sleep. He had found his first day out with his tutor, Ralph Gurney, enjoyable and stimulating so that his mind was now too active for rest. He tried reading the "Farmer and Stockbreeder", the only literature to hand, but found concentration difficult. After a few minutes, he gave it up, switched off the light and lie on his back staring at what would have been the ceiling if it had not been too dark to see it. In the house all was quiet, but in the distance he could hear the traffic on the Bayswater Road. It was not normally loud enough to keep him awake, but tonight it was one more reason for his being unable to sleep.

It had been his first day out of London, and from now on he could expect similar visits to other parts of the country; Kent, the Cotswolds, Wiltshire, perhaps even Devon or Cornwall; Kitchen, Kitchen and Drew had interests all over the southern half of the country. Considering the enjoyable day out and the prospects of more to come, he should have been looking forward to his year of pupilage. To his surprise, and illogically, he found the idea tedious and depressing. All that his visit to the Fens had achieved was to convince him that he did not want to be an estate agent. He was more determined than ever that somehow or other he would be a farmer – even if it meant starting in a very small way and working all the hours there were to scratch a living. It would be his own and he would be independent. Of course, it was interesting to meet successful farmers like Mr Holland and to have the opportunity of seeing at close hand a wide range of farming. His father had also had a good life managing the estate at Dunmere. But to be fully stretched and fulfilled, Robert felt he must be farming on his own. And he was confident that he could succeed.

The match at Beresford Park was in its dying minutes. The Park forwards forced yet another loose scrum almost under the posts. Out of a heaving mass of bodies and legs, the ball came out to the scrum half. Two Hospital players converged on him, but with a quick sidestep he managed to find enough room to send an almost perfect pass to Robert. He took it cleanly, and making one last effort charged for the line. Despite two tackles, he kept going forward and hurled himself over for a try mid way between the posts and the corner flag, taking one of the tacklers with him. That made the score 9–10, and all depended on the conversion, a comparatively easy kick, even though the ball was heavy and slippery. As usual, Roger, the fullback, came up for the kick at goal. He had already missed two easy penalties and Robert was not alone in quickly losing faith in his abilities. He took some time preparing himself, wiping the mud off his boot and controlling his breathing. As he kicked, there was the usual charge from the try line. The ball soared towards goal. It had sufficient height and strength, but it lacked direction, passing outside the near post by at least two feet. Almost immediately, the referee blew for time and the weary players wasted no time in making for the dressing room. It had been a hard, gruelling match, played in a persistent drizzle. With both sides playing it tight, the game had developed into a forwards' battle, as two evenly-matched packs slugged it out in the mud. At stand off, Robert had seen little of the ball and his one and only chance had been his try in the closing minutes of the game.

'I don't know why they continue to let Roger take all the place kicks and conversions. You would have kicked that last one and the two penalties easily,' said Peter, energetically soaping the top half of his body as he sat in the communal bath. '

Well, it was a wet, greasy ball,' said Robert. 'And, in any case, you can't easily suggest that as the regular place kicker at school you should be given a chance here. As new boys, we are fortunate to be in the team at all. Chuck over that soap when you've finished with it – if there's any left.'

'Here, catch,' said Peter. 'I shall have a word with Dave when I get a chance.'

Dave was the Park's captain, and it was because of his recommendation that Robert and Peter had been accepted as club members and eventually given a place in the senior side. He was an Oakfield old boy, three years senior to the two boys, but he was well aware of Oakfield's reputation for sport, and thought that as Robert and Peter had won their school colours, they were worth a trial with "The Park". He had not been disappointed. They were now regular members of the side, but still careful not to give offence to the longer serving members.

The visitors had been pinned in their own half for most of the game and had scored with a breakaway try and a doubtful penalty. However angry Peter may have felt over the missed goal kicks, the result should never have had to depend on them. There was a general feeling of disappointment in the changing room for a time, but gradually the usual jovial atmosphere returned. There were the customary gibes about missed chances and exaggerated claims about the punishment meted out in the set scrums. As one of the second row forwards, Peter had taken his share of knocks and had a large bruise on the inside of his thigh to prove it.

'It's a good job you didn't get kicked a bit higher up. It might have spoiled your Saturday night prospects,' said Robert.

'Unfortunately there's nothing to spoil, old chap. I haven't lined up any talent in London, yet.'

'You've been here nearly a month, ample time for a Casanova like you,' teased Robert.

Peter was not to be provoked. 'Talking of talent, did you notice those three girls on the touchline today? Quite put me off my stroke in the line-outs,' said Peter.

'They must be pretty keen to stand out in the rain watching a shower like us,' said Robert.

'They may be friends of some of our chaps, or, perhaps, "The Hospital" crowd. If so, they could be in The Grey Horse later on,' said Peter, suddenly becoming animated. 'Hurry up and get dressed, we had better get round there.'

'To be first in the queue, I suppose,' said Robert. 'Anyway, I'm not hanging around here long. I'm going to the theatre tonight with Mrs Hartley.'

'Oh, yes. I'd forgotten that,' said Peter. 'But you have plenty of time for a quick one. I would value your opinion if they turn up in there.'

'So long as you don't want me to take an active part. Remember, I'm already committed.'

'You never give me a chance to forget that,' said Peter. 'She must be something a bit special, this Margaret of yours. When are you going to introduce me? You should invite her to spend a weekend in London.'

'You'll meet her one day.' Robert had talked to Peter quite a lot about Margaret, but he had never gone into detail about her background and the family problems they were facing. He would have liked the two of them to meet. If only it had been a normal, conventional relationship, they could have made up a foursome. When at school, Robert had several times thought of inviting Peter to stay at Manor Farm during the holidays, but there were no suitable girls in Dunmere, except, possibly,

Celia. Robert smiled to himself as he wondered what Peter would have thought of Celia. There was no point in speculating, as in practice they could never have made up a party and gone out for the evening – a dance at Bridborough or a meal.

'Right, I'm ready if you are,' said Peter. 'You deserve a pint anyway for scoring that try. A pity that twit had to miss the conversion.'

Robert's worst fears were confirmed. He should never have allowed Peter to persuade him to come.

'Oh, it's just a friendly get-together, a few drinks and plenty to eat. Jose has invited some friends from the "Pud" school, so the nosh is sure to be good. After all, it will soon be Christmas and you'll be able to forget all about London for a couple of weeks.'

'Ten days, actually,' Robert had corrected him, when what he should have done was say, "No thank you" very firmly, and stuck by his refusal. From what he had seen of the nurses' Christmas party so far, he was going to need a will of iron. The three girls whom Peter and Robert had met in The Grey Horse after the hospital rugby match were student nurses and, during the past few weeks, Peter had become infatuated with Jose, the prettiest one of the three. She was certainly a good-looking girl, tall, slim, black-haired and with almost too-perfect features. However, it had not taken Peter very long to discover that she was decidedly cool, if not completely frigid.

'Cold as the end of an Eskimo's tool,' said Peter, quoting from the well-known rugby song. In his cruder agricultural way, Robert had suggested the use of a blowlamp. But, in spite of such a distinct lack of promise, Peter was hooked. He enjoyed a challenge and was determined to "crack it". He had told Robert, coming back on the team coach after a match at Bristol, that the nurses' party was going to be a final showdown. That, in itself, should have been sufficient warning to convince Robert that he would have been in safer company making up a bridge foursome with Mrs Hartley. However, he was familiar with Peter's exaggerated sexual exploits, and had not taken the threatened ultimatum very seriously. He now realised, as he looked round the common room at the nurses' hostel, that Jose would be an exceptional girl if a "large fissure" let alone a "crack" did not appear before the party was over.

It had all started innocently enough. A group of about thirty young people standing around with a glass of sherry, nibbling crisps and peanuts and trying to appear animated, making polite, but banal, conversation. It consisted almost entirely of everybody attempting to upstage everybody else. The girls prattled incessantly about themselves, trying to impress by dropping the names of producers they had met in the BBC club, or well-known riders in the local hunt point-to-point back home. They came from that sort of background. Daddy was either in the city or owned an estate in Suffolk. Mummy came up to London to shop or take in a show, staying in the family maisonette in Kensington. Training to be a nurse, or taking a course at domestic science college, was merely a front. An excuse to be in London with a licence to have a good time and, if possible, find a well-heeled husband who could give them the style of life they were used to at home. Mrs Denehurst would have been delighted to welcome anyone of the girls to Dunmere for the week-end if Robert had invited them.

With the exception of Peter and Jose and one or two other couples, nobody knew anyone else very well and most were complete strangers.

In the circumstances, it needed a potent injection of some sort to liven up the occasion. The catalyst was the rum punch. To start with it looked innocent enough and the bland taste suggested that it would prove to be innocuous. But after Peter had disappeared somewhere to the back of the establishment and returned to top it up with a couple of bottles, the effect on the punch and the subsequent effect on those who imbibed, was devastating.

A series of innocent party games culminated in a session of "Shy Widow". Robert remembered the game as it was played at Christmas parties in the old hut in Dunmere. A ring of chairs, all but one occupied by a shy, village maiden, dressed up in her party frock with a pretty ribbon in her hair. And, standing behind each one, an even more reticent village swain, his hair carefully parted and brylcreemed, as he eyed the familiar faces opposite. One boy stood behind the empty chair and winked at a girl who took his fancy who was then expected to leave her seat and rush to occupy the empty one in front of him. The boy behind made some pretence of restraining her while she played her part by making the escape look difficult. The triumphant youth was rewarded with a kiss from the girl whom he had known since childhood, probably sat next to in school and would never dream of kissing again until the next Christmas party. The game Robert remembered was an innocent young teenage frolic.

The version as played at the nurses' party was unrecognisable as the same game. The flick of an eyelash was sufficient to convince about half the girls in the room that the "wink" was directed at them. It was a question of who could fight their way to the empty chair first. And the rewarding kiss was no longer an innocent peck. It was not long before the game disintegrated completely, with couples locked in a long embrace without waiting for any encouraging wink. For a short time, some sort of order was restored when the food appeared. But neither nosh, nor order, lasted long. Dancing started, and Robert found himself doing a slow foxtrot with Diana. He was not usually very good at slow foxtrots, but, in spite of that and the additional handicap of a badly bruised knee, the legacy of a particularly vicious game against Harlequins that afternoon, he seemed to be performing extremely well.

He had a vague recollection of having met Diana somewhere before. She was quite an attractive girl, fair-haired and blue-eyed, with an elfin face, which did not match the considerable bulk of her body.

'I knew you would be a good dancer when we met for the first time in The Grey Horse,' she cooed.

'So that's where we met,' said Robert to himself. His conscience was telling him that it was time he disentangled himself from Diana. Perhaps he should suggest sitting down quietly for a while, but a quick look over Diana's shoulder put him off that idea. There were now very few couples dancing. Several were "sitting out" on the chairs and settees in the far, dimly-lit end of the room. It was difficult to see clearly in the semi-darkness, but it seemed to Robert as he tried to focus through the blonde hair on his shoulder that some couples had disappeared altogether, and he was pretty certain in his rather fuddled mind that they had not left the party and gone home. His geographical knowledge of the house was limited to an earlier visit to the cloakroom, but he recollected a back hall and some stairs. A staircase had a practical use; he was fairly certain that he knew the identity of one couple who had climbed unsteadily up there and he half expected to hear a loud "crack" which would prove him right.

He was now in a difficult predicament. Diane was becoming increasingly affectionate and her body, with its surprisingly ample bosom, was pressed close against him. She had put one arm around his neck, and her cheek nestled on his shoulder, temptingly close to his own face. A downward tilt of his head and their lips would meet. He needed to escape, but how? To have another drink? Very dangerous. To suggest sitting down? Fatal. To go to the cloakroom? That would mean passing the stairs and he could imagine the difficulty with that. The music stopped. For a moment, taken by surprise, they continued to hold each other in the middle of the dance floor, and then Diana took Robert by the hand and pulled him towards the door.

'Wait there, darling,' she said. 'I'm just going to powder my nose. Don't go away, I'll not be long.' She reached up, kissed him firmly on the lips, and disappeared down the corridor.

As soon as she had gone, he turned the opposite way to try to find an escape route. On the lower steps of the stairs, there were couples "necking" and, fumbling in varying compromising positions. If they wanted to do that sort of thing, and they obviously did, Robert wondered why they had not found somewhere more comfortable and secluded. He could hear giggles coming from the landing. Someone had been sick outside the entrance to the cloakroom. After some grovelling around, he managed to find his coat and the door onto the street, feeling righteous and cowardly at the same time. He and Peter had arrived together by taxi and he was not sure where he was. However that was a minor worry; he had made his escape, and that was all that concerned him. It was a dark, foggy night, and he decided to walk along the street and see if he recognised any landmarks. He felt terrible. His knee hurt, he felt sick, and whatever it was that Peter had added to the punch had given him a severe headache.

Gradually, the night air began to refresh him. When he reached the end of the street, he was relieved to find that it had brought him to the Edgware Road. He now knew where he was, and decided to walk through Sussex Gardens, past Paddington Station and along to the Bayswater Road. He was feeling guilty at having behaved unfairly to Diana. He blamed it all on London and the sort of depraved life it offered. He was not prudish, nor a kill-joy, but he despised the sort of girl he had met at the party – spoiled by rich, indulgent, fathers, selfish, feather-brained, and looking for a husband who could keep them in the luxury they had come to expect as a right. In London, the air felt dirty and second-hand. He longed for the fresh, pure smell of the country. He missed life on the farm; the noise of the horses in the stable, the smell of animals, the comfort of the farmhouse, the banter of the farm men and, above all, he ached for Margaret.

As he passed the end of London Street, a figure loomed out of the fog. In the badly lit street it was difficult to see clearly, but it was obviously a woman. As he approached, she stopped.

'Would you like a nice time, dear?' she asked. 'Just round the corner.'

As he walked on, Robert got a fleeting glance of long hair, mascara and lipstick, with a whiff of cheap scent. It was a fitting climax to an evening of decadence and dissolute behaviour.

It would not be Christmas for another two weeks, but there was already a gay, festive atmosphere in The Nag's Head at Askham Bryan. Long paper streamers snaked across the heavily-beamed ceiling. There was a fringe of holly round the bar, and the tinsel on the heavily decorated Christmas tree reflected the flames of an inviting log fire. A bunch of mistletoe hung tantalisingly over the door, kindling memories for the two old men playing dominoes in the corner and giving encouragement to any incoming reticent customers not yet emboldened by the liquid refreshments provided at the bar.

A dapper, sharp-faced man in a peak cap, breeches and leggings, twirled a glass of Scotch in his hand as he discussed prospects for the Saturday hunt meeting with the landlord. The only other occupant of the bar room was a long-haired rheumatic dog who decided that the fire was too hot, even for him, and, raising himself with difficulty, he padded over to cool down and continue his dreaming under the protection of an old wooden settle. Apart from the pageantry of Christmas, it was a typical weekday evening in The Nag's Head. Perhaps a little later, two or three farm lads may come in for a game of darts or merrils and if there was an NFU meeting in the village hall, the bar would suddenly be invaded by thirsty farmers who had made sure the chairman reached the end of the agenda at least half an hour before closing time. Otherwise, the village local was only busy on Friday nights, Friday being the traditional pay day, and Saturday nights, when even farmers' wives found time to relax; and whenever the darts team was playing at home.

The noisy arrival of a crowd of students was, therefore, welcomed by the landlord, but resented by the regulars, who regarded it as an intrusion of their domain.

'Not the end of term yet, is it?' asked the landlord.

'No, not quite. We are just celebrating the last day of exams,' replied a large broad-shouldered, bushy-haired lad, who was quickly recognisable as the gang's self-appointed spokesman. The students, from the agricultural college a mile up the road, traditionally celebrated the end of term examinations with a visit to The Nag's Head. A kitty was suggested, and the young men of the group fumbled for their silver and started to order the drinks.

Margaret had never been in a pub before, and had been hesitant about joining her friends for their celebration party. Being staunch Methodists, Harry and Emily were strictly teetotal, and she had consistently been warned by her parents about the dangers of alcohol, and the undesirability of associating with habitual drinkers, and had concluded that it would be rude and unsociable not to accept their invitation. Margaret had also been doubtful for another reason. She was sure that one of the boys, Tom, fancied her. He was a likeable, pleasant boy, whom she was pleased to have as a friend, but she was anxious not to become more closely involved.

Now that it was time to order a drink, she did not know what to choose. She noticed that two of the girls had ordered gin and "it". She knew about gin, a tipple she associated with Mrs Gamp in "Martin Chuzzlewit", but she was completely foxed by "it". She did not want to show her ignorance and naivety by asking, so she decided to take no chances by ordering an orange juice.

'Oh, come on, Margaret,' said the bushy-haired boy. 'You can do better than that. If you like orange, why not have a gin and orange?' And, not waiting for a reply, he promptly ordered one. Margaret sipped it carefully. It was quite pleasant and tasted mainly of orange, but even so she was suspicious and thought that if she drank it slowly, she could make it last most of the evening.

'You are not used to this sort of thing, are you, Margaret? You know, going into a pub or having a drink,' said Tom, who had made sure he was standing next to her. Margaret hesitated before answering, surprised at Tom's perception and understanding of her discomfort in unfamiliar surroundings. She looked at him, seeing in his kind, blue, eyes a genuine concern for her well being and, appreciating his good intentions, decided she could trust him.

'How do you know that?' she asked. 'In fact, I've never been in a pub before. I've been brought up a Methodist, and I've never drunk anything even remotely alcoholic – except mother's homemade wine. It's probably more potent than this,' she said, laughing.

Tom smiled sympathetically. 'Like me, a sheltered background and strict upbringing. It seems we are both innocents in an alien world.'

Margaret wondered if his proclaimed innocence extended to his experience of girls. He was a shy boy, and she thought that perhaps it did. She would have to be careful not to hurt his feelings. He continued to talk to her and as his confidence grew, prompted partly by the pint of beer, which he was drinking, and partly by Margaret's willingness to appear interested, he went on at length about his home on a small fifty-acre farm near Halifax, where his parents struggled to make a living. He had two older brothers, and there was no hope of his ever being able to follow his father on the home farm. The best he could hope for when he had completed his course at Askham Bryan was to become a head herdsman or manager on a large dairy farm.

'What you need to do is find a rich farmer's daughter who is an only child,' said Margaret.

'Oh, no, I couldn't do that. I should have to love the girl I marry,' said Tom, taking Margaret's light-hearted comment seriously. Tom obviously took life very seriously indeed, and Margaret, sensing the way in which the conversation might go, was relieved when they were interrupted by the suggestion of a game of darts. 'Boys versus girls,' shouted someone.

'Oh, no, that's not fair. I've never thrown a dart in my life,' said one of the girls.

'Neither have I,' added Margaret.

'All right, then, the boys will throw left-handed,' said Tom. All agreed, and each threw a dart, the one with the highest score to start the game.

It was on the walk back to college that Margaret became increasingly aware of Tom's feelings towards her. The game of darts had been a hilarious success; a happy occasion full of innocent fun and ending in dramatic farce when one of the girls who, for most of the game, had had difficulty even hitting the board, gave the girls victory by scoring an "impossible" double twenty with her final throw. This had earned her a kiss under the mistletoe, and they had all set off on their walk home with arms linked and an enthusiastic rendering of "While Shepherds Watched their Flocks by Night" in several different versions. They continued singing for most of the way back, but as they approached the poultry huts in the paddock close to the college farmstead, they quietened down and broke ranks. Margaret knew that two of the girls had special boyfriends in the group, and was not surprised when they dropped behind. She was not surprised either to find that she and Tom had been left together. It had been obvious from his behaviour all through the evening that he was "throwing a line" at Margaret, and their friends had made a tactful retreat. He slipped an arm innocently round her waist as they walked slowly into the college grounds.

'It's been great fun, but I'm pleased to have you to myself,' he said.

'I'm afraid you'll find me dull company,' said Margaret, not wishing to encourage him.

'You could never be dull as far as I'm concerned. I've wanted to talk to you for ages, ever since the beginning of term when we first met.'

Margaret wondered if talking to her was his only motive for being alone with her. The way she had caught him looking at her in the pub suggested more than just a desire for intelligent conversation. Not that she really minded. She was accustomed to boys chasing after her. Normally, she would have taken no notice, but she liked Tom, even if he was rather a bore, and she did not want to hurt his pride.

'There are plenty of other girls on the course, what's so special about me?' she asked.

Tom was not to be sidetracked. 'Oh, Margaret, you must know better than that. Everybody else seems to be aware of how I feel about you. I'm not very good at expressing myself, certainly not where girls are concerned, but I just find you the most attractive girl I've ever met. I think I may be falling for you seriously.'

'Don't be silly,' said Margaret, more sharply than she intended. 'We hardly know each other.'

'But we could get to know one another, if only you would give us a chance,' pleaded Tom.

They had now reached the student buildings. The girls' hostel was down a short drive to the left, but the boys' dormitories were on the other side of the farm buildings. They paused at the junction of the driveway, but Tom was in no hurry to go, and continued to stand with his arm now even more tightly round Margaret's waist.

'I turn left down here,' she said, waiting for him to drop his arm.

Instead, he drew her round to face him. He bent to kiss her. She offered no resistance, but just let it happen, not returning his kiss in any way. He held his lips on hers for a moment, but, realising that she was not returning his feelings, he stopped and said, 'I'm sorry, Margaret. I shouldn't have done that. I should have realised you didn't want me to kiss you.' He was obviously upset and embarrassed.

'No offence. But I've tried not to encourage you.'

'But I thought you quite liked me. You've always been friendly and seemed to enjoy my company.'

'Yes, I do, but only in a platonic way. I don't want to hurt your feelings, Tom, but you could never be anything more to me than just a friend.'

'You mean I put you off physically?'

'I didn't say that. But the fact is I have a steady boyfriend at home.'

'You mean you are engaged? You don't wear a ring or anything.'

Margaret found this conversation becoming difficult. 'No, we are not engaged yet, but we love each other, and plan to get married.'

As she said these words, she was suddenly overwhelmed by her love for Robert. All her old fears of losing him, of the impossibility of an engagement ever happening, of the difficulties they faced. She felt a lump in her throat, tears pricked her eyes and she said, in a faltering voice, 'You'd better go now, Tom. You've been very sweet,' and, reaching up, she gave him a friendly peck before rushing down the hostel drive, unable to control her emotions any longer. Once alone, she leaned against the college wall and burst into tears, saying to herself between the sobs: 'Oh, Robert, my darling, what's going to happen to us?'

Left in the driveway, Tom stood blaming himself for his clumsy behaviour, and yet perplexed by the intensity of Margaret's emotional outburst. For a moment, he was half-minded to follow and offer her some comfort but, thinking he might make matters worse, he decided against it, and walked slowly, and dejectedly, away, wondering if he would ever understand women and learn the secret of finding a girl-friend.

Chapter 19

Robert and Margaret were sitting holding hands on a seat in the waiting-room on York Station, surrounded by a pile of luggage. They were waiting for the 5.32 to Kirkley.

'Do you really think it's wise to travel on the same train?' asked Margaret, looking anxiously round the waiting-room to see if she recognised anybody waiting for the same connection.

'Why not? Why should anybody be surprised to see us together? It's perfectly straightforward. We are both travelling home for Christmas holidays and happened to meet on the station. If we did meet somebody we both knew, they would think it rather odd if we weren't at least talking together.'

'But what's going to happen when we arrive in Kirkley?' persisted Margaret. 'Dad is going to meet me, and suppose your father turns up to meet you. It could be very embarrassing for everybody.'

'Father isn't meeting me. He has an important landowners' meeting in Bridborough and he wouldn't miss that. I shall get Harold from the station garage to take me home. There's no problem.

'I suppose you are right. But I still feel nervous,' said Margaret, withdrawing her hand and shuffling down the seat further away from Robert.

'You didn't do that when we were sitting in the cinema,' he said. Margaret had a volatile personality, and he often provoked her just to watch her reaction, especially if he said something mildly suggestive.

'It was dark and cosy in there. I never knew there were double seats on the back rows,' she said.

'Well, you do now,' said Robert meaningfully. 'A good job there wasn't much competition from the film.'

This time, Margaret did blush.

'It was the first time we've been together in a warm, dark, comfortable place. And ten weeks is a long time to go without seeing you; I missed you terribly.'

'I think we should find somewhere even warmer, and more comfortable, when we meet in York for the Easter holidays,' said Robert. He watched her closely to see if she had realised what he was hinting at.

'How do you mean?' she said innocently.

'We could meet as we did today and then stay the night in York, travelling to Kirkley the next day.'

It was a chance for Margaret to get her own back. 'What would be the point of that?' she asked, as though not understanding the implications of his suggestion. 'We have had plenty of time in York today to do all we wanted to do, and it's still only twenty past five.'

Margaret turned towards him. He took her hand again and met her eyes. They both laughed.

'All right,' he said. 'Now, how about a serious answer?'

Margaret led him on a little further. 'Where would we stay?' she asked.

'I don't know. Anywhere you liked. The Station Hotel would be very handy, and we should be pretty anonymous there.'

'Oh, Robert, it would be marvellous, but you shouldn't tempt me.'

'We could have separate rooms, if that's what's worrying you.' Margaret did not react. She was remembering what she had debated with herself following their passionate lovemaking in Hagg Wood.

'My darling, don't forget, I was brought up a strict Methodist and you were brought up equally as strict. What would our parents think if they knew?'

'But there's no reason why they should know.'

'No, but that would be deceiving them even worse than our secret meetings.'

'So, the answer is "No,"' said Robert. He was quite resigned to the fact that she would reject the idea. It would have surprised him if she had said otherwise. He even felt guilty suggesting it, because it was completely out of character for both of them.

'At the moment, I don't see how it can be otherwise,' she said. 'But I'll think about it. I might change my mind, you never know. A lot can happen between now and Easter. And now we had better move. I'm still worried about our travelling together. There could be somebody from Dunmere waiting on the platform.'

The train from York to Kirkley was a slow one, which stopped at all the villages on the way. It was made up of old rolling stock with no corridor, and Robert and Margaret, having found an empty compartment, hoped that nobody would join them. For a few minutes, they were left alone, but just as the train was about to depart, a porter opened the door and ushered in a young lady, pushing her luggage in after her just as the train was starting to move away from the platform. It was Celia Heyford-Jones. For a moment, Robert was too shocked to respond but, recovering himself, he stood up and took one of her suitcases.

'Celia! What on earth are you doing here? Let me put this on the rack for you.'

'Hello. Thanks, Robert. I didn't expect to see you either,' said Celia, still rather puffed. 'Forgive me, I had to rush over the bridge. My Bristol train was late. I expect you are home for Christmas as well.'

'Do you two know each other?' asked Robert, as both girls hesitated, wondering what to say. He introduced them.

'I know you by sight, but we have never been introduced,' said Margaret.

Celia was at a disadvantage. She had no idea who Margaret was, and wondered if it was a girl he had met in London who he was bringing home for the holidays.

'Margaret's father worked at Manor Farm until recently. We've known each other for years. We were at Dunmere School together until I went to Oakfield and Margaret went to Kirkley Grammar School.'

'We met in the waiting-room,' said Margaret, thinking that some further explanation was needed. 'I'm also going home for Christmas.'

Celia settled herself on the seat opposite and both girls regarded each other closely. Margaret had only seen Celia from a distance, and would not have recognised her if she had not been introduced. She noticed her pretty red hair, and thought that if it had not been for the heavy rimmed glasses, she would have been quite attractive.

On the other hand, Celia would not believe the good looking, neatly-dressed girl sitting close to Robert was the daughter of a farmworker. She appeared nervous and ill at ease, but not in any way overawed. Celia noticed that they were sitting with their thighs almost touching, but as the remainder of the seat was full of luggage, it was, perhaps, unavoidable. Even so, if they had wished, they could either have made more room by putting their suitcases on the luggage rack, or have sat opposite each other.

As the journey progressed and they chatted easily about their respective courses, and Robert's life in London, the earlier tension between them eased. Robert was interested to hear about Celia's progress at Bristol University, where she was studying languages. He wondered if she had found a boyfriend there, but did not want to embarrass her by asking. He would have ample opportunity of finding out as they were sure to meet during the holidays.

Margaret was the quietest of the three, but when she did take part in the conversation, Celia noticed that she talked fluently and vivaciously, using her large, intensive blue eyes to great effect. She gave the impression of being an interesting and formidable young woman. The more she saw of her, the more Celia wondered about her relationship with Robert. They seemed to be on easy, friendly terms, which belied their difference in class, and was all the more remarkable considering that they could hardly have spent any time together since childhood. Celia also decided she would do some probing when she next saw Robert on his own.

For Robert and Margaret, the accidental meeting with Celia was an exciting, if nerve-racking, experience. It was the first time they had been together in the company of someone who was known to them. Margaret had a feeling of smug satisfaction when she thought back to the days when she considered Celia a rival for Robert's affection. She could not help wondering what Celia would have thought if she had seen them on the back row of the cinema. All through the journey, she felt that she was playing a part in a masque and that reality would re-assert itself when they arrived at Kirkley Station. But, even then, she would have to carry on the charade for the benefit of her father.

Robert still had a guilty conscience where Harry was concerned. He had not been looking forward to meeting him at Kirkley. It was an encounter, which would be even more uncomfortable following Harry's departure from Manor Farm. However, as soon as they arrived on the platform, he felt reassured as he witnessed the joyous meeting of father and daughter and saw the familiar grin on Harry's face when Margaret explained Robert's presence.

'You're looking well, Harry. The new life must be suiting you,' said Robert, as he shook his hand warmly.

'Aye, it took a bit o' getting used to, but ah'm settling down now.'

'A bit different from ploughing or carting mangolds?'

'It is an' all,' said Harry, with feeling. 'But ah still miss mi 'osses and a bit o' company. Ah don't see nowt o' mi old mates since ah left Dunmere.'

'And the new house, that must be a big change, too?'

'Aye, a grand spot it is. We rattle about in it though, like beans int' threshing drum,' said Harry.

'I can't wait to see it,' said Margaret excitedly. 'Come on dad, there's no time for you two to start discussing old times. I want to go home and see mum and the girls.'

'Yes, I must go too,' said Robert. 'Celia has offered me a lift home with the rector. I mustn't keep them waiting. Nice to see you again, Harry.'

'Goodbye, Robert,' said Margaret with a meaningful look. She hated leaving him in such a perfunctory fashion, but continued to play their charade, and Robert responded with a cheerful "Cheerio" as he picked up his bags and went out into the station yard to find Celia and her father.

Harry's remarks about the Jackson's new home were in no way an exaggeration. Birch House was only five minutes' walk from the station. At one time, it had been a small dairy farm on the edge of Kirkley, but as the market town expanded almost all the land had been sold for building, leaving the original farmhouse, some old buildings, garden, orchard and small paddock. George Coleman's plan was to convert the buildings into a bottling plant and dairy. For the time being, he was using the paddock to make hay and graze the aftermath with dry cows or young stirks, and Harry was nearby to keep an eye on these. It was a shrewd investment as, at a future date, he would, no doubt, be able to sell the land with planning permission for development.

The house was Edwardian, not particularly attractive but solidly built of brick and colour-washed white with black paintwork. There was a large kitchen, dining-room and sitting-room on the ground floor, and four bedrooms, which meant that the girls no longer had to share. But, the greatest luxuries of all were electricity, hot and cold running water, and, as George Coleman needed to be in easy contact with Harry, a telephone. This was especially welcome for Margaret, as it greatly facilitated communications with Robert.

Of course, they were woefully short of furniture and carpets and curtains, but compared with No 4 Oak Cottages, it was a palace.

Later that evening, Margaret was sitting with her mother in front of the fire, enjoying a cup of cocoa and a piece of Emily's fruitcake. Harry, who had to be up at four o'clock the following morning, and the younger girls, had gone to bed.

'This is one of the luxuries one misses at college. There is nowhere just to sit in comfort and relax,' said Margaret.

'How do you spend your evenings and spare time?' asked Emily, wanting to find out about her daughter's social life. Margaret had talked enthusiastically about the poultry courses but, so far, had said very little about how the students spent their leisure hours.

'We don't have much spare time. It's a hard slog. We concentrate a lot of work into one year. There's a great deal of reading to do and notes to write up.'

'Have you made any friends?'

'No one special. We all get along together very happily. Some of the girls have boyfriends on the agricultural course.'

'But not you?' queried Emily.

Margaret laughed. 'Oh, mum, you never stop trying, do you? No, not me. There's only one boy so far as I'm concerned, you know that.'

'How is Robert? Did you enjoy your day in York?'

Margaret was beginning to feel interrogated, but she told her mother about their meal in a smart restaurant, their visit to the cinema, and brought her up to date about Robert's life in London.

'But you will never guess who we met on the train. Celia Heyford-Jones.'

'That would be embarrassing for you. What is she like? I know her to nod to in the street, but we have never spoken to each other.'

'Friendly enough, but rather boring. Not particularly attractive. A bit of a snob I should say. I could see that Robert wouldn't be interested in her even if I wasn't around.'

'Or anyone else? You were worried that he might meet a girl in London.'

'Not any more. I know he loves me, but I do worry about our future. It helps being able to talk to you. But he still hasn't told his parents and, of course, dad still doesn't know. I feel very guilty when we all met at the station. And it's not going to be very easy to meet Robert this winter.'

'You'll be very busy at Uncle Gilbert's for the next few days,' said Emily. 'He told me they had more birds than ever to dress this Christmas, and I suppose Robert is going to Holme Green.'

'Yes, but not all the time. It is relatively quiet at this time of year, and he goes back to London straight after New Year.'

Emily was quiet for a moment. She had been waiting for an opportunity to talk to Margaret about Robert. She was well aware of the difficulties he faced, but was beginning to wonder if he was sincere when he talked of marrying Margaret. If he really loved her, why was he delaying telling his parents? It could be that he had met another girl in London, in spite of what he had told Margaret, and was now just stringing her along. After all, Emily did not really know Robert. She had known him well as a child, but she had seldom ever seen him over the past few years, and did not know what sort of young man he had grown up to be. She had no reason for believing he was anything other than honourable and well meaning, but she needed to know. Now that the Jackson family had moved away from Dunmere, she wondered if it would be prudent to suggest that Margaret should invite him home. It was highly unlikely that he would be seen by anybody in Kirkley who knew him, and even if someone did, she felt it was time to bring the whole business into the open. If Robert was not serious in his intentions, he should say so, and give Margaret a chance to meet someone else. She would never have a better opportunity than now, whilst she was at Askham Bryan. If he did intend to marry her, he should tell his parents and face the consequences.

'Where have you gone, mum? A penny for them,' said Margaret. 'I'm sorry, I was thinking...'

'I could see that,' interrupted Margaret.

'I was thinking,' continued Emily, 'about you and Robert. Would you like to invite him home sometime?'

It was now Margaret's turn to think. She looked round the room. No decent chair to sit on; a shabby settee through which you could feel the springs when you sat on it; and a scattering of pricked rugs, which she knew concealed the worst worn patches in the threadbare carpet. It was a much bigger and more attractive room than the kitchen at Dunmere, but she wondered what Robert would think of it compared with the opulence of Manor Farm. But that was stupid and irrational, she realised. He knew well enough the circumstances in which the farmworkers lived. If her humble upbringing and working class background had been an obstacle, he would never have become involved with her in the first place. He had reassured her on this point often enough, but it was when she came up against the practical realities of it that doubts arose in her mind.

Furthermore, she would have to tell her father and sisters – once Barbara and Joan knew, the whole neighbourhood would know. Whatever promise of secrecy they might give, she knew that the secrets of her love life would soon be the talk of the school.

'I don't know, mother,' said Margaret at last. 'Let me think about it. In any case, it would have to be after Christmas, as I shall be at Uncle Gilbert's for the next few days.'

'All right, as you say, there's no rush. Sleep on it.'

'You mean lie awake on it,' said Margaret ironically.

Chapter 20

As it left the hamlet of Darren Beck, the road to Newlands Farm crossed the brook, which gave the village its name, over a narrow stone bridge, and rose steeply towards the open moor. The farm's exposed position on the hillside had been purposely chosen by Gilbert Dawson as being a healthy, invigorating climate ideally suited for his poultry breeding enterprise. On a summer's day, when fleecy, white clouds floated across the hills and skylarks trilled in a clear blue sky, it could be a heavenly place to live and work. To the north and east, the arms of a narrow woodland planted mainly with larch and Scots pine enfolded the house and buildings, yet although protected from the prevailing winds, in winter it was bleak and cold, especially on a frosty morning, when the drinkers were frozen solid and the hens slipped on the icy patches round the fold units, their feathers plumped by a biting wind.

On the Wednesday of Christmas week, it was such a morning, and the poultry girls at Newlands welcomed the warmth and comparative comfort of the packing house where they were busy dressing poultry.

The week before Christmas was a time of year which Gladys and the girls hated. Gilbert's main enterprise was the pedigree flock of Rhode Island Reds, but the farm also carried a large commercial egg-laying flock, and every year chickens, ducks, geese and turkeys were fattened for the Christmas market.

Nobody enjoyed plucking and dressing poultry. The job had been made as pleasant as possible by converting some of the old farm buildings into a packing house. This was normally used for cleaning, grading and packing eggs, but at Christmas time it was temporarily converted into a place for dressing poultry. At one end of the shed, the girls sat on stools or benches in a semi-circle round a coke stove, dressed in jodhpurs and warm sweaters. Their legs and knees protected by old sacks, they sat hunched and uncomfortable with a bird on their lap, stripping off its feathers ready to be drawn and trussed. It was a boring, back-aching job, especially if a bird was "feathering", a stage when the feathers, instead of coming out cleanly, left a short, black "pen" sticking in the flesh. These "pens" had to be laboriously picked out one by one using a finger and thumb. The ducks and geese were the most difficult to dress. It helped to scald the birds in hot water, but the wet feathers quickly soaked through the protecting sacks, and it became a wet, unpleasant job. And there is nothing more unpleasant than the smell of wet feathers. When plucked, the birds were passed on for the next stage of singeing, drawing and trussing. The girls alternated between plucking and dressing, so that they not only had a change of occupation, but also gained experience in the various processes involved.

There were usually three or four girls working at Newlands, and none of them stayed for very long. The older, qualified, girls left to gain promotion or, more often, to marry, and the younger ones, like Margaret, tended to be temporary, gaining practical experience whilst at college, and providing a useful source of casual employment, as much of the work was seasonal.

'Well, Margaret, how have you enjoyed today? A bit different from sitting in a lecture theatre?' suggested Gilbert. Margaret had joined him and Gladys in the sitting-room, following her evening meal in the kitchen with the other girls.

'Apart from sore fingers and an aching back, I found it interesting, rather than enjoyable. But don't think we just sit around all day at Askham Bryan. We spend about half our time doing practical work on the farm.'

'Perhaps I chose the wrong word when I said "enjoyable". Nobody, in their right mind could enjoy dressing poultry. But I hope you're enjoying your course.'

'Oh, yes. It's great. Time goes so quickly; I can't believe I've been there a term and have only another six months to go.'

'And then what? Any plans for the future?'

'I suspect she'll be like most of the other girls and get married,' suggested Gladys. 'There must be plenty of boys to choose from at Askham Bryan.'

Margaret knew Gladys was fishing. She didn't know what she and Gilbert thought about her social life. They must have suspected that she had a boyfriend somewhere around, considering her frequent absences during the summer evenings.

Gilbert didn't give Margaret a chance to reply. She wasn't sure what she would have said if he had.

'We were wondering if you would like to come back here, permanently, when you leave college in July?' he said, coming straight to the point. 'I've been asked if I'm willing to stand for election as Chairman of the NFU Poultry Committee. If I agree, and succeed, it would mean regular trips to London, and a great deal of time away from home.

Gladys can take on more of the administration work, but she would need help in supervising the day-to-day running of the farm. We both think you would be the ideal person to do it.'

Margaret couldn't believe it. It was a wonderful opportunity. She was happy at Newlands, got on well with Gladys and, of course, it was near home. And if Robert was going to be at Cirencester, she would be able to see him when he came home for holidays.

'Oh, Gilbert,' she said. 'It would be marvellous,' and she rushed over to his chair to give him a hug and a kiss. Then she went to give Gladys a kiss as well.

'But what about the other girls? Do you think I can do it? What if I fail my exams?'

In her excitement and enthusiasm, she had not quite realised the implications of what was involved.

'You will pass your exams, with no trouble at all, but it wouldn't make any difference. We are sure you can do the job,' said Gilbert.

'We wouldn't have asked you if we had had any doubts,' added Gladys.

'I think we should have a celebratory drink,' said Gilbert, 'and start Christmas a few days early.' He went over to the drinks cabinet. 'You'll have a glass of sherry, Margaret, won't you?' he asked, suddenly remembering that, as Emily's daughter, she would not be accustomed to having a drink.

Gilbert was a methodist himself, but also a man of the world, and more broadminded than most.

'Yes, please,' said Margaret, and told them about her evening in The Nag's Head, but leaving out any reference to her embarrassing encounter with Tom.

Margaret came down for breakfast on the morning after Boxing Day in high spirits. The Jacksons had spent a quiet, family, Christmas, and Margaret had been glad of an opportunity to rest after a hard term and four exhausting days at Newlands. Her only disappointment was that she had not been able to meet Robert. But, at least, she had managed to telephone him at Holme Green before he, too, had returned home for Christmas to Manor Farm.

The confidence which Gilbert and Gladys had shown her by the offer of permanent employment at Newlands had greatly bolstered her morale. She had finally made up her mind that she would tell Harry about Robert. She loved him, she was sure he loved her, and whatever doubts her mother might have, she trusted him to tell his own parents. The one, redeeming, feature about having to do a boring, repetitive, job, such as poultry dressing, was that it gave plenty of time for thought, and she had considered at length the proposals made by her mother on the evening of her arrival home from college. She had decided that the crucial first step was to find out her father's reaction.

Harry was later home from his milk round than usual, delayed by people who wanted to adjust their milk order following the disruption over Christmas. Margaret waited for him to finish his dinner and have his customary ten-minute snooze before bringing up the subject she had avoided for the past year. She had agreed with her mother that she would talk to her father alone, and Emily remained tactfully out of the way, pretending to be busy in the kitchen.

'I've some important news for you, dad,' said Margaret, making an oblique start.

'Yer've already told me. We talked about yer job at Gilbert's on Saturday.'

'No, not that. Something much more important.'

'There's nowt more important than yer job, ah knaws very well,' said Harry. 'But go on.'

'I've got a very special boyfriend and we want to get engaged,' said Margaret, watching her father intently.

'A lad yer've met at Askham Bryan, ah suppose? It's a bit quick, isn't it? Yer ain't given yersels very long to get ti knaw one another.'

Margaret smiled, in spite of herself.

'No, don't jump to conclusions. It's not a boy I've met at college. It's somebody we've both known for a long time. A very long time.'

She paused, waiting for a reaction. She noticed that he became intense, puzzled, and waiting for a name.

'Robert Denehurst,' she said. It took a moment for the name to register.

'Master Robert?' he said at last. 'But yer've known him all yer life. Yer nivver said nowt t'other night at Kirkley Station.'

Whatever reaction Margaret had been expecting from her father, it certainly wasn't this.

'But you don't seem to be surprised,' said Margaret. 'I mean, you wouldn't really expect Robert to fall in love with a girl like me?'

'Why not?' asked Harry. 'Ah think yer a lass in a million. Why shouldn't he?'

Margaret was becoming more and more exasperated. It reminded her of David Copperfield when Mr Dick suggested that his aunt should "Give the boy a bath."

'I thought you would be cross and upset?' she said.

'Naw, why should ah be? If yer want ti knaw, ah'm very pleased. Ah can't think of a better lad to 'ave as a son-in-law. We allus got on well together.'

Margaret felt that this conversation was getting nowhere. Harry hadn't raised any of the difficulties she was expecting, and seemed oblivious to the problem of Robert's family and background.

'But think of the different backgrounds. You can't imagine that the Colonel and Mrs Denehurst would want their son to marry a farmworker's daughter,' said Margaret, wondering why she was continuing to raise doubts in her father's mind. If he was happy, why should she worry?

'That 'as nowt to do wi it,' said Harry. 'In the eyes of the Lord we're all equal. Christ was born in a manger, in a stable. Nowt very grand about that. Come to think of it, it doesn't say nowt about where t'bullocks were. They didn't 'ave 'osses in them days.'

'Oh, dad, you are marvellous,' said Margaret. She went over to sit on his knee, and, putting her arm round him, leaned her head against his chest and shed tears of relief and pure joy.

'Come on, lass,' said Harry. 'Ah dean't knaw why yer crying. Ah would 'ave thowt yer 'ad lots to be 'appy about?'

'Oh, I am happy. I am,' said Margaret. 'But I'm also worried about what Robert's parents will think. They won't see it the way you do.'

'That's for Robert ti worry about.'

'But he hasn't told them yet,' said Margaret.

'Well, yer 'have only just told me. 'e'll tell 'em when 'e's ready.' Margaret decided that there was now really no more to say. She was relieved to have got it all over, but was puzzled by her father's reaction.

'I'll go and see if mum wants any help in the kitchen,' she said. Giving her father a kiss, and leaving his knee, she went out to speak with Emily.

'He's always been like that,' said Emily when Margaret had told her about Harry's reaction to her news. 'He was just the same when he left Manor Farm and had no prospect of any work or anywhere to live. I nearly went potty with worry and he didn't seem to have a care in the world."The Lord will provide," he said, and went out to tie up his runner beans.

'It must be marvellous to have a simple faith like his,' said Margaret. 'But it's not going to help when Robert tells his parents.'

'Are you going to invite him here?'

'Not just yet. I don't want to pressurise him. I'm trying to be philosophical, like dad. He trusts Robert, just as I do.'

Chapter 21

Colonel Denehurst disliked the period between Christmas and New Year. Although the farm men came to work as usual, it seemed to be a stagnant period, with most of the time being spent catching up on routine jobs which had been neglected over Christmas and preparing for the New Year break.

The weather had not helped to allay the general feeling of malaise. It had continued hard, and cold, with grey skies during the day and keen frosts at night. John, Stephen, Robert and Nigel Heyford-Jones had been out shooting rabbits, which were causing a great deal of damage to a field of winter wheat, on the edge of Beech Wood. They hadn't had much success and the Colonel had decided that the best answer would be for the keepers to spend a day ferreting. Nigel had gone home and the men had joined the rest of the family for a pre-dinner drink round a welcoming log fire.

Mary was telling her mother about the New Year's Eve Ball, at Bridborough, to which she and Stephen were going with a party of friends.

'Why don't you take Celia and go with them, Robert?' suggested Marjorie. 'I don't suppose she's ever been to the Spa. I'm sure she would be pleased to go. There would be no problem about getting another ticket, would there, Mary?'

Mary had thought that her mother had, at last, accepted that Robert had no interest, whatsoever, in taking Celia anywhere. She looked across at Robert before replying, but decided to play it straight.

'No, I'm sure we could find one, but it's up to Robert to decide whether he wants to go.'

'What about it, Robert?' asked Marjorie. John and Stephen were still discussing the problem of controlling rabbits, but Stephen had not missed the conversation going on across the other side of the fireplace, nor the sudden tension it had created.

Robert had a difficult decision to make. He could stall for time and say he would think it over. He could say that he would love to go, but that he did not want to take Celia as his partner, or as there was nobody else he could take, there would be no point in pursuing it. But, of course, there was somebody else he could take, as Mary and Stephen knew well enough. Perhaps the moment he had dreaded, and avoided, for the past year had arrived. Now that Margaret was living in Kirkley it was almost impossible for them to go on meeting secretly, at any rate during the winter. They had both thoroughly enjoyed their day in *York* when, for the first time, they had been free to behave like any normal couple and wander round the streets and have a meal together. Sneaking out of the house to meet Margaret in a hole-in-the-corner fashion somewhere, like the hut in Hagg Wood, or to go for a walk and snatch a petting session in the grass, was neither fair to her, nor himself, or his parents. He decided it was too good an opportunity to miss. The time had come to speak up. He looked at his sister for a moment and held her eyes. She guessed what was going on in his mind and held her breath.

'I would love to go. But not with Celia as my partner,' said Robert eventually.

'But, why not with Celia? If not her, who? There's nobody else I can think of,' said Marjorie.

'You might not think so, but I can,' said Robert. He paused before saying, 'Margaret Jackson.'

Mary and Stephen exchanged glances and turned back to Robert. He looked tense and pale, but calm, determined and in full control of his emotions. There was a long silence, broken only by the crackling of the log fire and the heavy tick of the grandfather clock. It took a few moments for the significance of Robert's remarks to register with his mother and father.

'You can't mean Harry Jackson's Margaret?' said Marjorie in a quiet, almost strangled, voice, which was little more than an incredulous whisper.

'Yes, of course. I don't know any other Margaret Jackson.' Until now, the Colonel had been quietly drinking his Scotch, but suddenly he reacted, as though given an electric shock. He sat upright in his chair, and turning his piercing blue eyes on Robert shouted: 'Don't be ridiculous! I just can't believe what I'm hearing! It's out of the question!'

Robert stood his ground. 'Why? She's a perfectly respectable girl.'

'It is obvious why not,' said his father, a little less violently. 'You know well enough that people in our position would never dream of mixing with working class people. We have a sensible, working relationship, which is accepted by both sides, but it stops there. We would never mix with them socially. When have you seen one of the farm men invited here for dinner, or your mother asked to pop into one of the cottages for afternoon tea? Never, and you never would. So don't think you can suddenly take one of the village girls to a dance as your partner! I absolutely forbid it!'

'But why Margaret Jackson?' asked Marjorie. 'You don't even know her very well. I know you played together as children, but that was years ago. You don't know what sort of girl she has grown up to be. Very nice, no doubt. But not for you, darling.'

'There's something you and father need to know,' said Robert. 'I know very well what sort of girl Margaret has grown up to be because I've been seeing her regularly, over the past three years. We've been together as often as possible during the holidays and corresponded during term-time. She is a charming, intelligent girl. We have fallen in love and have every intention of getting engaged.'

The suggestion of taking Margaret to a dance had been bad enough, but what Robert was saying now was beyond all reason. He knew only too well the effect it was having on his parents. He had to fight hard to control his own feelings and maintain his composure. He would have liked to have said more but did not want to risk breaking down and making a fool of himself. Whatever happened, he intended to show determination and strength of character. Without waiting for any reaction, he rose and walked out of the room. Once outside, he ran upstairs to his bedroom, fell on the bed and buried his head in the pillow, no longer able to hold back the tears.

Nobody spoke immediately following Robert's departure from the drawing-room.

'I don't believe I heard all that,' said John eventually. 'It's like a nightmare. My son saying that he is in love with a farmworker's daughter. I don't believe it.' And, repeating himself, he said again, with even more emphasis, 'I just don't believe it.'

So far, Mary had sat quietly, occasionally glancing at Stephen, but concentrating mainly on her parents to see their reaction.

She knew what it meant to them, but she was equally aware of how Robert must be suffering now that he had finally spoken out. She was full of admiration for the way in which he had controlled himself and refused to be dominated by his father.

'I'm afraid, dad, you will have to believe it,' she said. 'I know it's true. In fact, Stephen and I have known about it for a long time.'

'Then why haven't you told us? Don't tell me you approve of Robert's behaviour? I hope you are not on his side?' snapped John, regaining some of his venom, and transferring his annoyance to Mary.

'It's not a question of sides,' she said. 'Robert would have told you long before now if he had thought you would have any sympathy or understanding. Judging by your reaction just now, he was quite right.

You don't appreciate his position at all. All that concerns you is your own pride – your status in the community.'

'Mary has a point, John,' broke in Marjorie before he could respond. 'We may be hurt and disappointed, but we need to discuss it with him rationally.'

She looked pale and shaken and was close to tears. She was probably more hurt than John. She, too, had her pride, but she also loved Robert dearly, and to some extent blamed herself. She felt that if she had been a better mother, he would not have drifted away, and would have been able to come to talk to her months ago. She now understood more clearly Robert's behaviour over the past two years. He had not shown any interest in Celia, because he was involved with Margaret. It also explained his long absences from home, particularly on days when the weather had not been suitable for walking round the farm. But she was puzzled to know how he and Margaret had been able to meet without being seen. She realised, too, why Margaret had not been with Emily to help at the last two Boxing Day dances. She could not remember when she had last seen Margaret to speak with. This was unusual, even though she was now away at college or working at Gilbert Dawson's. She was probably keeping away from Manor Farm, embarrassed by her relationship with Robert.

'I'm going to find Robert and speak with him,' said Marjorie. As she rose to go, John said, more gently, 'Don't be soft with him, Marjorie. He can twist you round his little finger any time he likes.'

Mary also stood up and went across to her father. 'I'm sorry dad,' she said, giving him a kiss. 'Perhaps I said more than I should have done, but we are all upset, and it hasn't been easy for me knowing about Robert but not being able to tell you and mother.'

After his characteristic, initial, outburst, John was now in a calmer mood.

'Well, my dear, there's something in what you say. Perhaps I am being autocratic, maybe snobbish. I dare say I shall have to believe that Robert is sincere in what he says. But I shall never accept Margaret Jackson as one of the family.'

'Never is a long time, John,' said Stephen, who had so far kept out of the family row. 'It took my father a long time to accept Mary. Remember? He was like all farmers and expected me to marry a rich farmer's daughter, someone who could bring money, or land, into the family. A lot of marriages amongst farmers may not be arranged in the true sense of the word – let us just say they are encouraged. Don't marry money, but love where money is.'

'Hold on a minute, Stephen,' said John abruptly, his pride again hurt.

'There's a vast difference between Mary and Margaret Jackson. Mary may not have neither land nor money, but she does come from a professional, middle-class background. Yours was more a marriage of equals.'

'Yes, of course,' said Stephen. 'But that isn't really the point. Perhaps I'm not putting my case very clearly. The fact is that it's common for parents to be disappointed in their children's choice of partner for one reason or another, apart from money. It could be worse. Suppose Robert found a worthless floozy in London, a prim, urban girl with no appreciation, or understanding, of life in the country? When you think about it, Robert and Margaret have a great deal in common. The only way in which they are not suited is that they come from different backgrounds.'

'And that is the most important thing of all,' said John emphatically.

'I thought the feudal system died when the industrial revolution started?'

'Not round here, it didn't,' said John. 'Anyway, I need another drink. What about you two?' and he walked over to the cocktail cabinet.

Upstairs, in his bedroom, Robert was back in control of himself. Whether his tears had been ones of anger, frustration or relief, he was not sure, perhaps a mixture of all three. He stood, looking out of the window, where he could see across the yard to the pond. He remembered standing there years ago on the day of the fight with Albert Lloyd. He now realised that his love for Margaret had started then – not love at first sight perhaps, but a strong bond of friendship and a mutual physical attraction, which had developed into sexual desire and finally to love.

He was startled from his daydreams by a knock at the door. He was not really surprised to see his mother. He went across to her, and, putting an arm round her shoulders, guided her to the bed where they sat for a moment, both too close to tears to speak.

'I'm sorry, mother,' he said in a tremulous voice. 'I know you think I've let you down. Margaret is not the girl you would have chosen for me to fall in love with. But I can't help that. I think she's a lovely girl; attractive, intelligent and kind. You must give her a chance.'

'But she's Harry Jackson's daughter,' said Marjorie incredulously.

'And that's all you and dad judge her by? If she were a farmer's daughter or the rector's daughter, you would accept her without question.'

Marjorie recognised that this was true. She had nothing to say against Margaret as a person. In fact, the opposite was true. She had always thought of her as a remarkable child considering her background, and wondered how Emily and Harry could have produced such a talented daughter. But, in spite of that, she could not bring herself to accept her as a suitable wife for Robert.

But it was not only Robert's choice of girl, which was of concern. Marjorie also considered his behaviour as dishonest and deceitful.

'Why haven't you told us before, instead of keeping quiet and meeting Margaret behind our backs all this time?'

'Well, for a long time, we weren't sure whether we were really in love. After all, we were very young. It may have been just a sexual attraction – an affair which would have never matured, and it would have meant upsetting you unnecessarily.'

'When did you realise it was serious?'

'Last Easter holidays. Since then I've been plucking up the courage to tell you. I knew I was behaving badly, but I was afraid you would stop us seeing each other. I could have told you, but not dad. It seemed unfair not to tell you both at the same time.'

'And Mary, how long has she known?' Robert laughed.

'At the Boxing Day dance three years ago. Mary caught me kissing Margaret in the maids' sitting-room. It was all fairly innocent then, even though we didn't think so at the time. I'm sure Mary thought it was just a mild flirtation. I told her it was serious when I was working at Holme Green during the summer.'

'And you really are sure now? After all, neither of you have been involved with anyone else. I know there aren't many girls around here suitable for you, which is why I encouraged you and Celia. When that didn't seem to work, I hoped you might meet a girl in London, or when you go to Cirencester.

'It was too late. I'd already fallen for Margaret. Peter Buckley did introduce me to some of his friends in London, but I wasn't interested. I found them urban, spoilt, shallow and very full of themselves. Despite all the difficulties, I thought how fortunate I was to have Margaret waiting for me here.'

Marjorie reluctantly accepted all that Robert had said, and saw no point in questioning him further.

'Well, darling, you seem very sure at the moment. But there's no rush. You both have your careers to think about. I don't know what to say. I need time to think and to speak with your father when he's in a more receptive mood. You know he always bullies and blusters, but he will be in a more rational mood when he has got over the first shock and had time to think about it.'

Chapter 22

Margaret was pleased to be back at Newlands Farm after the Christmas break. For one thing, she needed to earn some money, but even more importantly, she found that work took her mind away from her worries. She was also pleased because she was engaged in a job, which she enjoyed and which also gave her a great deal of satisfaction.

The incubator house was a pleasant, friendly, place to be. It had to be kept at a constant temperature about 60°F and, as good ventilation was also essential, the atmosphere was warm but fresh. There were twelve incubators, in two rows of six, along the walls. They were heated by paraffin lamps which had to be filled and the wicks trimmed regularly to guarantee a regular temperature in the incubators. They varied in size, holding from a hundred to a hundred and fifty eggs. Margaret was sorting eggs to fill one of the incubators. The eggs were from one of the pedigree pens, which had been trap-nested. This meant that each egg was separately numbered so, that when the chick was hatched, it could be traced back to its parents, and wing-banded accordingly. Every egg was carefully weighed and candled so as to make sure there were no hair cracks or other defects. Margaret discarded any thin-shelled eggs, and eggs which were excessively large or small, as these never produced healthy chicks. She had almost filled the incubator tray when Gladys came in.

'Are you free for a moment?' she asked. 'There's a telephone call for you. A nice young man, by the sound of him. Very polite, but he didn't say his name – something about it being a surprise.'

'Oh, thanks, I can come for a minute,' said Margaret, wondering who could be telephoning her in the middle of the afternoon. As she ran across the yard to the office, she hoped that it would be Robert but, at the same time, thinking he was taking a risk in 'phoning her at Newlands.

'Hello,' she said, a little apprehensively, looking over her shoulder to make sure Gladys had not followed her and that she was not being overheard.

'Margaret, I had to 'phone you,' the reassuring voice of Robert. 'Oh, I hoped it was you. But you are taking a risk 'phoning me here. I'm in the middle of sorting hatching eggs. It's not very convenient.' She sounded breathless and a little unsure of herself, the telephone emphasising her Yorkshire accent, which she still found difficult to disguise.

'I'm sorry, perhaps not, but it was essential, otherwise I wouldn't have dared to do it. I wanted you to know that I have told my parents about us.'

Margaret was overcome by a feeling of weakness, and apprehension, all thoughts of hatching eggs pushed to one side.

'Oh, my darling. Was it awful?' she said, anticipating the worst.

'As you would expect. Father was furious and mother very upset.'

'But what did they say? What's going to happen?'

'That's the trouble, I don't know,' said Robert. 'They said they wanted time to consider it. I know it must have been a shock, but I honestly don't know what there is to think about. They expressed their strong disapproval, but that was to be expected. Now we shall have to wait to see what happens next. But I'm relieved to have told them.'

'Yes, you must be. So am I. I mean I'm pleased that they know, even if it makes life more difficult for us. When am I going to be able to meet you?' she asked anxiously.

'I don't know. It's difficult when you are working there and I'm at home. And I don't want to make matters any worse. I'll ring you as soon as I know anything definite.'

'I'm going home on Saturday. It will be safer to telephone there. I hope we can meet before you go back to London. I do miss you.'

'I miss you too. I love you. We shall be together soon. The worst is over now, so don't worry.'

'I'll try not to. Bye-bye for now, darling. I must go. Gladys will be wondering who the mystery man is.'

Margaret walked thoughtfully back to the incubator room, wishing she could confide in Gladys, but confident that she would not have to keep her secret much longer.

After the Mothers' Union meeting in the rectory, Marjorie waited until the other members had gone. This was her customary practice, as it gave her an opportunity for a friendly gossip with Rosemary.'

'I'll just put the kettle on again. You sit quietly by the fire, I'll be back in a moment,' said Rosemary, taking a tray of empty cups into the kitchen.

Marjorie was content to just sit and watch the fire, alone with her thoughts. Since Robert's announcement about Margaret, she and John had taken opposing views about how they should handle the situation. Mary had strongly supported her mother but, for once, she had been unable to persuade John to modify his opinion. Marjorie had now decided to consult her friend, Rosemary, and possibly Nigel. At least she knew she would receive a sympathetic hearing, and she could rely on their discretion in not discussing it outside the family circle.

If Rosemary and Nigel were shocked by Marjorie's news, they gave no indication of it. It must have been unwelcome news for Rosemary, who still had hopes that one day Celia and Robert would get together. At least it explained why Robert had never shown any real interest in her daughter.

'It is John's attitude which is worrying me now,' said Marjorie. 'He says that if Robert continues to see Margaret, with the intention of eventually marrying her, he will cut short his pupilage in London, refuse to pay his fees at Cirencester, and stop his allowance.'

'What do you think?' asked Nigel.

'My view is that it will force Robert's hand and most likely bring them even closer together. I still think that, if he stays in London and Margaret is at Askham Bryan, there's a chance that one of them will meet someone else. After all, they'll be separated now for ten weeks, and although we could not realistically stop them seeing each other during the Easter holidays, their opportunities for meeting would be very limited. By the summer, Margaret would need to find a permanent job, which could be miles away.'

'That seems logical to me,' said Nigel. 'I think you are right. They are young and inexperienced. I should leave them alone. And it would be foolish and very short-sighted to ruin Robert's career simply because he has fallen for a girl you don't approve of. The two things should be considered separately.'

'What will Robert do if he can't go to college?' asked Rosemary.

'John thinks he should join the army. He believes there's going to be a war and would expect Robert to join up anyway.'

'What does Robert think? It's his life we are talking about,' said Nigel.

'We haven't told him yet, because we have still not agreed about it. And John also thinks that if we delay telling him until just before he goes back to London, he won't have the chance of discussing it with Margaret and being influenced by her.'

Nigel was beginning to think that John was being unnecessarily hard and unreasonable. He turned to his wife.

'What do you think, Rosemary?'

Rosemary had been giving it careful consideration, but for one who was being consulted because of her impartiality and fairness, she was not being very objective. Concerned for Celia's happiness, she still hoped that one day she might have Robert as a son-in-law. She had always had a high regard for Robert, a view that she still held despite his behaviour over Margaret, something which she did not believe was altogether his fault.

'I think John is being too hard and rigid, but I tend to agree with him about not sending Robert to Cirencester. He could live at home for a while and continue to work at Holme Green. As Marjorie says, Margaret will be away, and, perhaps, in time, they would drift apart.'

What Rosemary thought, but did not say, was that by continuing to live in Dunmere, Robert's chances of meeting another girl were greatly restricted, and during the holidays he would be sure of seeing Celia regularly.

'Well, Marjorie,' said the rector, 'I'm not sure if we have been much help. I think, on the whole, we agree with you. There's one thing I want to say, though, and I shall say it to John when I get the chance. If, in spite of everything, Robert does go ahead and eventually marries Margaret, you must overcome your prejudices and welcome her into the family. However hard it is, and however unsuitable you think she is as your daughter-in-law, she is Robert's choice. If they are blessed with children, they will be members of the Denehurst family, and I'm sure you won't want to be ostracised from your grandchildren.'

Later that evening, when Nigel was in his study preparing the New Year's Day services, Rosemary took the opportunity of passing on the news about Robert to Celia. It did not seem to be as big a shock to her as Rosemary had anticipated.

'Don't you remember, mummy,' said Celia, when I came home from Bristol, I met Robert on the train at York. Margaret was with him then – they were travelling to Dunmere together.'

'Yes, of course, I should have realised the significance of it.'

'I accepted it in all innocence at the time, but thinking about it now, they did seem to be on very easy terms, and when I got into the compartment with them, Margaret looked uncomfortable and embarrassed.'

'No wonder,' said Rosemary. 'But tell me, what is she like? I don't think I've ever seen her.'

'Well, you have, because she was helping Marjorie at the first Boxing Day dance we went to at Manor Farm. When I first met Robert.'

'But she was only a young girl then. What is she like now she's grown-up?'

'Well, I must admit, I was shattered when Robert introduced us. She was not at all what you would expect a farm labourer's daughter to be like. Very pretty – dark hair, blue eyes, good figure – but also quite sophisticated, and obviously intelligent. I can see why Robert is smitten; she's a very attractive girl.'

That was rather a blow to Rosemary; Margaret really was a challenge to her hopes. 'But, of course, completely unsuitable for a boy like Robert,' she snapped snobbishly.

'Suitable in every way except that she's a farmworker's daughter,' said Celia, equally haughtily.

'And do you think Robert will go ahead and marry her, even though his parents are against it?'

'I don't know. I hope not; but I think he can be very determined. He is, after all, John's son, and like him in some ways. I think it could be a very unhappy time for the Denehurst family.'

Following the Christmas holiday, Robert returned to London and the unrewarding prospects it offered for the next three months. The platform at King's Cross was as dirty and busy as ever; Mrs Hartley was arranging one of her regular bridge parties, and at the reception desk of Kitchen, Kitchen and Drew, Linda was sitting with her rehearsed smile and polite manner, both as artificial as her make-up.

Ralph Gurney had gone to Scotland for the traditional Hogmanay, and was still away. Robert sat, disconsolately, at his empty desk, with nothing to do, wondering why he had bothered to come back. He was in a troubled state of mind, as just before leaving home, his father had given him the chance of giving up Margaret or losing his allowance and the opportunity of going to Cirencester. He knew from his conversation with his mother that this was against her will, and he was also resentful about the timing of the announcement, which he considered cowardly and unfair. As far as he was concerned, there was no choice to be made. His love for Margaret was paramount.

He was not worried about not going to Cirencester. He had never wanted to be an estate agent in the first place, but he did have two problems to resolve. He did not want to join the army, and he had to find employment and think about an alternative career. He knew that, temporarily, he could work at Holme Green. This was satisfactory, as a stopgap, but it did nothing for his long-term future. He had been given until Easter to make up his mind and, although he was tempted to go straight back home and announce his decision, he thought it would be more sensible to take his time. If his father could be awkward, so could he. He would wait until the last possible moment before telling him.

However, his first priority was to contact Margaret. As he had nothing to do in the office, he decided to write to her, rather than telephone.

Margaret's immediate reaction to Robert's letter had been one of shock and disbelief. She had always expected that Robert's family, particularly his father, would be strongly opposed to their marriage, but even in her worst moments, she had never anticipated such an uncompromising reaction. She had discussed it at length with her mother, who now had no doubts about Robert's commitment to Margaret, even if it meant sacrificing his career and estrangement from his family. However, Emily could not really believe that, in the end, the Colonel would treat his own son so harshly. That he could be hard and self-opinionated, she had no doubt – the dismissal of Harry from Manor Farm was a constant reminder. But he was not completely ruthless, and she hoped that he would be influenced by Mrs Denehurst and Mary, who, she was certain, would not want the family to be permanently divided. However, she had not been able to convince her daughter that, in time, the Colonel would mellow, and Margaret had returned to Askham Bryan overwhelmed by the depth of Robert's love, and ashamed that she had even for one moment questioned his loyalty.

All that Colonel Denehurst had achieved by his intolerant behaviour was the opposite of what he had intended. Robert and Margaret were now drawn together in a bond of love, which, it seemed, nothing could break. And, furthermore, Robert would no longer be obliged to pursue a career, which he had never wanted to follow.

As the weeks passed, and the Easter holidays drew near, Margaret's thoughts turned to the future. The immediate prospects were encouraging. Now that Robert had made his intentions known to his parents, it was no longer necessary to keep their courtship secret. They were free to meet whenever, and wherever, they wished. But the long-term prospects were much less certain. Her own future was planned, but as far as she knew, Robert had no long-term plans at all. If he found employment, it could be miles away, and they would hardly see each other. If, in the end, he was forced to join the army, a long separation was certain. For Margaret, who had a volatile and impatient nature, this was a long time to wait, and something unforeseen could prevent it happening. Unlike her mother, she did not believe the Colonel would ever consent to her marrying Robert unless his hand was forced.

Once again, the idea of having a baby recurred. On a previous occasion, she had dismissed the idea as being selfish, disloyal, and against all her principles. But that was before the Colonel had taken such an uncompromising stand. To have a baby outside marriage would be a desperate step to take, but if Robert was willing to sacrifice his future for her, she was willing to sacrifice her principles for him. She could not believe that the Denehurst family, not even the Colonel, would turn away their grandchild. She decided to write to Robert, and agree to spend the night with him in York.

Chapter 23

Robert had played his last match for "The Parks", and he and Peter were having a farewell drink and meal together. They had booked a table at a French restaurant in Soho, but, before going on there, Robert had been saying his "good-byes" to his team-mates in The Grey Horse.

'You know I'm going to miss you,' said Peter. 'Next winter especially. We shall have to find a new stand-off half from somewhere for next season. There's nobody in the 'A' team good enough to promote. Young Jamie was a disaster when you were off, injured, the other week.'

'Somebody will turn up. They always do. After all, we arrived out of the blue last year. But I shall miss all this as well. Without having had you around and playing rugger every week, life in London would have been intolerable.'

'You shouldn't have got hooked-up with Margaret, and been free to put it about a bit, like me. You've missed out on the best years. There are plenty of girls around here panting for it,' said Peter, casting his eye round the bar to make sure he had not missed any recent arrivals with their tongues hanging out.

'You mean like Jose,' teased Robert. 'From what I remember of her she was not what you would describe as an easy lay.'

'No, but I cracked it in the end,' said Peter, taking a long drink of his beer as if still needing to recover from the effort of it. 'But what are you going to do about Margaret? Wait another eighteen months and then get spliced?'

On first acquaintance, Peter appeared to have a rather shallow character, being interested only in women, beer and rugby, but his flamboyant style, and exaggerated stories of his sexual exploits and treatment of opposing forwards in the loose scrums, was a front which concealed a much more responsible and serious nature. When Robert had eventually told Peter about Margaret and his family problems, he had found his friend to be sympathetic and supportive.

'As a matter of fact,' said Robert, 'she has agreed to our spending a night together in York.'

'You don't mean it?' said Peter, suddenly becoming serious. 'What about her Methodist principles?'

'It seems she has thought it through, and decided to go ahead, but I don't know why she has suddenly changed her mind.'

Not having met Margaret, Peter did not know what sort of girl she was, but it crossed his mind that she might be planning to trap Robert into marriage, even if it seemed to be all that Robert wanted himself.

'Well, if you really intend losing your virginity at last, I hope you know what you are doing, and make sure you don't get her in the family way,' warned Peter.

'If you can't be good, be careful; if you can't be careful, buy a pram. I know the risks well enough. I was going to ask your advice about that.'

'Don't worry, old chap,' said Peter, fishing in his breast pocket for his wallet. He held out a small square packet. 'Have this one on me,' he said. 'Hell, it's the last one, but your need is greater than mine.' And then in his customary, light-hearted, fashion he added, 'You know what to do with it, I hope.'

Robert laughed. 'But are you sure you don't need it yourself? I can always go to the chemist's tomorrow. There's plenty of time before I meet Margaret.'

'It's the least I can do. I just hope it's been worth waiting for. I'm still looking forward to meeting Margaret. You can't keep her under wraps for ever.'

'Well, if you promise to be my best man, you can meet her at the church. I'm not sure I could trust you two together before then.'

Robert was sitting in the reception hall of the Royal Station Hotel, in York, waiting for Margaret. He had purposely arrived in good time in order to register, and avoid her any embarrassment.

He had been a little apprehensive about booking a double room himself, but the receptionist had not made any comment about his wife and treated the whole thing as an everyday, boring, chore.

Robert looked round the elegant room with its lofty, moulded, ceiling, sweeping staircase, thick carpet and well-heeled clientele sitting, drinking their pre-lunch drinks. He wondered if he had been wise in choosing such an opulent setting. He did not want Margaret to feel overawed and, in any case, the cost of a double room, with the additional expense of lunch, seats at the pictures, and dinner, was really more than he could afford. His father's allowance had been generous, but that would soon be ending, and, if it had not been for the money he had saved from his wages working for Stephen, the whole plan would not have been possible. However, he wanted only the best for Margaret, and her happiness and pleasure were all that mattered. He felt that after all their struggles, illicit meetings, deceit, constant worry of being found out, times they had huddled together in the old hut, cold and uncomfortable, they deserved some comfort and luxury.

They had finished dinner by half-past eight. It was too early to go to bed, but neither of them had thoughts of anything other than going up to their room. They had waited all day for this moment, but now that it had arrived, they were both shy, each waiting for the other to undress first.

Margaret slipped off her shoes, and was standing in front of the dressing-table mirror combing out her hair. Robert had been rummaging in his suitcase, but he now crossed the room and, standing behind her, reached round to undo the buttons on the front of her dress, watching her reaction in the mirror. They ran all the way down and when he had undone the last one, she turned to him, and, as they kissed, all the inhibitions and nervousness were cast aside.

'I can't believe this,' said Robert, huskily, as they lay on the bed and he removed the last vital piece of her underwear.

'The last time I saw your bare thighs and midriff was in the Dunmere School playground eight years ago. There's something I've wanted to do ever since.' He bent and kissed her just above the mass of dark pubic hair, exactly on the spot where, when she was barely a teenager, Albert Lloyd had dropped his spittle from the top of the playground wall.

'I think that was the time when I fell in love with you,' he said, 'although I was too young to realise it at the time.'

'Do you know when I first fell in love with you?' she asked, but not waiting for a reply, added, 'when we accidentally met at the bramble patch in Beech Wood. When we parted, I wanted you to kiss me, but all you did was suggest that we meet again in the Christmas holidays. It seemed a long time to wait.'

'I do love you,' said Robert, looking into her misty, blue, eyes. 'Not just because I find you irresistible and want to make love to you, but because of everything you mean to me. Nothing else in life matters but you.'

'I love you, darling. Come to me. I want this just a much as you,' and putting her arms round him, she drew him down between her wide-open thighs.

The following morning, Margaret woke early. She was not sure if Robert was still asleep. She bent over and kissed him, allowing her lips to linger on his until he responded by parting them and slipping his hand under her nightdress. As he caressed her breasts, he could feel the hardness of her nipples under his fingers. She reached down under the bedclothes and undid his pyjama cord, gently stroking the inside of his thigh. Then she moved his hand down between her own legs. It was warm, moist and soft down there, as was her mouth as she continued to kiss him.

Robert now realised he was in danger of losing his self-control.

The conversation he had had with Peter flashed through his mind as his intense desire for Margaret welled up through the whole of his body.

As if reading his thoughts, Margaret whispered, 'Are you going to make love to me again, darling?'

'Not if you put your hand there. You know what will happen if you start doing that.'

Margaret knew well enough what would happen. She had relieved his frustration on many occasions as they lay together on mellow summer evenings under the elm trees in Hagg Wood. She removed her hand, pulled off her nightdress and, sitting astride him, started to move slowly up and down. Robert could no longer control himself.

He did not care any more what happened as he responded to the quickening tempo of her movements.

The dining-room was almost empty when they eventually went down for breakfast. The waiter showed them to a window overlooking the gardens. In the distance, the towers of the Minster stood sharp and clear in the pale morning sky and the daffodils on the grassy banks below the city walls danced to the tune of a gentle breeze.

'On a lovely spring morning like this you should be at Holme Green drilling barley, not lying in bed making love to me,' said Margaret.

'I thought it was the other way round this morning. Twice in twelve hours. No wonder I'm feeling a bit fragile.

'Peter never went out with girls on Friday nights. He said it affected his game on the Saturday. I know now what he meant.'

They were quiet for a moment, as the waiter brought in their toast and took their orders for the main course. Robert ordered everything; bacon, sausage, egg and fried bread. 'Well, it doesn't seem to have affected your appetite,' said Margaret. 'I'm not sure if I want to marry you after all, if I'm going to spend the rest of my life feeding you.'

'My appetite may not be affected, but I'm worried. I think we took an awful risk this morning.'

'Don't you think it was worth it? Didn't it come up to expectations?'

'Oh, darling, of course it did. It's not that. But think of the consequences. What would happen if you were pregnant?' said Robert anxiously. And the more he thought about it, the more worried he became.

'We should have to get married this year instead of next,' said Margaret.

'You don't seem to be very concerned. I think you planned to seduce me this morning. That's why you changed your mind about staying the night in York, isn't it?'

'Yes, that's one reason. But I also wanted you to make love to me.'

'But you also fully intended to get yourself pregnant?' said Robert incredulously.

'Yes. I don't think your father will ever consent to our marrying unless he is forced to, and I believe that not even he would want an illegitimate child for which you were responsible.'

'But that's something you can't be sure about. And what if I refuse to marry you?'

'But you wouldn't, would you?' she asked anxiously.

Robert did not reply. For a moment he concentrated on buttering his toast. He felt cheated. He had never really been angry with Margaret. She was the one with the volatile temperament. He now felt he was being weak.

'But why didn't you discuss it with me first?' he asked sharply, for once, showing his annoyance and disapproval.

'Don't be angry with me, darling. I couldn't bear that. I didn't discuss it with you because it would have put you in an impossible position. You would never have taken advantage of me, deliberately, to make me pregnant, even though you could understand the argument for doing so. This is something I had to take responsibility for myself.'

Robert could see that she was becoming upset by his critical attitude. She concentrated on drinking her tea, but he knew, from experience, that she was on the point of losing her composure. She usually managed to control her Yorkshire accent, but whenever she became emotionally upset, the flat As and fully emphasised Us as well as a liberal scattering of Hs crept into her speech. He did not want to embarrass her in public but, in spite of that, he said, 'What about your Christian principles? And what about the baby? What sort of life would it have, born a bastard in a close-knit, narrow-minded society like Dunmere?'

Up to now, Margaret had been convinced that in seducing Robert she had done what was best for both of them. However, she was now beginning to wonder, and question, what appeared to be rash and selfish behaviour. Her one and only object had been to be sure of marrying Robert, and that had excluded any consideration for the feelings of others. She was worried that her behaviour had created a doubt in Robert's mind.

'Oh, please don't go on about it,' she said. 'Maybe I was wrong, but my only motive was to try and influence your father.'

'Yes, I realise that,' said Robert thinking he had said enough and, not wanting to upset her any more, or spoil what had been, up to now, a harmonious and enjoyable time, with both of them almost overwhelmed by the physical pleasures of uninhibited love-making.

But he was, nevertheless, still not satisfied with Margaret's explanation of her irresponsible behaviour and total disregard for his own feelings. She had behaved badly and, for the first time ever, there was a definite coolness between them as they went up to their bedroom to pack their suitcases. They were quiet and subdued during their journey to Kirkley. Robert seemed cold and distant.

Margaret had never seen him in this sort of mood before. They would, normally, have taken advantage of being alone in the compartment. Margaret moved closer to him and took hold of his hand, but Robert ignored her gestures, and continued to sit in a stern silence. When they parted at Kirkley Station, he gave he an obligatory kiss, but there was no feeling of love, or warmth, in his embrace, and, as she walked dejectedly down Railway Street, she felt the prick of tears behind her eyes.

Whenever Robert returned to Manor Farm, he was reminded of the sights and sounds of childhood. It was friendly and comforting, like returning to the womb for warmth and replenishment. In autumn it was the sight of ripening corn, stirred by a gentle breeze which sent rippling waves of gold across the fields. In winter it was the ducks and geese, paddling thwarted, and perplexed, round the treacherous edges of the frozen pond. And, as Robert returned home now, on a bright, sunny, spring day, he was welcomed by the noise of rooks nesting in the swaying, churchyard elms; the lambs frisking in the park, and, when he entered the hall of the farmhouse, there was the nostalgic scent of narcissi, Marjorie's favourite flowers, which she always arranged in vases, mixed with sprays of flowering currant.

His mother's greeting was, as always, warm and loving. If she was anxious to know about Margaret and his future plans, she did not show it, and they were both careful to turn the conversation towards safe and mundane topics such as the Mothers' Union, the WI, and Marjorie's back-ache, a constant ailment which was always worse in the spring, aggravated by too much gardening. It was only later, when John came in for a cup of tea, that the conversation turned to what was uppermost in all their minds.

Robert had already made up his mind about his father's ultimatum. Although he was feeling angry and resentful about Margaret's behaviour, he would be seeing her as usual in the Easter holiday. He was not going back to London or to Cirencester. He was prepared for his father's question.

'So, you've made up your mind, Robert?' said the Colonel.

'Yes, I shall continue to see Margaret, and, if the consequences are as you say, I shall have to accept them.'

Marjorie looked at John. She saw no sign of any change in his attitude. He looked grim and determined.

'And have you made up your mind what you are going to do to make a living?' continued John.

'No. For the time being, I shall work at Holme Green as usual. But one thing is certain, I'm not going to join the army unless there is a war and I'm called up for military service.'

'That's a relief,' said Marjorie. 'The whole of my life has been dominated by "The Regiment". First my husband, then my son, whom I never see. I couldn't bear it if you were in the army as well.'

'You know my views about that, Marjorie,' broke in the Colonel sharply. 'And, as for you, Robert, I have no more to say. I shall write to Major Drew to tell him that you won't be going back to London, and also to cancel your entry for the Royal Agricultural College. You had better write to Mrs Hartley yourself. And now I've got work to do.'

He rose and stamped out, leaving Robert and Marjorie to finish their tea.

'I told your father that you wouldn't change your mind but, as usual, he was convinced he was right,' said Marjorie as soon as John had gone.

'What he never seems to have accepted is that I never wanted to go to London, or be an estate agent in the first place. It's no hardship for me to give up my career prospects. And money isn't important either. All I need to be able to do is earn enough to live on. My worry is you and father. I love you both – even if he doesn't realise it. I don't want to break up the family.'

Marjorie's heart was near to breaking as she saw more clearly than ever Robert's agony of mind. She took out her handkerchief and, dabbing at her eyes, said in a choking voice: 'My dearest boy, I never thought it would ever be like this. I know I spoiled you when you were a little boy. I may have been selfish in wanting to keep you to myself, but I've tried to understand and give you your freedom. I should never have found it easy to accept any girl as my daughter-in-law, but I was certainly not prepared for Margaret Jackson. How could you possibly imagine that I could ever invite Harry and Emily here for a social occasion, or go there for tea?'

'I understand your position, mother. I know what the Jacksons are like. I ran in and out of their cottage as a child, and, in those days, Margaret came here for tea. Of course it was different when we were children, but my intention would be to take Margaret away from here, where nobody would know what sort of background she came from. I think she is sophisticated enough to carry it off.'

'Yes, she's an exceptional girl. I know that. But although she is clever and attractive, she is still a member of the Jackson family. What about her sisters? There's already gossip in the village about Barbara's association with one of the village boys, and she hasn't even left school yet. How would you like to have Frank Wood as a brother-in-law?'

Robert was about to say that it was Margaret he was involved with, not her sister or the rest of the family, but he saw little point in arguing. Whatever he said would not change his parents' attitude, but it did increase his anxiety about his night with Margaret in York. He could imagine their reaction if Margaret really was pregnant.

Chapter 24

The land at Holme Green was working well. It had been ploughed in good time the previous autumn and a succession of hard frosts had broken the soil down so that it needed only very little cultivation to obtain the fine seedbed so essential for a crop of barley. Although most of the land was on a chalk sub-soil, there was a greater depth of topsoil than at Manor Farm, and the lower fields were capable of growing barley of sufficiently good quality to be sold for malting. Varieties suitable for malting did not yield as well as feeding barleys, but the selling price was considerably higher, and Stephen usually gambled by growing twenty, or thirty, acres in the hope of catching a favourable market. The remainder of his barley crop he kept for feeding to his pigs.

Robert had spent his first day back at work harrowing the malting barley land ready for drilling. By late afternoon, he had finished, and, as he drove into the farmyard to house his tractor, he met Stephen just back from Kirkley market.

'How has it gone, Robert?' he asked.

'Very well. All ready for drilling tomorrow,' said Robert, switching off the engine. 'What are you putting in?'

'Plumage Archer. It yields better than Spratt on this land and also gives a bit more straw. I know most people prefer a short strawed variety, but I need all the straw I can get for bedding.'

'We shall have everything sown by the end of next week, except roots. What are you planning to do then?'

'That's something I want to talk to you about. I don't want to stop now. We shall have an opportunity for a natter later on. You can give me a hand to feed the pigs as soon as you've finished with your tractor.'

Although it was April and the days were lengthening, it was still chilly in the evening, and Stephen, Mary and Robert were glad to have a fire to sit round after their evening meal.

'You know that where Margaret is concerned, we think that father has taken an extreme view,' aid Mary, pouring out the coffee. 'Whether he realises it or not, by behaving the way he has, he has given you more or less all you wanted except some sort of future career.'

Robert laughed and paused a moment before answering. In view of the present coolness between him and Margaret, he did not want to become involved in a discussion about their future.

'Yes, you are right, I suppose,' he said. 'Mother thinks so too. I appreciate your support. Without it, I'm not sure I could have coped with father. He worries me. He has made some stupid decisions recently. Sacking Harry Jackson, insisting on sending me to London, and failing to mechanise quickly enough at Manor Farm. I don't understand him.'

'Neither do I,' said Stephen. 'It's none of my business really, but I suggested to him some time ago that he should start farming. He has always said that farming is only prosperous during a war. He is convinced there's going to be one in spite of Neville Chamberlain. You would be only too willing to join him and he still refuses to consider it. Anyway, to return to you and my plans. Your future is uncertain. How would you like to join me permanently?'

'You mean work here indefinitely?'

'No. Not necessarily here at Holme Green. In the immediate future, yes. But you may remember some time ago I told you about my plans for contracting. I want you to get involved with that straight away. But I might rent or buy more land in the near future. Perhaps even a farm. If I did, there could well be opportunities for you there.'

'That sounds too good to be true. It's everything I could have hoped for. It would be marvellous,' said Robert enthusiastically.

'I'm delighted that you agree,' said Stephen. 'But one more thing. You need more experience, and perhaps some training. The National Institute of Agricultural Engineering, at Silsoe, is running short, intensive, courses on a whole range of implements and machinery. I think it would be a good idea for you to go on one, say after hay- time when you could most easily be spared.'

'I like the sound of that,' said Robert. 'I should feel I was doing something practical and worthwhile. It was so unproductive sitting in an office in London and following Ralph Gurney around like a lapdog. But have you said anything about this to father?'

'No, not yet,' said Mary. 'We wanted to see if you were interested first. But it has nothing to do with him now. It's your future we are discussing and he doesn't seem to be interested in that any more.'

News of Robert and Margaret's courtship spread rapidly throughout Dunmere and the surrounding district. Colonel Denehurst was a prominent, and well-known, personality. Whatever happened on the estate, and anything else with which he was associated, was discussed, and dissected, down to the last detail. His son's involvement with a farmworker's daughter was the most talked about event to have happened in the neighbourhood for years. For the men at Manor Farm it was an even spicier story than the dismissal of Harry Jackson, and was virtually the only topic of conversation for days. And, as it was the ex-wagoner's family who were again involved, it made the gossip all the more juicy. It was, of course, no surprise to Ernie.

'Ah allus knew summat like this would 'appen,' he said. 'Master Robert and young Maggie spent hours mucking about together when they were bairns. Ah reckon that they've been courting for a long tahm.'

The three labourers at Manor Farm were sitting having their lunch break in the shelter of a stonewall which they were repairing. Ted took a last bite at his sandwich and, with his mouth still half full, said: 'Cum off it, Ernie. It isn't all that long since yer reckoned 'e was courting t'parson's daughter.'

''appen 'e was laving it off wi' both on 'em,' said Ned. 'Ah'll bet Colonel is 'opping mad. 'e was nivver very 'appy about Robert helping us on t'farm and larking wi' t'village children.'

'There's nowt 'e can do to stop 'em,' said Ted. 'But it'll be missus who'll be most upset. She would be expecting Robert ti marry a posh lass from London, ah'll bet, or at least a farmer's daughter or someone from their own class.'

Taking a swig of his cold tea, Ernie put the bottle back in his lunch bag, wiped his mouth on the sleeve of his jacket, and said: 'Cor, Emily won't be able ti get through t'door-hole. 'er 'ead will be as big as a turnip. She allus fancied 'erself, did Emily.'

Ned was scraping round the bowl of his clay pipe with a penknife. He blew down the stem to make sure it was clear before filling up again with twist.

'Ah've all us thowt that Maggie is like 'er mother an' all,' he said. 'She 'as gotten a bit big-'eaded since she went away ti college. Mind on though, she 'as grown-up ti be a good-looking lass. A pair of good legs on 'er an' all. Good solid calves. Ah can't do wi women 'at 'as thin spindly legs.'

Having more or less exhausted the subject of Robert and Maggie, at any rate for the time being, the gossip led on to a general discussion about women's legs, as the three men gave their opinions and preferences about the figures of the girls and young women of the village. But they would, no doubt, return to their central theme another day. In newspaper parlance, the saga of Robert and Margaret would run and run.

But not everyone in Dunmere was as critical as the farm men. Those of a romantic nature compared it with the story of Cinderella – Robert in the role of the prince falling for a humble village girl. Others felt genuinely sorry for the Denehurst family, full of sympathy for a mother whose son had "kicked over the traces" and defied convention. In their eyes, a marriage between a boy and a girl from such contrasting backgrounds would never succeed.

There were those, but not many, who simply accepted what had happened and looked forward to a colourful and happy wedding day. An even smaller number, who kept themselves aloof from village gossip, expressed no opinions, and kept their thoughts to themselves.

The Easter break was proving to be anything but a holiday for Margaret. At Newlands, April was always a busy time with orders for hatching eggs and day-old chicks to be dealt with, in addition to the routine work on the farm. The young birds being retained as breeding replacements needed constant attention, with regular checking of temperatures and trimming of paraffin lamps in the brooders. Even a few hours without heat was sufficient to cause heavy losses, either because the chicks became chilled or, more likely, smothered as they massed together to keep warm.

Robert, too, was working long hours. As soon as the spring drilling was completed at Holme Green, he was away, almost every day, doing contract work for neighbouring farmers. During the years of depression, many tenant farmers had not been able to equip themselves with tractors and modern implements, and were still relying on horses for their cultivations. With the increasing cost of labour, they found it was more economical to hire a contractor. This was especially so on smaller farms, where it would have been foolish to invest in expensive machinery which was only going to be used for a few weeks, or even days, during the year.

It was ironical that now, when Robert and Margaret were, theoretically, free to meet, in practice the opportunities were even more limited. Robert now had the use of an old Ford van, which he used for carrying fuel, spare parts and equipment to wherever he was working. This would normally have greatly facilitated his arrangements for meeting Margaret on the occasions they were free, but since their night together in York, things had never been quite the same between them. It was almost as though each was making work an excuse not to meet and, when they did meet each other, there was a tension and coolness between them, which spoilt their enjoyment of being together.

At the end of the month, Margaret returned to Askham Bryan in a sad and anxious mood, regretting her decision to seduce Robert and attempt to influence his father. Since that fatal night, she had had increasing doubts about her future. She no longer felt certain of Robert's love, and hoped that a few weeks' separation would give them both an opportunity to find a way of overcoming their differences, and recapturing their mutual trust and happiness when she returned home in June.

Chapter 25

There is nothing more infuriating than a hen, which refuses to roost. Shutting up hens on free range can be a frustrating experience, as Margaret had discovered when going round the widely scattered hen houses at Newlands Farm. She quickly found that it was impossible to persuade a bird to go in through the pop hole. And, even if she did manage to usher it carefully up the ramp, instead of going into the house through the obvious open shutter, it would suddenly become excited, start to cackle and disturb those which had behaved rationally and gone to perch. Suddenly, instead of there being one stupid hen pecking about in the fading light, there would be ten or a dozen. The one essential virtue necessary to succeed was patience, a characteristic that did not come naturally to Margaret.

Margaret had finished her course at Askham Bryan, and was now working full-time at Newlands. Unable to meet Robert, who was taking a course at the NIAE, she did not mind the chore of shutting up, and quite enjoyed her compulsory stroll, despite the occasional reluctant hen. She had learned that it paid to wait until it was almost dark before setting out, and as she finally made her way to the farthest house on the edge of Darren Wood, a pale, crescent moon had already appeared above the trees. She was in no hurry and, as she frequently did on fine, summer evenings, decided to return home by taking a longer route. This led along a footpath, which cut through the wood and curved round to join the main road to Dunmere. She climbed over the stile, and when she had walked a short way into the wood, she was startled by a noise of rustling amongst the trees. She turned and saw a figure moving quickly through the undergrowth before emerging through the trees onto the path in front of her. It was Albert Lloyd.

'Well, if it isn't my favourite girl,' he said, grinning at her familiarly. 'Fancy meeting you out here. Where's that man of yours then? 'e 'asn't jilted yer already 'as 'e? Ah've 'eard all about it. Quite a catch, isn't 'e?'

'It's none of your business,' said Margaret sharply. 'Anyway, what are you doing up here? Up to no good, that's for sure.'

Albert dropped the sack he was carrying and it fell to the ground with a thud. It was bloodstained, and although tied round with a piece of binder twine, a few highly coloured feathers were visible sticking out of the top. Margaret side-stepped to walk past him, but he put out an arm to stop her.

'Don't run off yet, sweetheart. You and me 'ave some unfinished business. Yer nivver gave me that kiss yer promised,' he said in a slimy voice.

'What kiss?' said Margaret, now becoming a little alarmed. 'Let me get past.'

Albert now grabbed her firmly by the waist, his mood changing from one of familiar sarcasm to frustration and annoyance.

'Not so fast. Give us a kiss first, then ah'll think about it,' he said, pulling her roughly towards him.

Margaret was now really frightened. It was a lonely place to be with no help at hand. She was not sure what to do. Albert was not joking. She knew he could be nasty when roused and he meant to have a kiss. She also knew he had a reputation where girls were concerned, and he had always fancied Margaret. She found him revolting. There was a strong smell of pigs about his whole being. He was wearing a pair of dirty, baggy trousers, held up by a thick leather belt. His jacket, torn and frayed at the cuffs, was covered in oily and stained patches. He wore a greasy cap, and he had obviously not shaved for some days. When he pushed his rough, stubbled face towards hers, she could smell the beer on his breath, which reminded her of the occasion of the village dance, when she had last tangled with him. When he pushed himself against her, she could feel the hardness of his erection against her stomach. She stood still, too frightened to struggle. Getting no response as he tried to kiss her, he stopped a moment and said harshly: 'Come on yer little cunt, yer can do better than that. Ah'll bet yer don't kiss that young bugger Robert like that.'

He forced his mouth on hers again. She parted her lips, and as he inserted his tongue, she bit on it as hard as she could, at the same time bringing up her knee sharply into his groin. It was a stupid move to have made. Momentarily shocked and hurt, Albert stepped back, holding his mouth and doubled up in pain. Seeing her chance, Margaret set off running along the path, but she did not get many yards as Albert, recovering quickly, caught up with her and threw her roughly onto the ground.

'Yer shouldn't have done that, yer stupid bitch,' he said, now really roused and breathing hard. She tried to fight him off, but he ripped open the buttons on her blouse and fought to pull down her jodhpurs. Margaret now had no doubts about his intentions. He was like an animal. She kicked and screamed, trying to fend him off. He put one hand over her mouth and still tried to remove her underwear with the other.

Making one last effort, Margaret managed to wriggle from under him and tried to scramble to her feet, but, wrapping his arms round her legs in a sort of rugby tackle, she fell backwards onto the ground and, unable to check her fall, she hit her head against something hard sticking out of the ground. It was a severe blow and Margaret lay there not moving. Realising she was no longer resisting, Albert stopped tearing at her clothes. As he raised himself to look at her, he suddenly realised there was something seriously wrong. Her face was drained of colour, her eyes were closed, and there was a trickle of blood coming from the corner of her mouth. Albert panicked. For a moment, he thought she was dead but, as he watched her more closely, he realised she was still breathing.

Albert was a bully, but he was also a coward. His only thought now was to get away as quickly as possible without being seen. He ran off down the path towards the main road and Dunmere, forgetting all about his sack and its contents.

Gladys, sitting quietly doing her embroidery, looked up and saw that Gilbert had fallen asleep, his copy of the "Farmer and Stockbreeder" fallen onto the floor, his spectacles still on his nose. She rose from her chair without disturbing him, and went through to the kitchen to make their evening drink. As she mixed their mugs of cocoa, she decided to see if Margaret would like to join them before going to bed, and going back into the hall, called upstairs. There was no reply. She knew that it was Margaret's turn to shut up the poultry, and thought it rather odd that she was not back upstairs in her room. Returning to the sitting-room with the cocoa and biscuits, she woke Gilbert.

'You don't know where Margaret is by any chance?' she asked.

Gilbert yawned, stretched himself and looked at the clock. 'Isn't she upstairs? It's nearly ten o'clock and she's not normally late unless she's out with Robert.'

'It was her turn to do the shutting up, and I know she wasn't planning to go out tonight. Anyway, Robert is away in Silsoe.'

'The hens would be in ages ago,' said Gilbert. 'She can't be far away.'

'I know she sometimes goes for a walk on a nice evening, but even if she had, she should be back before now,' said Gladys, beginning to be concerned.

'You have another look round the house and I'll pop outside and see if she's gone to the brooder house or any of the other buildings,' said Gilbert, and he shuffled through to the utility room to find some boots.

When they met again, some minutes later, not having found her, they both became worried and puzzled.

'Well, she's nowhere on the premises,' said Gilbert. 'I think we had better follow the route she would have taken going round the hen houses. You go straight up to the far units near Darren Wood, and I'll go the other way round. It's a moonlight night. We shall not need a light. We'll meet half way round.'

They set off in opposite directions. 'If you see, or hear anything, give me a whistle,' he called as he opened the gate into the back paddock.

It was about half an hour later when they met.

'All the houses are shut up in my direction,' said Gladys.

'And in mine,' added Gilbert.

'What are we going to do now?' asked Gladys.

'Well, the only thing I can think of,' said Gilbert, 'is that she did what you say she quite often does, and went for a walk instead of coming straight back home.'

'But, even if she had, she should have been back home ages ago.'

'Have you any better suggestion?'

'No, I haven't,' said Gladys. 'I just can't understand it. Something unusual must have happened.'

'We're not doing any good standing here,' said Gilbert. 'I think we can assume she did go for a walk, in which case the obvious route from the far houses is along the path through Darren Wood and back onto the main road. Let's go and see if we can find anything along there. She could have sprained her ankle or something.'

It was darker in the wood, but the pine trees did not give a dense cover, and they managed to pick their way along the footpath. In the distance a vixen called, and the fallen litter beneath the trees crackled under their feet. Otherwise there was an eerie stillness, disturbed only by a frightened rabbit, which scuttled into the undergrowth.

'What's that?' asked Gilbert, suddenly stopping. 'Down there, by the side of the path.'

'What? Where? I can't see anything,' said Gladys.

Gilbert went forward, peering into the semi-darkness.

'A sack. It looks as though poachers have been along here,' he said, prodding it with his stick. 'But it's the wrong time of year for poachers, unless they've been visiting the breeding pens.'

'Why would they abandon their ill-gotten gains here?' asked Gladys.

'They must have been disturbed and gone off in a hurry.'

Gilbert bent down to examine the sack more closely, and Gladys went on ahead.

'Oh, my God,' she called. 'Gilbert, come quick.'

He hurried to join her. Margaret was lying on the path, just as Albert had left her. Her pale face expressionless in the moonlight, her blouse ripped and her jodhpurs pulled down below her knees.

Gilbert bent down. 'She's still breathing. I think she's unconscious,' he said. Neither of them referred to the vicious attack, which she had obviously suffered. Gently, Gilbert turned her head. There was a sticky patch of clotted blood under her hair. 'She was either hit on the head or, more likely, caught it on that tree root as she fell.' It was not a cold night, but he took off his jacket and wrapped it round her as best he could whilst Gladys pulled up her jodhpurs. As she did so, Margaret stirred and opened her eyes.

'Gladys' she said, in what was little more than a whisper. 'Thank God it's you.'

Gladys turned to Gilbert with a look of relief.

'Oh, Margaret,' she said. 'We wondered what had happened to you. But don't worry any more. We'll look after you now and get you home to a doctor. You can tell us what happened later.'

Margaret shuffled uneasily and tried to sit up. Gilbert put his arm round her and said, 'Just stay quietly where you are. Don't try to talk. Gladys will stay here with you whilst I go and get some transport and we'll have you home in no time.'

As Dr Bruce came downstairs he was met by Gladys, who had been too agitated to stay in the sitting-room, and was waiting, impatiently, for him in the hall.

'How is she?' she asked anxiously.

'Still in a state of shock, but other than a nasty blow on the back of her head, there doesn't seem to be anything else to worry about. You say she was unconscious about an hour?'

'Something like that. I can't be precise, because I don't know how long she had been there before we found her.'

Dr Bruce grunted and then said, 'I shall need to examine her more thoroughly in the morning, and also talk to her mother. I'll telephone Mrs Jackson now to reassure her. There's no point in her coming over here tonight. Margaret is better left alone to have a night's rest. She'll be feeling stronger in the morning.'

'Have you talked to her and found out what happened?'

Not in any detail. That's also better left until the morning when I can talk to her and Mrs Jackson. I'll also have a word with PC Hilton, and he can come over at the same time.'

In spite of Dr Bruce's telephone call and Harry's solid support, Emily had spent a restless night, and was still in a worried state of mind when Gilbert called to drive her to Newlands Farm. On arrival, she went straight up to see Margaret, and was relieved to find that she was well enough to be sitting up in bed and drinking a cup of tea.

'How are you feeling?' she asked, giving her a kiss on the forehead.

'Still a bit shaky and confused, but otherwise I'm all right.'

'Thank God you are safe and not too badly hurt. Do you feel well enough to tell me what happened? I've only heard part of the story from Gladys.'

Margaret told her mother all she could, but left out one or two of the more intimate details.

'You told Dr Bruce all this last night?' queried Emily.

'No. He said it was better for me to have a good night's rest, and that he would talk to me this morning.'

'He'll be here shortly,' said Emily. 'Is there anything you want to tell me before he comes?'

Margaret hesitated a moment before shaking her head and saying: 'No, not now. I'll talk to you again when he has been.'

For a moment they sat quietly, each with their own thoughts. Margaret was content to sit holding her mother's hand, whilst Emily was anxious not to press her daughter for information, which could wait until after Dr Bruce had been.

'Have you tried to get in touch with Robert?' asked Margaret eventually.

'Yes. Mary Langley gave me his telephone number first thing this morning. It was too late to try to contact him last night and, in any case, there was nothing he could do, but I talked to him at breakfast time.'

'I hope you didn't alarm him?'

'No, I don't think so. Naturally, he was very concerned, and was frustrated not to be able to come and see you.'

'You told him what happened and that it was...Albert Lloyd?'

'I told him all I knew at the time, and assured him you were not seriously hurt.'

Margaret squeezed Emily's hand. 'Thanks, mum. The last thing I want is to upset him. He was in a difficult mood during the Easter holidays, and with his being away in Silsoe, I haven't been able to talk things over with him since.'

Emily wondered what "things" there were to talk over. She sensed there was more behind Margaret's remarks than she was saying, and would have liked to press her further, but in the present circumstances, she thought it prudent to keep her suspicions to herself. On reflection, she now realised that Robert had seemed rather cool and aloof on the telephone. It was difficult to be sure, especially on the end of a not very good line – just a hint that all was not well between him and her daughter. She would not have thought any more about it if Margaret had not also implied that something had gone wrong between them. Perhaps it was no more than a lovers' tiff. She dismissed it from her mind, and went downstairs to wait for Dr Bruce.

As she sat in the kitchen drinking her coffee with Gladys and PC Hilton, Emily gradually recovered from the anxiety and strain of the previous night. Having found Margaret better and more cheerful than she had expected, she was certainly not prepared for the forthcoming shock when Dr Bruce joined them after having carried out his examination of Margaret.

'You can go up now, Brian,' he said to the constable, 'but don't question her too persistently and don't stay long. She still needs time to recover.'

Gladys poured out a coffee for the doctor and said tactfully, 'I'll go now and leave you two to talk. If you want me, I shall be in the farm office.'

As soon as they were alone together, the doctor said as gently as he could: 'I don't want to upset you further, Mrs Jackson, you've had enough to cope with already, but I think you had better be prepared for some disturbing news. Did you know that Margaret is no longer a virgin?'

'You mean, Albert Lloyd...?' Dr Bruce interrupted her. 'No. He didn't interfere with her in any way, thank goodness. This happened some time ago. Margaret is about ten weeks' pregnant.'

Emily was dumbfounded. She could not believe it. She was not sure what she felt; anger, hurt, resentment, compassion? She did not know. She just felt numb and speechless. Slowly, two things emerged from her confused thoughts. How could Margaret, and presumably Robert, have behaved so irresponsibly, and why had Margaret not told her? She must have known she was pregnant.

Dr Bruce waited patiently before continuing, realising for the moment that Emily was too stunned to say anything. He took a sip of his coffee, and then added, 'I'm arranging for her to go into hospital. She may well lose the baby, and she would be better under observation.'

To be told within the space of a few seconds that her daughter was going to have an illegitimate baby and then that she had to go into hospital was too much for Emily, and she suddenly, and uncontrollably, started to cry. All the pent-up emotions of the past few hours were released as she continued to sob and repeat to herself over and over again her disbelief.

Chapter 26

Margaret was lying in bed listening to the familiar sounds of early morning. Outside, in the yard, she could hear the rattle of milk churns as Harry loaded up his rully before setting off into Kirkley on his morning rounds. There was a paddle of feet on the landing and up and down the stairs as her mother called to her young sisters, to persuade them it was time to dress and have breakfast before going off to school. After the traumas of the past week, she was enjoying the comforts of home, trying to dismiss from her mind the horror of Darren Wood, the unhappy memories of hospital, and the nagging doubts about her future with Robert. She turned over and snuggled down between the sheets to wait for her mother. Breakfast in bed was a rare luxury.

'I'm getting spoilt,' said Margaret, as Emily put down the breakfast tray and plumped up her pillows.

'It's the last morning. You are well enough now to have breakfast downstairs. Dr Bruce suggested a week to convalesce, and you've had ten days.'

'I shall go back to Newlands on Monday,' said Margaret, taking a piece of toast. 'I think it will help to take my mind off things. I still have nightmares about Albert Lloyd. Is there any more news of him?'

'No. Brian Hilton promised to get in touch as soon as he heard anything. It seems he's just disappeared. He called in at home on the ...' Emily paused, trying to find a tactful way of expressing herself. '... on the night it all happened and he hasn't been seen since. He always was a coward and a nasty piece of work, even as a boy. It wouldn't surprise me if he has gone off to join the army. It would be a good place to hide.'

'They are welcome to him,' said Margaret. 'I hope, in a way, they don't find him. I don't think I could stand a court case – you know, having to give evidence and all the publicity.'

'Well, he's certainly influenced your life – all our lives. How do you feel about losing the baby?'

'I'm not sure. When I decided to spend the night with Robert in York, I was convinced I was doing the right thing. I wanted to have a baby as I believed that the Colonel would not want his son to be responsible for an illegitimate ch1ld and would have to agree to our getting married. Now, on reflection, I'm not so sure. I'm relieved, but, at the same time, sad not to be having Robert's child. I still love him, you know.'

'But didn't you think of the consequences? The disgrace to us all? The effect on your father, who has always worshipped you? I'm horrified to think that after the way we have brought you up you could even contemplate going to bed with Robert before you were married. I can't imagine him doing it either. But then actually plan, deliberately, to have a baby – a mistake may have been understandable, perhaps even forgivable, but a cold, calculated act. How could you?'

'I was desperate. I thought about it for weeks. I'd vaguely contemplated it a year ago, but dismissed it. It was the Colonel's uncompromising attitude which finally persuaded me.'

Emily thought for a moment. At least she could understand Margaret's logic, even if she did not agree with it. In any case, she believed that Robert would have married Margaret sooner or later whatever his father said.

She noticed that Margaret was not eating.

'Don't you want that piece of toast? You must eat to get your strength back.'

'I'm not hungry. I haven't been working or doing anything to give me an appetite. And I'm still very upset.'

Margaret had let down her hair, which swept down to her shoulders, emphasising the paleness of her face and the intensity of her blue eyes. She looked sad and haggard. Emily could not bear to see her daughter so wretched and unhappy. She moved the breakfast tray and, sitting on the bed, put a comforting arm round her shoulders.

'It's not all your fault,' she said. 'I'm to blame as well. I should have stopped you seeing Robert when you first came to tell me about him. I thought then that it could bring nothing but sadness and heartbreak.'

'Why didn't you? I fully expected you would.'

'I was weak. But I was also ambitious for you and, I suppose, too big-headed to admit that you can't break conventions. I just couldn't accept that we were not good enough even for the Denehursts. God knows why. The village people are right. I've become too big for my boots.'

'And you think I have as well, don't you?'

'Perhaps. I don't know. But what's wrong with ambition, initiative and hard work? You worked hard and we made sacrifices to give you a good education. You are a clever girl and came out top of your course. Why shouldn't you succeed? And what have the Denehursts got? Money and privilege.'

Margaret thought for a moment and said: 'Dad wouldn't agree. I remember years ago, when Robert went away to school, he said that I couldn't expect my friendship with him to continue and implied that I was "not good enough".' She paused, and then added anxiously: 'You haven't told dad about my being pregnant, and then losing the baby, have you?'

'No, not yet. I don't think I shall. It would break his heart. At present, only us and Dr Bruce know, and he won't say anything. I'm sure it's best kept secret. Imagine the gossip there would be if it ever became known in Dunmere.' She paused for a moment and then asked, 'What about Robert? Does he know you were expecting a baby?'

'No. I haven't told him anything yet – not even that I had missed a period. You mustn't blame him for what happened, it was my idea.'

Emily thought that he must, at least, take some of the blame, but she did not pursue it.

'You will tell him though? It would be immoral, and dishonest, not to.'

'I dread the thought of telling him but, of course, I know I shall have to. He's coming home at the end of the week. I shall tell him then, but he'll be very angry and upset. He's been cross with me ever since we made love together.'

To Emily, that came as a very revealing statement. She did not want to pry into the intimate details of their night in York, but, obviously, whatever was causing the rift between them started from then. She decided that, for the moment, she had said enough, and rose from the bed.

'I must go now. I don't want to tire you. I understand a lot more now than I did before our talk, but I'm still very upset. It's going to take us all a long time to recover and return to normal life.'

'Thanks, mum. And remember that whatever happens, I love you and dad.'

'As her mother took the breakfast tray and went over to the door, Margaret settled back into bed, grateful for her mother's support and confident that, given time, she would be forgiven.

A footpath led along the bank of the river Dun from Dunmere to Kirkley, but, for a mile or so, it passed through the Park, and this stretch was not a public right of way. However, Lord Heverthorpe was tolerant of the estate workers and their families using the path, and since their courtship had become public knowledge, it had become a favourite walk for Robert and Margaret.

Stephen's plan for Robert to attend the machinery course at Silsoe during the quiet period between hay time and harvest had not quite worked out in practice, and when Robert returned home, the hay harvest was still not finished. Robert spent all day Saturday carting the last field of hay at Holme Green and then on Sunday afternoon, he called for Margaret, and they drove to Dunmere with the intention of walking along the river path back towards Kirkley.

It was a hot, close, afternoon. A pervading scent of new-mown hay hung in the heavy atmosphere. Buttercups and daisies grew in profusion on the riverbanks and there was a constant drone of bees as they busily worked the clover in the uncut meadows.

A moorhen called from the reeds and clouds of midges danced above the rippling water.

After passing through the Park, Robert and Margaret climbed over the stile and decided to rest in the shade of a group of willows.

'I hope the walk isn't tiring you too much,' said Robert, aware that Margaret was still not back to her normal health. He noticed that she was more lethargic and less animated than usual, but whether that was due to physical exhaustion or the agitated state of her mind, he was not sure.

'No, I'm all right, but I shall be pleased to sit down for a while, it's so hot and muggy. You must be glad not to be haymaking.'

'Yes, I am. It's not my favourite job at any time – flies, sweat and hay seeds in your hair and down your back. Anyway, I'm pleased to be here with you.'

'That's the nicest thing you've said to me for ages. You've been cross and grumpy with me ever since our night in York,' said Margaret, and she leaned across to give him a kiss.

For a moment, he returned her embrace, then quickly drew back, aware that, although he wanted her as much as he ever had, once their emotions had been roused what he needed to say to her would prove to be impossible.

'There's something important I have to tell you,' said Margaret. 'But, first promise me you won't be cross.'

'How can I promise when I don't know what it is? But go on.'

'After our night in York, I was pregnant,' she said calmly and quietly.

Robert looked at her incredulously, too stunned to say anything. She saw that he had turned pale, and was obviously deeply affected by the news.

'But don't worry,' she added. 'You won't be obliged to marry me. When I was in hospital I had a miscarriage.'

If that came as a relief to him, Robert did not show it. His expression didn't change, remaining grim and tight-lipped. When he still did not respond, Margaret said bluntly and tactlessly: 'You would have married me if I hadn't lost the baby, wouldn't you?'

'Yes. I wouldn't have had any alternative. But it would have been no sort of basis on which to start our life together. I don't need to spell out the effect it would have had on our parents, and think of the practical implications.'

Margaret did not want to become involved in a hypothetical discussion. She was more worried about their future now that there was no baby to consider.

Ignoring the question, she asked: 'And now there is no baby, are you still going to marry me?'

A pair of wagtails were bobbing about on the flat stones at the shallow edge of the river. Robert watched them absently for a moment and then turned to Margaret. He could hardly bear to meet the beseeching look in her eyes. He wanted desperately to take her in his arms but, summoning all his self-control, he said, 'Not as I feel now. I just don't think it would work.'

Margaret had been prepared for his answer but, even so, she felt a prick of tears behind her eyes and a lump rising in her throat. She was determined not to break down or have an emotional outburst and managed to say: 'Why not? I love you and I believe you still love me.'

'You say you love me, but you have an odd way of showing it. All the time you behave as though you can't trust me. I know you've had a distressing experience during the past weeks, particularly the horrors of Darren Wood, but most of your troubles have been self- inflicted.'

'Come on, Robert. You can't say that. You wanted to go to bed with me. It was your idea to spend a night in York.'

'It wasn't my intention to have a baby,' he said sharply. 'That was all your idea. You didn't even discuss it with me.'

'You know why not. Because of your father. You were too scared to tell him about us,' said Margaret, goading him.

'No I wasn't. Maybe I delayed a long time, but you also delayed telling your father. You didn't trust me to marry you. That's what hurts. Now I've had time to think about it, I realise you never have trusted me. You thought I was having an affair with Celia. You even believed the idle gossip of people like Ernie and Ned rather than trust me.'

'But that was ages ago. That's all over now.'

'I'd like to think so, but every time we have a minor disagreement, or a difficult decision to make, you are never on my side. When I first went to London, you were worried because you thought I would find another girl...'

Margaret interrupted him sharply. 'And you thought I would meet a boy at Askham Bryan.'

'Well, you did. I've never heard the full story of this boy from Bradford, who you said you felt sorry for.'

'Halifax, actually,' said Margaret.

'Hull, Hell or Halifax, wherever you like,' said Robert, his anger rising. 'I didn't create a fuss about him. I trusted you.'

'Why bring him into it now, then?' said Margaret, her mood changing from one of feeling sorry for herself to one of defiance. 'Tom meant no more to me than Celia did to you. I only mentioned him because I was trying to be amusing about our night out to celebrate the end of term and Christmas.'

Robert was not to be diverted. 'Then this latest charade. You had to get yourself pregnant. You must think I'm pretty stupid not to see through that,' he said angrily.

Margaret was furious. 'That's a horrid thing to say. I sacrificed myself for you. Don't think I didn't care about losing my virginity. I'm not one of your village sluts, an "easy lay" as your friend, Peter, would say.'

'You did it for yourself, not for me,' said Robert. 'And now another act of deceit. Why didn't you tell me you were pregnant? Didn't I have a right to know? After all, I was only the father. Or maybe I wasn't. Is that why you didn't tell me?'

Margaret was now almost speechless with fury. 'My God, I just don't know how you could say such a thing. If you can say dreadful things like that, you are quite right. A marriage wouldn't work,' she said, trembling with rage.

As soon as he had said it, Robert had misgivings, regretting that he had lost control of his temper. It was an uncharacteristic outburst, which surprised him almost as much as Margaret.

'I'm sorry,' he said. 'I shouldn't have said that. It's only because I'm hurt and upset. I loved, and trusted you, and if you hadn't acted so selfishly and stupidly, our future together wouldn't be in doubt.

This was the reaction Margaret had feared and worried about ever since she had known she was pregnant. Her only hope now was that he would forgive her, but she could see by the intensity of his feelings and reaction that he was too deeply hurt to forget easily. In any case, forgiveness was not one of his characteristics. He was, after all, Colonel Denehurst's son, and had inherited a hard, stubborn, streak, which was normally concealed by a pleasant appearance and a charming manner.

Robert's apology caused Margaret to have misgivings of her own. She had a quick temper, but, unlike Robert, did not nurse a grievance and, regaining her composure as quickly as she had lost it, and knowing that she had behaved badly, said: 'You are not the only one who should be sorry. I'm equally to blame. Are you prepared to forgive me and make a fresh start?'

Robert thought a moment before replying. 'I expect I shall forgive you in time,' he said. 'But I don't see how we can continue as we are. Neither of us has been very happy during the past few weeks. I think it would be sensible for us not to see each other for a while.'

'So long as you don't mean for ever,' said Margaret. 'Do you remember, years ago, when we were just school children, you said you would always want to see me. I've never forgotten that.'

Robert smiled wistfully. 'Neither have I,' he said. 'If I remember correctly, I think you replied, "Always is a long time". Well, time is on our side. Let's give it a chance.'

This was more than she had hoped for. 'All right, so long as it's just a temporary parting. You will see me again, won't you?'

Robert did not answer her directly but said, 'Just be patient. And this time, trust me.'

Realising there was no point in further discussion, she stood up and brushing the grass from her skirt, said, 'I must go now. I promised dad I would go to chapel tonight. I haven't been for ages.'

Dark storm clouds were gathering over the hills behind Kirkley, and a sudden breeze rustled through the leaves of the willow. Robert stood up, too, and said, 'It's time we both went. There's going to be a storm soon. It's a good job we finished carting the hay yesterday.'

'I shall walk on to Kirkley along the riverbank. I need more time alone. It's only about a mile. I shall be home before it rains,' said Margaret.

She looked up to his face, not knowing how to part. 'Goodbye, Robert,' she said and then hesitatingly, reached up and kissed him gently on the lips, before setting off on her lonely walk home.

Robert stood and watched her go and then, with a heavy heart, set off in the opposite direction to Dunmere.

On reaching the stile, he recalled their parting when they had met at the bramble patch in Beech Wood. Looking back he saw that Margaret had reached the gate leading into the riverside meadow. He watched as she opened it and passed through. Then as she turned to close it behind her she looked back and saw him still standing by the stile.

He waved to her and she waved back, just as she had done in Beech Wood.

PART FOUR 1940

Chapter 27

The sun had disappeared behind a thickening mist, which rolled in from the Humber over the mud and shifting sand banks. The flat fields dissected by deep ditches and drains stretched monotonously to the horizon. There were no trees, or hedges, and the skyline was broken only by the soaring tower of Thornton church, renowned as the queen of many fine Holderness churches.

Two gangs of land-army girls moved slowly across a field of peas, turning over the cut swathes to dry before forking them into heaps ready for carting. They worked more in hope than expectation as there was no wind and the pale autumn sun, even before it was shrouded in the developing mist, did not have much power in its hazy rays.

'These rows get longer and longer,' said Audrey, a small, slight, girl with untidy hair and a pair of large round glasses through which she peered at the world in a rather owl-like fashion. Her long shafted fork seemed almost too much for her to handle. 'I wish I'd joined the ATS or the WAAFS,' she said wistfully.

'It's certainly a change from perming hair,' said Doreen, a much taller, glamorous-looking girl who, with her long blonde hair, gave every appearance of being more accustomed to working in a hair-dressing salon than on a farm. In fact, almost all the girls had been working in shops or offices until the outbreak of war and had chosen a life on the land rather than join one of the women's services.

'A girl I was at school with joined the WRENS,' continued Doreen. 'She was home on leave last week. Having a whale of a time she is. Down in Portsmouth. Dances and parties all the time.'

'Well, we don't do too badly. At least we can live at home and have our weekends free,' said Audrey.

'You might. I don't,' said Doreen. 'It's all right for you lot. The van picks you up in the morning and takes you back to Hull at night. You only work from about half past eight until four. Helen and I are stuck here all the time. I don't suppose we shall finish work until its dark.'

Most of the land-army girls worked in gangs and were sent to different farms, as needed, but Doreen and her friend, Helen, were permanently employed at Thornton Grange and cycled there every day from Thornton. When necessary they worked overtime, like the farm men and at hay time and harvest, often on Saturday and Sunday. The girls had now reached the end of their rows. Doreen stuck her fork into the ground and walked over to a pile of coats and sweaters lying on the headland. She fished out a bottle.

'What's in that? Cold tea?' asked Audrey. Drinking cold tea was a habit the girls had picked up from the farm men. A refreshing drink once you had got used to it.

'Only water. Do you want a swig? There's plenty left.' Audrey pulled a face.

'No thanks. I could down a shandy though.'

'I'll have a drink,' said Helen as she joined them on the headland. 'Then we'd better get moving again. The boss's truck has just arrived at the gate. He'll be over here in a minute.'

Audrey snorted. 'He won't say anything to you, Helen. It's always me he picks on.' Helen was an attractive dark-haired girl with widely separated hazel eyes and a generous mouth. She seemed different from the other two girls; better spoken and not as uncouth as Audrey. Her father was a doctor in Kirkella, one of the better suburbs of Hull and she had been to a private boarding-school.

'I think the boss rather fancies Helen,' said Doreen.

'I don't know about that,' broke in Audrey with a smirk on her face. 'I think it's Helen who fancies him.'

Helen blushed slightly but said nothing. It was not the first time her companions had hinted that their young boss treated her differently from the others.

'Well he'd certainly be a good catch. Over five hundred acres of top class land, a big farmhouse and a Colonel's son,' said Doreen.

'It isn't his farm,' said Helen. 'He doesn't own it, or even rent it. He only manages it for Stephen Langley, his brother-in-law. I suppose he could have some share in the profits.'

'Well he's obviously involved somehow,' said Doreen. 'And one day it could be his. His sister Mary, and Mr Langley don't have any family and I reckon Mary is now too old to have any children.'

'Come on, Doreen,' said Helen. 'She isn't as old as all that. About ten years older than the boss I should think. Anyway, he's coming over here now. We'd better change the subject.'

Robert Denehurst was making his way towards them between the rows of peas. Every now and then he took a handful of haulm, testing it for dampness and sniffing it to make sure it wasn't turning mouldy. The girls fell silent as he approached, concentrating on their work.

'If the mist clears and we get some sun this lot should be ready for cocking (putting into small heaps) in the morning,' he said.

Audrey, who had always had a smutty schoolgirl sense of humour and had still not grown out of it, just managed to stop herself from saying, 'I'm ready for cocking now.' It was the sort of remark she might well have made at home where her father was the landlord of The Fisherman's Rest, a rough pub in the dockland area of Hull.

'When will they be ready to cart?' asked Doreen anxiously, hoping they would not be ready until after the weekend. She was going to an RAF dance on Saturday night and did not want to be working late.

'It depends entirely on the weather but I doubt if it will be before Monday,' said Robert.

'Doreen is hoping to go to a dance at Wellersea on Saturday night. Mr Denehurst, are you planning to go?' asked Audrey rather cheekily.

'No. I shall be going home to Dunmere if we aren't working,' he said, being careful not to say anything which might be embarrassing. He had no intention of discussing his private life with the girls. He wondered, sometimes, how much they already knew and if they had heard the gossip about his past relationship with Margaret. He turned to Helen and said, 'You and Doreen had better carry on here when the van comes for the rest of the girls. You should get finished if you keep moving. I'm sure you'll welcome a bit of overtime, Doreen. Extra spending money for Saturday night.' And not waiting for a reply, he set off back across the field to his truck.

'He's a bit of a misery,' said Audrey as soon as Robert was out of sight. 'He never seems to go anywhere. Always at work. He looks as though a night on the tiles would do him the world of good.'

'He does look sad and careworn,' admitted Doreen. 'He's rather nice though. Lovely blue eyes. You think he's attractive don't you Helen?'

Helen not only thought their boss was attractive; she imagined herself in love with him and had difficulty in controlling her feelings, but all she said in reply to Doreen was, 'Yes, I suppose he is,' and stuck her fork firmly into the row of peas.

'He always seems to be going back to Dunmere. Do you think he has a steady there?' asked Doreen, trying to draw a more positive reaction from her friend.

'How should I know?' said Helen sharply, her guard slipping a little. I've always assumed he goes home to see his parents, and of course, to discuss plans with Mr Langley. His main farm is near Dunmere.'

'On the estate where Colonel Denehurst is agent?' asked Audrey.

'No. He owns his own farm there as well as this one. I know a bit about it because Mrs Langley told me when she came with her husband one weekend when we were working overtime. You remember Doreen?'

'Yes. I liked her. She seemed a good sort. Different from him. I reckon he's always after the money.'

'Does she look like the boss?' asked Audrey.

'There's a strong family likeness. You can see they are brother and sister but she's not so fair-haired as him and only medium height. About as tall as you, Helen, I should think.'

Helen didn't respond to that comment. There were times when she found the girls' prattle boring and tiresome. And in any case she didn't think they should always be gossiping about Mr Denehurst's family or his private life. It was no business of theirs. Towards the end of a long tiring day she was content just to concentrate on the job in hand. She marvelled at Audrey's energy and wondered how such a slip of a girl, not hardened by manual work, could be as bouncing at four o'clock in the afternoon as she was first thing in the morning. And considering there were air raids over Hull almost every night, even more remarkable. Quite often the alert lasted from dusk until the following morning and people living in the city spent their nights in an air raid shelter, frightened, cold and unable to sleep.

Later that evening, Robert finished his supper and carried his dirty dishes into the kitchen, undecided whether to wash them up or leave them for Iris Garbutt to deal with in the morning. Although he had been at Grange Farm over a year he was still not used to living alone. When Stephen had given him the chance to move to Holderness to look after his newly acquired farm, Robert had found it difficult to make a decision. The whole of his life, apart from his short stay in London, had revolved round the Dunmere estate. More importantly, it was where he had grown up and fallen in love with Margaret. Their separation had been a great blow to him and he needed to find a new interest in life although he didn't think anyone could ever replace Margaret. However, a move to Thornton would give him an opportunity to take more responsibility and widen his knowledge of farming. After much thought he had finally accepted but had not yet adjusted completely to his new life style. He now realised that, when living at Holme Green with Mary and Stephen, he had been spoilt, with a welcoming fire on cold, winter,evenings, a hot meal on the table, his washing and ironing seen to and above all warm companionship. He had decided against a living-in housekeeper as a luxury he couldn't really justify. All he needed were the basic essentials and Iris, who lived in a cottage with her unmarried brother just down the road, came in every day to do the housework and prepare meals.

Robert left the dishes and went for a stroll round the stackyard where there were two large Dutch barns. One was already full of harvested wheat but the other was empty, ready for the peas and later the straw. The outline of the barns framed huge black shapes in the mist but higher up the night was clear and a pale moon hung in the cloudless sky. A barn owl floated silently over the mist-shrouded pond and the whole farmstead was enveloped in an eerie silence. Suddenly the peace was shattered by the distant wail of a siren. Over to the west, the sky was lit by the criss-crossing beams of searchlights and when the air-raid sirens ended, Robert heard the distant drone of a heavily-laden bomber making its hazardous way up the Humber. There was constant sound of aircraft, day and night, but there was no mistaking that particular sound of an enemy plane as it headed towards the city.

When the noise of the aircraft faded there was silence for a time and then the distinctive thud of bombs. Now the searchlight beams were pierced by colourful flashes from the anti-aircraft guns.

'Some poor devils are catching it again,' said a voice behind him and startled Robert turned to see his foreman, Arthur Garbutt, behind him.

'Hello, Arthur, I wasn't expecting to see you out here,' he said. And then added, 'Yes, I wouldn't want to be living in Hull. We're lucky. They don't bother with us out here.'

'It always worries me when those girls go back there at night,' said Arthur. 'I'm surprised they don't do like Helen and Doreen and get lodgings in the village.'

'Young Audrey was as perky as ever when I went to see them in the pea field this afternoon. They're getting on well there. How is the wheat coming on?'

'Just about finished and then only the beans left.'

The two men were silent for a moment as they watched the searchlights sweeping the distant sky. There had been no more thuds, or explosions, and the anti-aircraft fire had stopped.

'I don't think we shall get much more activity tonight. I reckon I'll get off to my bed,' said Arthur.

'A good idea. Get some sleep when you can. They'll be back another night.'

'Good night. I'll see you, as usual, in the morning,' said Arthur and disappeared into the mist to walk back down the lane to his cottage.

Chapter 28

Margaret and James walked round the free-range poultry houses at Newlands shutting up the hens for the night. James was a corporal in the Royal Artillery stationed in the camp at Dunmere Park. He and Margaret had become friends after meeting at a dance at Kirkley. It was a mellow September evening. Over on the lower hill slopes a few rows of stooks still waited to be carted but most of the golden stubbles were striped with brown as the ploughs moved in for the start of the autumn drilling. Higher up the sheep grazed peacefully amongst the heather and bracken, oblivious to the haunting cries of the curlews. It seemed that the war had hardly disturbed the measured pace of life in the Yorkshire dales. The seasons followed their orderly pattern – harvest following hay time and autumn sowing following the harvest for the start of another farming year.

Soon the sheep would be brought down from the hills, the hoggs folded on the roots and the rams turned out with the ewes. The threshing machine would start icy winter rounds and already at Newlands the pullets were coming into lay.

But there were changes. Acres of grassland had been ploughed out to be planted with unfamiliar crops such as potatoes, sugar beet and linseed. Farmers went to demonstrations of new techniques. Powerful tractors and large, sophisticated, implements were replacing horses. After a decade of depression farming was moving quickly into a period of growth and prosperity.

And people's lives had changed. Convoys of army vehicles filled the country roads. On market days blue and khaki uniforms mingled with the corduroys and peak caps and in the public house bars, the quiet games of dominoes were disrupted by noisy crowds of soldiers and airmen.

'Don't you find this a bit of a bore?' asked James. 'Walking round every night putting stupid hens to bed. It must be very trying.'

'Not as bad as milking cows twice a day and, anyway, hens are not stupid' said Margaret. 'I'm not on duty every night any more than you are.'

'No, I suppose not. But this is your chosen occupation. I'm only in the army because I was called up. I don't intend to be a soldier for the rest of my life.'

'What will you do when the war is over?'

'I don't know. Finish my course at university and then teach perhaps. There's not much choice with a degree in French.'

Margaret released her hand from James', dropped the shutter over the pop hole of the last fold unit and walked over to inspect a water drinker. It was empty. 'Just as I thought,' she said. 'I shall have to have another word with young Rosie. She's not a bad worker – just forgetful. Daydreaming about her latest boyfriend no doubt instead of concentrating on her work.'

'Don't you daydream about me?' asked James putting his arm round her waist as they turned back towards the farmstead.

'All the time, darling,' said Margaret flippantly. She had only known James for a few weeks. She liked him and enjoyed his company but didn't want to become seriously involved. She thought a light-hearted response was the best protection.'

I don't know what to make of you sometimes. You never take my remarks seriously,' said James, a little petulantly.

'That's not true. I take your remarks very seriously most of the time but I'm not going to let you coax me into saying something I might regret later.'

'And what might you have said and later regretted?' persisted James.

'There you go again,' said Margaret stopping. He was much taller than her, over six feet. He had dark, wavy, hair and attractive brown eyes but rather too long a nose to be handsome.

'Don't tantalise me with those beautiful eyes,' he said when she looked up to his face. 'They would break any heart and mine dissolved the first time we danced together.' He bent to kiss her, his lips lingering on hers a long time. She pressed against his mouth warmly but kept her lips closed.

'Haven't you ever tried kissing with your mouth open?' asked James.

'You're full of leading questions tonight aren't you,' she said. 'But as you ask, yes. But it would have to be somebody very special.'

James was not hurt by this rebuke. He guessed that Margaret was not the sort of girl to fall in love easily. But he thought he was, perhaps, falling in love with her. Certainly he was strongly attracted and it was not only sexual. He wondered if she had another steady boyfriend, perhaps away in the forces. He could not believe that such an attractive girl did not have lots of admirers. Her behaviour puzzled him. In some ways she was warm and responsive but there was a definite reserve – a protective shell that he found difficult to penetrate. He felt that she was holding something back.

'I know I'm not special but is there someone who is?' he asked after a pause.

'No. There's nobody else,' said Margaret and then very quietly, almost as an after thought, she said, 'Not now.'

'But there was once? Somebody special I mean.'

'Oh, yes. Somebody very, very special.' Finding it hard to control her feelings, her voice faltered a little when she added, 'But that's over now.'

James wondered if it was. What she had just told him explained a great deal. She had obviously been deeply hurt.

'Would it help to talk about it? I'm a good listener.'

Margaret did not reply immediately. She was sure James was a sympathetic person and trying to be helpful. She also knew that if they continued to meet, and their friendship developed into something more serious, sometime she would have to tell him about Robert. Or at any rate part of the story. There were some aspects, which were so private she could never divulge them to anybody.

By now it was dusk and, as they entered the farmyard, Margaret made her decision.

'It's a very long story,' she said. 'Would you like to come in for a coffee. We may as well be comfortable while we talk.'

'That's a good idea. I'd love to.'

It was the first time James had been invited into the house. He wondered if he would be meeting Gilbert Dawson or Gladys or perhaps the other poultry girls. It was a long, low, house, the two ends being separated by the front hall. Gilbert and Gladys had their private rooms to the left overlooking the garden. The girls occupied rooms on the other side and to the rear, which led to the farmyard and buildings. They had their own bedrooms but shared a sitting-room and small kitchen where they could make hot drinks and snacks. Breakfast and the main midday meal were taken with Gilbert and Gladys in the kitchen.

As though reading his thoughts, Margaret said, 'Rosie and Nan are out tonight. It's their night off so we shall have the sitting-room to ourselves.'

She led the way in through the back door and, having brought in the coffee and some home-made biscuits, sat next to James on the settee.

'Who was this special person then?' he asked. 'A local boy or someone who moved into the area? A soldier, or airman, perhaps?' And then wondering if he was pressurising her he added, 'Don't tell me about it if it's painful to you. I just thought it might help to talk about it.'

'You're being very sweet,' she said, taking his hand. 'I think it's only fair to tell you but it's not going to be easy. I haven't really needed to tell anybody before. All the local people know about it, of course. And, as you can imagine, there was a lot of gossip about it in the village at the time.'

She stopped and took a drink of her coffee, undecided where to begin her story. 'As your unit is based in the Park at Dunmere, I expect you'll have met Colonel Denehurst, Lord Heverthorpe's agent and manager of the home farm.'

'No, we haven't met but I know who you are talking about. Wasn't your father waggoner there at one time?'

'Yes, and, of course, I was born in one of the farm cottages. Well, the Colonel's son, Robert, whom you won't know about because he now lives down in Holderness, and I went out together for a long time and planned to get married.' Here she stopped for a moment to let James grasp the significance of what she was saying.

So far James had not met Margaret's parents and knew little of her family background. He knew even less about the feudal way of life, which still persisted in the remote Yorkshire dales. But he knew enough to realise that a working class girl like Margaret would never be considered suitable for someone of Robert's position in society.

As she continued her story about her childhood days and how, as she had grown up into teenage, her friendship with Robert had developed into love, James began to understand her puzzling behaviour towards him. He suspected that Margaret was still in love with Robert and finding it difficult to adjust to a new life without him.

Wrongly assuming that Robert's behaviour had been typical of a spoilt, upper class, boy who had taken advantage of his position to influence a young girl flattered by his attentions and then deserted her when tough decisions had to be made, he said, 'As far as Robert was concerned that was the end of the romance.'

'Oh, no. It wasn't like that at all,' said Margaret, dispelling the implied criticism. 'Robert defied his parents and remained faithful to me. I mean he really did love me and I loved him. It was me who behaved badly and caused our separation.'

James waited for her to continue but, to his surprise, after a long pause, she suddenly let go of his hand, stood up and rushed out of the room. She was obviously very distressed and he wondered if he should follow in order to try to comfort her.

Deciding it would be more tactful to leave her alone, he finished his coffee and walked over to the window. All was peaceful in the farmyard as bats flitted about in the evening shadows. He felt cross with himself for having encouraged Margaret to talk. He realised that she had not told him everything and wondered what subsequent events had caused their separation. He was not going to find out – at any rate not tonight.

A few minutes later the door opened and turning from the window he watched her closely as she walked towards him across the room. There was an air of sadness about her and she seemed paler than usual. If she had been crying there was no sign of it. He noticed that, unusually for her, she had put some make up on. All it did was emphasise the deep blue of her eyes and make her mouth even more enticing.

'I'm sorry,' she said as she came close to him. 'I thought I was over all that. I think I am, really. It was talking about it to a kind, sympathetic, audience which brought it back to me so vividly.'

James was far from convinced that she had put her past behind her, but he put his arms round her and, as he kissed her upturned lips, she put her arms round his neck responding to his embrace. It was a new experience and welcome though it was he was not sure whether it was meant for him or Robert.

Chapter 29

'I'm going solo,' said Stephen with no more that a quick glance through his cards.

'Hold on a minute, not so fast,' said Kit shuffling carefully through his hand again. 'I'm going to risk misère.'

Kit Barton was an auctioneer by profession but he also farmed at Church Farm, near Wellersea, and, after a day at the cattle market, had invited Stephen and Robert to join him and his daughter, Ann, for supper and a game of cards. Ann was his only daughter. Her mother had died when she was a young girl and, since leaving boarding-school, she had stayed at home to keep house and look after her father. She was a short, stockily-built, girl with a rather dumpy figure and as the farm men said rather crudely, 'Plenty to get hold of.' Nevertheless, she was an attractive girl with naturally wavy auburn hair, grey-green eyes and a pretty mouth which when she smiled exposed small, even teeth. Having been forced by circumstances to take responsibility at a young age, she was mature for her years. But dominated by her father she lived a quiet life and, although now twenty-three, she had never had a boyfriend and appeared naïve when it came to attracting one.

The game progressed with Stephen becoming increasingly frustrated because with a hand full of high cards he had quickly taken the lead.

'I've nothing left now but high spades and Kit doesn't have any. Can't you take the lead from me, Ann? Surely somebody can get him down.'

'Sorry, Stephen,' said Ann. 'I think we're going to have to pay up.'

'You won't get me now,' said Kit. 'I reckon you'll have to sell that heifer you bought in the market today to pay me out,' he said, jokingly, as he threw his king of diamonds on Stephen's last spade.

'That's it,' said Ann. 'I think it's time for supper. I'll go and put the kettle on.'

'Anything I can do to help? I'm very domesticated you know,' said Robert.

'No, everything is ready to bring in. But you can help with the washing-up later if you like. I don't like to leave things until the morning.'

'It's time you found a girl and got married, Robert. You'll be turning into an old bachelor before long,' said Kit. It was meant as a lighthearted remark but, in the circumstances, rather a tactless one. Robert had still not recovered from his traumatic love affair with Margaret Jackson and was sensitive to any reference to girls or marriage even if not meant seriously. And Ann was in an equally vulnerable position, especially as she was becoming attracted to Robert. She escaped quickly through the door to hide her embarrassment.

Later, when Robert had gone to help Ann with the washing-up and Kit and Stephen were sitting having a whisky, Stephen asked, 'Is there anything going on between those two? I thought they looked a bit sheepish when you were teasing Robert about being a bachelor.'

'No, I don't think so.' Kit paused a moment. 'I haven't really thought about it. But no, I'm sure there isn't. Ann has never shown much interest in boys.'

'Perhaps she has never had much chance. She must be very tied looking after you and the house,' said Stephen pointedly.

'I suppose so,' said Kit defensively. 'But I try not to make too many demands on her. She has her own life ahead.'

Stephen made no comment. He was not convinced but he felt he had made a point. He knew too many widowers who had ruined their daughters' lives by expecting them to take the place of their wives.

Kit rose from the chair and walked thoughtfully over to the drinks cabinet.

'Are you ready for a top up?' he asked returning with the drinks bottle.

'No thanks, Kit. This is fine by me.'

Kit filled up his own glass and splashed in some soda.

'It's ten years since Emma died. We were never very close but I still miss her. It's only when someone has gone you realise how much they meant to you. I don't know what I would do without Ann but no doubt she'll leave me one day.'

'Haven't you thought of marrying again? You are still young enough. You might even have a son.'

Stephen made this last comment more forcefully than he had intended. The fact that he had no children of his own was a disappointment, which he found difficult to live with. He was fond of children and would have liked to have an heir to his farming business which was the main reason for his encouragement and generosity to Robert.

'I won't say I haven't thought about it,' said Kit. 'After all, I suppose I am what is regarded as a good catch. There are plenty of women – attractive, young, ones – who would say snap if I asked them. But I'm not interested enough in women and I wouldn't want to start a family again at my age.'

Stephen looked round the comfortably furnished sitting-room, with its fine Adam's fireplace, large Georgian-type, lavishly draped windows and thick pile carpet. There were some expensive pieces of furniture about too, including an antique pedestal table, large mahogany bookcase and chesterfield settee.

Stephen was too young to have known Emma well but he knew from what others had told him that she came from a cultured, professional background and the volumes in the bookcase suggested that she had been better educated than Kit. Certainly the sitting-room and the little that he had seen of the rest of the house made Stephen realise that she had had style, and tastes, not normally associated with farmers' wives.

'Was Emma a farmer's daughter?' asked Stephen.

'No, her father was an accountant. That's how we met. His firm used to do our books. She was a great help to me on the business side but she was not really interested in farming. She was a town girl and never liked living here.'

'I'm not surprised. It's a bit of god-forsaken country; cut off from civilisation, flat, cold, bleak and wet. But damn good land.'

'You've no regrets about buying Thornton Grange?'

'On the contrary. I think it will work out well. In fact I'd expand further if I had the money.'

'You'd better go and talk to your bank manager then. Mark Butler, isn't it? He used to be assistant manager at the Wellersea branch. I know him well.'

Not for the first time Stephen wondered if there was anybody in Holderness that Kit did not know.

'Yes, he's always been very helpful. Understands farming. But what I would like to do is form a sort of consortium rather than go it alone.'

Kit did not reply immediately and Stephen watched him closely wondering how he would respond to his rather obvious hint. Kit drained his glass.

'You must be ready for a top up now Stephen,' he said. And not waiting for a reply poured a generous portion into both glasses.

'If that was intended as an invitation, I'm not biting. Not at the moment anyway.'

'But you might. Perhaps if I twisted your arm?'

'I'll think about it. But there must be other farmers you could approach. Or even someone, not a farmer, but has money to invest. What about your father-in-law? Have you approached him?'

'John? No. He wouldn't take a chance. I've tried to persuade him to start farming on his own for Robert's benefit but he wouldn't even think about it. Anyway, we should never get on together. All he thinks about now is the Home Guard. He's like a lad with a box of toy soldiers.'

Kit laughed. 'Well, I'm sure if you had a word with Mark he would find you somebody.'

'I might just do that,' said Stephen looking at the clock on the mantelpiece. 'It's getting late. Those two are taking along time doing the washing-up. Do you think I should go and see what's going on?'

'You seem very anxious about them. Stop fussing. They're old enough to look after themselves.'

'Yes, I know. But I'm anxious about Robert. He was very hurt over the split up with Margaret Jackson last year. I don't think he has looked at a girl since. I just wondered if at last he's getting interested again.'

'I didn't realise it had been so serious,' said Kit.

'Oh, it was serious all right. Mary and I thought he was going to marry her. I don't know why he didn't. It's something I've never pressed him about.'

'It was his own decision not to go ahead?'

'Yes. As far as I know. John and Marjorie did their best to stop him but couldn't. I think they were relieved when he came to live down here, out of way.'

'You two look set for a long drinking session,' said Ann when she and Robert returned from the kitchen. 'How about a gin and tonic for me and something for Robert?'

'The same for me then, Kit,' said Robert. 'But it will have to be a quick one. I shall be in trouble from Mary if she thinks I'm leading Stephen astray when he comes down to the Grange.'

Conditions for spud-bashing were not good. It was a cold, foggy morning with a steel-grey sky. From the middle of the potato field at Thornton Grange, it was impossible to see anything other than the black, dying, potato haulm alternating with rows of white upturned tubers stretching to the horizon. Familiar landmarks were obliterated. It was like working in the middle of a bale of wool but less cosy. The stillness was almost eerie; the only sound the distant, familiar drone of an aircraft somewhere over the estuary. It wouldn't be foggy up there. Helen was reminded of Thomas Hood's poem which buzzed irritatingly round and round in her head.

'No sun. No moon, no proper time of day.' Six more potatoes in the bucket. Another six and the grand final; 'November.'

'Bloody November,' she screamed aloud, accompanying it with the thud of an extra large spud into her bucket.

The girls hadn't been at work for much more than an hour but Helen's fingers already felt like blocks of ice. Or they would have done if she could have felt anything at all. She stood up to ease her aching back and gloomily surveyed the never-ending rows still to be lifted.

In a few minutes Tom's tractor and spinner would materialise out of the fog to dig out yet another row. Somewhere behind her, and to the left, was a large barrel where the girls emptied their baskets when full. Later on, the farm men would come to take the barrels to the potato pit on the headland nearest to the road. These pits, which stretched for a hundred yards or so, were in the shape of an upturned letter V. In her flights of fancy, Helen imagined them as prehistoric monsters which would, at any moment, sprout wings and fly off to distant forests to feed. Probably on potatoes.

When work ended at four o' clock the fog was thicker than ever. Two of the farm men were collecting the last of the baskets and carting the full barrels to the potato pit. The van collecting the girls to take them home was already late and the girls were sitting on the headland cleaning themselves up and tidying their hair.

'Pass me that bag, Doreen, I'm going to take some spuds home,' said Audrey.

'You can't do that. It's stealing.'

'Don't fuss. Who's going to miss a few spuds out of this lot? Anyway, I regard it as part of the perks. I often took a boiling of peas home when we were harvesting. Nobody is watching and anyway, you can't see beyond the end of your nose in this fog.'

'Not you anyway,' said Helen laughing.

Audrey had a short, pug, nose hardly visible under her large glasses but she always had a ready answer.

'I wouldn't want a beak like yours,' she said. 'I don't know how you manage to kiss a bloke with a snout like that.'

Having filled her carrier bag with potatoes, Audrey was now rummaging in her handbag. 'I can't find my hankie anywhere,' she grumbled. 'Ah, there it is,' and she yanked it out by the corner. As she did so, a small, square, packet came out with it and fell on the ground. Helen and Doreen watched in amazement. There was no doubt about it. It was a packet of condoms.

'Oh, Christ,' said Audrey. 'I don't want to lose them. It would spoil my fun for a week.' And she picked them up casually as if they were a packet of sweets. Helen caught Doreen's eye in disbelief.

'Audrey, what are you doing with them? You don't use them, do you?'

'By God I do! I don't take chances. No riding bareback with me.'

'But do you let your boyfriends ...' Helen paused a moment searching for a suitable expression, 'go all the way,' she ended rather lamely.

'Yes, of course. Why not? Don't you? I thought everybody did these days. I mean, there is a war on.'

'But it's taking an awful risk. You'll catch the pox, or find yourself pregnant,' said Doreen.

'Well, I haven't so far. Anyway I feel sorry for a lot of the lads away from home. Likely to be killed at any minute. You should see some of the sailors when they come in with a convoy. They need a bit of fun.' And then, as an after thought she added, 'They ain't half randy when they've been away at sea for a few weeks.'

Helen looked at Doreen who shook her head. They said no more. But talking as they cycled home later, they agreed that she was a strange girl. A little simple, perhaps, and feckless but warm hearted and generous.

'I'm sure she thinks she is comforting the troops and helping the war effort,' said Helen.

'And enjoying herself at the same time,' added Doreen. 'I just hope nothing horrid happens to her.'

Chapter 30

At the Ritz cinema in Wellersea the house lights came on and everybody stood for the national anthem. Well, not quite everybody. The couples sitting in the double seats on the back row, mainly airmen and soldiers with their girl friends, disentangled themselves, grabbed their hats and coats and rushed for the rear exit. Robert and Ann did their patriotic duty by waiting for the final flourish of the drums and joined the rest of the audience in the crowded aisles.

'I hope you didn't find it too tedious,' said Robert. 'All the films are the same these days, either German submarines or Halifax bombers.'

'At least it ended happily. I can't bear sad endings. I'm a real softy and wept like a leaking tap over Mrs Miniver.'

They passed through the foyer and were surprised when they got into the street and the fog had cleared and it was raining. It was only nine o'clock but, because of the black out and the constant threat of an air raid, most entertainments finished early. Robert took Ann's hand as they groped their way in the dark along the High Street towards the car park, keeping as close to the buildings as possible to avoid the worst of the rain.

On a fine, moonlight, night Robert would have suggested a walk along the sea front and a wet Friday night in Wellersea did not offer much of an alternative. Most places were closed because of the war. There would, no doubt, be a hop of some sort in the Floral Hall but it would most likely be crowded with rowdy, half drunk, troops. Although he had known Ann for nearly a year it was their first night out together and Robert was anxious to do the right thing.

'I was making for the car,' he said. 'But, perhaps you would like to go to The Fleece for a drink. It's early to think of going home.'

'I'd love to,' said Ann. 'I told dad I wouldn't be late back. He's a real worrier if I go out anywhere. Not that I do very often but I don't think he will be getting too worried when he knows I am with you.'

'In that case we'll turn left here and cut through Finkle Street.'

The public bar at The Fleece was crowded but, in the cocktail bar, there were only a couple of air force officers and a group of farmers, one of whom Robert recognised as being a regular visitor to Wellersea Market.

As they settled with their drinks in front of a welcoming log fire, Robert's thoughts went back to the cold, bleak, days when he and Margaret had been glad enough to snatch an illicit hour together in the seclusion of the old, disused shepherd's hut in Beech Wood at Manor Farm. They had been difficult, heartbreaking, days but there was an excitement about them, which he still found profoundly moving.

He looked at Ann, her cheeks glowing and her hair dishevelled by the wind and rain, wondering if she, too, had memories. Perhaps a boyfriend away in the war. Up to now they had not been on personal terms and he knew nothing of her private life, but he didn't think she had known many boys and certainly had not had a serious affair. Although she was slightly older than he, she seemed young and innocent compared with the girls he had met when living in London. A girl's boarding-school in the quiet village of Hunmanby and life on a farm with no mother and a dominant father could not have provided many opportunities for romance. When she broke the silence it was as though she'd been reading his thoughts.

'You may find it difficult to believe, Robert, but this is the first time I've had a drink in a bar with a boyfriend.'

'Well apart from a few occasions with my friend, Peter, when I was in London, I haven't done much drinking in pubs myself.'

'With or without a girl?' she asked teasingly.

'In my case, without. But Peter always had a girl in tow. Sex and rugby were the only two things he was interested in.'

'What happened to him? Was he snared by some predatory girl looking for a husband?

'Not if he could help it,' said Robert, laughing. The thought of Peter being serious about a girl was something he could never imagine. 'I don't know where he is or what he is doing. Neither of us are very good at writing letters. The last I heard he had just got a commission in the RAF. It'll suit him down to the ground, if you'll forgive the expression.'

Ann laughed. 'Did you enjoy London?' she asked.

'I hated it. I'm a country bumpkin at heart. All I've wanted to be is a farmer. But what about you? Do you think you would like living in a city?'

'What chance is there of that? I don't know. Mother was a town girl and never liked living here. I think I'm like her in lots of ways.'

Never having known her mother Robert was unable to make any comparisons. It looks as though she had Kit's colouring and stocky build, but she had a much different personality. On first acquaintance, Kit was friendly, open and ebullient. But behind the bluff exterior was a guarded, secret, inner self, which Robert had not penetrated. He wondered if he ever would. Ann was the opposite. Reserved, quiet, unsure of herself and yet, underneath, she had a friendly, open, innocence.

When an hour or so later they reluctantly left the comfort of the lounge bar and went out into the hotel lobby, they found the weather was worse than ever. Sheets of rain lashed against the windows and a strong wind blew into the entrance porch. They had no umbrella and the car park was five minutes walk away.

'You can't go out in this rain, Ann,' said Robert pulling up the hood of his coat. 'You wait here while I go to fetch the car.'

'Don't be silly. I don't mind if I get wet.'

'Maybe you don't, but I do. It won't take more than a few minutes to run round to the car park.' And not waiting to argue he hurried off into the darkness. On his return, Robert was surprised to find Ann in conservation with Helen.

'Hello, do you two know one another?' he asked.

'We didn't, but we do now,' said Ann.

'We were both waiting for our chauffeurs,' said Helen, a little embarrassed at meeting her boss off duty.

'Helen's friend is in the RAF at Duffield,' explained Ann.

'That's quite a drive. Especially on a night like this. Anyway, if you're ready, Ann, we'll be on our way,' said Robert.

'Nice to meet you, Helen,' said Ann. 'See you again, perhaps. After all, we live near enough.'

'Yes, I'd like that. Bye for now,' said Helen and then called to Robert as he moved towards the door. 'I'll see you in the morning.'

'Early,' shouted Robert from the doorway. 'And don't be late,' he added, more in jest than earnest.

Driving back to Church Farm, Robert said, 'It was quite a coincidence meeting Helen like that.'

'Oh, I don't know. Not really. There aren't many places open at this time of night. Actually, I think she knew who I was but I don't ever remember meeting her.'

'Oh, well, it will give the girls something to gossip about tomorrow. They're always fishing to try to find out if I have any love life. It won't embarrass you, I hope?' said Anne.

'No. I don't mind. They'd find out sooner or later. Helen is a good girl. Hardworking and reliable. Without being snobbish about it she comes from a better class than most of them. Her father's a doctor in Kirkella.'

'A pretty girl, too,' said Ann. And just the type to interest an RAF officer.'

She wondered if Robert also found her attractive. It couldn't be easy having to keep a gang of young girls in order. It could create problems if he became too familiar and fatal if he started an affair with one of them.

On arrival at Church Farm, Robert stopped the car as near to the door as he could. Ann hesitated a moment before getting out. Robert wondered whether she was just getting up courage to face the rain, or whether she was expecting him to kiss her goodnight. Robert had wondered the same thing. He and Ann were sure to see each other regularly. It was one thing to be good friends but a more serious relationship could become difficult. He liked Ann and had enjoyed their evening out. He wondered if Ann had ever been kissed in earnest. One day, perhaps, he would find out. So far he had not felt that strong, sexual, attraction which he had always found difficult to control with Margaret.

'Are you coming if for a coffee and have a word with dad?' asked Ann. 'I don't suppose he'll have gone to bed yet.'

Robert hesitated. 'Thanks, but not tonight. If I come in and start talking to Kit it'll get late and I have an early start in the morning.'

'If you're sure. Thanks for a lovely evening. I've enjoyed it.'

'So have I. We must do it again, soon. If I don't happen to see you around I'll give you a ring.'

'I'll look forward to that,' she said and slipped quickly out of the car door into the driving rain. Robert watched her dashing for the shelter of the porch where she turned and waved.

Chapter 31

Stephen was feeling irritable. Nowadays, whenever he and Mary visited Manor Farm, he was in a bad humour. It hadn't always been so. Not until Robert had first started to work at Holme Green during the school holidays. The Colonel had never been happy about that. And when eventually Robert had gone to join Stephen permanently, John had been even more displeased, more so because he also believed that Stephen and Mary had been less supportive than they should have been over Robert's undesirable affair with Margaret Jackson.

'Do we really have to go to John and Marjorie's for lunch?' he said, taking off his muddy boots and padding through to the kitchen to find his slippers. Mary had already changed.

'We haven't been to Manor Farm on a Sunday for ages,' she said. 'We hardly go at all now that you are going to Thornton almost every other weekend.'

'I can't help that. Business is more important than pleasure. And anyway, it's not much of a pleasure to go to Manor Farm these days. John and I always end up having an argument about something or other. He seems to find fault with everything I say, or do. I don't know why. I used to get on with him well enough.'

Stephen didn't wait for a reply but set off up the back stairs to go to change.

'You'd better get a move on. We're already late. I'll go and get the car out,' called Mary as she heard the bathroom door bang.

It was a raw, foggy, November day. Not a good day for driving, not even on the quiet, country, roads of which Stephen knew every inch. He arrived at Manor Farm in an even worse temper than when they had left home but, after a pre-lunch drink sitting in front of the drawing room fire, he was feeling more relaxed.

'Don't settle down there too comfortably, Stephen,' said John. 'As soon as we've had lunch I want you to come and have a look at that riverside grass which you thought would be a good idea to plough out. We had intended to sow it with winter wheat but how we are ever going to get a decent seedbed I don't know. It's come up like leather.'

'Well leave it over winter and let the frost get at it and sow it with spring wheat. You'll have less trouble from wireworm,' said Stephen, thinking that he was really telling the Colonel something which he already should have known.

'That's all I want,' said John, crossly. 'You never said anything about wireworm when we discussed it before. Anyway you can come and have a look at it. You might be able to suggest something more sensible when you've seen it.'

'All right,' said Stephen reluctantly. 'But I shall have to borrow a pair of wellingtons. I didn't come prepared for this sort of expedition.'

He couldn't understand John. He must have had this sort of problem to deal with dozens of times. And, in any case, why couldn't he leave it to Bill?

It was the sort of practical matter that he should not be wasting time over and certainly not involving Stephen.

Although Mary would not have admitted it to Stephen, she was as concerned about her father's attitude towards him as he was. Left alone with Marjorie, following the departure of the two men, she said, 'I don't know if you've noticed it mother, but father and Stephen aren't getting on so well together as they used to. They seem to start arguing every time they see each other. I had quite a job to persuade Stephen to come today.'

Marjorie thought for a moment. 'Now you mention it, there perhaps is a coolness between them. But you know they have always seen things differently. They are not very much alike. John is a pessimist. Stubborn and slow to change. Stephen is the opposite. Optimistic, ambitious, forward looking and always willing to try new ideas and take risks.'

'Yes, I know,' agreed Mary. 'Admirable qualities I suppose but I'm worried about Stephen as well as dad. He's driving himself all the time. He never thinks about anything but work and making money. And since he bought Thornton Grange and become friendly with Kit Barton, he's hardened. It's a change I'm not happy about.'

'I've never liked Kit Barton,' said Marjorie emphatically. 'He behaved badly to his wife. I didn't know her well but she was a charming, sensitive, woman. I don't know why she ever married him. They weren't a bit suited. She came from a much better background than he did. I always think he is rather a common man.'

'Oh, I wouldn't say that,' said Mary defensively. 'He's been very helpful to Stephen and Robert.'

Marjorie snorted. 'He may be a successful businessman and a good farmer but I think he's getting too big for his boots. And what's more, I wouldn't trust him as far as the duck pond,' she said.

Mary was surprised by her mother's reaction and strength of feeling and asked if John felt the same way.

'He doesn't trust Kit either,' said Marjorie.

'So Stephen's involvement with Kit is another reason for John's attitude towards Stephen. Do you think there is a bit of jealousy as well? Father has always resented Stephen's success. And, of course, his independence. It can't have been easy working for Lord Heverthorpe all these years.'

'Nothing's perfect,' said Marjorie 'He's had a good life. Plenty of hunting and shooting, which he enjoys. And now, since the war started and the Home Guard, he's behaving as though he was back in the army again. There's no reason to be jealous of Stephen. He could have started farming on his own if he'd really wanted to. It would have been a struggle financially but the trouble is he's been too comfortable here. It's a pity he didn't farm for Robert's sake. Robert would never have drifted away from us then. We hardly ever see him these days and when he does come the love and warmth have gone. It's not the same as it used to be.'

Mary could see that her mother was becoming emotional and sorry for herself.

Marjorie had always spoilt Robert and thought that she could influence his life in any way she wished. His affair with Margaret, the defiance of his father and his decision to leave home had come as a shock to Marjorie.

'I'm sure Robert still loves you, mother, as much as he ever did but you've got to realise that he is grown up now. He needs his independence and the opportunity to make his own life. From what I hear that is what he is doing. Stephen thinks there may be something going on between him and Ann Barton.'

'Kit's daughter? I don't really know her. What's she like? She must have had a hard time since her mother died.'

'Oh, she seems a pleasant enough girl. Dominated by her father as you'd expect. Quite attractive. Lovely auburn hair and a pretty face but not much of a figure. She'd be a good catch though wouldn't she? A bit different from Margaret Jackson.'

'Thank goodness that's over,' said Marjorie. 'But Ann Barton. I'm not so sure about that as you seem to be. Plenty of money there of course and the only child. But hardly our type. I mean Kit may be making money but ...' and she hesitated, trying to find the right word.

'Not our class,' said Mary laughing. 'You really are a snob mother. You're a farmer's daughter yourself remember and I married a farmer. Ann's mother came from a professional background.'

'Well all right, I'm not going to make an issue of it now. I haven't even seen the girl since she was about twelve. If there really is something going on I shall have to suggest to Robert that he brings her over for the weekend. But I wish Robert would find himself a really suitable girl. I always hoped he would meet a nice girl in London.'

'I never saw any hope of that,' said Mary. 'He would only ever be interested in a country girl. At least Margaret had that in her favour and so does Ann Barton.'

'Well, I'm not going to interfere any more,' said Marjorie, much to Mary's amusement. 'I tried to get him interested in Celia. She was keen enough. Probably still is if given the chance. I've learned the hard way. You can't choose partners for your children. I just hope Robert has learned something from his experience, that's all.'

Mary did not pursue the subject further. She was far from sure that Robert's affair with Margaret was well and truly over.

Since the evening with Kit Barton, Stephen had been giving some serious thought to his future plans. He was not sure about Kit's response to his proposal about forming a consortium. Kit was a man well practised in controlling his facial expressions but Stephen was sure he had been interested but too careful in his dealings to give anything away. As usual, Stephen was keen to get things moving and, as he had not heard any more from Kit, he had decided to follow his advice and go and see his bank manager.

Mark Butler was an ambitious young man whose ability had earned him rapid promotion. He and Stephen had much in common and they had quickly established a good working relationship. And now that Stephen had farming interests both in Kirkley and Holderness, Mark's experience in the Wellersea branch was particularly helpful.

'I don't think it would be wise to borrow any more capital at the moment, Stephen,' said Mark after thumbing through some papers on his desk. 'I appreciate that you have got ample security but why don't you just consolidate for a year or two?'

'Come on, Mark, you're beginning to sound like old Jenkins,' a reference to Mark's former manager who had a reputation for refusing to lend money unless there was an absolutely solid guarantee only to ignore it and not lend any adventure capital.

'You know as well as I do,' continued Stephen, 'that now is the right time to expand. We're going to be short of food for as long as this war lasts and, in my opinion, a good deal longer than that. There'll be no cheap food to import for years after this lot's over.' He paused for a moment but as there was no response from Mark, he decided to press on.

'And in any case, I'm not going to ask for a loan. I've always been used to farming with my own capital. I don't take very well to paying interest. Especially not at your inflated rate of interest,' he added not losing the opportunity for a sly dig.

Mark ignored it. 'So what have you in mind if it's not money you want?' he asked.

'Well, I suppose indirectly I'm looking for capital but what really interests me is the idea of forming some form of partnership with someone who has money to invest.'

'You've already got one with Robert.'

'That's different. He's family and not what I mean by a partnership. Perhaps a better word is a syndicate. I'm not sure really. Which is why I've come to see you.'

Mark thought for a moment. 'What you want is a limited company. Possibly with two or three others involved?'

'Yes,' said Stephen eagerly. 'You must know people who have money to invest. We could start on a modest scale and if it goes well expand later.'

'What had you in mind to start with? More land?'

'No. I want to start a commercial pig unit or, perhaps, an intensive poultry enterprise. We wouldn't need any more land for that. Just sufficient investment capital to pay for the buildings and livestock.'

'Where would you site the buildings? At Holme Green or down in Holderness?'

'At Thornton Grange. That's the place to be for both pigs and poultry. Plenty of cheap grain and straw for bedding. And of course the potatoes and sugar beet will utilise the manure.'

'You seem to have got it all worked out,' said Mark. 'I shall have to make a few enquiries but I'm pretty sure I can find someone who may be interested. In fact I had a phone call from someone the other day that might well be a possibility. Are you willing to consider more than one partner if necessary?'

Stephen couldn't help wondering if Marks's caller had been Kit Barton. It would be like him to make an initial secret approach, and after all, it was Kit who had suggested that he should see Mark Butler.

'You don't need to tell me now if you're not sure,' said Mark, noticing Stephen's hesitation.

'Oh, sorry. I was thinking about something else,' he said thinking it prudent not to mention his true thoughts to Mark. 'I don't mind if there are more than two of us so long as we can establish a good working relationship.'

'Right. Leave it with me. I'll let you know as soon as I find somebody.' And picking up the telephone added, 'If you're not in a rush I'll get some coffee laid on and you can tell me your news. I haven't seen Mary for months.'

Chapter 32

Kit Barton looked over the door of the loose box and swore to himself. The heifer was going to calve. She was one which Sam Smith had bought in Wellersea market the previous day or to be more accurate, one which he had been obliged to accept when yet again, Kit had knocked her down to him when left without a genuine buyer. Sam and Kit had a private arrangement that if in trouble, Kit would knock down an animal to Sam even if he was not bidding. In return, Kit would take the animal home and look after it until the next auction.

Kit watched the heifer closely for a few minutes. There was no doubt about it. She was well bagged up, moving restlessly round in half-circles and occasionally switching her tail angrily over her back.

'Damn and blast,' he said to himself. He had an important meeting in Wellersea that night which he was now going to miss because of Sam Smith's bloody heifer. He closed the top door of the loose box and went to look for Walter. It was gone five o'clock but his stockman was not a clock-watcher and would perhaps still be bedding up. He found him in the fold yard.

'Walter,' he called. 'That heifer in the loose box is going to calve tonight. You'd better put some grit down. She's already dripping milk. We don't want any damage to her hips or pelvis if she happens to slip.

'Right. Ah'll see to her afore I go home.'

'And Walter. I'm going out tonight. Can you slip back later on and make sure she is all right? She looks to me as if she might want some help.'

'Well there's a problem there. Ah'm on fire-watch duty tonight. It's a bit late now ti try to swap duties wi anybody.'

'Damn. I'd forgotten it was your fire-watching night. Well, never mind, Ann can look in on her and ring the vet if necessary.'

By eight o'clock, Ann had become worried. She had been three times to look at the heifer. Mucus was hanging from her vulva and she was straining occasionally but there was no sign of progress. Ann was not very knowledgeable about cows. In fact, for a farmer's daughter, she was not very experienced in anything to do with farming.

However, she knew enough to suspect that something was wrong and decided to ring the vet. It came as a nasty shock when his wife told her that he had been called out to an urgent case and didn't know when he would be back.

Ann waited anxiously for another half hour, went back to have another look at the wretched animal and still found nothing different. She decided to phone her father in Wellersea. But as she lifted the receiver had second thoughts. She was reluctant to take him away from his meeting and did not want him to think she was incapable of coping with an emergency. She phoned Robert instead.

'How long is it since you said she had started?' asked Robert, taking off his jacket and shirt.

'About four hours. Maybe more. Should I have done something about it sooner?' asked Ann anxiously.

'No. Heifers can take a long time. There's no point in interfering too soon. You need bags of patience for this job. Can you go round and hold her head?'

Robert washed and soaped his hands and arms in a bucket of warm water and then cleaned up the area around the heifer's vulva before carefully inserting his hand passed the water bladder.

'Keep still, old girl. Let's see what we can find,' he said gently.

It was quiet and peaceful in the loose box. Outside it was a dark, moonless, night. The only sound was the drone of a distant aircraft. The naked light bulb, dangling from a stout beam, cast eerie shadows on the whitewashed walls. Cobwebs hung from the rafters and there was a warm smell of animals and straw. Ann found the whole atmosphere comforting and reassuring. She felt the wet muzzle and sweating head of the heifer pushed against her and wondered if she herself would ever be in labour.

'Is there anything wrong?' she asked after what seemed a long silence, surprised that she was talking in little more than a whisper.

'I can feel the head and a foot but there's no sign of the other one,' said Robert, struggling to feel even further into the uterus although his arm was already up to the shoulder. 'As I suspected, there's a foot bent back.'

'What does that mean?' asked Ann anxiously. 'Is there anything you can do about it?'

'Yes, don't worry. We can put that right but she's still very tight. When I've got the foot straightened out we'll tie a bit of rope on and pull the calf out. It's a big calf. I shall need your help.'

The meeting at the Fleece Hotel had finished and members were having a drink at the bar.

'We are making up a foursome at Harry's place for a game of cards. Are you joining us Kit?' asked his friend, Freddie.

'I don't know if I should,' replied Kit. 'I've a heifer calving back home. I left Ann keeping an eye on her.'

'You needn't worry then. She's a responsible lass.'

'Yes, I know. But she's not very practical about jobs on the farm. Why not give her a ring and make sure all is well?'

'A good idea. I'd like to join you if I can. I'll pop through into reception and use the phone. I'll be back in a minute.'

'You know Kit's changed a lot lately,' said Freddie as soon as Kit had left the room. 'He would never have considered staying if there was something important going on back at the farm.'

'He seems to lose his concentration when selling in the market,' said Harry. 'He got himself into a real tangle at Wellersea the other day.'

Freddie laughed. 'Only because he was taking bids that weren't there. But, come on, drink up. He'll be back in a minute.'

'When Kit returned a few minutes late, he was looking anxious and worried. 'I can't get through on the phone,' he said. 'I let it ring a long time, but there was no reply.'

'Ann was probably out looking at the heifer,' said Freddie. 'No need to worry. You can ring again later.'

'No. I think I had better be off home. I don't like leaving Ann on her own at night anyway. You never know with all these air raids.'

Back at the farm, Robert and Ann were watching the heifer as she muzzled and licked her new born calf. The birth of a calf, or other baby animal, was a common occurrence on most farms but Ann, not normally so closely involved, was moved and comforted in a way she found it difficult to express. Perhaps it was her maternal instinct but she suddenly found herself struggling to hold back tears of relief. She turned to Robert and putting a hand on his arm reached up and kissed him on the lips.

For a moment Robert was too surprised to know how to react but, understanding and perhaps sharing her emotions, he took her in his arms and for some moments they were locked in a warm embrace. Their moment of passion ended abruptly as the door of the loose box opened and Kit came in. He saw at a glance that a successful calving had taken place but was not sure how to respond to finding his daughter in the arms of Robert. The awkward silence was broken by Ann.

'I couldn't get hold of the vet,' she said. 'So I rang Robert. It's a good job I did because he's had a difficult calving to deal with.'

'I can see that. I'm very grateful to you, Robert,' said Kit. 'You'd better take him into the house, Ann, to get cleaned up while I tidy things up out here. A big calf, Robert. Any other complications?'

'A foot back. And she was very tight.'

'Well, thanks anyway. Put the kettle on, Ann, and I'll join you when I've given the heifer a drink and a forkful of hay.'

Later, when Robert had gone and Kit and Ann were about to go to bed, Kit said, 'I didn't know there was anything going on between you and Robert?'

'Well, there isn't really. It was the first time he has kissed me. It just happened on the spur of the moment. You don't mind do you?'

'No. Not at all. You are old enough to do as you like. It was just a bit of a shock. You've never shown much interest in boys. I suppose it's something I shall have to get used to.'

'You have nothing against Robert?'

'No. On the contrary. I have a high regard for him. For the whole family. Stephen told me that he hasn't shown any interest in girls since that *unfortunate* episode with Margaret Jackson. You know about that?'

'No more than you do. Mary told me a bit about it but that was before I had even met Robert. I gather she is an attractive, intelligent, girl. Not at all you would expect of a farm worker's daughter.'

'Ambitious, too, according to Stephen. But there's nothing wrong with that. Anyway, I don't know about you but I'm ready for bed. I'll just take a last look at the heifer. And thanks for your help.'

'It's Robert you need to thank. I'll see you as usual at breakfast,' said Ann, giving her father a kiss.

Later, when lying in bed, her mind too active to sleep, she thought about Robert and wondered if she was, perhaps, beginning to fall in love. As he was the first boy she had ever really kissed it was difficult for her to assess her true feelings but there was no doubt she was strongly attracted to him.

Chapter 33

Since their accidental meeting at the cinema in Wellersea, Ann and Helen had become good friends. Occasionally, when Helen had a free afternoon, they went shopping in town followed by tea at Church Farm. Once or twice on these occasions, Helen had thought of suggesting that Ann should invite Robert to make up a foursome with her and Tony, her RAF boyfriend, at one of the Saturday night dances in Wellersea.

She knew that Ann and Robert had been out together but she was not sure if it was a good idea to mix socially with her boss and thought he might well feel the same way. It was also difficult to make arrangements as Tony, who was a fighter pilot, was never sure when he would be off duty. However, she now felt that she knew Ann well enough to suggest that they should go to the dance the following Saturday night. Taken by surprise, Ann was not sure how to respond.

'It's a nice thought,' she said. 'But I'm not sure if I know him well enough to ask him. I see him quite often of course but we've only been out together a few times and always at his suggestion.'

'If you did ask him, do you think he would be embarrassed because I'm just a land-girl working at Grange Farm?'

'No. I wouldn't have thought so. You are only working at Grange Farm because of the war and, as a doctor's daughter and a public school education, you come from as good a social background as him. Tony says the war has broken down a lot of class barriers. There are chaps from all sorts of backgrounds in the RAF and they get on well enough together.'

'We get on well enough together in the land-army but Audrey and Doreen are always gossiping about people, particularly the Denehurst family. They would really enjoy discussing Mr Denehurst's private life. I mean the fact that I call him Mr Denehurst and not Robert shows it could be difficult for us to meet socially.'

'I'm sure you'd be very discreet,' said Ann. 'The other girls don't need to know.'

'Does that mean you are going to ask him?'

Ann thought for a moment. 'Why not? He can only say no. Anyway, a night out would be good for him. He spends all the hours there are at work. Until we went out together he had never been anywhere since he came to live here a year ago.'

Robin Butler had been as good as his word and found someone whom he considered to be exactly the sort of person to set up a partnership with Stephen Langley. He had suggested that they all meet at his offices in Kirkley and was now sitting talking to Stephen as they waited for Robin's contact to arrive.

'Aren't you going to tell me who this mystery man is?' asked Stephen.

Robin laughed. 'No, I'm looking forward to seeing the look on your face – both your faces – when he walks in.'

'It's someone I know then?'

'Yes. Very well.'

Stephen had always had a suspicion it would be Dick Barton and was now more than ever convinced that his hunch would be right. He was, therefore, completely taken by surprise when a few minutes later there was a knock on the door and Robin's secretary showed in Gilbert Dawson.

'Well, I must say I wasn't expecting you,' said Stephen, rising to shake hands warmly with Gilbert.

'Nor me, you,' said Gilbert with his usual affable guffaw. 'But knowing you are an ambitious man always looking to expand, I'm not really surprised.'

'You did say, Stephen, that you wanted someone with an interest in pigs or poultry. Well, nobody knows more about hens than Gilbert,' said Robin, 'and you know one another well enough to develop a happy working relationship.'

'I'm delighted to see you Gilbert,' said Stephen. 'But I always thought you were like my father-in-law and not in favour of intensive methods of keeping livestock.'

'You are right, up to a point, but I've been under a lot of pressure to "Get into the modern world" by young Maggie Jackson. She's come back from college full of all the new ideas and is eager for me to put them into practice.'

'Well, couldn't you do that on your own at Newlands?'

'Yes, I suppose so. We could put up some more buildings but I don't think you want too many hens under one roof as it were. There's always the risk of disease and I think it is sound management to keep the pedigree flock separate from commercial egg production. Robin tells me that you want to expand at Wellersea rather than at Holme Farm, which is ideal by me. Not too far away but far enough to keep the two enterprises apart. And I don't need to tell you about the advantages of having plenty of home produce wheat and straw if we go in for deep litter.

'Well, before you two get carried away,' said Robin, 'we need to talk finance. That's my side of the business and when we've settled that I can leave you to sort out the management details.'

On his way back to Newlands, following the meeting with Robin and Stephen, Gilbert decided to call and see Emily. He was pleased at being part of Stephen's plans but there was one aspect, which he had purposely not mentioned at their meeting. He needed to talk to Emily first. As always she gave him a warm welcome and he was soon sitting comfortably enjoying a cup of tea and a slice of chocolate cake.

'I'm surprised that with the rationing, and food shortages, you can still manage to make a cake like this,' said Gilbert.

'Well it's a bit of a struggle sometimes but we are fortunate not to be living in a town. As you do, we produce our own eggs, vegetables and butter. We live well enough. But anyway what brings you here? I don't see much of you these days. I suspect it's not just a social call.'

'No. You're right. You'll be surprised, but interested, to know that I've just come from a meeting with Stephen Langley. We're going into partnership and setting up an intensive poultry unit. Perhaps pigs as well later.'

Surprise was hardly the best way of describing Emily's reaction. It took her some time to appreciate the significance of Gilbert's news.

'Well, I'm delighted for you,' she said at last. 'But from what Margaret has said you've never been in favour of modern, intensive farming.'

'No. I know I'm a bit old-fashioned in my ways and if I'm honest I'm too old to change. However, you've got to think about the future and the young generation and it's Margaret I'm thinking about, which is why I've come to see you. I have no family of my own and nobody to inherit the business. You know I've always loved Margaret as if she was my own daughter. I've managed to help a bit in the past but I think the time has come now to set her up in a business of her own.'

Emily was well aware of Gilbert's feelings about Margaret and already felt indebted towards him. She was almost overwhelmed by this latest proposal and had difficulty in controlling her emotions.

'Oh, Gilbert,' she said. 'I don't know what to say. It's something I've never even dreamed about. But what about Gladys? She's been part of your life for over thirty years.'

'Don't worry about Gladys. I shall make sure she has all she needs for her old age and, like me, she's now ready for a quiet life with no responsibilities. It's the young ones we need to think about.'

'What do Stephen Langley and Robin Butler think about Margaret being involved?'

'I'll come to that in a minute. At present they know nothing. There's no reason why they should at this stage. It's my capital that's involved and we haven't discussed details of management. But you've raised an important point. After all the traumatic events of last year how do you think Stephen and Mary Langley would react to Margaret becoming directly involved in the day-to-day management? She would be the ideal person. She is knowledgeable, experienced and full of drive and energy but would the Langleys approve?'

'You mean because of Robert?'

'To be honest, yes. I don't know the full story of Robert and Margaret and I'm not going to pry but, as I understand it, the Denehurst family was greatly relieved when Robert went to start a new life in Holderness. My concern is that the new poultry unit will be at Thornton Grange, not here at Newlands.'

'So Robert and Margaret would be working together and living near each other.'

'Exactly. And, of course, I don't know what they would feel about that.'

'Neither do I,' said Emily. 'I don't think the Langleys would be too worried. The Colonel would be horrified but the Langleys have always had a high regard for Margaret and they were never opposed to the marriage in the way the Colonel was. As for Margaret and Robert I really don't know. So far as I know they have never been in touch since they separated. Margaret doesn't talk to me about it and I don't press her. As you know she sees quite a lot of James but I suspect that she is still in love with Robert and would welcome a reconciliation.'

'What about Robert?'

'I don't know any more than you. He certainly loved her at the time and since then doesn't seem to have any interest in anyone else. But Wellersea is a long way from here. He could have met a girl down there.'

Gilbert did not respond immediately and Emily continued to think about the significance of what he had told her. Naturally, she was delighted and thrilled for Margaret but the prospect of reconciliation between her and Robert was something she had tried to keep out of her mind.

'You aren't going to ask me to talk to Margaret about it, are you?' she asked, wondering if that was the reason for Gilbert's visit. She was relieved when he said,

'No. Not at this stage. You can tell her about my proposed partnership with Stephen Langley. It will soon be common knowledge anyway. But her possible involvement is just between you and me. I'll keep in touch and let you know how the partnership is progressing. And if you have any further thoughts about Robert and Margaret, let me know.'

Chapter 34

The Methodist Chapel in Kirkley was a large, bold, Victorian building with an impressive pillared entrance. It was separated from the street by a row of iron railings and a wide path, flanked by rose borders and small areas of lawn. At the top of the steps were double doors leading into a large vestibule from which two smaller doors gave access to two interior aisles. A narrow flight of stairs led up to the gallery. The chapel had been built during a period of great confidence when Methodism was fashionable and enthusiastic congregations filled the pews twice every Sunday. Behind the chapel, but attached to it, was a smaller building where committed parents brought their reluctant children to Sunday school and during the week it was used for meetings of the men's fireside, the mothers' union and choir practice. It was in this schoolroom that the chapel ladies ran a canteen every Thursday night for army and air force personnel stationed in the Kirkley area.

The Rev Paul Jackson was a young, energetic, minister who, in addition to running the chapel, was also chaplain to the army camp in Dunmere Park. The idea of starting a canteen was his wife's, Enid, inspiration. In spite of rationing, food in rural areas was more plentiful than in the cities. Farmers killed their own pigs, their wives made butter and almost everybody kept hens. There was plenty of fresh fruit and vegetables and, somehow or other, there seemed to be an ample supply of home-made pies, cakes, scones and buns.

Paul believed this to be the work of providence. A weekly happening of the parable of the two small loaves and five fish, which miraculously fed the multitude on the shores of Galilee. Emily Jackson, Gladys Cook and several other dedicated helpers knew otherwise. It was they who found the scarce ingredients, did the weekly baking and gave up their Thursday evenings to serve the grateful servicemen and did the washing-up. As Emily had said to Harry, when he was supporting the views of the minister, the Lord may send the sunshine and rain to grow the food but He never appeared with a large mixing bowl, or dish-cloth.

It was the Thursday before Christmas. The ladies had made an extra effort to celebrate the festivities by providing some seasonal extras in the form of sausage rolls, mince pies and even a Christmas cake. There was a decorated Christmas tree and coloured paper chains streamed across the ceiling and bunches of holly hung on the drab, cream walls.

The canteen opened at seven thirty and a few minutes later, Margaret dashed in with a basket of baking and produce from Newlands.

'Hello, mum. Sorry I'm late. Gladys can't make it tonight and she asked me to bring these for you.'

'I'm relieved to see you. We've been waiting for butter. We haven't finished making sandwiches yet. By the way, James arrived a few minutes ago with some friends. They arrived early. He seemed anxious to talk to you.'

'How did he know I was coming in?' asked Margaret a little flustered.

'I don't know. I didn't ask. I thought you must have made an arrangement. You'd better go and put him out of his misery.'

James and three of his friends were sitting at one of the tables, playing cards.

'You'd better not let Paul see you. He wouldn't approve of gambling on chapel premises,' said Margaret.

'We're not gambling. Just playing for matches,' said James. 'And, anyway, I need to see you as soon as we've finished this hand.'

'How did you know I'd be here?'

'Gladys told me when I tried to telephone you earlier.'

'Well, it's nice to see you anyway. Are you free all evening or do you have to get back to camp early?'

'Ask these chaps. We all travelled together and I shall have to go back with them when they're ready.'

'You can always walk. It's a fine night and not very far,' said one of his friends. 'Or, alternatively, you can go back in the truck and I'll entertain your girlfriend,' he added winking at Margaret.

'I've got a better idea,' said Margaret. 'I'll take you back in my van. Finish this hand and we'll go.'

'And what about our game? We'll be one short if you go.'

'Tough luck,' said James. 'I'll see you back at camp.'

It was a clear, frosty, night. Margaret had parked the van in a secluded gateway overlooking Dunmere Park. The rippling water of the river Dun was reflected in the moonlight and over the far side of the Park, the dim outline of the army huts were just visible between the trees.

'It all looks peaceful over there,' said Margaret. 'You're lucky to be camped in a lovely place like this. I shall always have memories of Dunmere.'

'Happy or sad ones?' asked James.

'Both.'

James waited but she did not expand and he didn't pursue it further. He now felt that whatever memories she had of growing up on the estate, they were slowly receding. He had already come to love her and although he knew that his love was not reciprocated he was hopeful that with care and patience it could be. The one thing that puzzled him was that if she and Robert had been so much in love why had they not tried to forget their differences and start again? It was something he had decided never to ask. If and when she was ready to tell him she would no doubt do so.

James returned to her original comment. 'Well, it's certainly different from Catterick. I shall never forget arriving there. Blowing a gale it was and bitterly cold in the huts. I should hate to be posted away from here and arrive somewhere like that.'

'Are you likely to be? You've only been here a few months.'

'That's why I wanted to see you tonight,' said James. 'I've been offered an officers' training course at Sandhurst but I'm not sure whether to accept it.'

'Why not?' interrupted Margaret. 'It's a marvellous opportunity. Congratulations. She gave him a quick kiss and then added, 'I wouldn't even hesitate.'

James took out a cigarette, lit it and took a long draw. 'I know you don't approve of my bad habits but it helps me to think,' he said.

'If you must,' said Margaret opening the window. 'And don't blow smoke all over me. Anyway, why do you need to think? You should be jumping at the chance and taking me out to celebrate instead of behaving like a wimp.'

'It's not as simple as that. I'm happy here. And I'm not sure I want the responsibility. And then there's the increased risk. The life expectancy of a subaltern in the last war was measured in days – even hours.'

'Don't be silly,' said Margaret dismissively. 'The last war was different. You aren't in the infantry or likely to be standing in trench, or dugout, being shelled and waiting to go over the top. This war isn't like that. You should know. You're the soldier. Not me.'

'All right. I'll stop making excuses and give you the real reason.' James took a last pull on his cigarette, opened the window a few more notches and threw out the butt end onto the frozen grass. Then putting an arm round her shoulders he said, 'If you must know, I don't want to leave you.'

Margaret braced herself for what she knew was coming next. She had been seeing James regularly for over two months. He spent most of his spare time with her and she had even had difficulty persuading him to go home to see his parents when he had a forty-eight hour leave. She was happy with their present relationship. She did not love James and didn't think she ever would.

Neither of them spoke for a few moments but, eventually, James made up his mind to finish what he had intended to say.

'I know. Because we've only known one another for a short time you think it is too soon to talk about love. Well, it's long enough for me to know. I love you and I don't want to do anything which will lead to our separation.'

'But that's not being rational. You could be posted away at anytime.'

'Loving someone as I love you isn't rational,' said James. 'If it wasn't for this bloody war I would be asking you to marry me.'

'If it hadn't been for "this bloody war" you would never have met me. And remember, it takes two to marry.'

'Yes, I know. I shouldn't have said that. But it's true, nevertheless. I've never felt like this about anybody before. I know you don't love me so you don't know what it's like.'

Margaret was truly hurt by that remark.

'How can you say that to me?' she said angrily. 'I have to live with my love every day. I try to forget. And sometimes when we are together I almost do. And then when you say I don't know what love is all about my memories come flooding back to me.'

'Oh, darling, I'm not putting this very well am I. I didn't mean to upset you. I was just trying to leave you in no doubt about I felt. I didn't want you to think it was just a quick fling. There are plenty of those around on the camp. So far as I'm concerned this is for real. I like to think that if I stay around long enough, then one day you might return my love.'

Margaret was calmer now after her outburst. She had never intended to reveal her true feelings in the way she had but, at least, James now knew that his chances of ever winning her affections were indeed slim. She put her head on his shoulder and took his hand.

'I'm sorry James. You'll have to be very patient with me and wait a long time. I don't want you to go away. You must know that. I just want things to stay as they are. But you have to be logical. Your love for me – and I do know it's sincere – is quite separate from going to Sandhurst. You must consider your future. When all this is over, leaving the army with a commission will make all the difference to your prospects for a career.'

'That's just what the adjutant said when I asked for time to think it over.'

'If you do accept, would you be based back here when you've got your commission?'

'I don't know. I shouldn't think so which is why I'm reluctant to go.'

'In that case we seem to be missing our opportunities,' said Margaret and raised her face towards his. They kissed passionately for a moment and then she drew back and said, 'I do wish you wouldn't smoke. Your mouth tastes of stale tobacco. You'll have to keep your lips closed when we kiss in future.'

Chapter 35

'You'll have to forgive me if I step on your toes Ann. I'm not very accomplished at this sort of thing and I'm out of practice,' said Robert, thinking back to his young teenage days at Dunmere and the disastrous evening with Peter in London.

'Don't worry about that. I'm just happy to be with you and, of course, Helen and Tony. I wasn't sure how you would react to my suggestion that we should make up a foursome.'

'Well, it was a bit of a surprise; but a welcome one. I've had a limited social life since I moved to Wellersea and, of course, the air-raids and wartime restrictions don't help.'

'Oh, I don't know. In some ways I think it does help. At least it's brought new faces into the area. We would never have met Tony or Helen if there hadn't been a war.'

'No. I take your point but I was thinking about the blackout and the petrol shortage. It's a long way for Tony to have come.'

'They seem to get plenty of petrol in the RAF. He's travelled with some friends from Duffield and taken Helen to meet them in the bar. Do you want to join them when this quickstep is over?'

'Why not? It'll be a relief for you not to be pushed round the dance floor and have your feet trodden on.'

Robert had, in fact, been in two minds about Ann's invitation to the dance. He enjoyed her company but didn't want it to lead to anything more than friendship. He had also wondered if mixing socially with Helen was a good idea. It was not easy maintaining the right sort of working relationship with the land-girls but Helen was a sensible, responsible, girl who he was sure would not gossip about their night out. He had also welcomed the opportunity of meeting Tony. Most of the young men of his age were away in the forces and the only male company he had were men involved in farming and there was a limit to the amount of time he wanted to spend talking shop.

However, Robert was certainly not prepared for the surprise he got when he and Ann went to join the group at the bar.

'Let me introduce you to some of my friends,' said Tony.

'You don't need to introduce him to me,' said a voice behind Robert's shoulder. He turned and couldn't believe it.

'Peter! How marvellous to see you. What the hell are you doing here?' he said as the two friends rushed to hug each other.

'I never expected you to meet someone you knew,' said Tony as equally surprised as Robert.

'Someone I know? He's my best friend. We were at school together and met again in London just before the war started. God it's good to see you, Robert. It's made my night.'

'And mine. But why didn't you get in touch. The last I heard you were in Cambridgeshire.'

'It's a long story which I'll tell you about later but for now we must not neglect our friends. Should I know anything about these delightful ladies?' he asked, wondering if Robert was still involved with Margaret. The last he had heard it was all off.

As Tony introduced the two girls, Robert quickly grasped the significance of Peter's question but he need not have worried. He hadn't changed and was soon ordering drinks for everybody and bestowing his charms on Ann and Helen.

'I'm sure you and Robert would like a few minutes together, you must have a lot to talk about,' said Tony. 'We'll take the girls off for the next dance.'

'Just this one,' said Peter already smitten by Helen's good looks. 'It's my turn after that. Don't let him monopolise you all night,' he said turning to her.

'You haven't changed at all,' said Robert as the couples moved onto the dance floor. 'Still an eye for a pretty girl.'

'And what about you? What happened to your Margaret? I thought you would be back together again by now.'

'I wish we were. But I can't tell you about it now. There'll be plenty of opportunities for us to get together now you're based at Duffield and I'll also explain why I'm living down here at Wellersea and not at Dunmere. And you can tell me about life in the RAF. How come you've moved from Cambridge?'

'I'm up here on a special assignment. I can't go into details; not even with you. But I'm only at Duffield for a few weeks and with luck, when I go back, I'll get my own squadron.'

'Promotion to squadron leader?'

'Yes. I've done some useful missions down there and anyway, in this game there are always vacancies arising, as you can imagine.'

'Are you enjoying life? I can't think of any other branch of the armed forces to which you'd be so well suited.'

Peter laughed. 'No, you're right in some ways. But enjoy isn't the right word. I must admit I get a thrill when I manage to cop a Jerry but it's pretty bloody at times. You're lucky to be out of it.'

'Yes, I know that. The army was never for me, much to the disgust of my father. I'm doing all I ever wanted to do. But we must arrange to meet again, soon, for a really proper talk. I'd like you to meet my parents and visit the old homestead at Dunmere. Are you likely to have any free time?'

'How far is it to Dunmere? I was intending to get in touch when I'd sorted myself out.'

'From Duffield? Not much further than to here. It would be nice to have a day together. Stay the night if you can.'

'I'd love to. I shall have to see how my schedule works out. My geography of these parts is a bit hazy. I wasn't sure how close you were to Duffield.'

'Tonight is just a fortunate one off. It really is good to see you. And now this waltz has finished I'm going to grab Helen for the next dance. I'm sure Tony won't mind.'

A couple of weeks after the dance at Wellersea, Robert had invited his friend to spend the following Sunday at Dunmere. They had spent a couple of enjoyable hours looking round the farm whilst his parents were at church and Robert had taken Peter up to Beech Wood, and the many favourite places of his childhood. They were now on the way back to join the rest of the family for lunch.

'It's odd, really,' said Robert. 'When we were away at school I didn't miss the countryside, or life on the farm as much as later when I was in London. I think being separated from Margaret was what made it so much worse.'

'But you were friends with her when you were at school.'

'Yes, I know. We've always been friends. But it was when we became old enough to fall in love that I really missed life on the farm. She was so much part of it.'

'Don't you miss her now?

'Like hell. Never a day passes without my thinking about her. I just can't accept that she deceived me that night we spent in York.'

'Come on, Robert,' said Peter. 'I did warn you. And anyway, it takes two to tango. From what you've told me it seems you were as much to blame as her. But, if you still love her, why can't you forgive and make a fresh start? It's in your own hands. You were the one who ended it. You can't expect her to come to you.'

'I know that. I just can't bring myself to do it. I suppose it's to do with pride and obstinacy, both of which I inherit from my father, as you will appreciate when you meet him. And anyway, I've heard that she's going around with an army chap based at Dunmere camp in the Park. I couldn't bear it if she turned me down.'

'For God's sake don't be such a wimp,' said Peter, more sharply than he had, perhaps, intended. He was beginning to lose patience with his friend. 'You are friendly with Ann but you're not seriously involved? Margaret may well feel the same as you. It wouldn't surprise me to learn that she's still in love with you. Never having met her it's difficult for me to judge. It's a pity we were never introduced.'

'That's my fault. I should have invited you to stay when we were living in London, but I thought you would have been bored in a small village, like Dunmere. Not much social life around here and, apart from Margaret, a distinct lack of talent.'

Peter laughed. 'It may surprise you to know but girls and the bright lights aren't all I think about,' he said. 'But when you take off to intercept the bombers, every day and night, not knowing if you'll be coming back, you take every opportunity there is to enjoy yourself. But let's not be morbid. I'm looking forward to your mother's roast beef and meeting Mary and Stephen.'

It was over coffee that Robert's comments about the Colonel's difficult character became noticeable, particularly his attitude towards Stephen. Conversation during lunch had been mainly about Robert's time in London and Peter's life in the RAF. John was obviously impressed by Peter and particularly the fact that he was an officer and shortly to be promoted to squadron-leader, something that interested John far more than the current state of farming or his problems on the estate.

However, Peter felt that his wartime experiences were dominating the conversation and, in an attempt to turn the conversation away from himself, innocently turned to Stephen and said, 'I understand from Robert that you are planning to start an intensive, livestock, unit at Wellersea.' But before Stephen could reply, John intervened.

'What's all this about?' he asked sharply. 'It's the first I've heard of it.'

'Well, I was going to tell you about it when my plans are a bit further advanced,' said Stephen. 'But I suppose you may as well know about it now as the subject's been raised. I'm going into partnership with Gilbert Dawson to set up an intensive poultry unit at Grange Farm.'

John was flabbergasted. 'Good God. What next? I thought it was a stupid idea when you started farming down in Holderness in the first place. What do you know about poultry and what are you going to use for capital?'

'Robin Butler is sorting out the financial side,' said Stephen. 'And nobody knows more about poultry than Gilbert. If this is successful, and I've every confidence that it will be, we may find somebody to join us in putting up a pig unit as well.'

All this was also news to Marjorie, but she quickly realised that as far as John was concerned it was like a red rag to a bull. Before she could try to say something to avoid a serious row, John pounced again.

'Borrowing more money? Starting something you know nothing about? You'll come a cropper my boy. This is going too far. And what about you, Robert?' he asked turning his disapproval to his son. 'You've never said anything about it, either. I suppose you also think it's a good idea.'

'As a matter of fact I do. I'm as excited about it as Stephen although, of course, I won't be directly involved. We shall need to employ somebody with the specialised knowledge and experience but I'm sure Gilbert will have some ideas about that.'

'It seems to me,' said John, 'that this is going to be the Gilbert Dawson show. He'll take over the whole thing, Stephen. I know his type.'

'Come on, John,' said Marjorie, at last managing to get a word in. 'Stop being vindictive and irrational. You've always had a high regard for Gilbert Dawson. We all know he is one of the most successful breeders of Rhode Island Reds in the country.'

'And he's also chairman of the NFU poultry committee in London,' said Mary, coming in to support her husband.

John snorted. 'I might have known you'd all be on Stephen's side,' he said petulantly. 'Nobody tells me what's going on in my own home these days.'

'No wonder,' said Mary. 'You're always against everything we say, or do. You seem to have lost interest in the family, and even the estate. All you think about these days is the Home Guard.'

John looked quickly at the old grandfather clock. 'It's later than I thought,' he said. 'You've reminded me I've got a parade in half an hour. I must go and change. No need for anyone else to move.'

He stood and went over to Peter's chair. 'I've enjoyed meeting you, Peter. Robert should have invited you to stay years ago,' he said. 'You chaps are doing a great job. I wish I were forty years younger; I'd have been up there with you. And good luck for your promotion.'

Peter stood to shake hands. 'Thank you. I hope all goes well with the Home Guard but, if we continue to shoot down Hitler's bombers I don't think you'll ever be needed,' he said.

When John had gone, Peter noticed that everybody relaxed.

'I'm sorry, Stephen,' he said. 'It seems I introduced a sensitive topic. I just felt we had talked long enough about me and the RAF. It's nice to be able to forget it for a while.'

Stephen laughed. 'Don't worry. You couldn't possibly have known and John would have had to be told about my plans sooner or later. He's sensitive about most things these days. At least you can now appreciate how Robert has suffered over the years.'

'I just can't understand dad,' said Mary. 'He's always said that farming is only profitable when there is a war on and a shortage of food. It's the ideal time for him to start farming on his own, especially with Robert so keen to be involved but, instead, he seems to have lost interest in everything but the Home Guard.'

Towards the end of the afternoon, Marjorie had suggested a cup of tea. Stephen was anxious to have a quiet word with Robert about Grange Farm and Mary suggested she should take Peter on a tour of the garden whilst her mother put the kettle on.

'I'm so pleased to have the opportunity to talk to you on our own,' said Peter in the privacy of the rose garden. 'It always seemed to me that Robert was dominated by his father and now I can appreciate why. He must have had a difficult time both over his career and his affair with Margaret. I think, from talking to him, that he is still in love with her. I know it is a difficult situation for the whole family but does he discuss it at all with you? I know he always appreciated your support in the past.'

'Yes, he did confide in me when he was younger but he never talks about Margaret these days. I think you could be right, though, but I hear that he's becoming friendly with Ann Barton who would be much more acceptable to my parents as you can appreciate.'

'I met her at a dance with Robert but they are just friends. She may be keen on him but there's nothing in it on his side. But do you think Margaret is still in love with Robert?'

'I don't know but I would think it is quite likely. I've always thought that they would get together again, one day.'

'I would like to meet Margaret. How far is Newlands from here? I could possibly call in on my way back to Duffield.'

'You would have to take a short detour. Only three or four miles.'

'Could we arrange it? Perhaps ring up Gilbert Dawson. I realise it would be difficult to phone Margaret herself but Stephen must be in regular contact with Gilbert.

Mary smiled. 'You seem very persistent. I believe you're plotting something. Some devious scheme.'

'You think it's none of my business?'

'As Robert's friend I can understand you wanting to try to help. As a matter of fact, I'm also interested to know how things stand between them for reasons that I can't divulge, even to you. If Stephen can arrange a meeting for you, promise to let me know what happens.'

'Yes, of course. But it might not be for a week or so. I should like to see you all again anyway. I've enjoyed my day.'

Margaret had no idea that Peter was based at Duffield, or that he had visited Robert at Dunmere. It was, therefore, a welcome surprise when Gilbert told her that he was on his way to meet her. All her best clothes were at home so she dashed around trying to find something a bit more glamorous than the breeches and sweater that were the standard wear for the poultry girls. All she could find was an old, blue, dress. She brushed back her long, dark, hair allowing it to fall onto her shoulders and put on a little lipstick. She didn't think her appearance was all that important but she wanted to look her best for Robert's sake.

She opened the door to a tall, dark, attractive RAF officer. 'This is the nicest thing that has happened to me for ages,' she said. 'I've heard so much about you from Robert and always hoped we would meet one day.'

'It seems I've waited years to meet you,' said Peter stooping to kiss her upturned cheek. 'I can see now why Robert kept you in hiding. He wouldn't have stood a chance.'

Margaret smiled, showing her prominent teeth, her wide, blue, eyes reflecting the joy of meeting him. My God, thought Peter, no wonder Robert was hooked and not interested in any of the girls he met in London. But what was he doing to let her go now.

'Come in, Peter and I'll put the kettle on. Do you want to meet Gladys and Gilbert while you're here?'

'I'll pay my respects before I go. But it's you I came to see. Robert showed me all your childhood haunts this morning but there was something missing. Meeting you brings it all alive. He always said you were so much part of the farm and his childhood and I know now just what he meant.'

Margaret was touched by that remark and wondered just how much Peter knew. Probably everything.

'He was always so grateful to you,' she said. 'His life in London was bad enough but it would have been impossible without you. Anyway, excuse me a minute while I fetch the tea. I might even manage to find a biscuit.'

'Just a cup for me. I had a huge helping of Marjorie's roast beef not long ago.'

Margaret's absence gave Peter an opportunity to consider his strategy.

So far he had been greatly encouraged, first by Mary's co-operation and now by Margaret herself.

He could see she was a sensible, honest, girl he could be frank with. She suited his style.

'I brought some home-made biscuits with me,' said Margaret on her return from the kitchen. 'You may not want one but I do. I've got to go and feed up shortly. You can come with me if you like. Robert always said there was nothing you liked better than being out in the country-side,' she added teasingly.

'Don't believe everything Robert said about me,' said Peter, laughing. 'I would have loved to go with you but I've got a good excuse to decline. I've got to be back for duty tonight and my time is limited.'

It was Margaret's turn to laugh. 'You're exactly as Robert described you,' she said handing him his tea. 'Anyway does he know you were coming to see me?'

'No. And as far as I know, John and Marjorie don't know either. I thought it was prudent to keep it a secret until I'd met you. I wanted to see what your reaction would to my acting as a go between.'

'Are you bringing an olive branch or just hoping to take one back with you?'

'I don't know yet. Perhaps a bit of both. I'm told you've got a new boyfriend.'

'I suppose you mean James. Well, yes. But he is just a friend. At any rate as far as I'm concerned. He's leaving here next week. Going to take an officer's training course at Sandhurst.'

'Are you sorry?'

'I shall miss his company but it's a great opportunity for him. And now it's my turn to ask a leading question. I hear Robert's got a new girlfriend. Ann Barton is it?'

'Yes. I met her last week. But she's not important. Just like James. Someone to go around with.'

There was a moment's silence as Peter thoughtfully sipped his tea and Margaret, wondering where the conversation was leading, helped herself to another biscuit.

'Sure you won't have one?' she asked.

Peter shook his head and waited a moment before saying, 'I won't beat about the bush. I've only been with you a few minutes but I already know I can be honest and straightforward with you. Robert is still in love with you. He tells me he always has been and always will be. Do you still love him?'

Margaret was overcome. Unable to control her tears she said, 'I'm sorry, Peter. Pass me your handkerchief. I can't describe how I feel. Relief and happiness I suppose.' She dabbed her eyes and added, 'I've spent months waiting anxiously for him to get in touch. Of course I still love him. The stupid fool. He was the one who finished it.'

'Yes. I know. He told me. He told me everything.'

Margaret thought for a moment. Apart from her mother Peter must be the only other person to know about her pregnancy. She didn't blame Robert. Who else could Robert have confided in? However, she was sure that Peter would keep their secret.

'What will you tell him when you see him again?' she asked, now more composed. She passed back the handkerchief. 'Thanks. And forgive me. It's no way to treat someone who is trying to help.'

'Don't worry. I understand perfectly. I shall tell Robert again what I've already told him once. That he needs his brains seen to. But what I do is more important than anything I might say to Robert.'

'What are you going to do?'

'I have a plan in mind which now I have talked to you I can put into operation. Trust me and leave it with me. And now I'd better pay my respects to Gilbert and Gladys before I set off back to Duffield. It's been lovely to meet you at last and I look forward to seeing you again. Robert doesn't know how lucky he is.'

Margaret smiled but didn't respond to the compliment. 'It's been marvellous to meet you, too. Robert is fortunate to have such a loyal friend. And now I'll take you through to meet Gilbert.'

On the way back to camp, Peter was able to give some thought to his next move. He knew that the last thing John wanted was reconciliation between Robert and Margaret. However, now that Robert was completely independent and old enough to do as he liked, there was nothing to stop the two lovers marrying. Having talked to Mary, Peter was sure that she and Stephen would give their support. He had no doubts that Margaret and Robert were still in love and there was no one else involved but he was still puzzled to know why they had not forgotten their differences and got together again months ago. He concluded that Robert was to blame. He had almost admitted it himself but had still done nothing about it. Peter knew Robert well enough to know that even he would have difficulty in persuading his friend to make a direct, personal, approach to Margaret. Somehow he had to arrange for them to meet and, as far as Robert was concerned, it must not appear to have been pre-planned. Having met Margaret he was confident that for Robert just to see her as all that was necessary. He now knew exactly what he was going to do but as he would be returning to Cambridge in ten days time, he needed to act quickly.

The partnership between Stephen and Gilbert was now well established and they had reached the point where the needed to appoint someone to oversee the building of the poultry units and then manage the whole enterprise. Gilbert was sure that Margaret was the ideal choice and he had arranged to visit Holme Farm to put his ideas to Stephen.

The two men were sitting in Stephen's office looking at the plans for the battery and deep litter houses.

'Would you mind if I asked Mary to join us for a few minutes?' asked Stephen. 'I think she might have a useful contribution to make to our thoughts about appointing a manager.'

'No. Of course not,' said Gilbert, wondering what was in Stephen's mind.

'Firstly then, Gilbert,' said Stephen when Mary had joined them, 'do you have anybody in mind? After all you are the expert and have a wide range of contacts. I would rather consider names of people known to us before we decide to advertise.'

'As a matter of fact I do,' he said. 'But I'm not going to find it easy to tell you as you will understand in a minute. It's someone you know well. Margaret Jackson would be the ideal person.'

There was a brief silence and then Stephen burst out laughing and turning to Mary said, 'What did I tell you? Great minds think alike.'

'You mean, you've been thinking the same as me all along?' said Gilbert with one of his guffaws. 'You don't know how relieved and pleased I am. But you must see the difficulties as I do.'

'You mean because of Robert,' said Mary. 'Yes, we've discussed it endlessly. We hoped you might know more than we do because of your friendship with Emily.'

'Well I'm sorry to disappoint you but Emily doesn't know any more than we do. Margaret never mentions it.'

Mary looked at Stephen before turning to Gilbert and saying, 'This is where I think I may be able to help. Did you wonder why Robert's friend, Peter, was so anxious to meet Margaret?'

Gilbert thought for a moment. 'No. It was really none of my business. But perhaps I do now. Am I right? He wants to knock a couple of heads together.'

'Something like that,' said Stephen. 'I think if we wait for a week or so we may know a lot more than we do now.'

'I don't know just what Peter is going to do,' said Mary. 'But you are right. He would like to see Robert and Margaret together again and is now working on it.'

'If they do get together again it will solve our problem,' said Gilbert, 'so let's hope Peter is successful.'

'I'm optimistic,' said Mary. 'I think he has a lot of influence over Robert. They are certainly very good friends and Peter impressed us all. Even John. He has the advantage of not being involved with the earlier troubles and brings a balanced view with no preconceived ideas. Anyway, all we can do is wait and if you don't want me for anything else I'll leave you two to continue your discussions. I'll join you for a drink later if I'm asked.'

Robert woke and, for a few minutes, lay uneasily in the dark before getting out of bed. He felt as though he had not slept all night. Never had he heard so many planes droning steadily, but relentlessly, in the sky over the Humber towards Hull. He switched on the light. It was gone six o'clock but he was sure he hadn't heard the all-clear siren following the previous night's air-raid warning. Switching off the light, he went over to the window and drew back the blackout curtains. It was still dark but over to the west the sky above the city glowed ominously red. There was now no sound of aircraft, no gunfire and no flashes in the sky but he knew that there had been a terrible air-raid over the city. Certainly the longest, and worst, he had experienced. As he went down stairs to make a cup of tea, the all clear did sound. As usual, he went outside to check on the livestock before coming in again for his bacon and eggs.

Listening to the news on the radio told him nothing he didn't already know but when, an hour later, the van bringing the land-girls from Hull had still not arrived he became anxious and went over to the Dutch barn where Arthur and the girls were loading straw.

'It seems you'll have to manage on your own for a bit,' he said. 'No sign so far of the van bringing Audrey.'

'Have you tried phoning anywhere?' asked Arthur, only too well aware of what was on Robert's mind. 'The War Agricultural Committee office might know something, or even the police.'

'I thought I would try to ring Audrey herself. Do either of you girls know her telephone number? Doesn't her father run a pub in the dock area?'

'Yes. The Fisherman's Rest,' said Doreen, 'but I don't know the phone number. It will be in the Hull phone book.

'Thanks. I'll go and try.'

Back in the office, Robert found the number and tried the telephone. Just a dead line. He tried the War Agricultural Committee office. Another dead line, so he turned his attention to the morning post which, miraculously, had arrived, even if later than usual, whilst he was in the buildings. Amongst the usual brown official envelopes he was pleasantly surprised to find a personal letter in writing that he recognised as

Peter's. It was brief and exciting. An invitation to join him and some friends for a celebration lunch at The White Swan, in Duffield. No mention of Ann or who else had been invited. He wondered if Helen's friend, Tony, would be there. Or even Helen herself. It was unlike Peter not to include any girls and even odder he didn't say what they would be celebrating. Perhaps Peter's promotion to squadron-leader.

Whatever, it was something to look forward to and cheered up what had, so far, been an anxious and depressing morning.

Chapter 36

It was two days before Robert heard anything from the War Agricultural Committee. He was in the kitchen having a hot drink and sandwich before going to plough the sugar beet land when the phone rang. The call was from a clerk in the ministry office in Beverley.

'I'm ringing with some bad news,' he said. 'As I'm sure you know there was a severe blitz on Hull on Tuesday night. Our office there received a direct hit and the whole of the city centre was on fire until late yesterday afternoon. I'm sorry we've been unable to ring before now.'

'I fully understand,' said Robert. 'I suspected something serious had happened. I tried telephoning your Hull office several times and also the home of the land-girl who should have been with us.'

'You mean Audrey Milner?'

'Yes. Do you know anything about her? We've been worried ever since your van failed to arrive yesterday morning. Is she all right?'

'I don't know any details but is seems she is in hospital, suffering, I think, mainly from burns and shock. The pub where she lives was burnt out and I believe her mother and father were both killed.'

Robert had feared bad news but this was worse than anything he'd imagined. He felt shocked, weak and helpless. There was nothing he could do.

'Thank God Audrey was not killed. Was she at home at the time the bomb fell?'

'I don't know. I don't think so. It seems unlikely as all the customers were killed, many of them sailors from a convoy which had docked that day. We'll keep you informed of any news but I'm sorry you won't be getting any land-girls for some time. Our van will certainly not be on the road again until next week at the earliest.'

'That's the least of my worries,' said Robert. 'It's Audrey I'm concerned about. We all have a high regard for her here. Anyway, thank you for phoning and please let me know if you receive any news of her. Her friends will be devastated.'

Later, when Helen and Doreen were on their own, riddling potatoes, the conversation turned yet again to the dreadful news of the air-raid and Audrey in particular. They were relieved to know that at least she had not been killed.

'Do you remember when Audrey told us about going out with the sailors when they were on shore leave?' asked Doreen. 'I'll bet that's why she wasn't at home when the pub was destroyed.'

'I've been thinking the same thing,' said Helen. 'It's ironic isn't it. Doing a good turn to the troops, as she called it, probably saved her life.'

'She's a strange girl but I'm very fond of her. Always so full of life and energy and whatever Arthur might say, a hard worker. I wonder if she'll be back.'

'Oh, she'll be back. But she will have to start a new life. No family. No home. She should come and join us out here. I feel so desperately sorry. I worry all the time about Tony and his friends in the RAF. They face death every night. It seems that civilians are now in the front line as well.'

'It puts a different complexion on sorting spuds,' said Doreen. 'I know I grumble about being in the land army but it certainly has its compensations.'

It was about an hour's drive from Newlands to Duffield and Margaret was enjoying the journey across the wolds. The landscape was very different from the moors and dales around Dunmere with large open, cultivated fields stretching to the horizon and substantial farmsteads, most of them surrounded by a belt of trees to give shelter from the cold east winds which blew in from the North Sea. Many of the fields were still bare following the harvest but others were already sown and showing rows of pale green as the winter wheat shimmered in the sunshine.

As it was Sunday morning the roads were quiet. No farm vehicles and, so far, no military convoys. As she drove through the villages small groups of worshippers were standing in groups outside the church after morning service which brought back memories of her childhood and teenage days attending chapel and then, in the afternoon, sneaking out from home to meet Robert in Beech Wood. The leisurely drive gave her plenty of time to think about the day ahead. She was not sure what to expect. In her telephone conversation with Peter he had simply invited her to meet some friends for Sunday lunch at the White Hart Hotel and making sure that she could get there without difficulties over transport and petrol rationing. The only vehicle she could use was the farm van which had Newlands Pedigree Rhode Island Reds printed in bold letters on the doors. Not very elegant but she was grateful to Gilbert who had not only been pleased for her to use it but had also provided the petrol.

There was another aspect of Peter's phone call, which she found puzzling. He had emphasised that she must arrive promptly and to ask for him at the bar where the barman, George, would be expecting her. There was no mention of other guests but she was confident that Robert would be one of them, a prospect that excited her but one she tried to put out of her mind in case she was disappointed. However, this had not prevented her from wondering what sort of reaction she would get from Robert if they did meet. She knew that, so far as she was concerned, it would be the culmination of her hopes and happiness. She would welcome him with open arms and everything forgiven. Margaret arrived in good time and after a leisurely visit to the ladies cloakroom she found her way to the bar.

It was surprisingly quiet even for a Sunday. A small group of airmen were sitting at one of the tables and what looked like three farmers were standing at the bar talking to George. As she approached, rather self-consciously, he turned from his customers and said, 'Are you the young lady for flying officer Buckley's party? He's expecting you in the private room at the back.'

'Yes. Thank you,' said Margaret, pleased that the barman had been well briefed.

'Through the door in the corner and down the corridor to the first door on the left,' he said.

Margaret found the door open and wondering just what she should expect was surprised, but also relieved, to find Peter there standing alone looking out of the window which had a view of the car park. She realised that he must have seen her arrive. He came across the room to greet her.

'Am I the only one?' she asked as he bent to kiss her.

'So far, yes, but I'm pleased you're here in good time.'

She looked round the room expecting to see some sign of lunch or drinks but there were only a few unlaid tables and some dining chairs, nothing to indicate a party of people.

'I'm so pleased we're meeting again so soon,' said Peter. 'I apologise for my vague phone call. Not quite honest either. There will only be one other guest.'

And noticing that Margaret was puzzled about what was going on, added, 'Robert will be here in about ten minutes time. We shall see him arrive. That's why I'm standing here with a view of the car park.' Peter's motives were now clear.

'Oh, Peter, I don't know what to say. I half expected you were plotting something following your visit to Newlands. It's so kind of you to make a meeting with Robert possible. You can't begin to know what it means to me but I must admit to being nervous. Silly isn't it when it's someone I've known all my life and loved for years?'

'No. I understand perfectly. But don't worry. Trust me. I wouldn't have arranged all this if I wasn't sure that Robert will be just as thrilled as you are. As soon as he arrives in the car park I shall leave you here on your own. I think it's better if I'm not playing gooseberry. He's had a similar invitation to yours but has no idea he will be seeing you. I won't be far away and I'll join you after you've had a few minutes together. We can then see about a drink and some lunch.'

Robert arrived at The White Hart in a happy frame of mind, pleased to be seeing his friend again and celebrating, what he was sure was, his promotion. He parked his car and had no difficulty in finding the barman and following his instructions. He found the door to the private room open and bounced in. He was completely stunned to find Margaret standing waiting for him. He stopped for a moment and simply stood gazing at her in amazement not knowing what to say. In that instant, not more than a few seconds, the whole of his life flashed through his mind. Margaret too, although she was expecting him, just stood quietly facing him across the room and then instantaneously they rushed to meet one another. He took her in his arms and for a minute they hugged in silence.

'Oh, my darling,' said Robert eventually. 'I can't believe it. You've no idea what seeing you again means to me. You're looking as lovely as ever. Life without you has been hell this past year.'

Margaret, holding back tears of joy, could not trust herself to speak. She raised her face to his and he bent to kiss her. Gently at first and then with uncontrolled passion as the old feelings of love and desire overcame them both.

After some time, Robert suddenly withdrew from their embrace.

'But why are you here?' he asked. 'I thought I was meeting Peter. Some sort of celebration with his friends.'

Margaret laughed. 'Oh, he's here. Tactfully keeping out of the way.' And she went on to explain his friend's plot. But Robert was still mystified.

'But how did he come to meet you in the first place?' he asked still holding her in his arms. Margaret told him about his visit to Newlands and that she suspected the involvement of Mary, Stephen and Gilbert.

'After talking to you and meeting me, Peter was sure that we were still in love and was determined to bring us back together. I hope you still do love me because I've always loved you and always will.'

'More than ever if that's possible. I've been a stupid, obstinate fool. I should have come back to you months ago.'

Going back in her thoughts over those months, Margaret recalled their last meeting by the river.

'Do you remember what you said when we parted on that hot, June, evening and I asked you if you would always want to see me?'

'I shall never forget. I said always is a long time. Let's give it a chance. Well, thanks to Peter that time is now over. We'll be together for the rest of our lives.'

'Oh, darling. It's wonderful for us just to be together,' said Margaret. 'But don't you think we should go and find Peter?

'Yes. The least we can do is buy him a drink and some lunch. But I want to talk to him anyway. I need to know when he'll be free to be best man at our wedding.'